WINCHESTER UNDEAD

WINCHESTER OVER and WINCHESTER PREY

« DAVE LUND »

A PERMUTED PRESS BOOK

ISBN: 978-1-68261-230-9

Winchester Undead:
Winchester Quarry (Book Three) and Winchester Rue (Book Four)
© 2017 by Dave Lund
All Rights Reserved

PERMUTED
PRESS

Permuted Press, LLC
permutedpress.com

Published in the United States of America

WINCHESTER: QUARRY

PROLOGUE

March 6, Year 1

Jessie knew this was the end, but she couldn't fail, she wouldn't fail. The barrel of her M4 smoked in the cold air, shot after shot putting down bodies in the large horde of undead surrounding her. Standing on the roof rack, she quickly changed magazines as the bolt locked back, looking down at what was to be her death altar in the sun. *No. I have to live. She depends on me being alive ... I'll continue to shoot until I'm out of ammo, then I'll fight with my hands and knife until they are all dead.*

Another magazine change and another twenty undead lay on the ground, their skulls ruined in a black mass of oozing puss on the pavement. Steam poured from under the hood of the SUV stranded in the road. On the last magazine for her M4, Jessie began counting the growing number of gathering undead against the number of rounds she had left for her pistol. *If I can't win ... I have to save the last round for me.*

CHAPTER 1

The Mountain Warfare Training Center (MWTC), Bridgeport, CA
December 26th, Year 1

Captain Jason Krapf hated being away from his little girls, especially during Christmas, but the consolation remained that after this round of deployment workups he would have a full week of leave at home, Camp Lejeune in North Carolina, before he and his unit deployed again. Not that he minded; after all, this was the payoff for his hard work—to reach a position in the Marine Corps Special Operations Command (MARSOC) so he could lead his own twelve-member Marine Special Operations Team (MSOT). In reality, Master Gunnery Sergeant Jerry Aymond, better known as Chief, led the men, but Krapf was the officer in charge and had the exceptional privilege of leading some of the best trained, most dedicated, and hardest working men in the Marine Corps into battle ... again.

The mountain was colder than he remembered from their last training cycle at the (MWTC). Melting snow by using his personally owned Jet-Boil, the warmed water would reconstitute the MRE: freeze-dried winter Meal Ready to Eat. It had been four days since the MWTC cadre's Snowcat dropped the team off for their training cycle. The redundant communications using the team's radios kept them in contact with the Reconnaissance Operations Center, (ROC) as well as Range Control. Besides being needed, as they operated alone on the mountain, taking the radio into the wild was good practice for Staff Sergeant Charles "Chuck" Ski. Aymond had made him carry the slightly larger PRC-152 radio instead of the small handheld Motorola radios that the cadre used, and that the team could have used as well.

Each man carried a full combat load, although there was no live ammo, but all the ammo weight was simulated with blanks. Although it made the packs slightly lighter than the full live ammo load-out would, it was close, and physically taxing, especially in the high, thin air.

Krapf looked at the wristwatch that was clipped to the front of his armor carrier. *Nearly time for the second check-in of the morning and the first team movement of the day.* Finishing his mushy MRE, Krapf stowed the trash in his ruck and made his way across the snow to where Ski sat with the radio.

"Morning, Captain."

Krapf crouched in the snow, under the edge of the tree cover of their encampment, listening to Ski's side of the radio conversation. Normally the check-in would take under ten seconds, but first Ski had difficulty raising anyone on the radio net, and once he did, the transmission was cut off.

"Captain, Reconnaissance Operations Center stated there is a situation and to stand by for fifteen mikes."

"Fifteen minutes? What sort of situation do they have? Their breakfast is late?"

"No idea, Sir."

Krapf shook his head. This training cycle had been fraught with inconsistent bullshit from all the supporting elements and his own chain of command had swayed back and forth with conflicting directives; at least their training would be similar to their deployment in that regard.

"OK, give them five and try again."

Krapf walked off, plodding across the surface of the deep snow with his snowshoes to where Master Gunnery Sergeant Aymond stood.

"Chief, Ski had some strange traffic on the net for check-in; was told to stand by fifteen mikes due to some sort of situation. Something is off. Rally up, I have a feeling that once he reaches ROC they'll want to pull us off the mountain for some reason."

Aymond nodded and left to prepare the team for movement. Krapf looked at his watch again; the digital display was blank. He shook it, which accomplished nothing. Aymond returned. "Team's ready to move."

"Thanks, Chief. Time check? My watch just shit the bed."

Aymond checked the face of his analog watch. "You have ten more minutes."

Gunnery Sergeant Williams, standing nearby, looked at his watch. "Hey, my watch is dead too."

The team was beginning to form up where Aymond and Krapf stood next to Ski, who sat on the snow.

"Ski, instead of waiting for the ROC, check in with Range Control."

"Already tried, but I'll try again, Sir."

Ski punched in the frequency change and tried to raise Range Control on the radio again. After three attempts, someone responded. Krapf could hear the reply for himself, it being yelled into the mic. "Get the fuck down here!"

"That sounded like small arms fire in the background, Captain."

"Chief, saddle up, we're walking to extract and might have to hump it all the way down."

Krapf looked into the sky; the contrails of the aircraft passing overhead usually gave a good indication of the winds at altitude, which gave them a guess at the weather for the day. Staring at the crisscrossed white trails in the sky, he spotted a large aircraft passing overhead, lower than usual. The shape was unfamiliar to him; it looked like a military aircraft, not a commercial airliner, but it wasn't one he readily recognized. They were far enough into nowhere that it wouldn't be unlikely for a prototype aircraft to fly overhead; what was unlikely was that it would happen at night. Thick black plumes trailed the aircraft, looking vile in contrast to the snow-white contrails above. Just as the team began to move down the mountain, they were covered by an oily substance that pelted them from the sky. It fell against the fresh snow, making it looked flecked and dirty. The team looked at Aymond, who looked at Krapf.

"Chief, I think this was sprayed by that aircraft."

"Like a crop duster?"

"Bigger ... much bigger."

CHAPTER 2

Big Bend National Park
March 2, Year 1

Jessie sat naked on the bed in her cabin, crying into her hands. The boots she had been wearing, covered in mud, sat next to the door, which was closed and locked. Her M4 rifle lay on the bed in front of her, and her wet and muddy clothes hung in the bathroom. The cabin was the one that she and Bexar had stayed in for their honeymoon a decade before. Now that day felt like two lifetimes ago, the ancient past, like something from a dream half-forgotten. The cuts and scratches on her hands and arms stung with her falling tears.

Oh my poor Bexar, how could I be so stupid?

Jessie raised her head and stared at the rifle. Inanimate, cold ... nothing but a tool for survival, but she felt a pull towards it, the pieces of her broken heart yearning for a release from the pain. One the rifle could give her. *No more pain,* she thought. A sweet escape from a life of hell; a life that had turned badly. Looking around the small room, Jessie remembered snapshots of her and Bexar together that first week after their wedding. Lazy mornings drinking coffee and making love, afternoons hiking the "must see" trails around The Basin, followed by evenings sitting on the ground at the trail on the west side of the parking area, snuggling under a blanket and watching the sun set into a sky colored in deep reds, oranges, and purples with a bottle of wine beside them.

My little Keeley, I'm so sorry. I love you so much.

Gradually the sobs slowed and Jessie looked at her rifle again. The broken and melted remains of the Yaesu HAM radio sat on the table next to the bed. Her hopes of reaching out for help dashed, burned and melted by the lightning storms of the day before. Her eyes drifted back to the rifle.

My adult life started here; it should end here.

Jessie's hands reached for the rifle, the steel receiver cold in her hands. She looked at the cuts and scrapes on her hands and arms, then down her breasts and to her stomach.

Oh God, Bexar! I can't do this, I can't do this alone ... the last of us still lives, growing inside of me. That has to live; I have to live. I need help.

CHAPTER 3

Superconducting Supercollider Facility, Ennis, TX
March 2, Year 1

Bexar blinked slowly, his eyes reticent to adjust to the dim light. Every thump of his beating heart throbbed through his head in surges of pain.

I don't know where ... a bed. Beeping ... I don't know what's beeping.

Gently Bexar turned his head, the disposable paper pillow case crinkling beneath his ear. An eternity passed before his eyes focused on the shape beeping in the dim light. A monitor, lines spiking with each thump of his heart. Suddenly, with a whirring noise, a tightness formed around his right bicep. Confused, Bexar looked at his arm, which was strapped to the side rail of the hospital bed. An IV stuck out of his wrist, taped to his arm, and the tightness was from a blood pressure cuff. Bexar looked back at the monitor, his awareness slowly dawning.

A hospital? What the fuck happened?

Bexar looked left and saw a drawn curtain hanging from the ceiling. His head throbbed and he began to realize that his right leg ached badly. He tried to sit up but couldn't achieve more than just raising his head off the pillow. He calmed himself and took note of his situation.

I'm nude, there's a tube running out of the end of my dick, and my right leg is swollen, bruised and wrapped in a bandage, and hurts like hell.

The stuck on-pads for the heart monitor tugged at his chest hair and two straps ran across his torso, binding him to the bed. As the pressure cuff began to inflate again, Bexar reached across his chest and pulled the Velcro apart, letting the cuff fall off his arm. The monitor sounded an alarm, showing no blood pressure.

Bexar saw a dark-haired woman step through the curtain. She wore camouflage pants and a t-shirt, the pistol grasped in her hands raised and pointed at Bexar's face.

"Whoa, drop the weapon, lady!"

The woman lowered the pistol and smiled, holstering it on her right hip. She walked to the monitor then turned to speak to Bexar, who was suddenly self-conscious about being nude.

"Officer Reed, welcome back to the land of the living. We thought we lost you there for a while, but I'm glad to see you awake."

"I don't understand. I don't know where I am."

"Officer, you were shot and the wound was badly infected by the time you arrived. We had to cut away some of the infected tissue and muscle then start you on a heavy round of antibiotics. You had severe dehydration, walking pneumonia, and a few other issues. You've been in a coma for nearly two weeks." She looked at her watch. "Thirteen days in all."

"I don't remember getting shot. What happened? Where is this place? Am I in Houston or Temple? This doesn't look like any of my local hospital rooms. Who are you? Could I get some clothes, please?"

"You're in a safe, underground facility. Chivo and his team rescued you from Big Bend National Park during a battle with a renegade gang of survivors. They said you regained consciousness during the drive, but the blast was significant and we figured you had at least a concussion ... we were concerned you would have some memory loss."

"Oh fuck." Bexar stared at the bland white acoustic tiles of the ceiling, remembering the battle, burying Keeley, and seeing Jessie.

"What about Jessie—where is my wife?"

"You were the only survivor from the blast."

"No, I saw her; I saw her being dragged out of a cabin."

"I'm sorry."

Bexar frowned at the woman. "You didn't answer my question. Who the fuck are you? What underground facility? Groom Lake? Where's Cliff?"

The woman's eyes appeared weary and compassionate. "My name is Amanda Lampton, and we are not at Groom Lake ..."

Amanda was cut off by a man who stepped into the room, "Madam President, Wright is on the SATCOM ... they think they found Cliff."

President Lampton turned and walked out of the room.

"Glad to see you made it, mano."

Bexar looked confused.

"The name's Chivo. I'm part of the team that pulled you out of the park."

The spark and expectancy drained from Bexar's eyes. Chivo had seen the look before, in battle, with men he had fought with. In Vietnam they called it "the thousand yard stare."

"Hey mano, let's try getting you up and around. But first we need to pull this thing out of your tube snake. I'm not going to lie; it's going to sort of suck, but you'll feel better once it's out and we get some clothes on you. Generally speaking, it's best not to have your dick sticking out while talking to the first female President," Chivo said with a laugh.

CHAPTER 4

Mountain Warfare Training Center
March 2, Year 1

Four men entered the large room and shrugged out of their modular tactical vests, which carried their heavy armor, ammo, and gear. Sweat-drenched shirts clung to their chests. Riggers belts worn on their Marine Corps Combat Utility Uniforms (MCCUU) held holstered pistols. The current standing order was that every Marine shall be armed at all times; it was put in place by Captain Krapf before he was killed on a patrol three weeks prior.

"Chief, three new walkers in the camp—all put down and dragged to the burn pile."

Aymond looked up from the map section in his hands. "Any new signs of survivors?"

"No, nothing. This place is fucking dead; it's us and only us."

He nodded in response. "Get some chow, switch out your socks, and take your rest before relieving the watch."

"Aye, Chief."

Aymond surveyed the guys in the room, each of them maintaining and cleaning their gear before lying down to rest for a few hours. All top level communications had been down for sixty-six days. Only during the first day, the day of the attack, did the MSOT get any information from the chain of command. The team walked off the mountain that day to find pandemonium. It would have been his fifth deployment, the second with this team, and his first as the team's Chief, the top enlisted man on the team. Only eight men of the original fourteen remained, including himself.

If we stay here we'll die. If we leave we'll die. But if we leave we might find other survivors; we might have a chance to help someone.

He reached into his pocket and pulled out a heavy coin, his team's challenge coin, and set it on the desk. "Always Faithful, Always Forward."

We have to go.

Aymond looked at the map and flipped through the pages; sunlight filtering in from the high windows was the only light in the room. The generators ran dry of fuel on the thirteenth day after the attack, or as they were calling it, Z-Day.

Z-Day. Fucking zombies ... out of all the things to give a single fuck about in this world it had to be zombies.

He set the pages against each other and lined them up, tracing a line south towards San Diego. Aymond unfolded an old California driving atlas that they'd found in an abandoned vehicle near the camp housing and traced the route with his finger.

Dammed near five hundred miles ... five hundred miles. Three fuel stops if we can keep things rolling well ... but it never rolls well; I have to plan for five stops. How long will that take? How long will I be able to keep the guys safe?

"Hammer. Get your ass over here!"

Ryan Hammer left his half-assembled M-4 on his cot and walked to the Chief's desk.

"Ryan, get your squad and sweep the immediate area then pull the sentries. Have everyone in here in an hour for a team meeting. Everyone."

Hammer nodded, quickly assembled his M-4, and left to carry out his orders.

CHAPTER 5

Chivo helped remove the catheter as gently as they could, which was still an exceptionally uncomfortable task for Bexar. Not solely because a section of tubing was being pulled out of his penis, but that another man was holding his dick while pulling a tube out of it, and Bexar could only grip the bedrails and grit his teeth. Eventually he was unhooked from all the monitoring equipment and freed from the hospital bed. Chivo pointed to a chair with a pile of clothes. Brand new ACUs, Riggers belt, t-shirt, underwear and socks, and a new pair of boots. His green blanket poncho and shemagh sat on the table next to Bexar's AR-15, his pistol, big CM Forge knife and his go-bag. All of his gear appeared to have been cleaned and the pistol and rifle were loaded with a round in the chamber.

Chivo helped Bexar stand and shakily take the few steps to the chair where his new wardrobe awaited.

"Thank you Chivo ... means goat, right? That can't be your real name."

"It's real enough," Chivo replied with a hint of a smile.

Bexar had to use the table to steady himself while dressing, threading the nylon belt through his belt loops.

"Wait, I remember now, you cut through my heavy SOE belt. This thing is a piece of crap."

"Well mang, this will have to do. We did save your ass, you know."

Bexar gave Chivo a half-hearted smile. A few moments later the stiff new boots were laced tight, his pistol holstered on his hip, and the big knife on his belt. Bexar slung his AR across his chest.

"Standing rule," Chivo said, "you will always be armed. Keep your shit clean, keep it loaded, and keep it on safe or holstered and always be ready."

"Ready for anything, ready to work, play, etc. ... yeah, got it."

"Whatever, just try not to overdo it. The stitches in your leg are still healing and a shit-ton of good it would do you to pop them now."

Chivo handed Bexar a large plastic bottle. Bexar turned it over and read the label: "Norco?"

"Yeah, take two now and use them as needed. Just don't take more than four a day and you'll be healed up soon."

Bexar did as he was told before dropping the pill bottle into his go-bag. The levity of getting him out of bed and dressed fell away from Bexar like a curtain had been drawn. Keeley, Jessie, his whole family was dead. *Malachi is dead. Jack is dead.* All the people whom he loved, all the people he'd promised to protect were dead. Bexar took a deep breath, fighting back the urge to cry. *Push it down, bury it deep ... sorrow, love, and pain are luxuries that are no longer afforded in the new world.*

Bexar limped behind Chivo, out of the infirmary and into a brightly lit corridor that could have been the hallway of any corporate office in America. Ten minutes later Bexar was shown where his bunk was and where the mess hall was located. The tour ended in the command room where the President, another woman, and two other men he didn't know stood. All of them wore mismatched military clothing, they were all armed, and they all huddled around a large glass table top that looked like a computer screen.

CHAPTER 6

MWTC
March 2, Year 1

The remaining members of the MSOT huddled around the Chief's desk; nearly half the team had been killed. The near thousand people who had lived and worked at the training center were all either missing, dead, or reanimated dead, which were put down for good by the few still living.

"As you know, our recon patrols have found that we are practically isolated and abandoned. Comms don't appear to be down, as far as we can tell, just that no one is answering on the other end of the line. Also, I'm sure you know by now that Chuck picked up a piece of a BBC shortwave broadcast yesterday that was a news report about the attack and the rising dead. We don't know how old the report is, but we do know it is on a recorded loop. My point, gentlemen, is that we are done with the previous directive to shelter in place. Without contact from any in our chain, or anyone at all, for that matter, we need to seek them out, rescue if need be, and set a base of operations at a location we can maintain longer than this facility. My first choice is to point east and head home, but Camp Lejeune is the wrong direction for immediate information. Therefore, Twentynine Palms is our destination. If it is overrun, we will then proceed to Camp Pendleton. Then, if need be, The Recruit Depot and keep heading through to find any remaining Special Operations Command (SOCOM) elements at Coronado. However, I want each of your opinions and agreement on our plan of action."

Aymond looked at each of his men individually. One by one they nodded approval. The last man, Chuck, summed up the team's feelings: "Zero fucks left, Chief. Let's roll."

"Good. Wheels up in forty-eight hours. Put together the three best M-ATVs we have—pull parts off the others if needed. We have to assume that we are completely on our own, simply because we are. We are going to have to fuel at least three times if we roll all the way to Coronado, and there will be no fuel depots, no bowsers. We will be improvising, gentlemen, so creative solutions that work are to be expected. Assuming that the EMP affected the rest of the country, there will be no power but there will most likely be plenty of abandoned vehicles. With three trucks we'll need nearly one hundred and fifty gallons of diesel for each fuel stop, if we run them dry. However, with zero support we operate with a reserve, never less than a quarter of a tank."

Each of the men stood with the small notebooks they kept in their utilities pockets in their hands, taking notes.

"Hammer, you're in charge of food. Assume worse case. Let's call it fifty miles a day or less and we have to go all the way to Coronado, so ten to fourteen days on the road. Also assume that each stop is looted, overrun, or otherwise not a resource. Include needed water for each man and be sure to count it against the vehicle's allowed weight."

"Roger that, Chief."

"Ski, you're still on comms. Check the intra-team commo and the 150s in the trucks. Bring spare parts, batteries ... be creative."

Ski smiled with a thumbs up.

"Holmes, take care of your long rifle needs first, then you'll still continue the role of team armorer. Spare parts, spare weapons—use your best judgment. What do we have mounted on the M-ATVs?"

Tom flipped through his notebook, "I know we have two M2s, one M240, and an MK19. We might have a MILAN or BGM-71, but I'll have to double check that they're still operable."

"Check on them. How do we stand for ammo on the crew weapons and ammo for each man's personal weapons?"

"Roughly forty thousand rounds of XM193, another twenty thousand rounds of 9mm ... if the crates are full we have fifty thousand rounds of 50 cal and roughly two thousand rounds for the MK19. I never looked for any of the TOW missiles since they weren't needed."

"Check on them. Ammo first, water second, fuel third, then food, in that order. The rest we'll figure out as we need. The rest of you, team up and help your buddies. Find our problems, find solutions, and bring them back in twelve hours. In thirty-six hours I want to be spaced out for inspection and loading. This isn't a Level Zero meet and greet, this will probably suck, and we are all we have, but we will succeed."

Each of the men walked off, donning their combat gear before stepping out into the cold mountain air to complete all that needed to be done.

CHAPTER 7

SSC
March 2, Year 1

"We believe Cliff is alive. If you look at this overhead, 'CLIFF' is written in the snow and the roof of this home has a large 'X' marked in the snow. Smart, since we don't know of any other aircraft and he knew we would be looking with the Keyholes."

All eyes were on Clint while he spoke and flipped to the next PowerPoint slide. Even with the collapse of society, even though the dead had risen to hunt the living, Bexar was bemused to see they couldn't escape giving slide presentations.

"What are those other lines?"

"Madam President, we believe those are tracks left by reanimates."

"They seem to go towards the house that we believe Cliff is in," she said.

"That is correct. And if you look in the fenced-in portion of the yard," Clint zoomed the image in, "you can see there is a pile of corpses hidden from view of the road."

Bexar was stunned by the resolution of the imagery. Google Earth was incredible when he thought about it, but the military grade overheads were like watching TV in high definition; they could read a book on the ground from a satellite in space.

"That's one reason why we believe he's still alive."

"Clint, what about the aircraft?" President Lampton asked.

The slides changed on the large screen. Clint flipped through them until stopping on another overhead view. Snow covered the dirt and aircraft, but it was obvious even to Bexar what he was viewing.

"We know that Arcuni called 'Mayday' before we lost contact with him. As you can see here, the aircraft impacted at a high velocity before sliding to a stop in this small creek. Look at the debris trail. I believe that the aircraft was brought down by shoulder- or vehicle-mounted anti-aircraft munitions."

"How is that?" the President asked.

Clint scrolled the overhead away from the destroyed fuselage. "Notice that the debris field starts all the way back here. This is roughly a mile from where the aircraft impacted. It was shedding parts and pieces before crunching in. The problem is that I can't figure out why the aircraft was even flying at this heading; there are no obstacles to overcome, and that puts the C-130 headed away from Groom Lake."

"So we don't know?"

"No ma'am."

"What's your best guess?"

"My best guess is an RPG or something else that is shoulder-fireable, easy to use, and easy to buy. We don't know that there were any other survivors besides Cliff. If you look in this frame, next to the fuselage, there are three bodies that are similarly dressed, but they're not any of our guys."

The President turned away from the slide and looked directly at Clint. "Who are they?"

"I don't know, except to guess that they are part of the Tribe of Man or whatever that cult is calling itself. My guess is that they were responsible for downing the plane and went to investigate their prize. Cliff and any other survivors killed them then fled the wreckage."

"Why all the footprints in the snow?"

"They appear to be from reanimates. As loud as that crash would have been, every walking corpse from miles around would be drawn to that location."

Bexar watched the briefing, still in awe of the technology and a little amazed that anyone could have survived a crash of that magnitude.

"Madam President, how do you want to proceed?"

"Clint, help me out. I want to give Cliff and his team support, but don't know how we can."

"Ma'am you can't; but we can," Chivo said, looking up from his notes. "Apollo and I can travel overland and conduct another rescue op."

President Lampton looked at Apollo, who agreed. "Are you sure?"

"We both know Cliff, and we owe him."

"OK, get with Clint and take whatever gear you need from the stores. Go get him."

Chivo and Apollo thanked the President and excused themselves to begin preparations.

Bexar stood and limped to the front of the room where Clint stood. "This satellite, can you zoom in to Big Bend—to where I was? I have to know about my wife."

Clint squinted. "This is a national level asset ..."

The President cut him off. "We'll analyze the imagery from the next pass that goes over that section of Texas. Until then, Clint, could you pull up the most up-to-date imagery we have?"

"Yes ma'am, but it's nearly two weeks old." Clint clicked off the screen, entered a lengthy password, and began the search for the coordinates.

Bexar watched, nearly holding his breath. "There, that's The Basin. The smaller buildings with the orange roofs to the south of the parking area ... zoom in there."

Clint zoomed in far enough to see that a vehicle appeared to be driving towards the road that led out of The Basin. There were bodies spread out on the ground around the parking area between the cabins, and chunks of a vehicle scattered outward from the explosion in all directions. The destruction was evident; two of the cabins were no longer standing, just piles of rubble.

"There, those three in the middle, zoom in there."

Clint centered the view on the three figures and zoomed in to a tight view of the bodies. The image slowly resolved, and in stark contrast against the asphalt surface were three, mostly nude women. One was missing a portion of her skull; the other had an obvious broken neck. The woman in the middle ... Bexar began to tremble; the woman in the middle lay on the ground covered in blood. That was his Jessie, his best friend, his lover, his wife; her body lay in the open, undignified. She was gone forever.

Bexar dropped his head into his hands and sobbed. Clint zoomed out and looked at the vehicle on the road, the same that Chivo and Apollo had arrived in. The image must have been captured just after the IED exploded and just after their extraction of Bexar. Lampton put her hand on Bexar's shoulder. "I'm so sorry."

Wiping the tears from his face, Bexar looked at her, defeated, angry, barely whispering, "I want to go with them."

The President squeezed his shoulder and nodded. "Go."

Bexar stood. The pain, the sorrow, the savage battle to survive the last two months of hell began to wash away, giving way to rage. Pure anger, resolve, *fuck'em all. No more ... no more pain, no more sorrow, nothing but vengeance. No peace until I can kill every last walking corpse I find.*

Amanda Lampton watched him, lost in thought, and saw the change on his face as he left the room. Clint stood next to her. Now alone, she wrapped her arms around him. "What do you think will happen to him?"

"He'll probably die. I've seen that look before. That man is out of fucks to give, but before he takes the boat ride to Valhalla he's going to be dangerous. I'll give Apollo a heads up; they might be able to keep him in check."

CHAPTER 8

Cortez, CO
March 2, Year 1

Cliff blinked away the sleep in his eyes; sunlight filtered through the curtains of the bedroom window. Shaking and weak, he slowly pulled himself up to sit on the side of the bed, wrapping himself in the heavy wool blanket. Gingerly walking into the bathroom, he stood on the scale. Even with the blanket he was thirty-five pounds lighter than before.

Five days ago he had raided a pharmacy, which had already been looted of any narcotic pain killers, but large bottles of antibiotics and Z-packs were still on the shelves behind the counter. Those he took, along with all the over-the-counter pain killers he could find. In the store, a few cans of soup and Vienna sausages remained; those went into his pack along with a handful of syringes, three vials of cortisone, and a jug of powdered Gatorade. It was all he could find. Once back in the house, he'd started with a Z-pack, gave himself a painful shot of cortisone in his left knee, and took a handful of Tylenol.

He was hurt, he was sick, and he was in pain. He was relieved that there was no longer any blood in his urine, but Cliff was fairly sure he had pneumonia. There were no doctors, but long ago his training had prepared him for this. He was extensively taught and could triage himself. What he really wanted was an IV and some bags of saline solution; sadly the pharmacy didn't have those. He had no desire to attempt a raid on a hospital or clinic; he assumed that they would be like both epicenters where people had flocked after the attack—probably still teeming with the undead.

Slowly, Cliff walked down the stairs and into the garage to the propane grill. Lighting the grill, he began warming a can of chicken noodle soup while melting snow for water to mix with his Gatorade. An old-style glass and mercury thermometer stuck out of his mouth while he stirred the soup, waiting patiently before checking his temperature.

101.5. Well at least the fever has broken.

Overall, Cliff knew he was lucky. First he'd survived the crash, which was due only to blind luck, then he was able to evade capture, and finally he had set up a safe hiding place that provided good shelter. At first, the undead that had congregated around the house were a problem, a big red flag that someone was living inside, but those "people" were now completely dead and piled in the backyard out of sight.

If he was going to complete his mission, he had to conduct reconnaissance on the cult. He needed to figure out if they were still at the school, as the captured member had said. Then he needed to plot their patrols, compile a number of enemy combatants, locate the survivors, and plan a rescue. A rescue, assuming the captured Cortez survivors were still alive. If they were, he knew he would save them. He wasn't sure how yet, but he would get them to safety. But that plan was in the future. The immediate "now" required his full attention; the immediate now was his road to recovery, and it started with chicken soup.

CHAPTER 9

Big Bend National Park
March 3, Year 1

Jessie took the calendar off the wall and flipped the page back to February. We left the park on Valentine's Day, the 14th. We came down the mountain the day before, so the 13th, and we had sex the night before, so the 12th.

Jessie flipped the pages of the calendar, counting the weeks as she went, marking the end of each trimester until she stopped on October.

So, October 28th ... that's my due date, assuming the baby doesn't come early. Keeley was four days early. Oh God, those last few weeks were miserable! I can't imagine trying to do that by myself, much less going through labor alone. What if I die during delivery and the baby lives? Oh God, alone and crying for food ... no. I can't think about that. I have to live, I will live, I will live for my baby.

Jessie flipped through the pages of an old road atlas she'd found in the saddle bag of one of the motorcycles. She turned to Nevada and found what she thought was Groom Lake. It wasn't exactly marked on the map, but she knew it was north of Las Vegas. Using her fingers as a guide, she used the map scale and paced out the roads, turning the pages back until she ended back in the middle of Big Bend National Park.

Twelve hundred miles ... shit. That's over twenty-four hours of driving back when the world was normal. It took us three days to get to Big Bend from Maypearl, and that should have taken less than a day. It'll probably take a week to get to Groom Lake, maybe two. Damn. I have to get ready, I have to prepare, food, water, fuel ... diapers. Oh my God, baby supplies. I have to start gathering baby supplies! Clothes, food, formula, bottles, diapers ... everything!

Overwhelmed by it all, Jessie curled into a ball and lay on her bed. There was so much to do—too much to do. The longer she waited, the harder the journey would be, and the higher the chance she would get caught going into labor without help, out on the road. She needed to leave soon, she needed a list, a detailed list, and to take care of things one little piece at a time ... just like building a Cadillac.

Jessie smiled. For the big parts, I'll need a buddy with a mo-bile home.

CHAPTER 10

"Major, SSC reports the same and came to the same conclusions. At the minimum, Cliff survived the crash, maybe others too, and they're most likely sheltering in this home." The airman switched slides to show an overhead photo of the house with the large 'X' in the snow on the roof. "The OGA team that went through Texas is mounting a rescue attempt, driving to Cortez."

Wright nodded; he did not have personnel or anyone with the training to conduct a rescue operation. Besides, with the increased and increasing number of civilian survivors in the facility, he had his hands quite full. New survivors seemed to arrive daily. The civilian groups divided themselves into "towns," the bunk rooms they were in, assigning each of them with names like "North Las Vegas" and "Undeadville." Regardless what it was called, each town elected a representative, then together they had elected a "Mayor of Groom Lake" to head them all. So far the civilians had been a strong asset. Some of them were quite skilled in jobs that were desperately needed for the facility; others were able to contribute by working as janitorial staff or cooks. There was a concern that, since the civilians far outnumbered the military men, they could attempt a coup and overthrow their authority, or that one of the civilians would try to become a dictator or warlord, but so far the relationship between the military side and the civilian side was quite amicable.

The President was quite clear that Wright's mission was to continue what Cliff had started: provide a safe haven for survivors, uphold the Constitution, and protect the people put in his care. Cliff seemed to know the facility fairly well, but

Wright didn't. Currently two of his airmen were tasked with exploring and mapping all the places and passageways belowground that connected to the main facility. Once they were done, they would continue the operation topside. Deep down, he didn't believe in the conspiracy theory, but there was a part of him that hoped his men would find the infamous S4 facility: a hangar, built into the side of the mountains, that contained an alien craft. Who knows? A few months ago he didn't know that the belowground facility existed here, and he certainly didn't know that the facility in Texas was there. Of course, he also never thought the dead would rise to hunt the living, so at this point he wouldn't be surprised by anything they found in Groom Lake.

Suddenly, the room went dark. Emergency lighting glowed in the hallway, the computers all went blank and off, and the ventilation system's constant hum was missing in the silence. Before anyone could respond, the lights turned back on and the computers began rebooting.

"What the hell was that about?"

Wright looked at the airmen in the room. They all shrugged.

"Get Texas on the SATCOM and see if Clint knows anything about it. Cliff said that all the generators for this facility were nuclear-powered and would last another twenty years, so if that's wrong, we might be in trouble—especially if the whole facility shuts down."

Wright pointed at one of his airmen. "Ask the mayor to check with his people to see if any of them are ex-Navy. Perhaps one of them was a power plant guy on a sub or a carrier and knows something about nukes. If we can find the reactors then maybe he can inspect them."

With a "yes, Sir," the man left the room. The rest of the airmen went off to complete their orders as well. Wright leaned against a table. *I have no idea how this is gonna work, there's no way humanity is going to survive all this.*

CHAPTER 11

Bexar walked into the storeroom where Chivo and Apollo were loading M4 magazines out of an open case of ammo. Lindsey was busy stacking cases of MREs next to four large blue barrels, which Bexar presumed held water.

Chivo looked up at Bexar. "Heard you want to ride with us, mano."

"Yeah, I can't just sit here. I need to get out and do something useful."

Apollo looked at Chivo and shrugged, then turned to Bexar. "We better run some drills with you ... but first we need to get you kitted up."

Lindsey pointed at a cart. "Bexar—bring that and follow me." She placed the last case of MREs on the stack and walked away, down a dimly lit aisle, racks reaching the ceiling, full of various goods and supplies in crates and boxes. Bexar limped along behind her, pushing the cart as told.

A half-hour later Lindsey and Bexar returned the cart, now full of gear. Apollo stood and stretched, a large stack of thirty-round M4 magazines loaded and stacked neatly next to where he had been seated. Standing next to the cart, he talked Bexar through what each piece of gear was for and how to assemble it, explaining why certain pieces of gear went where they did. Once complete, Bexar stood wearing his new gear, most of it foreign to him. Although he was an experienced Peace Officer he had never served in the military; he wasn't even a SWAT guy, he was just a cop. The closest he'd got to most of this kind of gear was bumping into the tacticool wannabes at the local rifle range.

Chivo and Lindsey set out to strip down the MREs from the packaging to save weight and space in their vehicle, while Apollo spent time running some basic tactical drills with Bexar, assessing what he did, and more importantly, what he didn't know.

"Good. So you can shoot, move, and transition. You understand 'field of fire' and 'area of responsibility;' that will save us some time." Apollo put on his lightweight bump helmet and had Bexar follow him into the next room, another large storeroom, extinguishing the lights as they entered.

"Flip down the NODs—the night vision on the front of your helmet. The switch is here ... good. Now look at me." Bexar looked at Apollo, who was mostly visible in the green light glowing from the reticles of the night vision.

"Press this button on the DBAL."

"What's a DBAL?"

"Dual Beam Aiming Laser—the boxy thing on the rail of your rifle ... watch me."

Apollo raised his M4 and pressed the button on the top of the DBAL mounted to the quad rail of his rifle. It emitted a bright laser beam. "You use this to aim and shoot while using your NODs, since it's damned near impossible to use the traditional sights on your rifle with the NODs flipped down."

They set up a stack of new Humvee tires across the aisle and took turns firing their rifles at it, sighting in the DBAL's laser to match the point of aim with the point of impact. Afterwards, they spent another hour practicing some small group tactical movement skills. The training finished up with a lesson on the basic operation of the radios the team used for intra-team communications. Returning to the neighboring room, they found Chivo and Lindsey finishing the stripping and prep of the MREs.

"Alright mano, the check list is complete. We've got the trauma bag, some extra parts for the M4s, a spare rifle, pistol, and general load-out for Cliff, if he needs it, but I'm not sure how we're going to get this all to fit."

Bexar looked at the large pile of gear. "What about extra fuel for the vehicle?"

Chivo looked at Apollo. "The kid's got a point, you know."

CHAPTER 12

Aymond plotted a primary route, a secondary route, and a tertiary route, and marked all three on his maps. Normally he would have refrained from drawing the route lines, but he wasn't too worried about the OPSEC, or operation security. The enemy was already dead and couldn't read a map. The rest of the team were done prepping the M-ATVs and gathering the rest of the gear they needed for their overland expedition.

"Hey Chief, we didn't even roll this heavy when transferring FOBs in the Stan."

"I know, but then all the gear we needed was already at the Forward Operating Base. We have no gear but our own; the trucks *are* the FOB. This is going to be more dangerous than driving across to the Hindu Kush."

"If the Zeds wore some fucking man dresses then it would be just like old times."

Aymond smirked but tried to ignore the remark. "Ops brief in thirty mikes. Spread the word."

"Got it, Chief." Gonzales walked out of the door to tell the rest of the team about the briefing.

Aymond took the time to inspect the fully armed, lightweight, 4x4 transports, aka M-ATVs, checking off items from the list he'd created. They were set for everything but water and fuel, even though those were priority items. They could only carry two hundred gallons of water, so they would have to find clean water at some point. With all the fuel cans they could find, they only had one hundred gallons of spare diesel. That would fill two of the big armored trucks only once. One of the guys mentioned that they should watch for tanker trucks on the highway and snag fuel from those; Aymond had to admit he hadn't thought about civilian tanker trucks transporting diesel when the EMP hit. They should be found abandoned in place and easy to get fuel from. Even just one semi-truck with its saddle tanks could probably refill all three of his trucks at once. If this was a traditional Marine Corps operation, then refueling bowsers would either follow his convoy or be strategically placed for fuel stops, but this was no traditional op. There would be no mobile fueling depots every three hundred miles, there was no logistical chain of command—hell, he wasn't even sure there was a Marine Corps left, much less anyone else.

Slowly the rest of the MSOT members wandered in and took seats in the folding chairs around Aymond's desk.

"As you all know, we're departing the MWTC and checking bases starting with Twentynine Palms and on through to Coronado if we need to. We're still operating in the blind. We have no support, we have no intel, and from what we've seen so far, we should consider this a convoy headed into enemy-held territory. If we end up going all the way to Coronado and our SOCOM family is gone, we'll set a temporary FOB while we stock up from the Naval supplies, then point to Camp Lejeune. We're wheels up at sunrise; get some sleep, double check your gear. I don't know what we can expect, except that I think this trip might suck. It looks like civilization is broke dick and our mission is to find anyone left who can help us unfuck it."

"Hoorah, Chief!"

The men stood and continued going through their gear, getting mentally ready for the task ahead and getting some sleep. Aymond looked through his maps again. "Goddamn, this is going to suck ass," he muttered.

CHAPTER 13

Cliff stood in the garage of his new home, as he had grown to consider it. Whoever used to live here didn't have many tools, but they did have a stud finder, hammer, nails, and a utility knife. That was all he really needed at this point. Returning upstairs, Cliff looked at the rooms and guessed that the master closet probably wasn't a load-bearing member of the home. He marked the stud locations and neatly cut out the long strips of sheetrock between each one. Once the sheetrock strips were stacked in a pile, Cliff began prying the studs out of the closet wall. Two hours later, Cliff had a pile of strong used lumber and sheetrock.

Cliff cut the strips to length and covered the two large windows of the master bedroom, nailing the sheetrock in place. Now no light could enter, but more importantly, no light would leak out if he was using a candle at night. Using the 2x4 studs and nails, he barricaded the exterior doors, except the door to the garage. The sliding glass door to the backyard was covered with sheetrock and crossed with more of the used lumber. Someone might break the glass of the sliding door, but they would have a hard time getting inside.

Still sick, Cliff took numerous breaks throughout the process of fortifying his home, but finally the task was complete. He could enter and exit through the garage by unlatching the garage door opener and sliding the door up by hand.

Although he still needed time to fully recover, Cliff knew he couldn't stay in his new home/fortress forever. Wright either found his message or he didn't. Cliff had to assume that he didn't. He would need to conduct more raids for supplies and medicine, but first he needed to start a detailed reconnaissance of the area and the movements of the cult. He wanted overhead imagery, but that not being an option, he needed a local map. In the digital age, it would be tough to find a detailed paper map of a town; they were becoming more rare with each passing year. If he could find a phone book there would probably be a small map in the front, but those were scarce as well. A police car or a fire truck would probably have one, as both police officers and firefighters tended to keep detailed paper maps as backups to the computer systems in their vehicles.

A spotting scope or high-powered binoculars were also needed, so he planned to raid a sporting goods store or a hunting supply shop. Even a camera shop would be an option, although the EMP would have broken all the digital cameras. He could still use one with a long lens as a spotting scope. His concern was that if the cult had RPGs, wouldn't they also have night optics? So far the members he'd killed didn't have any, but he couldn't rule them out.

Cliff found a blue school kid's backpack in the house and stuffed it with two bottles of water and a few cans of Vienna sausages, then began digging around the closets for some blankets that weren't brightly colored. Thirty minutes later, Cliff had a dark red and a dark grey wool blanket; he cut a hole in the middle of the grey one so he could wear it like a poncho. It would keep him warm and break up his outline, helping him hide. Even in March, Colorado was quite cold, so the red blanket went into the backpack as well.

Geared up and ready to leave, Cliff looked out an upstairs window and saw the sky burning bright red with sunset. He walked downstairs to the garage, shut the door to the house, and slowly raised the garage door as quietly as he could before sliding into the bitterly cold wind and quietly lowering the door back down.

At least it isn't as bad as Chechnya. But then again, I had a satphone and could call in the Calvary if I got stuck ... focus. Got to focus.

Cliff crouched next to the trash cans and scanned the area.

Walk too close to the homes and chance a corpse surprise attack; walk in the open and I'll have nowhere to hide if I'm surprised by a patrol.

Cliff scanned the neighborhood and thought about the truck hidden in the trees behind him, but decided he would walk the neighborhood to recon the area before coming back for it. He picked up a rock and threw it at the galvanized metal trashcan across the street, which fell over with a loud crash, breaking the silence in the still neighborhood. Crouched and well-concealed, Cliff slowly counted to thirty, waiting to see if there would be any undead responding to the sudden noise. When no reaction came, he decided to stay close to the houses in case a patrol drove by. Walking through the yards, he was sometimes startled by a dead face thumping against a window, snarling and snapping its teeth at him as he passed out of reach beyond the glass.

Cliff slowly made his way south. When he reached Empire Street, he stopped and crouched behind a large tree, studying the cars in the driveways around him. If he had to refuel his stashed truck, all he would need was a hose and container to syphon gas. Even if the tanks were only half-full, here was all the fuel he would possibly need. While scanning the homes for any signs of a shed that could contain a lawn mower, or more importantly, a fuel can that he could use, he saw headlights bounce through the intersection two blocks away, turn right, and travel towards him.

CHAPTER 14

After a few minutes of discussion, Chivo and Apollo settled on using the old Defender 90 that they had taken from the gun club in El Paso. The vehicle had, thus far, proven to be reliable and they liked the thought of using something smaller and lighter than one of the Humvees that sat in storage in the motor pool. Now considering themselves a team, albeit a mostly unproven and mismatched one at best, they loaded the packs into the back of the interior compartment. Each pack had enough food, water, ammo, and other gear to give the wearer a minimum of seventy-two hours of survivability, while keeping the weight to just fifty pounds.

The majority of the gear was loaded onto the large roof rack and packed into weatherproof Harddig cases, including the same fifty-caliber rifle that Chivo had used in The Basin to rescue Bexar. Also piled in was a multitude of other supplies, most of which was communications gear, although the VideoScout was left behind as there were no drones, no aircraft at all for that matter. In any case, nothing would be flying overhead that could give them live video feeds. After a heated discussion between Apollo, Chivo, and Lindsey, Lindsey won out and would join the team for the rescue mission to Cortez.

"Commo check, over." Apollo's voice played in each of the other's ear pieces and each member responded for the communications test. The team was lucky to have access to the MBITR, their Multiband Inter/Intra Team Radio. It was a solid upgrade from the PRC-117 that Chivo and Apollo had taken from storage at

Fort Bliss. Now they were able to communicate with each other using line-of-sight transmissions and also with the SSC or Groom Lake by using the SATCOM. One of the large Harddig cases secured to the roof rack held everything that Cliff would possibly need. Everything from underwear and boots, to a complete tactical load-out and M4 rifle. They had no idea what waited for them on the topside, except that the journey was probably not going to be as easy as the previous one from El Paso.

Bexar felt a little overwhelmed by all the gear. His experience in law enforcement hadn't prepared him for the amount of equipment and the complexity of the radio system he now wore. He wanted to wear the simple chest rig with AR magazines, but Chivo was adamant that the team wear a full load-out, including armor plates. He argued that the aircraft had been brought down by a hostile force and that they might end up having to fight the same.

Through the earpieces each of them wore, Clint's voice came through clearly on the team's frequency. "Video topside shows light activity in the park above. The last satellite pass showed a large group of undead northwest of our location. I'll help you route through when you get closer, but that will be a few minutes. I'm still analyzing the shots to determine which direction they're moving."

Chivo keyed his radio. "Roger, thanks for the intel. We're wheels up in five mikes."

Each of them made one last check through their gear, press-checking their rifles and pistols, verifying that a round was chambered and the safety flipped on before climbing into the Defender. Chivo was at the helm; he drove to the bottom of the ramp and punched in the long security code he had written in his small notebook, which activated the opening sequence, releasing the massive steel hatchway that led topside. Bexar sat next to him in the passenger's seat. Chivo wanted him to help navigate, since he was familiar with this part of Texas and with the laminated map grids he held in his lap, along with a civilian road atlas. Lindsey and Apollo sat in the back, with the team's gear piled around them. Lindsey lightly rubbed the back of Apollo's neck as a line of early morning sunlight spread harshly across the ramp, blinding the four of them as they drove topside.

CHAPTER 15

Cortez, CO
March 4, Year 1

Cliff moved quickly from behind the tree to the edge of a dark wooden privacy fence, propping his rifle against the corner post as the headlights traveled slowly towards him. Waiting for the distance to close, Cliff saw that the vehicle was another rusted old pickup truck and there appeared to be only two people in it, both sitting in the cab. He took a deep breath and let it out slowly, flipping the selector switch on his rifle from safe to three-round burst. Driving closer, the truck's headlights washed over Cliff's rifle barrel which protruded from the corner of the fence. Either the driver saw Cliff or it was just stupid luck, but the truck slid to a stop not thirty feet from where he knelt. The driver's face sited firmly in the reticle of his rifle's optic, Cliff squeezed the trigger. The windshield shattered, blood erupting from the driver's head and spraying the broken glass. Cliff was happy to see the passenger do exactly what he had hoped—open the door and try to run away. Once more, Cliff gently squeezed the trigger of his M4 and the second man fell to the ground, blood pooling on the pavement from the three new holes in his head.

The truck, still running, sat in place; the driver's dead foot resting on the brake pedal. Cliff quickly made his way to the open passenger's door and climbed into the cab; the seat was covered in glass fragments, bone, and blood. He pushed the gear selector up into "park" before opening the driver's door and shoving the body out of the truck and into the street. Leaning back in the seat for support, Cliff kicked the windshield out completely before dragging the bodies to the back and dropping them into the bed.

The gauge showed a half a tank of gas, and if that was to be believed, then he was in luck. The noise was sure to bring the undead around and maybe more cult members, so Cliff decided to abandon his recon of the neighborhood and try to find some of the supplies he needed elsewhere. He wanted to get back towards the pharmacy he had raided before. There was a Walmart near there, but that was one place he would never want to attempt, as he assumed it would be teeming with the undead. However, Cliff had thought he'd seen an outdoors store near there as well.

Driving quickly towards his destination, Cliff was surprised at the lack of undead on the street. He expected to see more, or at least a few, but there just weren't any to be seen. *I wonder if the cult has been culling the herd or what the deal is ... maybe they're all trapped in the homes.* Cliff continued to wonder about it until he realized that he really didn't care. It didn't matter why; he should just be happy that there weren't many undead around to cause him more problems. His optimism fell to the wayside as he passed Walmart; there were hundreds of undead bumping around the cars in the parking lot and he could only assume many more were trapped inside. Passing quickly, Cliff saw the sign for Shooter's Country. The glass windows were broken, the front door propped open, and except for a single SUV, the parking lot was empty. He slowed and drove past, looking at the store, before looping in the parking lot and backing into the handicapped spot by the front door. He left the motor running and the driver's door open when he exited the truck.

Broken glass crunched under Cliff's boots as he stepped into the interior of the shop, his rifle up and ready, scanning for any threats. The gun cases were all broken, not a single weapon left. The shelves of ammo were likewise bare. Behind the counter, up on the higher shelves, sat a couple of Nikon spotting scopes. Those were just what he needed. Well, he only needed one, but hey, at these prices who could resist getting two. On the shelf below them was a generic gun cleaning kit, a couple cans of Gun Scrubber, and two large bottles of Break Free. *Everyone wanted guns and ammo, but no one took the tools to keep them clean and working. Fuck that. A clean M4 is a happy M4.*

The new supplies, spotting scopes, and cleaning gear went into plastic shopping bags. Cliff walked out into the pale light of the rising sun and his still-running truck. Driving back to the neighborhood of his new house, Cliff turned north two blocks early and parked in the driveway of a different house, next to a large fifth-wheel RV, which he hoped would block the view of the truck if another patrol glanced down the street. He left the bodies in the bed of the truck.

CHAPTER 16

Big Bend National Park
March 4, Year 1

Jessie felt ready, emotionally prepared to start her long journey. The day before was spent cataloguing her supplies and digging through the rubble of the ruined cabins for any more gear that survived the blast and the bikers. Much to her amazement, the last remaining wall tent was intact, the heavy plastic box having protected it from the rubble of the collapsed cabin. After some debate, she decided to take Jack's FJ45 Land Cruiser instead of Malachi's International Scout. The FJ was the larger four-door version and could simply hold more gear; regardless, the Scout reminded her of Keeley's death every time she saw it. Malachi's specially built off-road trailer was also left behind. Not that it wouldn't have been useful; she just couldn't think of a good enough reason to haul it along.

Of all the things she had, of all the supplies she catalogued and organized, the one thing she wished she had was the shortwave radio. In Terlingua, Bexar said he wished he had it, but it had been in the RV, which was totaled. Jessie realized that even though the RV was wrecked, the radio could have survived the crash. It was a long shot, but it was worth checking it out on the way, since she would be passing right by it. Besides the radio, on her list were prenatal vitamins and a long list of baby supplies. She would be the only guest at her baby shower and the gifts would consist of items scavenged from stores as she found them. She thought back to Keeley. Before she was potty trained she used something like three to five diapers a day for nearly three years. *That's over five thousand diapers*, she thought.

Jessie sat on the ground next to the FJ. She felt stupid, letting Bexar knock her up again. Now she was a single mother at the end of the world. She began to hyperventilate. She closed her eyes and focused on her breathing, forcing herself to calm down, remembering that for thousands of years before modern medicine, women had had babies. They didn't have disposable diapers and they made it just fine. *I'll make it. There are many weeks until October; I'll raid every store I see and start baby prepping. Formula, bottles, everything I could ever need ... a nursery scavenger hunt.*

With one more deep breath, Jessie wiped the tears from her eyes and stood. If she was going to leave in the morning, she needed to double check her gear list and locate anything essential she was missing. Along with the tent, she found the old green Coleman stove in the cabin rubble, along with three cans of fuel for it. *See! Our prepping wasn't so bad. Some of it survived and I'll survive too.* Jessie placed her hand on her belly. *Don't worry, little peanut, you and me are in this together; we'll make it.*

CHAPTER 17

"Chief, the team's loaded—weapons hot and ready to roll."

"Thanks, Hammer. Move it out."

Aymond made a circular motion with his head and climbed into the passenger's seat of the lead M-ATV. The sun was beginning to crest over the eastern mountains. The cold air hung heavy around them as they left what had become their home over the past few months. He always had this feeling whenever he had to leave an FOB while deployed—even the worst, most desolate places became home after you lived there awhile. What made it worse was that no matter how bad the conditions were, no matter how much time you spent improving your position, and no matter how much better the return back to civilization would be, this was the place where you lived and fought, the place where your teammates died. It was sacred ground and it always hurt to leave it in enemy hands.

The enemy ... the enemy was death ... worse than death. It is the legions of the dead tirelessly marching forward in battle against the living. Aymond looked out the thick, bullet-resistant windows at the buildings of the MWTC, scanning the battle improvements, Hesco walls, and shooting platforms, confident that the dead would soon overtake what they had fought so hard to get.

The large armored trucks lumbered along the asphalt at a conservative forty-five mph, as per the plan. The goal was to conserve fuel more than to save time. Time was something they appeared to have in abundance; fuel, on the other hand, was a scarce commodity to be cherished and preserved. With the gearing of the big trucks and the heavy loads they carried, forty-five mph was their best guess for the highest possible fuel mileage. Driving towards the rising sun, the convoy turned right onto Highway 395, towards the tiny town of Bridgeport. As close as it was, with their slow speed it would take nearly an hour to drive into the first town on their route. Due to the lay of the mountain range, even though their destination was south of where they sat, they had to travel east first.

Initially, they entertained the thought of traveling overland instead of using the roads, as the trucks were built with that task in mind. But without any support or recovery crews, the risk of losing a vehicle to damage or rolling over was too great. No, their route would lie across improved surfaces—roads, even dirt roads, and highways. The problem was that roads and highways go places. Places have people, and people quickly become members of the legion of Zeds. Zeds always mean problems. The entire MWTC staff and six of his own MSOT were lost to the Zeds during the first few days of the attack. All of those men and women, fellow Marines, had to be put down. At first they dug individual graves, but after conditions continued to deteriorate, the individual graves turned to mass graves until finally the surviving members had to resort to simply burning the bodies. With hundreds of bodies, and more Zeds shambling to their location every day, digging graves by hand with only eight people was simply impossible.

Each of the little roadside spots on the highway looked like it had been hit by an airstrike. Staring out the window at the countryside rolling slowly by, Aymond let his mind drift and wander into the desert around them. He was surprised to hear the voice of Ryan Hammer, his driver, come through his earpiece.

"Heads up—Zeds on the road. We're entering the edge of the town."

The operation briefing laid down the ROE, rules of engagement. While in convoy, they were to use the vehicle-mounted heavy weapons sparingly to conserve ammo, and to avoid driving over bodies if at all possible. They couldn't risk damaging their only means of transportation by running down Zeds like they were in some crazed video game. At no point would anyone dismount from the vehicles and engage the enemy on foot, unless absolutely necessary. If a Zed can't reach you, it can't bite you, and it can't reach you when you're inside an M-ATV.

Just like back in Iraq, the convoy didn't slow for fear of ambush; they just swerved around the half-dozen undead in the road as they entered the town. The view through the windshield was unbelievable. Aymond was amazed at the extent of the destruction. The town lay in absolute ruins; many buildings stood only as burned-out shells.

This must have been where that last large wave of Zeds came from, he thought.

Hammer swerved the heavy truck around another group of undead before reaching the town's far edge. They exited the town; a ribbon of asphalt pierced the open desert around them. Abandoned vehicles were sparse and easy to drive around without having to slow much. Aymond hoped that the rest of the journey would be this easy, but they had a long way to go and many more towns to cross. He keyed the radio. "Check in, over."

"Dagger Two, Dagger One, we're good, over."

"Dagger Three, Dagger One, are we there yet? Over."

Aymond smirked. If Kirk was anything, he was a perpetual smart ass. It hurt his career path in the conventional Marine Corps, but once he made it to Force Recon and started rotating through MARSOC, he found his place in the world. Aymond felt lucky to have him after the heavy losses of the battle to win the MWTC.

Waxahachie Creek, TX

Chivo drove through the damaged gate at the park entrance and turned right, reaching the highway. The tiny town of Bardwell lay ahead and the team was zipping along at fifty-five mph. It seemed fast to Bexar, nearly too fast; they had agreed to hold it to forty-five. But he was only the navigator; he had to assume that Chivo was well-trained in advanced driving techniques. Nevertheless, it was still hard for Bexar to let go of being the driver. He hated being a passenger.

Bexar took a deep breath, held it for a couple of seconds, then exhaled slowly. None of them wore seat belts, which also felt odd to him, but trying to get a seatbelt around all the gear they were wearing, plus his rifle, just wouldn't work. Never mind that his lap was full of map sections and the atlas. It reminded Bexar of being a rookie working the night shift; he never wore a seatbelt in the patrol car—he would get stuck in the car with the seatbelt wrapped around something on his duty belt. If you're diving out of a car to chase a suspect or have to get out of a "death chair," as cops called the driver's seat, because you were ambushed, well, suffice it to say wearing your seatbelt simply was a no-go.

"Bexar, eyes up, man. We're hitting the edge of town."

At first glance the town looked nearly pristine. No signs of fire damage, no burned-out buildings, just a town empty of people and movement. Along the main highway through the town all the cars that had presumably been on the roadway were pushed against the buildings, into the windows and store fronts. The paint on the sides of the cars was scraped off, the vehicles all badly damaged. Light poles were knocked down and flattened, like a huge snow plow had come through town and blindly cleared a path for intrepid travelers.

"What the shit?" Bexar said softly.

"We've seen this before, on our previous drive here. A big pack of undead came through, pushing through cars and anything else in their way, like a bulldozer. There were more than we could count on I-10; fucking huge herd of them, destroying everything in their path like an Old Testament plague." Chivo shook his head and signed the cross across his chest.

He slowed the Defender as they entered town. Except for the damage left in their wake, there was no sign of the dead now, discounting the truly dead, whose bodies rotted in the sun. Bexar stared at the damage as they passed. He noted that the vehicles were all pushed away at the same angle from the middle of the road, same with the light poles, which were broken off at the base.

"We're driving in the same direction the herd of dead went."

"How do you know that?"

"Look at the path of destruction. Everything is pushed forward and out from us. We're driving towards the ass end of this mess."

Apollo, listening to the conversation in the front seat, keyed his radio. "Clint ... have you figured out what direction that large pack of undead is traveling?"

"Not yet. But the last pass showed them congregating at a larger city to your northwest."

Bexar flipped pages in his binder of map sections. "That's probably Waxahachie; we pretty much have to go through the city before taking a route around."

"Fucking awesome," Chivo mumbled as he eased the Defender back to forty-five mph, exiting the town. The small Texas highway only had a couple of vehicles that had previously been on the road; they were all pushed off into the side ditches.

"Say what you will about the dead, but at least they were nice enough to clear a path for us."

Everyone turned to look at Lindsey. "Hey ... just saying."

Big Bend National Park, Chisos Basin

Sweat dripped from her face as Jessie finished loading the FJ. *This is why Bexar was always the family Sherpa; this is no task for a pregnant woman.* The job complete, she sat on the ground, surveying the scene around her. The park had always been a happy place full of fond memories, but now all she could see around her was death and pain. Even if the world righted itself once again, Jessie knew she was never coming back here. There was no way she could handle the pain of the memories.

Standing slowly, nausea washed over her body in waves. Jessie steadied herself on the side of the SUV, taking deep breaths, trying to keep her breakfast down. With Keeley, she had never been one of those "I'm so happy being pregnant—everything is awesome!" kinds of women. She was sick for most of her first pregnancy and secretly Jessie hated those women, the Internet Supermoms of Creativity and Joy. She didn't know how they did it; right now it was all she could do to simply keep food in her stomach.

Jessie climbed into the driver's seat, started the motor, and drove down the hill towards the exit of The Basin. Twenty minutes later she stopped at the gas station near Panther Junction, took the empty gas cans and the hand-cranked pump and got to work. Fifteen minutes and minus one stomach-full of breakfast later, the fuel tank of the FJ was full along with her three, five-gallon gas cans. She suspected that this would be her last easy fuel stop. Jessie lifted the gas cans onto the roof rack, next to the jugs of water. *My problem isn't fuel, it's water. No fuel and I can walk; no clean water, I get sick and die.*

Turning west, Jessie drove towards Study Butte, passing the turnoff for The Ross Maxwell Scenic Drive for the very last time. The desert drifted by outside her windows and before she knew it she was pulling into Study Butte-Terlingua. About a dozen undead milled about near the gas station. In the road for the turnoff towards the Terlingua Ghost Town lay part of a burned corpse and its motorcycle.

Jessie drove into the gas station's parking lot, shifted the truck into neutral, set the brake and climbed out, leaving the motor running. After their scare in Marathon with one of the trucks not wanting to start, she would take no chances. Surprisingly, the glass doors of the gas station were still intact. She banged on the doors a few times then leaned against them to hold them closed. Facing away from the store and towards the fuel pumps, she watched the undead shamble closer to the FJ and to her. With her rifle up, she started picking off the undead closest to her and her vehicle. She felt a hard thump against the doors behind her. Putting down the last of the parking lot undead, Jessie turned to see half of a dead woman's rotting face snarling at her, gnashing its teeth and clawing at the glass door. Jessie stepped back and pulled the door open quickly. The woman fell forward and Jessie fired her rifle once, putting her down for good. Propping the door open, she threw a rock from the sidewalk into the store and waited for a response. After counting to one hundred and hearing nothing, she walked into the dark interior.

Behind the counter were plastic shopping bags; she grabbed a few and walked through the aisles. Towards the back of the store was a small selection of diapers. Those went into the bags, along with the lone package of baby wipes and the whole rack's worth of single-dose Tylenol packets. *Fucking Tylenol. I might as well take Skittles. I wish I could take Advil while I'm pregnant ... hmmm ... Skittles.* Jessie walked through the candy isle and put an entire box of Skittles and then Sour Straws into her bag.

The undead woman she had killed in the doorway lay face down on the sidewalk, but she also politely served to hold the door open. Shopping trip complete, Jessie walked back into the sunlight to see that her running SUV had attracted a crowd.

She walked towards the edge of the store and yelled, "Hey, over here you rotting assholes. Look at me!" Every pair of milky-white dead eyes snapped to Jessie, followed by their owners' shambling gait across the parking lot towards her and away from the FJ. Her hands full of loot, the rifle hung on the sling across her chest, she waited until the first of the walking corpses were nearly within grasping distance before she quickly moved away and back towards the FJ. Rounding the back of the SUV, a lone corpse stood between her and the driver's door. It moaned and reached with its rotting hands to grab her, but Jessie side kicked the corpse in the pelvis, folding the undead man over at the waist. She grabbed the driver's door handle and slammed the door open against the man's face, knocking him to the ground. Before he could stand up again, Jessie was already in the FJ, letting the clutch out and pulling out of the parking lot, towards the Terlingua Ghost Town and the destroyed trailer.

Cortez, CO

On the roof of his house, Cliff lay with a dark blanket covering his body. He was on his belly, propped up on his arms, the blanket draped all the way to the front edge of the spotting scope. His hands held a small notepad and pen, marking distances in each direction from the house, creating a range card so he could accurately hit targets with enough hold over on his rifle sights, if everything went to hell and he was under siege. *Everything always goes wrong. Fucking Murphy and his laws; if I ever meet that bastard I'm going to kick his ass.*

Facing west, Cliff could see out to the highway. *Three hundred and fifty yards to the edge of the pavement,* he thought as he jotted down his estimate. A sketch and notes were marked on the lined paper. Cliff knew those shots would be harder, the optic on his rifle having no magnification, but with his M4, it was a very doable shot and fell within his well-honed abilities. Cliff pulled his face away from the eye piece and blinked slowly, resetting his vision before looking at the sun marching across the western sky. *Looks like there's about four hours until sunset ... four hours of sleep.*

Still concealed under the blanket, Cliff slowly slid down the roof, over the main portion of the house and onto the garage roof, then climbed into the open second-story window. Melting into the shadows of the room, he watched out the window to see if anyone had noticed or if there was any reaction to his movement. Fifteen minutes later, Cliff lay in the master bedroom, the alarm on his watch set. His first task was to recon the cult—start trying to figure out their movements, times, and schedule of operations. In order to do that he had to stay in place during the daylight; he would have to move at night to avoid being seen.

Italy, TX

Idling in the middle of the highway, the Defender sat indifferent to the marked lanes of travel. Lindsey and Bexar stood on each side of the SUV, rifles at the ready, watching for any movement. Apollo stood rear security while Chivo stood on the roof rack with his binoculars to his face, slowly scanning the scene ahead of him. Lindsey's area of responsibility included a squat two-story apartment building; Bexar scanned the front of the small "supermarket" grocery store. He wasn't sure if it was the sunlight playing tricks on his vision or if he was really seeing movement in the shadows of the dark windows. Apollo's rifle remained silent, the tagalong undead not close enough to make a difference yet.

"Hey Chivo, you might want to wrap it up. I think the grocery story is overrun and I don't want to hang around to see if they figure out how to work the doors."

Chivo climbed down onto the back bumper of the Defender before taking his place behind the wheel, and each of the others returned to their previous spots as Chivo shifted into gear and continued west, into the tiny town of Italy, Texas. The highway curved and turned into Main Street, passing small, stucco-fronted homes. They entered the two-block-long downtown section. The cars were again pushed out of their parking spots and into the fronts of the businesses and buildings. The signs and light poles were knocked forward, and, as before, they followed the same path the group was driving. Speeding through the town at a respectable forty mph, they quickly exited downtown and reached the four-way intersection of Highway 34 and 77. Chivo stopped, ironically obeying traffic laws. It would have been comical, had any stop signs still been standing. While idling at the intersection, Apollo called up from the back of the SUV, "We're cool now, but in about five minutes our 'friends' will arrive by the dozen."

"Roger. OK, Bexar, which way?"

"Straight takes us to I-35, which takes us into Waxahachie; turning right puts us on Highway 77, which takes us into … Waxahachie."

"So we're stuck regardless?"

"Sort of. We need to get to 287, and that goes through Waxahachie, but personally, I don't think we should be going anywhere near that place. Compared to Italy here, Waxahachie is a mega-metropolis."

Apollo keyed his radio. "Clint, are you still on station? Over."

"Roger. Go ahead, over."

"How do the overheads of Waxahachie look? Over."

"Stand by … shit."

"Clint?"

"The SATINT just went offline. I can't pull anything up and I'm not sure why."

Every head in the SUV snapped around when the first walking corpse slapped the back glass at the living occupants it wanted for lunch.

"Fuck this noise, just pick one, Bexar."

"Straight, then. We'll try I-35."

Chivo drove away quickly, leaving the gathering dead grasping at the empty air for a fresh meal. Two minutes later Chivo stopped next to a large Western-themed gas station.

"Holy shit. Look at that."

Bexar smirked, "I know, everyone in town hates that dome building, especially since it's built up to look like the Starship Enterprise."

"No ass hat, the cars. Look at the fucking bridge."

Pushed over the edge of the bridge, cars had fallen to the pavement below. Their previous occupants, now undead, tried to walk on their shattered bones. The dead streamed across the bridge like a solid wall of corpses and flies; the sheer force of the number of them pushing cars, signs, and anything else in their way over the railing and onto the pile of wreckage below. Bodies, crushed by the passing horde, lay smeared along the concrete barrier of the bridge.

Apollo gaped at the scene through the windshield. "That's fucked up. Let me guess; they're headed towards Waxahachie, aren't they?"

"Yup," Bexar replied, nodding his head.

"What if we just drive straight ahead?"

"I don't know. The map doesn't show much; the road's too small."

"Fuck it, mano. Straight we go. It's better than jumping into the critical mass march of the undead."

Chivo let the clutch out and drove towards the overpass, weaving around the cars and leftover body parts that had been pushed off the bridge.

"You realize that all the roads in this area most likely lead back towards I-35, right?" Bexar said to no one in particular.

Terlingua, TX

The Wagoneer still sat in the middle of the highway and Jessie stopped the FJ next to it. The body that Bexar had stuffed into the driver's seat still lay half-out of the open door. Rifle in hand, Jessie walked out into the desert where the destroyed RV trailer lay torn open. A month hadn't passed, yet it seemed like a lifetime ago that her family, still intact, set out for Groom Lake together. Most of the outer shell of the RV was solid, but Jessie couldn't fit into the crushed interior space with her rifle. So, she laid it on the desert floor and climbed onto the top of the RV. She lowered herself through the open side door, which was now pointed up towards the sky. Digging through the jumbled mess and broken cabinets she found the hand-cranked shortwave radio—and it appeared to be undamaged. She lifted the radio out the door and onto the top of the RV before pulling herself up and out. From the top, she saw that the FJ, which she had left running, had attracted some uglier members of her fan club. She climbed down and gathered her rifle, took a kneeling position, and began slowly putting down the undead for good. One by one they fell, seven in all. Jessie walked back to the FJ, set the radio on the dash, and looked at her road atlas. She wasn't exactly sure where Groom Lake was, but she knew it was near Las Vegas because Bexar had tried telling her about Janet Airlines, a semi-secret commuter airline run by the government to ferry workers from Las Vegas to Groom Lake every day. A few minutes later, she found what she thought might be her destination on the map, tracing back from Las Vegas to I-40. She opened the New Mexico map page then continued to trace the Interstate east across the state. Looking at the different routes, she decided that since I-25 was large enough to show on her atlas and it bridged I-10 to I-40, it would be a good path to follow for now.

Jessie held the Texas map open in her lap and retraced highways from I-10. She realized that she would need to go back to the gas station and stay on Highway 118 instead of heading straight into Terlingua. *Dammit Bexar! You were going the wrong way. We might be together; maybe Keeley would be alive ... if you knew what the fuck you were doing for once and where we were going.* Tears fell onto the paper; she shook uncontrollably, mad at Bexar, mad at herself, and her heart aching for her little girl.

Near Bridgeport, CA

Aymond and the remaining members of his MSOT kept rolling at a steady forty-five mph after exiting the small town. He watched out the tiny side window; the thick bullet-resistant glass made the terrain look a bit odd, but there wasn't much to see anyway. This part of California was rugged and also quite under-developed, which meant there never were many people in the area to begin with. This is why the U.S. Government had used this area for training; there wasn't much land available for commercial development. It was a give and take that left the three M-ATVs driving through a landscape that could have been Mars.

The cars abandoned on the highway were sparse, and Hammer maneuvered the heavy truck around them with ease. About every third vehicle there would be one or two walking corpses, or Zeds. Per the ROE that Aymond had placed on his team, they ignored the threats and drove past in an effort to save time and ammo. The dead might have come from the vehicles on the road or from the small clusters of homes and businesses placed every few miles. Aymond didn't know, and quite frankly, he didn't care. The Chief wasn't completely sure, but after the battle to win control of the MWTC from the dead, he was certain that their trip to Twentynine Palms would be bad. If they had to go through San Diego, it would be even worse than anything they had ever experienced in their three tours in Afghanistan. The drive produced the same feeling of impending battle that riding a convoy to a new Forward Operating Base in The Stan had. The men seemed to have the same thought, each of them passing the time in their own way. Some played cards, others slept. Sleep is a luxury in wartime, so like warriors throughout all of history, they slept before the battle. The stress, mixed with anticipation, was palpable in the heavily armored truck.

Terlingua, TX

Her eyes puffy and red from tears, Jessie strained to see ahead through her windshield. The wind gusted against the side of the vehicle, nearly pushing her out of the traffic lane, not that staying between the painted lane markings on the road actually mattered anymore, but some things are so ingrained that they are hard habits to break.

Dust, thick dust, also blocked her view; slowly she turned left at the intersection where the half-eaten biker and his wrecked motorcycle lay, to travel northbound on 118. She had nothing but unending miles of desert ahead of her until she reached the town of Alpine. There was no real way around the town; she would have to drive through it and hope for the best. It would be the first *real* town that she would drive through since arriving in Big Bend National Park months ago. She could shelter in the desert that spread out before the town if conditions didn't improve, but she thought it might be best for her to drive through while the storm continued to blow sand across the desert landscape. She didn't know if there would be any paint left on the FJ by the time the sand storm was over. Slowly, nearly blinded by the storm, Jessie drove onward into the dust, her destiny unknown.

Near Italy, TX

The civilian atlas was unfolded across the entire dash of the Defender. Bexar traced his finger along a small line that he believed to be the road they were on. *I wish we had Malachi's GPS; that would be handy. All of this high speed gear and they didn't have a turn by turn GPS system ... fucking government.*

"OK guys, good news and bad news. Good news is I think I've figured out what road we're on and we are actually going in the right direction. Bad news is that we still hit I-35 outside of Waxahachie. We don't, however, have to drive through the middle of town ... we're also really close to where my friends and I had our prepper group cache site."

"Anything useful still there?"

"No, just the two friends we buried."

Outside of Lee Vining, CA

The convoy had traveled nearly fifty miles without incident, until they drove past the middle school on the edge of town. The small town saw tourists for the Mono Basin and it appeared to be a popular spot. Hammer slowed as Aymond keyed the radio. "Going weapons hot—stay tight back there ... Ski, light 'em up."

Like agitated workers on strike, a mass of undead crowded the road ahead by a gas station which sat next to the first hotel on the road. The convoy would pass the gas station as they entered the town. In the back of the lead M-ATV, Ski opened fire with the electronically controlled mounted M2. With controlled bursts, the fifty-caliber rounds ripped the crowd of walking Zeds apart, blood, bone ... whole pieces of bodies littered the asphalt. Every fifth round was a tracer, shining like a laser arcing through the air, raking fire back and forth, decimating the dead. The rounds also peppered the roadside motel, which began to smoke from the burning hot tracers, catching the building on fire.

Ryan Hammer picked the spot that had the least amount of bones and body parts and threaded the trucks through the small gap. The handful of undead that "survived" the automatic fire bounced off the fenders and sides of the heavy trucks. The rest of the M-ATVs followed Hammer's trail through the carnage and the convoy slowly sped back up to a blistering forty-five mph, leaving the hotel and a host of the undead burning in their wake.

CHAPTER 18

Cortez, CO
March 5, Year 1

The sun sat low against the western mountains. Cliff readied his gear. The school kid backpack held a few bottles of water and some cans of Vienna Sausages that he'd scavenged from the home's pantry. The dark-colored blanket he used for camouflage doubling as his poncho was worn over his shoulders. With all of his gear on, Cliff conducted a rattle check, shaking back and forth then hopping up and down. The gear moved more than he would have liked, especially the backpack, but nothing clanked and nothing clinked. Gear rattling is not a sound found in nature; therefore it is a tell-tale giveaway that a human is on the move nearby.

Armed with a ten-year-old Chamber of Commerce map, Cliff picked out a spot to spend the rest of the night and the first day of his recon mission. After climbing out of the window above the garage and closing it behind him, Cliff lowered himself to the ground. The *new* truck lacked a windshield. He took the time to break out the tail lights, turn signals, and brake lights. He disconnected the horn and drove south towards the heart of Cortez with the headlights off. He needed stealth, not an accidental horn blast or bright red lights glowing in the darkness behind him, inviting unwanted followers.

The cult member that he had interviewed before the unscheduled skydiving lesson was administered confessed that the cult was based at a school. The other survivors had said that the middle school was where the survivors were located before it had been overrun. He believed they had been at least partially rescued.

So that left only a handful of other school buildings to recon. The grade school on 4th Street was as good a place as any to start, so that's where he headed.

Hanging back a few blocks from the school, Cliff was disappointed to see that the neighborhoods were mainly comprised of one-story homes—low vantage points. But at least with the trees still bare, his line of sight was better than it would have been later in the year. At the end of Harrison Street, Cliff found a large open lot. He followed the dirt drive southward until reaching a fence line. Ditching the truck among the brush near some trees, Cliff climbed over the fence into the back area of some two-story apartments. To his right, a row of homes stood between him and the front of the school, hiding him well on one side. The sun had set and the darkness gave him more cover than he could have hoped, especially with his shape disguised by the blanket. Sneaking around to the front of the next to last apartment, Cliff gently walked up the metal stairs, as quietly as he could. Back against the wall, he tried the door to the apartment; it was unlocked. He pushed the door open slowly. The living room and kitchen were in view; a card table had been knocked over and blood was smeared on the kitchen wall. *Well, shit*, he sighed.

Cliff reached under the blanket and drew his knife. He kicked the door frame a couple of times, making enough noise to attract the undead but quietly enough not to be heard from the street. As Cliff had guessed, a moan erupted from the back of the apartment, followed by a walking corpse crashing through the hallway and into the living area. The poor bastard must have been significantly obese before he died and reanimated, because he was now a massive pile of rotting shit. Before the fat corpse could stumble out onto the porch, Cliff closed the distance and plunged his knife into its skull, which split open like a ripe melon. The knife pulled out of the skull with a wet slurp as the now truly dead corpse fell to the carpet. Thick black pus covered the knife blade and Cliff's hand. Maggots crawled through the mottled and hanging skin, making the mounds of rotting flesh ripple with movement. Cliff shut and latched the apartment door then threw up on the carpet. *Goddammit, these things are getting worse.* Cliff had to leave the body where it was. First of all, he didn't want to touch it; and secondly, if he pulled it outside it would be obvious that someone was in the apartment, and stealth was his only ally in Cortez. He continued down the hallway. The back bedroom's window faced north and the school could be seen through the bare trees.

Cliff pushed the bed away from the wall and flipped it up on its side to get it out of the way. He raised the window shade slightly, just enough for the spotting scope's field of view to be unobstructed. Then, he retrieved the card table from the kitchen, along with a folding chair, and set up for a long night and day of recon. Assuming that the cult had at most a limited number of NODs, they would probably only be active in the daylight; but then again, he hadn't expected them to have a shoulder-fired rocket that would take down a C-130 either.

With his small notepad in hand, pen ready, Cliff propped up on the table with the spotting scope. The blanket was draped across his body and to the front of the scope, breaking his form in the shadows, just in case one of the nuts with the cult was trained in counter-sniper techniques. He sat and waited patiently for signs of movement.

Highway 396, CA

The endless desert mountains were punctuated by an occasional home, farm, building, or business, but the monotonous drive continued on and on at forty-five mph. It had been five hours since the convoy left the MWTC, and the sun was hanging low to the west. The only excitement after Lee Vining was that the men wanted to take the turn off for Mammoth Mountain to see if any of the resorts were still up and running. They knew the answer, but to an enlisted Marine, there is always some glimmer of hope, especially when passing a ski resort. There had to be some possibility of civilization, or he would lose his mind. Both Bishop and Big Pine, Indian reservations, passed by with hardly a whimper, only a few Zeds for the convoy to weave around, some bouncing off the trucks as they passed. They were getting low on fuel and it was quickly nearing time to set up a secure location for resting during the night. Aymond had toyed with the idea of hot swapping drivers and rolling continually, but everyone needed a break. Even the guys who had no other task during the past day except riding in an M-ATV would need a reprieve from the noise and vibration, not to mention it would do them good to get out to stretch and move around freely.

When Highway 14 split off of 395, the sign pointed left for China Lake. *China Lake! How could I have forgotten about China Lake? ... Probably because you're not a naval aviator, dumbass.* The convoy passed another sign, showing the direction for the Inyokern Airport, a civilian field. Aymond shook his head and keyed the radio. "Dagger Actual, Dagger Two, Dagger Three, over?"

"Two, over."

"Three, over."

"Dagger Actual ... we're going to pull into Inyokern Field to bivouac. Eyes up and continue to follow, over."

"Two, clear."

"Three, clear."

The convoy took the exit off of 395 and drove into the small desert town. The area appeared completely deserted; not a single body in sight, no burned-out buildings, nothing to indicate anything was amiss. *Makes sense. If I was a civilian who lived next to a large naval installation and an EMP hit, I would head to the installation for help and shelter.* The convoy passed through the town without incident and turned onto Airport Road. The road ran past several fenced-off driveways leading to the small hangars; Aymond was looking for a way through one, but at the end of the road they found yet another gate. He keyed the radio.

"Dagger Actual. Gonzales—check in, over."

"Go, Chief."

"You and Snow take the bolt cutters and get us a way in."

A few moments later Gonzales and Snow strode past the lead vehicle and to the gate. With a few cuts to the chain link, Snow slid through the hole in the fence, opened the control box to the gate, flipped the release handle over and pulled the gate open. The convoy drove into the field. Gonzales tied the middle of the hole in the fence back together using 550-cord; Snow slid the gate closed and flipped the lever over to engage the security lock.

Driving across the ramp, Aymond called Stop to the convoy in front of an old WWII-era Kodiak hangar and keyed the radio.

"Hammer and Happy, you're with me to clear the hangar. Ski and Davis, recon south for hostiles and supplies. Snow and Kirk, you two take north."

No one responded, but they didn't need to. By the time Aymond stepped out of the lead vehicle, the divided groups were already headed in their assigned directions. Ryan Hammer and Mike Happy formed up with Aymond.

Ten minutes later the Kodiak hangar was clear, nothing found inside except a handful of aircraft and tools. The North team returned, but Ski and Davis weren't back yet. There had been no gunfire or radio calls, so unless they had both had an aneurism at the same time, they were probably okay.

"Aymond. Ski and Davis—what's the hold up?"

"Chief, found something. We'll be back in two mikes."

From the other side of the small rows of hangars Aymond heard an engine cough to life, and black smoke billowed into the air above them. A moment later an absolutely ancient-looking fuel truck slowly pulled around the side of the hangars, driving towards the rest of the team. Davis drove as Ski hung off the running board.

Dark, oily exhaust filled the air behind the lumbering truck as it ground to a halt beside the M-ATVs.

Ski jumped off the running board. "Chief, this thing is full of Jet-A. That's jet fuel—that'll run in the M-ATVs, right?"

"Yup, good find. You're now in charge of the fueling detail. And turn that fucking thing off before it fills the whole desert with black smoke, telling everyone in the area someone is on the airport."

Ski turned towards Davis and made a cut sign across his throat. The motor shut off and the area fell silent. The black smoke dissipated in the wind.

Near Alpine, TX

The dust storm finally abated, but it cost Jessie a lot of driving time. She reached the southern end of Alpine, Texas, just as the sun was beginning to set. Stopped again in the middle of the highway, Jessie had the road atlas unfolded across the entire dashboard before finally pinpointing her location. *I have to drive through the middle of town, but do I want to do it now or in the morning? Maybe I can find a spot to sleep tonight ... or maybe there is an ambush waiting for me.* Jessie sighed, pushed the unfolded map into the passenger's seat and, with a deep breath, put the FJ in gear and drove into Alpine. She didn't know much about the town except that Sul Ross University was there. Following the road signs, Jessie turned left after the tracks, drove through the middle of town, then turned right and back onto 118 traveling north. Undead moved aimlessly through the town's center; Jessie didn't count them, but guessed there to be at least seventy. The shambling corpses turned to follow her SUV as she passed. Jessie took a turn onto a side street and drove slowly for three blocks, nearly idling the truck while in gear, letting the walking cadavers just start to catch up to her then making sure that they made the turn behind her vehicle. Once she had become the leader of a macabre parade through the neighborhood, Jessie sped up, turned left and then left again, and headed back to 118, hoping that she was able to shake her undead tail. On the north end of town, she slammed on the brakes. A squat metal building sat to her left with a sign that read, "Road and Bridge Department." *Perfect,* she thought.

Jessie drove into the open gate, got out, closed the gate behind her, then parked with the metal structure blocking the view of her vehicle from the road. She scanned her surroundings and saw three pickup trucks and two large silver fuel tanks on stands at the back of the property. *First the building.* Jessie tried the door and found it unlocked. She slowly pulled the door wide and propped it open with a rock. She banged on the door a few times, then backed up and waited by the front of the FJ with her rifle braced on the top of the vehicle's hood. Soon a man in camouflaged coveralls lumbered out, a dead man, a walking corpse. Jessie let him clear the doorway before firing a single shot into his forehead. His skull exploded backwards before he hit the ground. She waited, counting slowly to one hundred. Nothing else came out of the building. Five minutes later, she was confident that the small office space was clear. The covered equipment area housed front loaders and backhoes, but those were of no use to Jessie. The five-hundred-gallon tank at the back of the property with "UNLEADED" painted in stencil was, though. Jessie used her gas cans to top off the FJ's tank, then refilled the cans with gas from the gravity-fed tanks. Jessie checked the trucks parked at the back of the property. All three of them had red gas cans in their beds, all three about half-full. Not wanting to chance bad fuel, Jessie poured the contents out and refilled them from the large fuel tank. She lashed them on the roof rack with the others, parked the FJ by the office building, grabbed her bag, and went inside for the evening, looking forward to a meal of MRE surprise washed down with powdered Gatorade.

Outside Waxahachie, TX

Bexar stood on the roof rack of the Defender, the binoculars to his face as he surveyed the scene at the intersection with I-35E. In the fenced-off businesses' lots on either side of him, walking corpses clawed at the fences, trying to reach him and the rest of the team. After close to five minutes, Bexar climbed down and sat in the passenger's seat.

"As far as I can see ... they're all on the northbound side of the Jersey barrier. Well, most of them; there are a few on this side, but nothing like the other side. Also, looks like the access road goes up and over the Interstate instead of under."

"What are the other options?"

Sitting in the very back, on top of a case of MREs, Lindsey spoke up. "What if we just follow the access road on this side and see if it gets any better up the road? Maybe if we get out in front of them we can outrun them."

Bexar shrugged as a sign of indifferent support.

Chivo put the Defender in gear and turned left, heading the wrong way on the access road. The handful of vehicles left in the road didn't pose a large risk for the team, as the SUV was easily able to drive around them, swerving once into the grass for a bit before continuing north. The mass of walking corpses off to their right was staggering. Thousands and thousands of them marched silently northward, death's soldiers ready to bring the war to whomever they found. Some lunged over the concrete barrier between the lanes of travel as they passed, but the team drove too fast for any of the dead to catch up. Bexar, following the map, directed Chivo onto the Interstate, ignoring a Do Not Enter sign on the exit ramp. More vehicles littered the roadway here, causing the group to slow. Twice the undead grasped onto the hood of the Defender, only to fall off as they tried to crawl towards the windshield.

Exiting via an on-ramp, Chivo followed the access road around and up onto Business 287. The road, a small highway, had only a few undead in sight. The tension in the Defender fell away as they drove further away from the horrible march of dead.

Bexar traced his finger along the map. "We'll meet up with the regular 287 in a few miles, and thank God we're away from that fucking horde of corpses."

Chivo nodded. "That explains why we haven't seen more of those things walking around until now. It's like they're attracted to one another; they all seem to move in the same direction. Weird. It would suck to be stuck in that mess—you'd be lucky if you had a chance to kill yourself before being ripped apart."

Chivo piloted the Defender onto US 287, continuing northwest towards Colorado. Apollo snored in the back of the SUV. Now that they were away from the mass of undead, he needed to nap so he could take over driving for the night shift.

CHAPTER 19

Cortez, CO
March 6, Year 1

Cliff finished the bottle of water then pissed into the empty bottle. Screwing the lid on tightly, he tossed the urine-filled container over by the upturned mattress. So far, he'd been correct in assuming the movement would be light at night. There appeared to be a few patrols out, but there wasn't much else. Unless his hunch was wrong; maybe there wasn't much activity at all and the high point of the day was right now. He wouldn't know without watching for longer, which was the point of conducting the recon, but the meth he had found on the other cult members meant that they would be really unpredictable, possibly staying awake for days on end before crashing. One guess he did get right was the location of the school the cult was operating out of, unless, of course, they were using more than one.

The sky was beginning to glow from the rising sun; Cliff was facing the wrong way to see it, but the sky was definitely getting lighter. Checking his watch, he made sure to note what time the sun rose, just as he noted the time it had set the previous night. Watching the days get longer would help him keep track of the season by adding roughly a minute to every day. *What about daylight savings? I have no idea what day that is this year.* Cliff had a moment of concern before realizing how stupid that worry was. Time zones were basically a thing of the past; local time was all that mattered and it would be set by the sun, until things started to come back together for society.

SSC

"No, I don't know why, but we've lost all ability to communicate with any of them; even the communications satellites are only giving me spotty connectivity."

"So you're saying that we can't see what's going on and we may not be able to talk to anyone about it?"

"That's it exactly, Amanda."

"Dammit."

Near Mansfield, TX

"What do you mean you can't get a lock?"

"I mean that it's like there's no satellite out there. I can't get any signal."

"Are you sure you have everything plugged in right and you're using the right azimuth?"

"Fuck you, Apollo. Yes, I'm doing it right."

"OK, OK. So SATCOM is down. How likely is it that all of this would fail simultaneously all on its own?"

"Pretty fucking low, mano. Pretty fucking low."

Bexar, standing on the roof rack with the binoculars, called down, "I think if we just go for it we can figure it out along the way."

"Sure, for now, but then there's Fort fucking Worth. That'll be worse than El Paso, man."

Apollo shrugged. "We can't talk to anyone, and we have to drive through a large city to go help a guy we haven't seen in years. We can sit around and bitch about it or we can move along, Bexar. What other routes do we have?"

"I don't know; the roads around Fort Worth are screwy—I never got used to them. We might be able to backtrack and get a different route, but I'm not sure on that. Pretty much all the small highways and FM roads hit the Interstates and go to the big cities. It isn't like West Texas where there is nothing and more nothing along the roads."

Lindsey stood at the rear of the Defender, keeping guard for any undead tagging along. "I'm not getting stuck on a highway sign again; all three of you can fuck yourselves before that happens."

Chivo looked at Apollo, who could only raise his hands to give the universal sign of: "I don't know what her deal is."

"If we go back we might run into that huge herd of those damned things again," Bexar said before climbing off the roof.

"White Bread is right, you know."

Chivo nodded.

The early morning was cold. A strong wind blew out of the north, low gray clouds a gloomy overwatch for their dangerous task. They all climbed back into the Defender, Bexar keeping the navigator's spot up front and Chivo getting behind the wheel again after sleeping for a few hours while Apollo drove through the night. The night drive was slow, very slow; Apollo often had to backtrack and get on the other side of the highway due to collisions blocking the road. Throughout the night the undead would appear like ships in the mist into the green world illuminated by the NODs Apollo wore. Apollo wouldn't chance driving into the grass off the road surface; if they rolled the truck or got it stuck it could cost them their lives.

Near China Lake, CA

The M-ATVs were full of Jet-A, which the manual confirmed they could run on, assuming civilian Jet-A was similar to the military's JP-8. Aymond thought it was; actually he *hoped* it was, to be honest with himself. Once the men were up, the sentries were released from guard duty so they could eat breakfast. Just more MREs, but still better than the cold weather MREs since all of them had run out of fuel for their Jetboils over a month ago. In short order, the convoy was moving out, the previous night's sentries taking the opportunity to sleep in the back of the trucks.

Ski flipped the clutch lever for the gate opener, and once again the gate slid back easily, but this time he didn't take the time to close it behind them as they left. There was no need. Five minutes later, the M-ATVs pulled off the road by another gate, this one for the Naval Air Station. It was a simple, low-tech gate with a chain and a lock. Ski made quick work with the bolt cutters and pushed both the gates open. No way to really secure the gates behind them, but Ski wrapped the chain around the two sections to hold them closed.

The heavy armored trucks drove along the dirt road south of the runways, dust billowing behind them, before their wheels reached the paved runway surface. Aymond made the decision to break into the facility and to use the runway instead of driving onto the facility in the normal fashion. Given the lack of flight activity yesterday afternoon, throughout the night, and still this morning, Aymond's hopes that the facility was intact and had survivors was slim at best.

The runway seemed to stretch on forever, but eventually the convoy pulled onto the flight-line. F-18s sat on the stained concrete. Some of the tires were flat; one of the aircraft's nose gear had collapsed, and their Super Hornet sat nose down with some serious damage from the fall. There was no activity—no flight ops, no personnel, and no movement. Only the heavy diesel rattle of the three M-ATVs filled the desert air.

Aymond pointed and Hammer drove. The convoy followed towards the other side of the maintenance bays, off the flight-line, and eventually onto Sandquist Road, southbound towards the housing, commissary, and headquarters. If the runways were long, this road seemed never-ending. But eventually they reached Inyokern Road and turned left towards the main base facility. Looping around the traffic circle, they pulled alongside of the commissary and the exchange. The parking lot was roughly half-full. Hammer drove towards the front of the building. "Chief, they look open! Look at all those people inside."

Aymond squinted to peer into the dark building just as the first of the undead stepped through a broken door. He keyed the radio. "Heavy weapons—go hot, follow out." The air burst with heavy machine gun and grenade fire.

Scores of undead streamed out of the shattered doors as the convoy shagged ass out of the parking lot, bouncing over the curbs and back onto Inyokern Road.

"Secure weapons, check in."

"Two's good."

"Three's good, but there's a metric fuckton of Zeds that followed us out of the parking lot. Think they'll keep coming, Chief?"

Aymond had no idea. "No they'll stop shortly. Don't worry about 'em."

Hammer slowed the convoy down to forty-five mph as they turned onto southbound 395 again.

After a few moments, Hammer, normally quiet, glanced at Aymond. "Chief, some of those Zeds were kids. Like, *little* kids."

Aymond didn't respond, he just frowned at the windshield, focusing only on the desert that was in front of them, and the thought of reaching a large city, like San Diego. *We're so fucked ... but we have to keep trying.*

Near Fort Davis, TX

Jessie woke before the sun rose. She had to pee again. All of the unpleasant parts of being pregnant are quickly forgotten once you finally hold your child, but quickly return to mind once pregnant again. She remembered how often she had to pee when she was pregnant with Keeley. She peeked out of a side window and saw that there was no movement in the fenced equipment yard, so she unlocked and opened the door into the frigid desert air. She tossed her bag into the passenger seat of the FJ, pulled her pants down, and squatted against the front fender to pee, her AR across her lap. *Toilet paper. I need to scavenge up some damn toilet paper. Well, at least I don't have to worry about needing any other feminine products for a few months.* Jessie would have taken the toilet paper from the restroom inside, but the toilet was overflowed with so much nastiness that her sensitive nose couldn't handle it right now. For once she wanted to try to keep down the MRE crackers she had eaten for breakfast.

She unsecured and opened the gate to the highway, climbed into the FJ, took a left and continued north on her journey. A half-hour later she quickly drove through Fort Davis. There wasn't any visible movement besides a handful of shambling dead, but nothing like Alpine had been. Zig-zagging through the desert mountains twenty minutes later, Jessie passed the McDonald Observatory on her way to I-10, and what she hoped would be smooth sailing. This part of Texas made BFE look like a thriving city, but only another hour passed before Jessie had to stop at the intersection of 118 and I-10. Cars sat on their roofs, having been pushed over the metal railing and falling to land wrong side up. Pieces of bodies and gruesome red smears on the pavement punctuated the twisted metal. Jessie drove around the vehicles to reach the westbound side of I-10, only to be greeted by a gas station that was abandoned long before the end of the world. More vehicles were on the pavement on the northern side of the road, likewise appearing to have been pushed off by some coordinated force.

Jessie threaded the needle before taking a left to get on I-10 towards El Paso. The highway here was clear; no corpses roamed the road, and all the vehicles were off the pavement. The wrecked traffic looked to have been pushed towards Jessie. The sides of the vehicles were smeared with blood and gore, pieces of the undead littered the pavement, and flesh had melted into the asphalt as the sun heated the surface. *Well, maybe this is good; maybe they all went towards San Antonio. Just maybe I'm catching a break, for once.*

Groom Lake, NV

Wright stood in the radio hut, staring at the consoles in disbelief. "What do you mean you can't connect to anything? What about the SeeMe?"

"Nothing, Sir."

"What about the SATCOM link to the SSC?"

"That's down too."

"Well, what do we have that still works, Sergeant?"

"We can still conduct line of sight comms, spotty high frequency signals over the horizon, and broadcast on shortwave bands, but we've lost all satellite connectivity."

"Why?"

"I don't know, Sir."

"Fuck." Wright stormed out of the room.

In the hallway, Wright looked at the clock on the wall and realized he was now late to the welcoming reception for the newly arrived civilians who had just been released from quarantine. Running down two flights of stairs and traversing a long hallway, Wright entered what they had begun referring to as the "civilian side of the house." It had a real name, but since that facility had basically been given over to the civilian leadership while the military stayed in the other facility, it made sense. To be honest though, Wright didn't care. He was frustrated and preoccupied that he was now cut off from communications.

Wright walked into the auditorium just in time for the Pledge of Allegiance to be recited, followed by a speech from Jake. Originally from Cortez, Colorado and now the elected leader, they called him "Mayor" of the civilian house. Seeing Jake at the podium, Wright was reminded of Cliff. He couldn't even check on Cliff using overhead imagery or make contact with the rescue party headed his way from Texas. Effectively, Wright was isolated from everything outside of the dry lake bed, except for broadcasting a shortwave message, which amounted to nothing more than a beacon to any rogue survivors to come join his merry band of misfit toys. *What is behind all of this? Or is it 'who' is behind all of this? Shit!*

Wright stayed just long enough for Jake to point him out so he could wave at the civvies before he turned and walked briskly back towards the radio hut. If the problems did turn out to be because of a *who*, they were in trouble.

Westbound I-10 in Texas

It all made Jessie uneasy. The roadway completely clear: vehicles, cars, trucks, semi-trucks, all pushed into the ditches, all of them smeared with dried blood and gore. Crushed bodies, undead bodies, she presumed, lay against the vehicles. *There is no way anyone could survive a massive push like this.* Trying to conserve fuel, Jessie kept her speed at a steady fifty-five mph. She could have driven as fast as she wanted, she could have even traveled the posted speed, which she thought was eighty mph, but all the road signs had suffered the same fate as the vehicles. Not a one was left standing.

Approaching Van Horn, Jessie decided to take the exit onto what she thought would be Business I-10, which went through the middle of town, presumably. Her guess was correct, and the tiny town of Van Horn filled her windshield. Vehicles sat abandoned in the middle of the road, but no blood, no gore, nothing to show that the massive herd of walking corpses had taken the exit off the Interstate. She slowed, staring at the truck stop on her left. Numerous semi-trucks sat next to the bright yellow building. Squinting into the shadows, Jessie saw movement between the trucks. She stopped the FJ and watched to see if it could possibly be real people, survivors. The first of the group stepped around the front of the large Freightliner and shambled towards the FJ. Jessie rolled her eyes, frustrated with herself for even hoping that there could possibly be any chance of finding another survivor. *There have to be more like me, there have to be others. It just can't be that I'm all alone.* Jessie let the clutch out and quickly drove away from the truck stop, into the heart of Van Horn. She saw walking corpses milling about in the parking lots of small, long-abandoned businesses, seemingly permanent residents of the middle of nowhere Interstate hotels.

Swerving around an abandoned oil field truck sitting on flat tires, Jessie slammed on the brakes. The yellow and black sign of a dollar store was in front of her. Wiggling the shifter into neutral, she set the parking brake and climbed out of the FJ with her AR-15 and walked towards the glass front of the store. The irony wasn't lost on her; before the attack it would have been odd to go shopping with an AR slung across her chest, but now it was the norm. *If a mall ever opens up again, there should be gun racks hung in the dressing rooms for your convenience.* Jessie shook her head and tried to focus. Too familiar was the threat that dealing with the end of the world had become routine, nothing but a joke and a nuisance. She knew that it would spell her death, and her unborn child's death, if she got too comfortable. She looked back over her shoulder. The local undead population had left their hotel rooms to bid her a fond welcome to Van Horn. *I better hurry.*

Jessie peered into the dark interior of the dollar store. The shelves looked ransacked, which would make sense, but at least she didn't see any movement. She banged on the glass of the last remaining window with the muzzle of her rifle and waited, slowly counting to ten. *No movement: good for me.* The front doors had been pried open and broken off their hinges. Broken glass crunched beneath her boots as she stepped into the store. She scanned the aisles and grabbed a shopping cart. Fortunately, the selection of diapers and baby formula was still there; she quickly filled her basket with everything on the shelves.

Diapers of every size, from newborn to size five, baby bottles, nipples, everything that would fit was tossed into the cart. Jessie's baby shower would be one of action and need. She glanced towards the FJ and saw that the first of the undead welcoming committee was arriving, interested in her running vehicle. *As long as they haven't seen me yet, I'll be OK.* As quickly as she began the shopping trip, it was over. She pushed the overflowing cart towards the ruined store front, stopped at the doors, stood in the shadows of the store interior, raised her rifle, and braced her arm on the red plastic handlebar. One by one, with each press of the trigger, the undead in the street fell to their final rest. *Breathe, aim, squeeze, breathe, aim, squeeze.* Jessie kept a steady pace until something pulled sharply at her ankle. Startled, she screamed in fright.

The torso of a corpse clung tightly to her ankle, pulling itself towards her thigh. Its face had rotted away, and its lipless mouth snapped with blackened teeth, its nose a gaping hole. Without thinking, she pulled the AR to the front, flipped the selector switch all the way around, and yanked on the trigger until the bolt locked back. The crawling corpse's skull lay ruined in a heap of black gore, and a single hole smoked from the toe of her boot. Jessie stared at the hole in her boot, holding her breath. No blood came through, it didn't hurt, but her heart rate was so high and with the adrenaline dump she probably could have cut off a hand without feeling any pain. Jessie sat on the cashier's counter, ignoring the undead shambling towards the front of the store, and pulled her left boot off. There was no blood and no marks on her sock. Removing the sock, she was glad to see all five toes wiggling on her foot. She stared at her boot and realized how lucky she had been; a round had punctured the toe of the boot, but passed just beyond her actual toe. Jessie pulled her dirty sock and boot back on, angry at her mistake but happy that God smiled on children, drunks, and idiots.

Her shopping cart crashed to its side as the first of the horde of undead closed in on her position, the wheels catching debris on the sidewalk. Jessie pulled her AR to her shoulder, aimed, and squeezed the trigger. Nothing happened. The trigger didn't move. She leapt to her feet, standing on the counter, rotated the rifle right, and saw that the bolt had locked back on an empty magazine. Depressing the release, she rotated the rifle back the other way while reaching in her cargo pocket for a fresh mag. Slamming the magazine into the well, Jessie thumbed the bolt release, slid her left hand along the forestock, and pulled the trigger, ripping through the face of the closest aggressor with a full auto burst. Realizing her mistake, she thumbed the selector back to semi and jumped off the counter to retrieve her spent magazine. Quickly, she took aim and fired as another dozen undead staggered across the parking lot towards the front of the store. The nearest threats put down, she pulled the shopping cart upright and quickly reloaded as much of the looted baby supplies as she could back into the basket. Pushing hard, Jessie nearly ran with the cart into the street and to the waiting FJ. Driver's door open, Jessie grabbed and threw everything across the seat and into the floor of the passenger's side. Just as she threw the last jug of baby formula into the FJ, the cart bumped and pressed into her side. She turned and, drawing the pistol from her hip, fired a single round at point-blank range into the skull of a very large dead man, who wore a blood-stained flannel shirt and a John Deere ball cap. Blood and blackened brain matter sprayed back at her. She had no time to care. A seemingly infinite line of undead trudged towards her from all around. She climbed into the driver's seat, slammed the door shut, and drove west, dodging the advancing mob as she went. Jessie found I-10 just as she'd left it, barren of all life—cars, trucks, and everything else shoved into the ditches and desert around her.

Ten minutes later, Jessie rolled to a stop in the middle of the road. Her hands shook uncontrollably as she dropped her head onto the steering wheel and wept.

US-287 outside of Fort Worth, TX

The pace slowed considerably; apparently traffic was backed up before the EMP made sure that none of the vehicles would move again. Chivo drove around as much as he could, taking the shoulder most of the time, until they passed over I-30. There they had to avoid a six-car pileup against an exit lane divider. A motorcycle lay on the ground, the shoulders and head of the dead rider exposed, full face helmet rocking back and forth as gloved hands desperately reached for the Defender as it passed.

Bexar held the civilian map folded over to the Fort Worth expanded view and gave directions as best he could. "Take the ramp right, it'll be 287, 377, and I-35W all marked on the same road, but keep an eye out—it seems like this shit is always under construction. It's been a few years since I've been through here, so I have no idea if this map is up to date."

Chivo shook his head and concentrated on the road ahead, scanning side to side as he drove. It reminded him of when he had worked doing personal protection and security details for visiting VIPs. It was high stress and exhausting to be the driver, constantly scanning for threats large and small, ready to react fast enough to avoid or survive an attack from anywhere.

Merging onto I-35W, Chivo continued the slow task of driving around all the stalled vehicles, while the undead bounced off the fenders of the SUV. He couldn't risk running one over; bones can puncture tires, so he tried his best to swerve so they would hit the sides of the Defender as they passed.

"Bexar, this is I-35, right?"

"Yeah."

"So what's wrong with this picture?"

Bexar looked around before it dawned on him. "All the cars and undead are still here."

"Exactly."

"So either that massive corpse herd took a detour, or we've managed to get in front of them."

"Right, so what do we have to assume?"

"That they're behind us."

"And?"

"If we stop, we'll be overrun."

"Yes, young Skywalker. An operator of you make we will," Chivo said in a really bad Yoda impression.

"Shit. Well, we won't be on I-35 for long, maybe we'll be lucky and the undead will prefer to use the Interstate system instead of smaller highways."

"Yeah, but we can't assume that. What we can assume is that they'll catch up if we delay, so we have to put enough distance between us and them to give us room to stop for fuel and any problems that come up."

Bexar nodded as Chivo continued their zig-zagging course, threading the Defender between the abandoned vehicles on the highway. In the back, Apollo was asleep once again, Lindsey curled up in his arms. Bexar sighed heavily. *I don't think there will ever be anyone else for me. Jessie was it; she was all I could have or would have wanted.*

Bexar's digression into self-pity crashed back to reality as a body landed on the hood from the overpass above, its head shattering the windshield. "Holy shit!"

Chivo yanked the steering wheel back and forth, rocking the vehicle hard, but the body wouldn't move, its jaws snapping at the shattered windshield right in front of Bexar's face.

Chivo slammed on the brakes. "Dude, open your door and get that fucking thing off our car!"

Bexar did as he was told. He drew his big custom-made knife from his belt, plunged it through the windshield and into the forehead of the gnashing corpse, then climbed out, walked to the front of the Defender and pulled the body off the hood to the pavement, where it landed with a wet thump. Shortly after, the drive continued, Lindsey now sitting straight up, eyes wide open in surprise while Apollo still snored softly beside her.

Thirty minutes later, and with no more sudden guests surprising their traveling party, Chivo took the exit for 287 to continue towards Colorado while the bloody, shattered windshield blocked most of Bexar's view.

Cortez, CO

So far, Cliff's notes showed that there were at least thirty different men and one woman who had entered or exited the school. All of them wore surplus military cold weather gear; occasionally one of them would not have their jacket buttoned up and they appeared to be wearing white shirts with black ties. The woman wore a heavy, full-length black dress. Still hidden beneath the dark blanket, Cliff glanced at his watch. Just a few more hours until sunset. After sunset he would need to sleep for a couple of hours before moving locations. He needed to check out a few other places around town that he had marked on his map. A short yellow school bus pulled to a stop in front just before a bearded man wearing a black beret stepped out of the school. He was preceded by two men with AR-variant rifles who stopped and stood guard, facing outwards. Following the man were five women and two young-looking girls. On the man's beret, a silver cross glistened in the sunlight. The entourage climbed into the bus and were followed by their sentries.

The bus drove south and out of Cliff's view, but in the still air it sounded like the bus turned westbound a few moments later. Cliff looked at his map and noted two other schools in that general direction, as well as a church. After finishing the notes and descriptions of what he'd just seen, he set the alarm on his watch for two hours and laid his head on the table. This was going to be another long night.

Highway 395, near Johannesburg, CA

Aymond noted that the gauge on the dashboard indicated the engine was running hotter today; he guessed it was probably due to using jet fuel instead of the lower grade diesel fuel. The convoy rumbled into the tiny town of Johannesburg after fleeing China Lake. Aymond pulled a small notepad out and jotted some notes. They had to treat the approaches to towns and military installations as they would hostile enemy territory now. High Level Threats, he noted. He needed to start watching the population numbers on the town signs to see if he could get a general pattern to determine threats in relation to population size. It seemed obvious that a larger population would mean that there would be a larger threat present, but he could no longer make any assumptions, not again, not ever. This was unlike anything he had seen in over twenty years of service. Johannesburg passed without any problems, a small handful of undead meandering towards the sound of the rumbling M-ATVs as they passed. Endless desert greeted them at the other edge of the town as the convoy continued their slow ride towards help. *If we survived, there have to be other Marines that survived ... or someone, anyone.*

The minutes ticked by into hours, punctuated by small towns and seemingly random homesteads. Most of the small towns had Zeds stumbling about, but others showed no signs of life and seemed to have been abandoned for hundreds of years, frozen in time. At no point did Aymond, or anyone else, see any signs of survivors. It was as if the ragtag leftovers of a once-proud MSOT were the only live remaining humans in all of California.

Eschewing an approach through the town of Twentynine Palms, the convoy turned onto the highway to the east, driving towards the Marine Corps Air Ground Combat Center. Even the acronym was a mouthful, MCAGCC, so like other Marines, Aymond simply referred to it as "Twentynine Palms." Only Joshua Tree stood between them and a familiar Marine Corps installation. Aymond keyed the radio; the radio etiquette had become lax over the last two days of travel. "OK guys, we're close, but we're not going to charge ahead into Twentynine Palms like we did China Lake. After Joshua Tree, we're stopping at the compound gate and actually running some recon."

Each of the senior men of the two following M-ATVs radioed acknowledgement to the transmission. The tension in his own M-ATV seemed to rise; Aymond imagined that it was just as bad in the two behind him.

"Hammer, as we near the installation, slow the pace to thirty mph alongside the fence line, and even more as we near the gate."

Ryan Hammer nodded, concentrating as he drove around two wrecked cars in Joshua Tree. A few turns later and the convoy was northbound on Adobe Road, coming alongside the southern edge of the fenced-in main section of Twentynine Palms. The base was huge, hundreds of square miles used for training, but the main section was tiny, just large enough to house those assigned there, equipment, an airfield, and not much more.

Aymond gazed intensely out his window at the housing on the southern end of the installation. Many of the homes were burned completely to the ground; only a few of them were still standing, and those appeared to be damaged. Long sections of the fence were down.

"Hammer, slow it down some more." Aymond keyed the radio. "Doesn't look good, but we're going to slowly approach the main gate. Dagger Two take right side responsibility, Dagger Three the tail; we have everything to the front."

The electronically controlled heavy weapons of each M-ATV turned towards their area of responsibility. Aymond peered through the windshield using a pair of binoculars.

"Jesus, look at that."

The front gate was fortified, but it appeared to have been hastily constructed using Hesco barriers and some of the armored vehicles from the base. Between the convoy and the fortified position, burned-out vehicles lay alongside incredible carnage—bloody viscera, gore, limbs torn from bodies, all strewn about the burned and blood-soaked asphalt. The barriers and vehicles were black with chunky, dried blood.

"Hammer—turn us around," Aymond keyed the mic. "Circle back, follow lead, we're going to go through one of the sections of downed fence and see if we can locate any survivors. Eyes out for fuel bowsers."

The convoy made a wide U-turn, driving onto the desert beside the road to get the large trucks pointed back the way they'd come. The second M-ATV's heavy weapon turned and now took the threat responsibility to the convoy's left, without the need to be told.

Slowing, Hammer drove the lead M-ATV over a downed portion of fence, through the sand, around a children's playset and into the ruined neighborhood of duplex housing.

CHAPTER 20

Groom Lake
March 5, Year 1

Wright nearly fell into the room with the force he used to throw open the door to the radio hut. "At NORAD we could track everything in orbit. Can we do that here?"

"Yes, Sir."

"Are we currently doing that?"

"No, Sir. We haven't had the manpower to continue the transmissions and survivor coordination and take care of tracking orbital objects. Besides, we figured it was relatively moot now."

"How many more people do you need to man the radios and bring the tracking back online? I need you to be able to compare historical plots with current plots, looking for any orbit degradation or orbital debris where there should be an asset."

"At least two, but five or more would be better so we can have rotating shifts."

"OK, I'll have you people by this afternoon. Cease all other projects. Everyone is on our satellite problem until I tell you otherwise. I think our orbital assets have been, are being, and will continue to be attacked. I cannot believe that we lost two primary systems with all the redundant controls inherent in their design, outside of a Kessler syndrome. It is too unlikely. Also, figure out some other method of communicating with the SSC. Both of these are tied for top priority. Split into teams if need be, just get it done—as in yesterday!"

Before anyone could answer, Wright was gone, door slammed closed behind him. Wright's entrance, reaction, and exit seemed to suck all the air out of the room. Every airman sat as if in suspended animation, completely still, until a half-second later when the room erupted in frenzied action.

Wright practically jogged down the stairs and across the long hall to the civilian side of the complex. He burst into the auditorium where Jake was wrapping up the welcoming ceremony and indoctrination. "Jake, I need at least five people who know how to work radios to report to the radio hut now."

Jake, on stage behind the podium, blinked twice before turning to the audience. "Bill?"

Bill stood.

"Get a team together, any other HAMs you can find, or people you can teach."

Jake turned his attention back to Wright. "Anything else, Major?"

"Get your council together and meet me in D2 in thirty."

"Will do."

Wright left the auditorium and headed back to the radio hut, leaving Jake standing on the podium. He looked out at his audience, which consisted of the newly added survivors, twenty-two in all.

"Once again folks, that was Major Wright. Don't let him fool you, he's a great guy, he just has a lot going on right now, seeing how he's basically in charge of rescuing the United States. With that said, signups are in the mess hall. You have to sign up for at least one detail, and the most undesirable details will be assigned by your group designators. Our 'fresh air activity' time is at three p.m. each day until summer, when we will choose a better time to go topside for a break. Any questions?"

The new community members applauded, just happy to have security in their lives again and be of some use. Jake's wrist was sore by the time he was done shaking everyone's hands as they filed out to their new bunks. Jake glanced at the clock on the wall and went to gather the council members, leaders elected by each designated group. The updated survivor count stood at sixty-four; every week a few more made their way to Groom Lake.

Who would have thought after more than a half century of extreme secrecy that the government would be calling people home to Area 51, like a lighthouse in a storm. Now I need to figure out a good excuse to go investigate the mountainside across the lakebed; this Sector 4 business sounds intriguing. I bet it's true ... but I bet it isn't aliens. It's never aliens.

Jake chuckled at the thought that in another life he could have had his own TV show after living in Area 51. He could have made up stories of lizard people, it could be *anything* and he would have been on TV making a ludicrous amount of money. Jake stopped at a door, knocked gently, then opened it. "Group A" was stenciled on it along with a rough sketch of a bottle of steak sauce being poured over the head of a zombie. About two weeks prior, the groups had begun creating logos and humorous names for themselves. What place did Jake have to say "no" to that? It kept moral high. Basically locked in an underground prison, people needed something to keep their spirits up.

Twentynine Palms, CA

The M-ATVs drove right through the landscaping of the duplexes and onto the asphalt residential streets on the other side. Half-burned bodies lay scattered on the sidewalk and driveways. Children, women, men, it was nearly impossible to tell what they once were except for their approximate size or the presence of a weather-tattered toy. Slowly the convoy made their way out of the neighborhood and east to Condor Road. To the south lay the other gate into the installation. It was completely blocked off with Hesco barriers and an up-armored Humvee with mounted M2. Just as with the main gate, outside the fence the perimeter was filthy with body parts, bloodstains and scorched pavement. Fifty-caliber shell casings littered the ground around the Humvee. Aymond surveyed the aftermath of a battle frozen in time. It was impossible to tell who'd won, but there were uniformed bodies face down on the pavement near the Humvee. It was obvious they had been there for some time, as weathered, torn, and scavenged as they were. Hammer turned the lead M-ATV to the north and continued towards the interior of the installation. The rest of the housing was much the same as the first, bodies scattered amongst the burned-out debris of what used to be homes. The commissary and exchange were also mostly burned down. Destruction here was on par with what Aymond had studied of Europe after WWII. The convoy continued onto Del Valle Drive, passing the neglected football field.

Aymond pointed and Hammer nodded, taking the turn onto 1st Street. Two blocks later, he stopped the M-ATV in the middle of the intersection. The hospital appeared heavily damaged, windows on the upper stories broken, marks from fire and smoke marring the outside walls, but there was a lot of movement on the ground level. Through the broken sliding glass doors of the main entrance, people began streaming out into the late afternoon light.

Aymond raised his binoculars. "Hammer, get us the fuck out of here!" Then he keyed the radio. "Weapons hot, headed north!"

The big M2 on Aymond's M-ATV opened fire in controlled bursts as Hammer turned and drove north as quickly as the large armored vehicle could move. The M2 on the second M-ATV took the task of suppressing fire against a force that didn't shoot back, but showed no fear, no concern, and had an unfaltering need to feed on human flesh. As the second M-ATV cleared the intersection, the last M-ATV, mounted with the big Mk-19 belt-fed grenade launcher, began a siege of the front of the hospital. Pieces of cement block began falling onto the undead below. The number of walking corpses never seemed to end; they continued to stream out of the ground floor, trailing the convoy as they sped northward, away from the countless Zeds.

"Hammer, go west. We need to get back to Del Valle and then go north ... head for the airfield." Aymond keyed the radio. "Stay weapons hot. We're dashing for the airfield to regroup."

Both of the following vehicles acknowledged the radio transmission as the convoy rattled north at a blistering sixty mph, the vehicle-mounted weapons occasionally firing at groups of undead that were too close for comfort.

Westbound I-10

Jessie squinted into the setting sun. *Should have looted some sunglasses too.* The time of day snuck up on her—not having a working watch will cause that—but Jessie knew she needed to pay better attention to the sun's position. Even though I-10 had been completely clear so far, she could not risk driving at night and she definitely couldn't risk charging headfirst into another town like before. Just the thought of half of a corpse clawing its way up her legs made her heart rate jump and gave her a shudder. The ones she could see she could manage, but she'd never thought about half of a body crawling its way across the ground. *Who am I to think I should bring a baby into this world?* Jessie shook her head. No, she absolutely could not afford to think like that. She had to survive, she had to be tough, and she needed to be somewhere safe to give birth. There was nothing more to say. If it was safe enough to give birth, then hopefully it would be a safe enough place to live, at least for a while, free from the threat of the undead. Area 51 was her last hope. The only place in America that she knew to be safe. *You don't know that it's safe, you're just assuming it's safe because of that guy on the radio. What if you're wrong? What if it's a trap?* Jessie frowned at the thought. No, she had to believe. She had to believe that there were good people in this world still, that Cliff was who he claimed to be, and that refuge could be found there.

Passing the exit for another Business I-10, this one in Sierra Blanca, Jessie chose not to drive into town. She needed a spot for the night, even if she slept in the FJ; she needed to be safe, hidden and safe. Glancing at the gas gauge, she realized she also needed to put more fuel in the tank from the gas cans on the roof. After passing the ramp back onto I-10 from the business spur, Jessie glanced in the side-view mirrors and didn't see anything coming up the ramp, so she stopped in the middle of the Interstate, put the FJ in neutral, and set the brake, leaving the engine running. Her belly was just barely starting to show in her pregnancy. Climbing up the side of the FJ to retrieve the fuel cans was still a doable task, but in a few more weeks it would be more difficult; a few more weeks after that and it would be nearly impossible.

The now-empty gas cans were placed back on the roof rack and tied down again. *I need to top those cans off before I get to El Paso. For El Paso, I need full fuel and no stops. I can't imagine that it could be safe, or even sane to drive into that damned city.* Jessie stared straight ahead. A few miles later, I-10 turned sharply to the left and off the Interstate. Suddenly, a rest stop came into view. With all the signs pushed over, she'd had no idea she was near one. Slowing the FJ, Jessie turned and drove up the exit. It was more of a picnic area; there were no buildings or restrooms, just sheltered picnic tables with small grills available for families wanting to stop for a couple of hours to throw a party. *Who in the hell actually stops on a trip and goes to the trouble of lighting a grill with charcoal they just happened to have with them to cook burgers or chicken or steaks or whatever in the hell they have in the cooler?*

Jessie drove over the curb and onto the grassy area, driving slowly past five vehicles parked in the picnic area. None of them appeared to be occupied. She stopped in the middle of the drive and got out to check the vehicles. All of them had been abandoned, all were locked. There was no sign of any people, alive, dead, or otherwise, in the area. Climbing back into the FJ, she drove across the field to the truck and RV parking where there was a lone RV. Jessie pulled alongside the front of the Winnebago and peered through the windshield into the dark interior. Setting the parking brake, Jessie climbed down and knocked sharply on the windshield before quickly getting back in the FJ. A moment later, with a thud, a small corpse slammed against the windshield of the RV with enough force to cause it to crack. *Holy shit!* The small girl, wearing a Princess t-shirt, looked like she could have been five or six years old when she died and turned. Jessie closed her eyes. *If I leave her alone, she will beat on the windshield until it breaks, and then she'll be loose ... fuck it.*

Jessie leveled her AR to fire a single shot through the windshield and through the little girl's skull, its contents exploding backwards into the interior of the RV. The now-dead corpse of the little Princess slumped over the dash of the RV, black pus oozing out of the large hole in the back of her skull.

Jessie climbed back into the FJ and drove across the field, across the parking lot, and past the picnic tables, stopping near the fenceline on the north side, where she parked the FJ facing the escape to westbound I-10 and then began to sob. Wave after wave of grief crashed through her; she couldn't control it, she couldn't breathe. Her body shuddered so violently in sorrow that everything else vanished. She hadn't shed this many tears since they'd lost Keeley.

US-287 near Decatur, TX

They rested long enough for everyone to take a piss, and for Chivo to swap places with Apollo, then the merry band of rescuers were on their way again. Everything was calm, although Lindsey declined Chivo's invitation to snuggle before he fell asleep, and Apollo refrained from punching him. The sun hung low against the western sky, enough light outside for Apollo to see without using his NODs. Bexar tried to rest his eyes and maybe even get some sleep, but he couldn't. Every time the Defender rocked slightly as Apollo drove around an abandoned vehicle or a walking corpse Bexar's heart rate would jump and he would sit up, ready for the threat, but there would be no threat. Well, there were many threats, but it was their directive to ignore as many as they could along the way.

The shattered windshield lost more glass fragments and had begun to whistle softly in the air passing over the SUV.

"OK, guy, what do you know about Decatur?" Apollo looked over at Bexar.

"Umm, it's a smaller town and that's about all I know. I think I've driven through it once or twice and that's about it."

"Great, thanks for the hot intel."

"Dude, you asked and now you know more than before ... and knowing is half the battle."

"Seriously, stop talking," Apollo said with a straight face before flashing a big grin at Bexar.

The handful of roads that crossed 287 in the small town went under the highway, so they didn't have to worry about any suicidal undead landing on their ride again. Apollo didn't tell Bexar the story about Odin; he figured it would only rattle the guy more, and he was right. Apollo could sleep anywhere. He'd had to be woken up to fight in an active battle before, sleeping through the initial explosions and gunfire. To Apollo, and to Chivo, war was a way of life. They were warriors and had been their entire adult lives, from the time they enlisted in the Army after high school to when they'd fought with Delta; the job titles didn't matter, they went to war. Some wars the American public knew about, but most they didn't.

"I can tell you this, Apollo, these nice freeway overpasses come to an end soon. Most of this highway is rural, but it also becomes the main drag for a lot of the small towns we'll bump into." As if on cue, the freeway changed. The overpasses were gone and were replaced with cross-overs in the medians and intersecting roads with stop signs.

"Well shit, man. Guess I don't get to relax like you tonight after all."

The last bit of sunlight fell beneath the horizon as the sky turned from red and purple to the dark blue of twilight. Apollo flipped down his NODs. "Try to get some rest, dude. We're going to have a fight at some point, and we'll need you there; you won't do us any good if you haven't slept."

Bexar nodded. He knew Apollo was right. Trying again to relax, Bexar curled up against the side of the door and closed his eyes. Soon his body gave in to the exhaustion of the day and he fell into a sleep full of dreams about burying Keeley and seeing his wife before the explosion. Dreams are the realm where warriors are built or destroyed through victories and pain.

Twentynine Palms, CA

At the gate to the airfield, Ski quickly cut through the fence to make a hole just large enough for him to slip through with his gear on, then jogged to the control box for the sliding chain-link gate. Inside the box, he flipped the lever and pulled the gate open to allow the three M-ATVs to pass, then shut the gate behind them and locked the lever back in place. Before driving off, Ski used a handful of zip-ties to secure the hole in the fence; he didn't want any of the Zeds getting lucky and falling through the hole.

Relatively secure, the convoy drove away from the gate and the horde of Zeds possibly close behind, and towards the flight line and maintenance hangars. The first hangar stood open and appeared empty. The second hangar was ringed with Hesco barriers, full of rocks, sand, and dirt. A front-end loader sat nearby, as did a Humvee.

Aymond signaled Hammer to stop and keyed the radio. "Davis—stay on the Mk-19. Everyone else dismount to clear the hangars. Rally on me."

Hammer shut down the M-ATV and climbed out, along with all but Chris Davis, who swung the grenade launcher towards the hangars, providing security to the rest of the dismounted MSOT. Aymond walked to the far side of the third M-ATV and knelt. The other six men stood around him as he used a gloved finger to draw in the sand.

"Snow and Kirk, take the eastern hangar, the rest of you are with me for the western hangar. Someone lived long enough to erect the Hescos. Hammer, take the M-ATV around towards the front of the barriers ..."

"Uh, Chief?"

"Yeah, Kirk."

"We don't have to do anything." Kirk pointed west.

On top of the Hesco barrier stood two men in badly worn utilities, waving their hands above their heads. Aymond keyed his radio. "You have eyes on, Davis?"

"Roger that, Chief."

The two men climbed down the front of the barriers and walked towards the M-ATVs.

"Thank God you came. We didn't know how long it would take for a QRF to arrive from San Diego, but we figured it would eventually happen."

Aymond eyed the two Marines. "You two are the only ones here?"

"Yes, Master Gunnery Sergeant, we're the only two left on the airfield."

"Relax Corporal, some things have changed in the last few weeks. We're not a Quick Response Force. We were at the MWTC when the attack came, and we're trying to get to San Diego. What were your orders?"

"Secure the field and wait for replacements. Those two 18s over there were the only two aircraft not ready to fly when the sprayers came overhead. Everything else flew out."

"What's wrong with those Hornets?"

"No idea. We're motor pool guys—we don't touch those things. A team from their squadron was supposed to be en route with parts, tools, and techs, but we haven't seen them yet."

"Great. Hate to tell you this, but you two are the first living persons we've found since we left the MWTC."

The smiles fell from both of the corporals' faces.

"I don't understand."

"Neither do we, Corporal, but we're going to find out."

The sun began to set as the MSOT enjoyed some physical fitness time. Some of them jogged up and down the runway, while others improvised a pull-up bar in the empty hangar. The two maintenance corporals brought a fuel bowser around from the tanks to the north and topped off the M-ATVs' fuel tanks. The evening was relaxing, the first chance the MSOT had to wind down since leaving the MWTC, although that also entailed swapping stories with the two E-4s. From their perspective, the fight for Twentynine Palms had been absolute hell. The surrounding civilian communities flooded the base after the attack; some of them were already bitten and infected. No one understood what that meant in the first couple of days, and by then it was too late—the base was overrun with Zeds from both outside and inside the gate. Secure behind the inner airfield fence, the E-4s stayed hidden, though Zeds would trickle in occasionally. One of the men constructed what could best be described as a machete on a stick, using spare F-18 parts. It was quite possibly the most expensive improvised weapon ever made, but according to both of them, it kicked ass.

CHAPTER 21

Cortez, CO
March 5, Year 1

Night finally came and Cliff's watch beeped softly in his ear. As part of his training, Cliff had learned how to transition from sleep to awake smoothly without a "start," and without moving a muscle. The beeping stopped and Cliff remained perfectly still, his head resting on the table, the blanket covering his form and the spotting scope. Even under the blanket it was quite cold; the open window allowed the cold breeze to filter into the room. Barely breathing, Cliff listened for any changes outside of his blind. Confident that everything was as it should be, he pulled the blanket back slowly, exposing the front element of the spotting scope. The school was still in view. The bus wasn't there, but an old Jeep sat idling with its headlights on by the front of the school. Two men, dressed as the others before, in surplus military clothing, climbed in the Jeep, made a U-turn and drove north away from the school. *That must be the night patrol.* Cliff wrote the details in his notebook. It was time to move locations, but with a patrol driving through the streets he didn't want to chance using the truck he had stashed nearby. By now, surely the group would notice that two of their own were missing, as well as their vehicle; not to mention the others that he had killed prior to those.

The spotting scope went into his book bag and the blanket became his poncho once again. Cliff dug through the bathroom cabinet until he found what he was looking for: black shoe polish. *Dry as a bone.* Cliff took a sip of water then spit into the tin of polish, working the saliva in before smearing the polish on his face. Luckily, the bathroom mirror had survived the zombie apocalypse. In short order, every portion of Cliff's exposed skin—face, ears, neck, hands, scalp—was covered in polish. In simpler times, before the attack, Cliff would not have dared use all black shoe polish as face paint, even if it was for camouflage, but simpler times these were not. The shoe polish tin went into the book bag with the spotting scope, wrapped in a small towel so it wouldn't clank as he moved. After jumping up and down, followed by a hard wiggle, Cliff was satisfied that his noise discipline test was complete and his gear silent. Out the door he went, stepping over the bloated, fat corpse he'd left in the living room.

Cliff traveled south across the parking lot of the apartment complex, keeping the row of buildings between him and the road by the school. Reaching the main east-west road, Cliff crouched behind a telephone pole next to a short picket fence. No headlights in either direction, but he couldn't count on the cult members always using headlights. He had to assume that they had NODs. If they had a FLIR Thermal Sight rifle scope or any advanced device, he would be in serious trouble. All the undead he had killed had been about whatever the ambient temperature happened to be. Somehow they didn't freeze solid, despite the brutal temperatures. In any case, he would be the only non-cult, warm body in all of town, unless there were survivors still being held prisoner nearby.

Letting the seconds tick by into minutes, Cliff felt confident he could cross the road. Two deep breaths, and he was up and running the fastest forty-yard dash he could muster. He dropped into the drainage ditch at the edge of the green space across the street. Cliff was now angry; angry for being wet, angry for being cold, angry for being wet and cold in March in Colorado. Lying flat on his belly, Cliff slowly slid up the rocky surface until his head barely poked over the top. He counted off the seconds silently while watching for any reaction to his dash across the road. When there was none, Cliff crept along the bottom of the ditch to get farther away from the road before sliding up the side to watch again. Two deep breaths, and again he was on his feet, dashing across another road, vaulting over a split-rail fence, rolling to a stop, and lying flat in the scrub bushes. Again he froze, watching to see if there would be any reaction to his movement. Inching away from the thorny stems, Cliff was now even angrier; angrier for being wet, cold, and pricked everywhere with thorns.

Cliff rolled to his back and pulled the thorns he could find out of his skin. Ten minutes later, he slowly crawled across the field towards a trailer park. Each movement revealed thorns he had missed. Reaching the edge of the trailer park, Cliff waited once again. He had time, all the time he needed; what he didn't have was any help if he was detected. It could have been worse, much worse. At least he wasn't worried about enemy air support showing up, and at least he wasn't in a swamp. Cliff hated swamps. Piss in the water and a virus swims up your urethra to kill you. No, this was much better than a swamp.

Two deep breaths and back on his feet, Cliff dashed between the single-wide trailers of the park. Slowly, he made his way across the back of lots, as far away from the road as he could be. Jumping two fences, Cliff found himself under the back porch of a manufactured home, staring at a building across a field to the west. The building looked a bit like a church; in the parking lot was the small yellow bus he had seen the day before. Cliff pulled out his notepad and made notes about the scene. With the porch overhead, distance and darkness his allies, Cliff sat up, rifle across his lap, spotting scope in his hands. Using the graduated reticle, he estimated the distance, made more notes, including the number painted on the front bumper of the bus, just in case there was more than one. He waited.

Three hours later the two bodyguards exited the church with a third man, who Cliff assumed was the driver because he climbed into the bus and started it. One of the bodyguards nodded and the man with the beret walked out of the church to the bus by himself. The church might be where the women stayed and maybe the children were there; Cliff had no idea, but with the bus leaving and traveling west again, he didn't have time to investigate the church. Obviously, the man was the more important target. Sunrise was coming quickly and the bus traveled away from his location; if he was going to have a chance to get home, eat, and rest, he had to go back to the truck now.

US-287

Apollo drove carefully; the rest of the people in the Defender slept while he drove. Homes, small businesses, farms, and ranches dotted the highway along the northwest route. Their progress slowed due to the number of abandoned vehicles on the road. Walking corpses continuously bounced off the fenders of the SUV, and twice Apollo accidentally drove straight over one, jostling the sleeping team as the tires bumped over the bodies. Luckily, the highway bypassed the small towns along the route, so there weren't any real surprises, just more of the same song and dance—driving around the undead and the cars they'd failed to bring with them to a very active afterlife.

The odometer read seventy miles since Decatur, and his watch showed that it'd taken three hours. The Defender sat idling on the highway, the heart of Wichita Falls just ahead. "Bexar, wake up," Apollo whispered while nudging his navigator out of a loud, snoring sleep. Waking with a start, it took a few moments for Bexar to clear his head and focus on where he was and what he saw.

"Bexar—we're at Wichita Falls. Take a look ahead."

Bexar flipped the NODs down on the bump helmet he wore, turned them on, and waited for his eyes to adjust to the green glow of the scope. The shattered windshield blocked some of the view, but ahead of the SUV, the abandoned vehicles rippled like waves in a pond. It took a moment to realize that the ripples were the undead filtering through the vehicles on the highway.

"Holy shit. They're coming this way."

"Yeah, I know. Check the map; we need a way around all of this. I think you have about five minutes before they get here."

Bexar unfolded and refolded the large civilian road map until he found the section he needed. Squinting at the road signs, it took him a moment to find their location.

"OK, turn around. Highway 79 is behind us about a mile, mile and a half. Take it south."

Apollo spun the wheel, made a three-point turn, and drove back the way they came, up the wrong way on a merging ramp and onto the wrong side of the highway until he reached 79. He still had to dodge cars and the undead, but there were far fewer than before.

"Keep going south until we reach FM 1954. Take that west, and we'll eventually hit Highway 82. Take 82 southbound—it turns west and will get us to the same place eventually. We'll have to go through Lubbock instead of Amarillo, but we'll be able to skip Wichita Falls."

Apollo nodded, dodging another walking corpse. The vehicle traffic and undead in the roadway became more sparse the farther away from the city they drove. Bexar looked at his watch, a new one from the SSC that thankfully still worked, and noted that it was just before midnight. Sectioning off the atlas using his thumb, he guessed it would take about fifteen hours at this speed to reach Cortez.

They approached Seymour, Texas. Although the main highway bypassed the town, they needed to stay on 82 and go straight through. Bexar's mind drifted to the plight of these small towns. Someday, if anyone survived long enough to be so lucky, teams of people would need to go door to door to eradicate the undead and relieve the living. Thankfully, Bexar knew that this would not be their task. If they found survivors en route, great. Otherwise their mission was one of rescue, and it required as quick a response as they could give. They were already running days late; hopefully they would find Cliff alive, but as of now, that was more up to him than them.

Seymour was a ghost town. The town center, where the team turned west, was a burned-out shell; a large fire had ravaged the town. Bodies lay immobile in the road and all around the buildings. Bexar watched the macabre scene roll by through the green glow of his NODs. Everything appeared dead, actually dead. Not a single corpse could be seen, only bodies littering the ground by the dozens. Bexar didn't see the city limit sign with the population number, but Seymour, he thought, couldn't have had that many people before the attack.

Deftly, Apollo threaded the Defender through the horror of Seymour before he was able to break free and increase their speed on the country highway. Farmland passed by outside their windows, the occasional home or small business dotting the endlessness. A green sign said "Benjamin, Texas. Population of 258." The courthouse sat in the middle of the silent town; it looked surprisingly like the courthouse in Grayson County. Grayson County reminded Bexar of Malachi and Amber, the first casualties in his group at the hands of the undead. Now he was the last survivor. Bexar sighed heavily, turned off his NODs, and stared into the darkness. Slowly, his eyes adjusted, and by the time the Defender was out on the open highway again, Bexar could see the stars—more stars than he had ever seen. *No more light pollution*, he thought. *Maybe I'm seeing the world and the stars as the ancients saw them.*

CHAPTER 22

Keeley laughed and laughed, banging her sippy cup on the tray, watching the yellow cheese crackers break into dust, her little hands slamming the cup down on the tray with a *thud, thud, thud, thud* ... Jessie startled awake and screamed when she saw the macabre face banging relentlessly against the driver's side window. *Thud, thud, thud.* The face had no lips, no nose; one eyeball was missing, fallen from its socket, the other was milky white like maggot flesh. *Thud.* The teeth gnashed and snapped at the glass. *Thud.* Jessie, shaking, tried to start the FJ, but the truck just lurched forward a few feet and didn't start. *Thud, thud.* Remembering the clutch, Jessie slammed her left foot on the pedal and turned the ignition again. The chilly engine roared to life. She pushed the gear shift into first and let the clutch out gradually. The rear tires spun in the dirt as the FJ drove forward and bounced over the curb, leaving the window-banging corpse to its own fate. Behind her, the eastern horizon glowed with the impending sunrise. The dim yellow headlights of the FJ provided just enough illumination for Jessie to drive. As she caught her breath, her heart ached with the fading dream of Keeley making a mess when she was still a baby. *She will always be a baby now, my poor baby girl.* Tears streamed down Jessie's cheeks; she clung to the last shreds of the dream as she absentmindedly rubbed her belly with her right hand. Her left hand was firmly placed on top of the steering wheel, guiding her forward.

The vehicles in this area were still pushed into the ditches, so the road was clear for her to drive however she wanted. *Maybe that'll be the only one I see today.*

She wiped her cheeks with her shirt sleeve and knew that wasn't true. By the time that Jessie saw another town off to the left side of the highway, the heater had finally warmed the cabin up from the cold desert air. The sun was high enough that she turned the headlights off. Jessie had no idea what town she was passing, as the road signs were all flattened into the desert floor, but it was small. She pulled the atlas off the seat next to her and held the steering wheel with her knee. She knew I-25 would get her to I-40, and that I-25 was on the other side of El Paso, across the New Mexico border, but much of I-40 was a mystery to her without a map of Arizona. Even without road signs she would know El Paso when she hit it. Hopefully, there would be signs to follow after that; otherwise she would be in a bit of a jam. Jessie was already in a part of Texas she hadn't driven before. Bexar was the usual bus driver for the family.

Exit after exit passed by on the deserted Interstate for the small farming communities along the Rio Grande. By the time that Jessie's tears had dried and the FJ was warm, she was at the edge of El Paso, Texas.

The Interstate was still clear, but off the Interstate to either side there were hundreds of bodies moving amongst destroyed neighborhoods and strip malls. Sections of concrete barriers on the sides of bridges had broken away; more chunks of the jagged edges of the bridges tumbled off as the FJ bounded across them at a steady fifty mph. Jessie had forgotten about trying to find fuel after the frightful wakeup call she'd had. The gauge showed that she was already down a quarter of a tank, and she hadn't refilled the used gas cans yet. She had enough for now, but she feared running out completely in a part of the country where there wouldn't be any vehicles that she could siphon from. The large overhead Interstate signs remained intact, which was a blessing, since if one of those had fallen it might have blocked the road, making Jessie have to backtrack along the surface streets where there were still hundreds and hundreds of undead teeming about in a churning sea of death.

Jessie was making good time. In El Paso, there had been no ditches for the cars to be pushed into, so she had to slow considerably and drive around the mangled remains of vehicles pressed against the barriers. She caught herself holding her breath as she drove, and had to constantly remind herself to breathe while concentrating on the road, the signs, and the hazards. That drive had been more stressful than any Houston traffic she had ever been stuck in, but as abruptly as it had begun, she was past the center of El Paso, and back on I-10 headed into New Mexico.

Twentynine Palms, CA

Since it was certain that gunfire would bring Zeds streaming towards the sound, the sentry rotations were instructed to use knives or the corporal's improvised weapon to dispatch them. Bullets were to be spent only as a last resort and would alert the entire camp to assist.

Corporal Simmons, mechanical whiz kid, had spent most of his middle school days cutting history and math to be in shop class, which the shop teacher allowed because he could see Simmons' talent and potential. What he missed in the other required subjects he made up with his creative ability to fabricate, repair, or build anything and everything in between. Aymond thought about his old CJ sitting in his driveway at home at Camp Lejeune. *If we survive; if things go back to normal,* he thought, *Simmons will be on my short list to help finish the build.*

Sunrise was met with more MREs and Simmons crawling around the M-ATVs doing some basic servicing. Their trucks were in good shape, but a lube job and filter cleaning never hurt anyone. Freed from riding in the M-ATVs, the MSOT spent time cleaning their personal weapons, the rest of their gear, and the crew-served weapons mounted on the M-ATVs. Once the mission was explained, the resident Corporals Simmons and Jones opted to join the ragtag group of operators. Marines are riflemen first, and whatever their day job is second, so if Aymond could scare up some more M-4s, Jones and Simmons could be combat effective. Regardless, bringing your own mechanics along is always a good idea.

Jones, still not used to the loose command structure of the MSOT, properly informed Master Gunnery Sergeant Aymond of an unimproved road south of the middle of the runway that would lead them to a series of unimproved roads and back to the highway. They would have to cut some fence, but they would be able to skip the main base and all the Zeds they accidentally baited out of the hospital. Believing the route was a winner, by 1000 hours the M-ATVs were loaded, including some more five-gallon jerry cans of fuel and a few more cases of MREs that Simmons and Jones had acquired. The convoy increased by Jones and Simmons in their Humvee bounded across the flight line, taxiway, and runway, into the desert, and onto the unimproved road heading southwest. Eventually, they intersected with other unimproved roads near the mountains to the south, and an hour later the convoy was back on 62, the Twentynine Palms Highway, headed towards San Diego. Like thousands of Marines before them, the lessons learned by coming to Twentynine Palms would help them immensely in their next battle; unlike the

Marines that came before them, the lessons took less than twenty-four hours and included a security briefing by an E-4.

TX-82 Lubbock, TX

Apollo stopped at the exit for the loop. The sun glowed in the rearview mirror and it was time to swap places with Chivo. Lindsey complained that she was bored and was quickly chastised for it; as soldiers know, boredom can be quickly punctuated by intense terror. For Bexar it was like commenting how slow a shift was going in the police world—simply uttering those words out loud would bring the sort of non-stop shenanigans that are typically reserved for episodes of police reality TV shows.

Lindsey didn't care; she was still bored. All she did was sit in the back and only got to climb out during one of the allotted rest and bathroom breaks. Chivo, behind the wheel with dawn breaking over the horizon, took the Defender off Highway 82 and onto the 289 loop around Lubbock. They only needed to travel to the very top of the loop to reach Highway 84, and as luck would have it, that section was largely undeveloped outside of light industrial complexes. There were no shopping malls or Walmarts teeming with people anywhere to be found. As quickly as they were on the loop, they were off of it and heading northwest on 84. No longer an elevated freeway, the highway was crossed by intersecting roads and private driveways. More of the undead shuffled amongst abandoned vehicles, but Chivo kept to the now standard operating procedure of weaving through the bodies and vehicles as best he could. If they had to dismount and engage in a ground fight with the walking corpses, it could be a losing battle. Everyone was better served by moving quickly through the fray and on towards their destination. In that regard, this drive reminded Chivo of working in The Stan. Move fast, blow by the threats in a soft vehicle, a civilian vehicle like a Hilux or 4Runner, and be gone before any insurgents could attack. The destination mattered, not the journey. The "journey" was for conventional troops with broad assignments, not for the special missions and tasks that the MSOT served. Swerving across the road to the shoulder, Chivo drove past a small group of undead, who turned to follow the passing vehicle. Chivo still didn't know how long one of the walking corpses would continue in a specific direction, but he hoped they would eventually cease. Otherwise, once the convoy stopped they would have a really big problem.

The small towns along the way, Littlefield, Muleshoe, and Clovis, all told the same story. No signs of survivors, burned-out buildings, and the undead roaming the streets. It seemed that every town had burned. Chivo's best guess was that in the beginning, right after the attack, survivors had sheltered in place in their homes and tried to cook indoors due to the undead threat. Since the electricity was off, they probably used gas grills. Carbon monoxide would quickly fill the air and kill a family in a home that way; certainly, if the grill flamed up or tipped over it would take the house with it. With first responders nonexistent, the fires would go unchecked and burn house to house, building to building, before extinguishing by themselves from lack of fuel, or maybe a rain storm. Chivo seriously doubted a rain storm, though. The flat desert of West Texas didn't look like it had much rain ever, much less a miraculous downpour that would douse a raging fire.

With each passing mile, more and more vehicles sat along or on the highway; countless corpses walked through the roadside parking lots, and bodies littered the ground. By now, the carnage and gore rolling by the windows of the Defender was nothing new; it had actually become routine. It is amazing how quickly people can adapt to horrible conditions and destroyed lives. Chivo had a long Special Forces career both in and out of the military which cushioned him against this nightmare, but he wondered how Bexar and Lindsey were holding up. Lindsey at least had Apollo, but Bexar had no one. All alone in the new world order where the dead rule the earth.

The gas gauge fell just past the halfway mark and Chivo decided now was as good a time as any to stop and fuel up. At the last fuel stop, Bexar had showed the group a trick on how to syphon gas easily. The sign said "Fort Sumner." Whatever. It appeared to be yet another small town in the desert.

"Look alive back there. Stopping for fuel. Bexar, care to take care of the jerry cans again? I'll use the first cans to fill the truck. Apollo and Lindsey—take security?"

Everyone answered positively. Apollo was just waking up from a good half day's worth of sleep after his night shift driving. With any luck, they would reach Cortez by the evening.

Chivo left the Defender running, setting the brake as he climbed out. Apollo and Lindsey rolled out of the back of the SUV, rifles in their hands. Bexar got out and walked to the first car in his path. He noticed absently that it was a rental car; there was a small barcode sticker on the back window. At the front and rear of the Defender, rifle fire filled the air as Lindsey and Apollo began picking off the curious dead as they approached the team. Bexar used the butt of his big CM Forge blade to break the window of the rear driver's side door so he could reach in and unlock the rental car. The bottom of the rear seat came out next, thrown onto the roof of the car so it would be out of the way. A few hits with the butt of his knife and the fuel pump unlocked from the top of the gas tank. Bexar pulled the pump assembly out of the way, and was looking to see how much gas was in the tank before inserting a section of garden hose to syphon with when he started laughing.

Chivo walked over to Bexar with two of the jerry cans. "What's so funny?"

In his bad Cop-Spanish, Bexar answered, "su tiene cocaina" as he pulled out a tightly wrapped brick of cocaine from the gas tank. "These things had a street value of about $20k apiece. You guys want to party? Or maybe make some side cash? Maybe we can talk the undead into trying a few lines; they'd get all paranoid we might be narcs and leave us the hell alone."

Bexar threw one of the bricks of cocaine across the road yelling, "Fuck! Fucking world sucks!" before stomping off to the next car, a red Ford F450. This one was not a rental. Repeating the process, Bexar found the gas tank full of gasoline instead of drugs. A few minutes later, three of the jerry cans were full, the Defender was full, and Bexar slid under a pickup to cut the fuel filler hose to finish the task. The superduty truck's big tank refilled the used jerry cans, which were then lashed back on the roof rack. Apollo and Lindsey spent two magazines each keeping the undead at bay for the half hour it took Bexar to fill the gas cans and the Defender.

Everyone back in the vehicle, Chivo drove past the pile of undead that Apollo had dropped about thirty yards in front of them. Fort Sumner passed by the windows, just as the other small towns did, Chivo dodging walking corpses and worrying only about the destination. Reaching I-40, Chivo took the on ramp and found that the Interstate was completely clear. Everything was pushed forward and off the road, all the signs were down, and dried blood painted the dented and crushed sides of the vehicles in the ditches.

Bexar smirked. "Well, we have that going for us, which is nice."

"No mano, the vehicles are pushed westward, not east."

Lindsey interrupted from the back of the Defender, "So we're driving *towards* the undead surge. Fucking great."

I-10 Las Cruces, NM

Jessie followed the signs and took the exit for I-25 from I-10, turning northbound. The vehicles on the roadway were sparse, but they were still in the road. *Nothing big has come through here ... yet.* The *yet* that slipped into her thoughts gave Jessie pause. She didn't mean to think it, but her mind just added it, as if she already knew what that meant; she hadn't seen the worst of it.

Undead milled about on the surface streets on either side of the Interstate, but so far the walking corpses on I-25 were few and spaced far enough apart that she could maintain close to fifty mph, driving mostly on the shoulder. The farther north she traveled from Las Cruces, the more scattered and barren the landscape and road became. *I wish the radio worked.* She shook her head at that. *Even if it did work, what would be left for me listen to?*

The sun continued its constant march across the sky. The Interstate was practically clear of vehicles, and in a short time, Jessie saw a sign for Truth or Consequences. The frontier town names were always the best. The big green sign on the side of the road stated she was a hundred and fifty miles from Albuquerque. *So three more hours, plus or minus, before I turn onto I-40.God, I hope I-40 is as easy as I-25.*

Jessie stopped and fueled the FJ from the gas cans on the roof rack, then refilled the gas cans from two nearby pickup trucks. She only had to put down three undead during the time it took her to do all of this by herself, so with a full tank of gas, full gas cans, and feeling easier about the drive, she opened up the FJ to sixty mph. She just had to make it to Groom Lake. She felt so close to safety.

Jessie's mind wandered as she drove, deciding to name the child either Malachi or Bexar if it was a boy, but she couldn't decide on a girl's name. She tried not to think about going into labor on her own; she had to make it to safety and help before that happened. The image occurred again of her dying giving birth while the baby made it just long enough to die next to her body. It made her shiver. Nausea swept over her and a tear streaked down her cheeks as she passed the southern outskirts of Albuquerque.

The sign said two miles to I-40. *Almost there— finally almost to I-40.* The dashboard of the FJ was a simple affair, but it still had gauges for the battery level and temperature. A soft thump came from under the hood of her truck; Jessie looked at the hood and didn't see any obvious signs of a problem, so she kept driving, weaving from shoulder to shoulder, driving around vehicles, the undead, and other wreckage. A red light flickered to life on the dash. Jessie looked and saw it was a warning light for the temperature, the gauge below it climbing at a rapid rate. *Oh shit, oh shit! What do I do?* At the ramp for the flyover to reach I-40, Jessie rolled to a stop and shut off the engine. Around her were several cars and a gaggle of undead. Jessie climbed out with her rifle and picked off the three closest walking corpses before unlatching and raising the hood of the FJ. She looked at the engine. It looked like an engine to her. Jessie had no idea what could be wrong or how to fix it. *Dammit Bexar, this is your job.*

The increasing number of moans grew closer; a hand grabbed Jessie by the shoulder. She kicked hard and stepped away from the groping hand. The hood of the FJ fell closed. As she had feared, the hand was attached to a corpse. She raised her rifle and fired multiple times. The gruesome face exploded in a black mist. Hatred burned in her eyes. *Fuck the dead*, she snarled Looking left and right, Jessie realized how bad her situation was. She stepped on the bumper and climbed on top of the hood, then over the windshield and onto the roof rack. Standing on top of the roof rack, she could see an ocean of the undead, dozens and dozens of them shambling through the vehicles on the Interstate towards her position. Feeling panic rising in her throat, Jessie closed her eyes and counted her breaths, slowly regaining her composure. From every side and closing in, Jessie saw her fate. Her rifle hung limp on the sling across her body.

Tears streaked down her face; she placed both her hands on her rounding belly. Her fetus was only a peanut clinging to life within her body, but a life it was, a child, *her* child. She wouldn't give up, she had to win; she had to win for her child. Clutching the rifle, Jessie took a deep breath, angry at God, angry at fate, but she had to try, she had to fight. With each pull of the trigger, she began killing the undead about twenty yards out. The ones nearest couldn't reach her; she would worry about them later—she would figure out a way. Stepping across the cases and gas cans lashed to the roof rack, Jessie continued to fire, changing magazines when the bolt locked back, determined to survive. If she had to kill every last zombie in the city with her bare hands and a knife, she would. Her child demanded her best.

I-40 Albuquerque, NM

The Interstate well-cleared of all obstacles by the mob of undead preceding the convoy, Chivo kept the Defender's speed up as they neared the middle of the city. He cocked his head to the side.

"You guys hear that?"

Lindsey shook her head, but Apollo responded, "Sounds like small arms fire."

Bexar couldn't hear it; the crushed windshield made too much noise in the blowing wind.

"I don't see anyone ahead of us ... Apollo, anything following?"

"Nope."

All four of them scanned the scene outside their windows. Bexar saw the overhead road sign pass by. "Chivo, next exit right, that's I-25. Take it; keep right, and head north."

"Got it. Man, I can really hear the shots now. Someone is really getting after it, and it sounds light, like an M4."

All of them kept scanning, but they didn't see anything.

Chivo took the off ramp and kept right to take the flyover ramp to I-25.

I-25 Albuquerque, NM

The bolt on Jessie's rifle locked to the rear on her last magazine. She let go of the rifle and let it hang on the sling while she transitioned to her pistol, continuing the constant cadence of scan, breathe, shoot ... scan, breathe, shoot. She looked down at yet another walking corpse limping close to the FJ. *Scan, breathe*, but before she could squeeze the trigger its head exploded in a black mist. Half a second later the deep crack of a rifle filled the air. Jessie froze. One by one the undead around the FJ lost their heads in a grotesque combustion followed by a distant rifle report. She used the pistol to put down the few undead pressed against the FJ, which was smeared with dark blood, skull fragments, and the black pus of undead brain matter. Moments later, Jessie could hear the rattling pop of a motorcycle's exhaust. Jessie's ears were ringing from all the gunfire, but she could tell it was getting closer.

Shit ... again? More bikers? Goddammit! Jessie turned towards the sound of the approaching motorcycle and raised her pistol, steeling herself for a hard battle against another gang. An ancient-looking bike rolled up alongside the FJ. The rider pulled the filthy bandanna down and said, "You might as well lower your pistol, sweetheart. My daughter has you in the scope of her rifle and you saw how good she is."

A woman? My daughter?

"If you want to live, you should climb down and get on; otherwise, we'll just let you sit on your perch, but we won't help you with the dead anymore."

Jessie blinked hard. Long, dirty blond hair stuck out beneath the knit cap the rider was wearing and trailed down the back of the worn leather jacket she had on. All Jessie could do was nod, climb down from the FJ, and climb on the back of the motorcycle. She wrapped her arms around the rider's waist. The bike threaded through the vehicles, avoiding all the headless corpses, and accelerated sharply before driving down an entrance ramp and off the Interstate.

CHAPTER 23

"Amanda, I have a link up. We have contact with Groom Lake again."

The President of the United States stood over Clint's shoulder wearing utility trousers, a brown t-shirt, and no bra. Not the sort of working clothes that most Presidents wear while in office, but she didn't care. Besides, Brooks Brothers was probably unavailable for a tailored fitting.

"The satellites are back online?"

"No, but the Secure Terminal is up. It's secured VoIP."

"Voice over Internet Protocol ... but how on earth is the Internet still up?"

"It isn't. Well, the civilian one isn't. The major installations are connected via fiber. Off-site communications is made using an Enhanced Crypto Card (ECC), and then a satellite link. This facility and Groom Lake are connected."

"What about Apollo and his team?"

"They're still in the dark. At this point, if they can get to Colorado then back to Groom Lake, they'll be contactable."

"Why didn't we do this yesterday?"

"I tried. My ECC didn't work; I had to do some major work to get anything to run."

Groom Lake, NV

In the radio hut, a phone rang with a strange electronic warble. The Air Force team and the civilian radio operators all stopped and stared at the phone at the end of the room. Bill, nearest to the phone, picked up the receiver.

"Uh, hello?"

"Who is this?"

"Umm, Bill. Who is this?"

"Clint. Get me Major Wright."

Bill cupped his hand over the receiver. "Get the major in here!"

SVoIP

"This is Wright."

"Major, this is Clint. The SSC is still secure, but we've lost all satellite access. What is your status?"

"We're nominal, but having the same access problems. My team is working on the tracking to figure out what happened to them—what sort of failure it was, and whether or not we can fix it."

"Major, have you ever heard of Have Dragon?"

"Have ... no. What is it?"

Clint took a deep breath and waved to Amanda to sit next to him.

"Have Dragon is a deep black project to design launch-ready objects that will disrupt satellites. Satellite killers. It began as a proof of concept program with DARPA, the Defense Advanced Research Projects Agency, but actually went into real production about eighteen months ago because China launched their own version of the same device."

"OK ..."

"Do you know about Blue Skies?"

"Yes, well sort of; I know there are about a dozen Air Force officers in orbit, or *were* in orbit at least."

"Do you know what those Air Force pilots were actually doing in orbit?"

"No."

"They were sent to capture the Chinese satellites and bring them back for study."

"So, are you telling me that we have lost access due to a deliberate act of sabotage?"

"Yes. Well, most likely."

"But, early imagery showed that China was overrun by the dead."

"Before the attack, one of the scenarios tossed around was that China might sacrifice nearly half of their population as part of a "false flag" operation and as a means to regain control of their rampant overpopulation problem."

Amanda listened to the exchange; all of this was news to her. Clint had brought her up to speed on a lot of the secret programs, but the incredibly large number of projects made it hard for him to cover them, if he even knew all of them. Some database somewhere might have information on most of them, but she didn't even know where to start looking. It didn't matter; her first priority was protecting the surviving citizens, followed by trying to create a safe place for society to restart from. Some place with access to navigable waterways, farmable land that didn't require significant irrigation efforts, and that had available raw materials, primarily lumber. Amanda wasn't sure such a place still existed in modern America. That was the United States of 1840, not the United States of the twenty-first century.

"But that is an act of war!"

Amanda's attention was drawn back to the conversation.

"It is, Major, but so was the EMP; so was spreading the virus."

"The U.S. has maintained biological warfare be met with the nuclear option."

"That's true, but we don't have access to those assets now, even if they are still available. This isn't the 1980s; we don't have crews on standby like that anymore. There is our sub fleet, the surface fleet, and a small handful of Minutemen sites left. So, assuming that a B-52 crew doesn't materialize out of thin air, those are our only assets with nuclear weapons. So far, all my attempts to contact any of these units have failed. We can't use Extremely Low Frequency (ELF) communications because we can't make contact with the transmission station in Clam Lake or Michigan. All we can hope for is that one of our subs surfaces and uses High Frequency; then if we have the right conditions maybe we can pick it up."

"We need people on the coasts."

"Sure. There's a lot that we need, but we have to focus on what we have."

Amanda ignored the conversation again. *Nuclear war ... I'm the first woman President and I might be the first to order a nuclear strike post-WWII ... God help me.*

Cortez, CO

Cliff reviewed the notes he took during the recon mission. The more he thought about it, the more the church concerned him. Why would the group keep women and young girls away from the school? The school had protection, people, patrols ... the church had nothing. It stood alone and out of their direct control. He didn't know why, but the church really bothered him. Clint had learned to trust his intuition over the years. He couldn't do anything about the situation yet. Before he could deal with the church, Clint needed to organize another recon mission, this time to two more schools, including the middle school the survivors were using.

CHAPTER 24

Chivo stared out the side window, looked forward and slammed on the brakes. The Defender skidded across the pavement and into an overturned semi-truck.

"Everyone OK?"

"Just fucking dandy, Chivo, thanks," Bexar answered, shaking his head to clear it.

The windshield was truly done now. The four of them climbed out of the Defender and looked at the damaged front end.

Apollo kicked a front tire. "Well, at least the tires didn't flatten. I don't think we're in that much trouble here. The headlights are fucked but we weren't using them anyways." He then climbed into the driver's seat, backed the Defender away from the tractor-trailer, and turned the engine off so he could inspect the vehicle.

"You two take guard. Chivo, why don't you walk around the damned thing and see if there's a way through."

Lindsey stood near Apollo, her rifle in hand. Chivo walked north and around the overturned semi-truck. Bexar walked south a ways, looking into car windows to see if there was anything worth scavenging.

The sound erupted like a tornado—like a hundred roaring trains coming straight at them. All four of them looked west and saw nothing but a dark cloud, a wall of dust headed closer by the minute.

His leg still sore from being shot, Bexar limp-jogged to the west side of the roadway and peered over the concrete barrier. "Holy shit. It's a solid mass of fucking undead."

Apollo ignored Bexar; it didn't matter to him. As long as they weren't on the bridge with the four of them, it didn't affect him. All that mattered now was trying to bend the radiator support out so the engine-mounted fan didn't contact the radiator anymore.

Chivo watched the approaching wall of fumes from the other side of the semi-truck uneasily. *At least it looks like they'll pass through ... we'll be safe up here.*

The cloud preceding the undead swept over the group. The smell was worse than Bexar had ever experienced; rotting flesh with excrement, like it had cooked in a hot car for days. Bexar gagged and threw up on the pavement. His mouth hung open trying to catch his breath; he then accidentally swallowed a handful of flies. The massive black fog was partly dirt kicked up by the mass of bodies, but mostly flies, heavy black flies feeding on the flesh of the walking corpses. Maggots wriggled their bloated white bodies into the putrid skin and flesh, growing to become more flies, leaving their own larva behind. Bexar threw up again and fell to his hands and knees, dry heaving. He pulled his shemagh over his face, wrapping it around his head to block his mouth, nose, and ears from the flies. The ground shook violently; the vehicles on the road vibrated and shimmied down the sloped roadway. Pieces of the concrete barriers began to crack and fall off, the Defender with them.

Bexar yelled at Apollo and Lindsey, but as loud as he yelled, he couldn't even hear himself. The noise of the thousands of undead passing below drowned out all other sound. Bexar felt it happen more than he could see it; the dust and flies were so thick that he could only see a few feet in front of his face. Scared to run blindly, Bexar crawled on his hands and knees until he saw the edge of the cracking roadway.

The bridge, the semi-truck, the Defender were gone, fallen into the mob of undead below. Seconds felt like hours, minutes felt like lifetimes. Eventually, the dust began to clear, the entourage of flies following their mobile feeding and breeding grounds.

The Defender lay partially exposed in the rubble, the semi-truck covering much of the vehicle. Chivo stood on the far side of the embankment, where the bridge had ended, his shemagh also over his face. He had his rifle shouldered, scanning the debris below. Among the rubble twitched hundreds of crushed undead bodies, some dead for good, some merely trapped and destroyed, but still very much alive in their way. Bexar saw her first. Lindsey's arm and head were barely visible in the broken concrete under the semi-truck. She was dead. He fired a single round, splitting her skull apart to make sure she had peace after death. Chivo did the same for Apollo.

Chivo's voice crackled in Bexar's ear. He had completely forgotten that they had comms. *I should have used the headset to warn them.* Defeat washed over Bexar, his knees felt weak, he sat down on the pavement, staring at Lindsey's body and the crushed Defender.

"How copy?"

Bexar looked up and saw Chivo pointing at his own ear.

"10-9 … sorry, repeat."

"OK, stay there. I'm coming to you. One piece at a time—watch your ass up there; I need you alert and your head in the game. We'll have time for our friends later, but right now you have to be straight. Get fucking straight, mano!"

Bexar stood up and turned his back to the broken edge. He scanned for any incoming threats from the south and waited for Chivo.

Albuquerque, NM

Jessie climbed off the motorcycle. The driver swung her leg over, pulled her knit cap off, pulled down the bandana that covered her face, and closed the overhead door.

"Holy shit. Look at you—you're a hot mess."

Jessie just blinked at her. The woman standing in front of her looked about forty years old. She wore filthy jeans, leather boots, a black t-shirt, and a broken-in leather jacket. Her hair hung nearly to her waist.

"OK, I get it. I'm Sarah; my daughter Erin should be here shortly. Who are you?"

"Jessica … Jessie Reed."

"Alright, Jessie. So what's your deal, sightseeing in New Mexico? You seemed to know where you were going."

"I, well … I'm headed for Groom Lake."

"As in Area 51? Why the fuck would you do that?"

Jessie turned. A girl, no older than fifteen, walked out of the shadows across the concrete floor with the largest rifle that Jessie had ever seen thrown over her shoulder like it was a shovel.

"Uh, yeah, like Area 51. We were going there because of Cliff."

"We who?"

"Bexar. My ... my ..." Jessie sat down on the floor. *I can't do it, I just can't do it anymore.*

Sarah nodded to Erin, who came back with a bottle of water and handed it to Jessie.

"Just relax for now; we'll get your story when you're ready. Until then, we'll figure out what to do about your ride."

Twentynine Palms, CA

The M-ATV and Humvee convoy of four drove west on Highway 62 at a steady forty mph, rolling through the town of Joshua Tree and Yucca Valley with no problems. Aymond understood why the towns were deserted. All the residents had fled to the installation.

The small communities along the route until they hit the mountains were equally deserted, as if one day everyone had simply left their cars and their homes and flown away. They rolled down the other side of the mountains. Huge windmills dotted the area, spinning slowly in the wind, generating power for no one. *If they are able to generate any power at all.* Aymond wasn't sure; he didn't know if windmills would survive an EMP. Mechanically, they looked fine from miles away, but if their generators had ceased ... it really didn't matter if there were no other survivors to use the power anyway. The MSOT's spirits were lifted by the two new corporals joining their merry band of travelers. *If we found two people on an overrun installation, we'll probably find more in San Diego, and more elsewhere. There might be a chance that there are people left everywhere: survivors.*

After turning onto I-10, Aymond had expected to find a parking lot of abandoned vehicles in the road. Instead, many of the smaller vehicles were pushed off into the ditches. The larger vehicles were badly damaged; dried blood was smeared along the sides and the western-facing ends of the vehicles.

Reaching the town of Banning, the convoy encountered the first underpasses of their journey. The first M-ATV drove under, followed by the second; a Zed dropped from the bridge above onto the windshield of the last M-ATV.

"Holy shit, Chief! A fucking Zed just fell onto our windshield from the bridge above!"

"Any damage, Davis?"

"I don't see any ... just blood smeared across the windshield after the fucking thing bounced off."

"Do we need to stop?"

"Hell no, Chief!"

Davis wanted to stop. It creeped him out to have Zed blood smeared across his windshield, but he couldn't risk losing face in front of the team. Besides, he didn't want to pull over next to a town anyway.

The same thing happened with each overpass they cleared. A walking corpse would inevitably fall off the bridge and land on Davis's M-ATV. By the third body he was no longer startled—just pissed that he was the third in line and the one catching all the jumpers.

In Beaumont, they turned south to head over more mountains. Away from I-10 and away from the towns, the number of abandoned vehicles diminished, but more importantly to Davis, no more Zeds splattered onto his windshield.

Albuquerque, NM

Chivo stood with his back to the edge of the collapsed bridge, scanning for any threats that came up the road. The mass of undead that had pushed the bridge over were mostly gone, the parade of death and gore becoming a limping and stumbling gaggle of bodies shambling by, detoured by the incredible piles of rubble.

Bexar glanced over his shoulder. *They have a really hard time climbing over the rubble; they're basically stuck.* He turned, shouldered his rifle, and fired half a dozen shots, dropping four of the shambling dead trapped in the debris. Chivo made his way to the side of the bridge that Bexar could only refer to as "downwind." The remaining horde of bodies hit the debris and pushed out on either side, failing to navigate all the broken concrete and crushed vehicles. The Defender lay partially destroyed near Lindsey's and Apollo's bodies.

At the sound of a rifle firing, Bexar spun around to see a body drop about thirty feet behind him. Chivo walked up the incline of the road towards him. Bexar's life in law enforcement had given him the experience to read people's emotions and actions, but Chivo's face was a complete mask, absolutely unreadable.

"Alright mano, looks like we're on the leather express until we find another ride. I think if we stay on the side of the road where that mass of dead passed we'll be OK, or at least better off than on the other side. First, we need to pull gear and salvage what we can out of the Defender. Come with me."

Chivo walked down the road towards where he could lower himself to the road below. Bexar gave him cover until he found his footing, then Chivo returned the favor as Bexar climbed down. The road beside the overpass was thick with abandoned vehicles. Faces slapped against the inside of closed cars as they passed, each of them startling Bexar. Chivo appeared impervious to any emotion whatsoever. *I wonder how he can flip a switch like that. How does he turn it off?* Bexar wondered.

Reaching the broken mounds of concrete and rebar, both of them carefully climbed over the rubble, mindful that there could still be undead active and trapped beneath the collapsed bridge. Neither of them wanted to survive just long enough to get bit.

Surveying the scene ahead of them, they faced the ruined Defender. A rasping moan behind them caused them both to spin in place to address the threat. Chivo kicked the corpse, knocking it over before firing a single shot. Its rotting skull exploded across the pavement. Dozens of undead were closing around them, followed by dozens more, and more after that. The first horde of undead may have passed, but a new one simply took its place at the bridge, now an altar of ruin and death.

"Fuck, mano. Come on!"

Chivo turned north and started a steadily paced trot. Bexar, never much the runner, was quickly gasping for breath after only a block, limping hard with his still-healing leg. He was used to a thirty-pound duty belt, but he wasn't used to the higher altitude and a combat load-out that weighed more like fifty pounds. For once in his life, Bexar wasn't the chaser; he was the chased. He didn't like it at all.

Focusing on each step, Bexar kept Chivo centered in his vision, matching the fast-trotting jog step for step. Bexar's eyesight became obscured; dark curtains edged towards the center, white flashes popped just on the edge of his peripheral vision. *Don't look down, don't look back ... focus, focus, focus, focus, focus ...*

Bexar ran right into the back of Chivo, who had stopped suddenly in the middle of an intersection, nearly knocking him over. Chivo wasn't even breathing hard; Bexar gasped for breath like a guppy out of water.

Chivo scanned the urban world surrounding them. More dead streamed out of the alleys and around the buildings to either side. The horde they'd outpaced while on the jog was beginning to close on them. Bexar tried to raise his rifle and control his breathing, but that only resulted in chucking up the remnants of the last MRE he ate. Specs of vomit, spit, and snot flecked across the front of Bexar's load carrier and AR magazines.

"This way, Bexar!"

Chivo dashed towards a building to the east. Bexar tried to keep up but was quickly left behind by Chivo's much faster sprint towards possible safety. Reaching the target, Chivo held open a heavy metal door, pistol up and firing, the rounds cracking in the air as they flew past Bexar's head.

Bexar never stopped running; he fell through the open door and hurtled into the darkness. Tables and chairs were thrown aside by Bexar's crashing body, and he lay sprawled, dry heaving on the floor. Chivo closed the door, turned a deadbolt, and flipped his NODs down. All he could hear was Bexar dry heaving what was possibly left in his stomach onto the floor. *Probably not the first time that has happened here,* Chivo chuckled in his thoughts.

Bodies thumped against the door, the moans barely audible through the heavy cinderblock walls of their safe haven. Then a louder moan sounded, very human and reverberating in the darkness.

"Get a fucking hold of yourself. Jesus Christ, Bexar, suck it up and shut the fuck up!"

Bexar gulped air and held his breath, his stomach still spasming, trying to be quiet, but all he could hear was his own heartbeat thumping in his ears.

Two Miles South

If society had still been standing, the three of them might have shared some coffee, or more likely Sarah and Jessie would have shared stories over coffee while Erin did her own thing, ignoring and judging her mother as teenage girls are wont to do. As society was not still standing, the three of them sat on an oil- and grease-stained concrete floor inside a mechanic's shop of some sort. Erin's rifle, roughly the same size that she was, lay on the floor; an M4 with a very short barrel lay across her lap.

Jessie had just met the two of them a couple of hours ago, but already they felt like family. Jessie brought both of them up to the here-and-now of her story, from Bexar running into the house still in uniform, to losing Malachi and the battle against the bikers at Big Bend. With every triumph, each failure, Jessie's emotions felt like a train with no conductor, gaining speed out of control on the way down the mountain, chugging around turns and passes without being able to stop or slow down.

Erin watched passively, glancing around the darkened interior every few moments. Sarah held Jessie's hand.

"You're pregnant?"

"Yes. Well, I think I am ... I haven't seen my OB yet to confirm it."

Erin stared at Jessie for a moment. She had no siblings, she had never really cared for a newborn before, and she didn't understand why her mother reacted so strongly to the news.

Sarah wrapped her arms around Jessie. "We'll help you. We have to help you ... we have to help you for your baby's sake!"

"Thank you. But, how will we get to Groom Lake? We can't all fit on your motorcycle."

"We have to fix your ride."

"I don't know how."

Erin rolled her eyes, stood and peeked through a small hole in a paint-smeared window. "Mom, there's about three hours or so to sunset. We have time to check on it if we stop fucking around."

Sarah nodded. "Stay here. We'll be back soon."

Jessie smiled weakly. Sarah threw her leg over the big motorcycle; Erin climbed on the rear and leaned back against the sissy bar, the short-barreled M4 clutched in her hands. Deftly, Erin gave the rifle a quick press-check and verified the safety was on before Jessie pulled on the chain to roll the door up. The motorcycle barked to life, echoing throughout the workshop. Erin raised her rifle as the motorcycle rolled into the harsh sunlight, firing rapidly at the encroaching undead as they rode away. Jessie lowered the door and sat quietly in the dim light, the sound of the bike getting fainter.

Twenty minutes later, the low pops of Sarah's motorcycle grew in volume. A horn honked twice, and Jessie pulled sharply on the chain, quickly raising the overhead door. Erin rode the motorcycle into the shop, followed by her FJ, steam pouring out of the hood.

Chivo and Bexar

"Did you hear that?"

"No ... I can't hear shit."

"That's because you're a fat cop."

Bexar didn't respond; for once he actually agreed with someone when they said that. As hard as he'd trained in the gym, Bexar was outmatched. Chivo wasn't even breathing hard. Slowly, Bexar stood, the dry heaves mostly passed; his skin flushed hotly in the cold air, sweat drenching his face and beard.

Bexar flipped the NODs down and looked around. He was still getting used to having them at his disposal. Up till now they hadn't been a tool that he would immediately think of. Even with the NODs, the green flash of a screen was mostly black, so little light was available in the interior of the building. Feeling down the quad rail on his rifle, Bexar found the thick square sitting on the outboard rail and pushed the button to turn on the IR light. With infrared on, he swept his rifle across the room. Mirrors glittered and flashed in his goggles. To his right, Chivo used the outside wall as a guide, and to protect his flank. Bexar followed suit and began down the other wall, stepping slowly and deliberately. Chairs and cocktail tables lay strewn about the room. Bexar continued scanning, lingering on the open doorways that bled into the darkness of the other rooms. The solid wall gradually turned into curtained partitions. Bexar gently peeled one of the floor-to-ceiling curtains back and found a wide booth with a low table. A glistening metal pole went through the middle of the table, reaching the ceiling. *A fucking strip club?*

Bexar glanced at Chivo. He was at the mirrored bar, checking behind it for any threat. One by one, Bexar cleared the small VIP rooms. He found no one, which sort of made sense, with the attack having occurred the day after Christmas.

"Bexar, I'm about to throw a bottle to see if we get a response," Chivo's whispering voice cracked in the radio earpiece.

Bexar turned to face the rest of the strip club; he could see Chivo at the bar with a bottle of something in his hand, which he threw towards the stage. It exploded in a loud crash, showering the stage and poles with liquor and shattered glass. A loud moan erupted from behind the stage and a single woman shambled out from the darkness of an open doorway, right into one of the poles.

Chivo wasted no time and a single rifle shot cracked through the building. The undead woman, wearing only a G-string, crumpled to the ground, her skull painting the mirrors behind her in blood and pus.

"Bexar, I'm checking the back, you go up front—and give that young lady a good tip, she's trying to work her way through school."

"Fuck you, and if that was the only bottle of Jack Daniels you broke, you and I are going to have problems."

They looked at each other in the glow of the illuminated green, surreal world in which they stood. Bexar could see the smirk on Chivo's face as he disappeared into the back of the strip club.

Cortez, CO

The sun fell closer to the western horizon. Cliff, up and awake, cooked his breakfast on the grill in the garage. He had to be careful not to build up too much carbon monoxide; he could pass out and possibly die, so with a single burner on low, the chili slowly warmed as he stirred the brown goop in the can.

His mind absent from the activity, Cliff's thoughts drifted in and out of operational details and the overhead map he held in his memory. *I have to check out the middle school; there could be stores left from the survivors. Or the cult might have cleaned it out; they could be using the school. Either way I have to determine what the status is.* Besides the women and girls from the first night of surveillance at the elementary school, Cliff had not seen any activity that would lead him to believe that there were any other persons in the town besides the cult members. The survivors and those they'd abducted had to be somewhere. The town just wasn't that big; he had to find them and get them out, and then somehow get them back to Groom Lake.

Groom Lake, NV

Bill continued to man the radio systems, mainly sticking to the high frequency HAM bands. One of his assistants continued broadcasting on the shortwave emergency frequencies and the weather stations, hoping that there might be weather-monitoring radios that couldn't pick up other shortwave transmissions. He sent continuous details on how to contact the facility using HF radios and channels available to many civilians with HAM radio sets. Bill's first concern was that the fellow HAMs probably already knew this and were trying to cobble together a radio with parts that had survived the EMP; the other was that there might be people hearing the shortwave broadcasts with malicious intent. Wright assured Bill that the facility was prepared for any sort of attack and could go into a fully defensive posture: locking the doors and blocking all access from the outside. With the subterranean nuclear power plants, Wright said that they would be safe and able to live on the stores for something like twenty years.

Twenty years without seeing the sun. Twenty years … *there is already little left, what would be left after twenty years? Nothing. Like a movie, like the book "On The Beach," everything would be dead; everything would be gone.*

Bill shuddered as a chill traveled down his spine. Behind him the airmen worked at a feverish pace, pulling communications satellites from past radar tracks. Bill didn't quite understand what they were doing, but the airmen said that was what they used to do back at NORAD, so he assumed they knew what they were looking for.

"Holy shit!" one of the airmen half-yelled, startling the bustling communications room. "Look, this is the track from last month; this is the track from last week. The transponder track is here, but the skin track is here. There is another object without a transponder and it's closing distance."

Bill walked to the airman's console; the others huddled around as well. "What does that satellite do?"

"It's one of the communications birds we have up, one of the latest."

The screen refreshed. The radar track of the object ran overlaid with the transponder track of the geostationary satellite. The unknown object was closing the distance at what appeared to be a breakneck speed, but what in reality would take a number of days. The time stamp on the corner of the screen showed that these images were recorded two days ago. The transponder track, then the radar track, vanished from the screen.

"That's about the time we started noticing communication issues."

Bill looked at the blank screen, the time stamp in the corner continually updating as the track continued to play. "I don't get it; they both disappeared."

"Exactly. The unknown object appeared to collide with our bird, which destroyed them both to the point of being too small for this radar system to track."

"So it was attacked?"

"Either that, or by happenstance, a few weeks after the initial attack on the U.S., some random object in space rammed a communications bird. This one is recorded; I'm checking the tracks on the other birds now."

SSC

"So we have no idea if there are any naval assets that survived or are still in play or anything?"

"No."

"How do we find out?"

"Generally the fleet is kept in the loop via SATCOM. Subs are kept in contact using very low frequency radios, similar to whale song, but much lower frequency ... out of our hearing range. But there are only two transmission sites in the U.S. for those comms, which are often patched through using SATCOM. We have neither control of those facilities nor SATCOM use right now."

"So what can we do?"

"Depending on atmospheric conditions and distance, we could establish contact using standard HF communications. Not very reliable for what we're trying to do, though."

"OK, so let's say we make contact with a ship. Let's say it is a whole carrier group. What then? We're still here; we're still stuck."

"First, we can direct recon missions over the U.S. to find survivors and secure facilities for replacement, rearmament, etc. Then we can send them towards China and 'Better Korea' to see if my theory is correct."

"Fine, Clint. Let's say that your theory is correct. What then?"

"My advice, babe? Fucking level the country into a pile of nuclear waste then focus on rebuilding ours."

CHAPTER 25

Cortez, CO
March 6, Year 1

Cliff dropped to the ground and slowly made his way over the fence and towards where he had stashed his second truck. Another night and another recon mission; another twenty-four hours holed up, trying to figure the crazies out.

Heading west, Cliff made a slow and deliberate drive towards the middle school. He would have to figure out where to stash the truck when he got there, and from the survivors back in Groom Lake, it sounded like the school had been overrun by the cult members. *I wish they at least had an idea of how many assholes I'll be dealing with. Right now it's a total guess. Could be ten, could be a thousand ... probably closer to ten, though.*

Diamond Valley Lake, CA

Passing through a few small towns without further incident, the team drove on as night slowly fell across the west coast. Aymond called for a halt, then stood on the roof of the lead M-ATV, scanning the horizon using his binoculars.

"All we have is farmland and random homes."

All the team members took the opportunity to get out of their lumbering armored vehicles and stretch their legs while pulling security for the convoy stopped in the middle of the road. Aymond climbed down from the roof and circled his finger overhead while climbing back into the passenger's door of the lead M-ATV. Five minutes later, the four trucks roared to life, driving slowly forward to a dirt road and a locked gate. Quick work with the bolt cutters and the convoy was in the fenced-off farm land. Aymond didn't know what crop was half-dead in the field, it could have been marijuana for all he knew, but he didn't care. What he cared about was that he had a fenced-off area free of buildings or other roads. He had the opportunity to create a safe spot for the convoy to bivouac that night.

While the moon rose in the night sky, the first security watch set up on an M-ATV's roof. The rest of the team, including the two new members, slept on the ground, protected by the circle of their high-tech covered wagons.

If we don't start making progress, it will take a week for us to reach San Diego ... a drive that wouldn't have taken us longer than a day before the attack. Aymond checked the map and his pocket calendar, checking off another day and making some notes on the notepad. Tomorrow they would fuel up and drive hard.

Albuquerque, NM

Erin slept softly, curled into a ball on a ratty couch. The hood of the FJ propped up, Sarah pointed out what the components were. The belt that turned the accessory drives and the water pump was shredded.

"That was probably the thump you heard, the belt hitting the hood."

"So now what?"

"Jessie, girl, don't worry about it. Belts are easy; we can raid a parts store in the morning. All we need to know is the length and width."

"How are we going to know the length?"

Sarah smiled and routed a piece of 550 cord around the pulley system before tying the end off, making a loop roughly the length of the belt. With the parachute cord and a piece of the old belt, it wouldn't take long to flip through the rack at a parts store to find a replacement and a backup.

Long into the night, the two of them talked, Sarah now telling Jessie her story. From Tennessee, she and Erin had set off cross-country in an attempt to find Sarah's father in Northern California after her home near Knoxville was overrun. Sarah's tale was one of utter sadness and destruction. Along the way, she and Erin had gained and lost three vehicles, including Sarah's prized CJ Jeep, which explained to Jessie why she knew what was going on with her FJ. The motorcycle was the last vehicle they'd found, just after entering New Mexico on foot. Erin's dad, Sarah's ex-husband, had taught her how to hunt, and took her hunting every October. Which further explained to Jessie why that sassy-bitch of a fifteen-year-old could shoot so well. *I'm fairly sure I was that bitchy when I was fifteen, and the world hadn't ended.* Jessie made a mental note to give Erin more space. She would figure it out, or Jessie would get used to her. Sarah had just agreed to ride to Groom Lake with her, so she would have to put up with Erin at least for the short term.

"Now, get some sleep if you can. We'll need to run the raid first thing in the morning, before the sun heats up the deaders too much."

"Why does that matter?"

"For one, they smell worse in the sun. But also, they seem to move a little slower when they're cold."

I hadn't noticed that. Oh my God; what is summer going to be like?

Fantasy Lounge

Chivo passed the bottle back to Bexar, slapping him in the chest with the square bottom. They sat in the darkness to conserve batteries. The NODs were flipped up on their helmets, which now sat on the bench next to each of them. Their feet were propped up on the low table of a VIP room.

Bexar took a long drink, the Tennessee whiskey burning his throat. "No, seriously. At one hundred mph, you are outrunning your siren. It's safer to split the traffic than go around it. So anyways, I get to the area, and I'm not really sure where the others are because the radio traffic is sporadic yelling, running, and fighting. So with the siren off, I'm rolling slowly through the neighborhood, when a guy matching the description pops out from behind a vehicle, never sees me, and starts running down the middle of the street right in front of me, holding his pants up while he runs. So I drop the clutch and, like a rocket, I'm on the guy. Matched his running speed and was about to kick him over, when he looks over his shoulder at me and cuts right in front of the bike."

"No shit?"

"No shit. I run him the fuck over, he breaks the mirror off my brand fucking new ride, knocks me over, I go tumbling to the ground, scratching my brand new motor and scuffing my boots. He's lying on the street, my bike is on the ground, and I'm up fast. I peeled off my helmet and threw it into a yard, and he's lying there bitching about me running him over. I'm standing over him, cursing him out for damaging my new bike, when the rest of the patrol team chasing him catches up. One of them pulls me aside; they hook him up and drag him to the ER for a release before going to jail. Luckily, my video showed his dumbass move, so I didn't get in trouble, but he got charged for the damage. Fucking turd."

Chivo roared in laughter before passing the bottle back to Bexar. And so the night went, finishing the bottle of whiskey, each story more outrageous than the first. Stories Bexar would have never heard outside of a movie, as he wasn't an elite operator like Chivo, and stories Chivo would never have heard because he wasn't a cop, nor included in the inner circle behind the thin blue line. Stories that both of them only told their buddies and only after a few stiff drinks.

Cortez, CO

In another cold home, Cliff used his blanket to construct another hide in which to conduct surveillance. If someone with the cult had counter sniper training, they would have noticed the window of the home was now open, but Cliff had to take the chance, believing it was unlikely. It was a less risky gamble than letting the window fog up with the humidity of his breath while hiding.

If this was a real op I would have cameras and listening devices up and a drone overhead. I would be monitoring video and audio from a secure location, far enough away that I wouldn't be known as a threat until we struck ... this is a real op, dumbass. Get in the game.

Cliff closed his eyes and took a deep breath, focusing on a moment of meditation to center his mind. Opening his eyes, Cliff peered through the spotting scope. No movement in the area, no movement from the school; the doors stood open and unguarded.

Six hours later, the dark night sky was beginning to glow faintly. Checking his watch, Cliff saw that it would be sunrise soon. With zero movement the entire night, it was time to gamble. Cliff couldn't sit behind the scope staring at nothing any longer, no matter what his training was telling him to do.

Gathering his things into the backpack, the blanket poncho over his shoulders, Cliff slowly made his way out of the house and towards the middle school. Creeping from cover to cover, eventually he crouched in the shadow of another shed. He gazed at the vast expanse ahead of him, checking the road in front of the school. It would be a hundred-yard dash. Moving fast or moving slow—it wouldn't matter. There was no cover, no shelter, nothing but open space between the marginal comfort of the shed and the open doors of the school.

Once more, Cliff scanned the area around him before taking a deep breath and launching out of his crouched spot. Rifle in his hands, blanket flapping like a cape behind him, he sprinted as fast as he could towards the open door, eyes front, eyes focused on the darkened opening ahead. Cliff exploded through the doors into the hallway of the school and slid to a stop. He turned to glance out the door at the path he'd just traveled. Focusing on slowing his breathing, he scanned the outside world, watching for any reaction to his mad dash.

Nothing.

The double set of doors stood open. Leaving the outside set wide, Cliff closed the interior doors and stuck a broom through the crash bars. A little security is a bonus, but he couldn't risk closing the outer doors; someone would probably notice that.

Turning his focus to the dark interior, Cliff slowly made his way through the hallways of the survivors' former home. The notepad in his breast pocket contained a layout with labels and information he had gathered from the survivors. Every interior door was standing wide open.

"REPENT" was painted on the wall of a classroom in tall letters. That was the first indication of any activity that he found. The paint didn't seem right. He approached and scratched at it, then sniffed the flakes under his nails. Something was indeed wrong with the paint; it was blood.

His senses now on high alert, Cliff slowed down his tour of the abandoned middle school and began looking closer for any clues that could help. He assumed that the survivors wouldn't have written on the wall in their own blood. Danger hung in the air like a heavy fog.

CHAPTER 26

Albuquerque, NM
March 7, Year 1

Jessie woke with Erin gently shaking her shoulders. "We're headed out for the raid, and you're in charge of holding down the fort."

Blinking hard, it took a moment for Jessie to realize what was going on. She didn't mean for Sarah and Erin to go in search of parts for her FJ without her, but before she could object, the motorcycle roared to life and sped out the open door. Jessie walked to the chain, unhooked it, and lowered the rollup door.

Morning sickness, she thought, *more like all the time sickness.* She grabbed yet another MRE from the FJ and cut open the green plastic bag. Black letters spelled out the meal of the morning: "RAVIOLI." *Yum.*

Scrunching her nose, Jessie started with the cookie and the large crackers. The instant coffee packet fell on the floor; she looked at it, really wishing she could have some coffee. *Screw it, if my mom smoked while pregnant I can have some dammed coffee.* A few minutes later, the heating packet warmed the small cup of water up a little while the instant coffee dissolved.

Finishing the coffee, Jessie took the M4 rifle apart, wiping down the bolt carrier before pulling the pin and dropping the bolt carrier group apart into pieces and cleaning each piece. A small bottle of Breakfree was all she had to lube the rifle. *Gun oil needs to be on my list, and I bet Erin has some.*

Done with the rifle, she strained to try to hear the sound of Sarah's motorcycle, but heard nothing outside the metal walls. Long plastic spoon from the MRE in hand, Jessie tore the top of the ravioli package apart. The smell struck her hypersensitive pregnancy nose, causing her to immediately throw up the little breakfast she had already eaten.

"Goddammit!" Jessie threw the vomit-covered MRE pouch across the shop; it landed with a wet thump against the wall.

Fantasy Lounge

Both Chivo and Bexar were a little slow moving around the interior of the strip club. With Bexar's ear against the metal door, he strained to hear any moans or movement from the undead that had chased them here the afternoon before. Hearing nothing, he turned the latch and slowly cracked the door open.

A long sliver of sunlight pierced the darkness. Blinking the tears out of his eyes from the harsh glare, Bexar peered into the morning sun. A couple of undead shambled by on the street, but the huge mass of undead from the previous day had gone elsewhere. Somewhere far away, hopefully. But Bexar wasn't sure. The mass that chased them yesterday seemed to have appeared out of nowhere, as if the undead had waited in planned ambush.

Another bottle of Jack Daniels was stuffed inside Bexar's pack, as was a bottle of tequila in Chivo's. Bexar laughed at the tequila. "Mexican guy with tequila? Dude, that's racist." Chivo answered with a middle finger. Slowly, Bexar opened the door further before sliding into the sunlight; Chivo's hand was on his shoulder through the movement, then he broke left to cover his area of responsibility. Bexar took point. He thought that the raised highway might give them some added protection as they made their way back to the ruined Defender. They could look for a replacement vehicle along the way. They cautiously proceeded around disabled vehicles on the highway, giving each a wide berth, as some of the owners still hung around next to their rides, even in death. At each rise, Bexar thought they were at the bridge, but apparently they had run much farther yesterday than he realized. Finally nearing the collapsed bridge, Bexar estimated the distance to have been almost two miles.

Bexar stopped and crouched in place. Chivo crouched in response and made his way to Bexar. On the road below, next to the collapsed bridge, was a bright yellow school bus. A large brush guard was welded across the flat nose of the bus, and steel bars protected each of the windows, including the windshield, which was missing. Blood was smeared along the battered sides, and the stop sign was missing. Two people stood on the roof, facing away from the highway, rifles in hand. Two more appeared from the rubble, carrying gear they'd scavenged from the Defender.

"What the fuck?" Bexar whispered to Chivo. "Drop 'em or what?"

Chivo scanned the scene, holding his left hand up to signal "stop." The people on the roof of the bus were women, one young and one older. Behind the wheel was a young boy, probably early teens. The two men, one much older than the other, carried the equipment from the Defender to the waiting open door at the rear of the bus. Black smoke rattled out of the tailpipe and the bus shook a little while idling.

A shot pierced the air. One of the women had fired her rifle at an approaching corpse, its skull bursting as it fell backwards into a heap on the pavement about thirty yards to their east. She fired again and again; the other woman began firing at corpses. The men on the ground threw the looted gear into the back of the bus as quickly as they could.

The younger man leapt into the back of the bus, while the older man pulled a pistol out of his waistband and began firing, turning around to face the ruined bridge.

Sliding forward, Bexar peered over the ruined edge of the roadway and saw at least a dozen undead flopping through the rubble towards the old man, some of them getting close. The younger man made his way to the front of the bus and began yelling at the women still perched on the roof. They quickly climbed in through a hole and disappeared into the interior.

Focused on shooting into the rubble, the old man didn't see the corpses closing in on him from the south.

"Shit."

Bexar rose into a kneeling position and picked off the corpse closest to the old man, the rifle round cracking loudly as it passed his head. The old man spun around and saw the dead closing in behind him, the nearest now crumpled on the pavement with a ruined skull. Bexar stood and began firing rapidly; Chivo joined him, giving the old man the chance to dive into the back of the bus. The bus lurched forward and onto the curb next to the raised roadway. Through the broken windshield and bars Chivo saw them waving him on.

"Fuckit mano. Time to go."

Chivo leapt over the barrier, dropping onto the roof of the bus. Bexar joined him with a heavy thud, denting the thin metal. As they climbed through the hole cut into the roof, the child in the driver's seat let the clutch out, shifted gears and turned an impossibly large steering wheel. The old bus rattled loudly as it accelerated, turned east at the next intersection, and moved out towards the rising sun.

Albuquerque, NM

The distant rumble of a motorcycle brought Jessie out of her trance-like state. Quickly, she reassembled her rifle and did a functionality check as she stood ready to pull the chain and raise the door. Magazine seated in the magazine well, Jessie ripped the charging handle back just before the motorcycle honked.

Once inside, Erin and Sarah climbed off the motorcycle. Erin's short M4 hung from the single-point sling across her chest. Jessie dropped the roll-up door, pushing the chain into the locking slot. Erin took her backpack off and pulled out three fan belts, a section of large flexible hose, some bottles of oil, and assorted things from the parts store. Sarah did the same; it seemed they'd had a successful run.

"Jesus. What all did you get?"

"If we're traveling together to Groom Lake, we'll have to be ready. We have replacement radiator hose, oil, tire patch kits, cans of Fix-a-Flat, tape, wire, and a few other knick knacks we might need." Sarah listed parts, holding up each item as she named it.

"I didn't think about that."

"Figured you didn't, although you look trimmed for war with all the shit you have in your Toyota."

Jessie nodded at Erin's comment, which was true. Ammo, food, water, shelter; she was set. Vehicle problems? She was not. *If I could go back, I would spend more time with Bexar in the garage and learn how to do all of the mechanical things. I should have learned about vehicles.*

"There was a bunch of gunfire towards the north," Erin said.

"Did you two see who it was?"

"No, and we've been around long enough to know it is better to not find out. Besides, the deaders will start showing up to gunfire."

"Erin—they'll what?"

"Sound, they're attracted to sound. Gunfire travels for miles; they'll have every deader in this part of the city zeroing in on them by now. Fuck that. They can deal with it."

Jessie glanced at Sarah who shrugged. *Her daughter, her rules* Jessie thought.

Thirty minutes later, the FJ was repaired, the radiator topped off, Sarah and Erin's gear loaded into the back (including the huge fifty-caliber rifle that Erin had), and they drove out of the metal building with Jessie behind the wheel.

In The School Bus

The whole bus shook every time the kid shifted gears, the gear shift nearly as tall as he was. Black smoke poured from the back of the bus, filtering through the missing windows and bars. Chivo made first contact, wiping his face with his shemagh and extending a hand towards the old man.

Nearly having to shout over the old diesel motor, he said, "My name is Chivo, and that was our ride and our dead friends back there."

"Well Mr. Chivo, thank you for your assistance. If you hadn't stepped in, I would have been got. When we get back to the compound we can talk about the stuff. For now, I'm Jeff, that's Brandy, the kid behind the wheel is my nephew Danny. This is my daughter, Amanda, and her husband, Terry Don, otherwise known as T.D."

Chivo smiled at each of them, although both Brandy and Terry looked at him cautiously.

"This is Bexar." He nodded at the acknowledgement. Dust and fumes filled the bus. All but the first three seats were missing. Brass casings rolled around on the bare floor; a homemade rebar ladder extended from the floor to the hole in the roof. Bexar pulled his shemagh over his mouth and nose, coughing at the dirty air.

Bexar didn't check his watch, but he estimated that they had been driving for close to half an hour. He glanced at the dashboard, but the speedometer was broken. Guessing that the bus averaged about thirty mph as it lurched hard from side to side to miss the undead in the street, Bexar figured they couldn't have traveled all that far from where they had been.

Bexar keyed his radio. "I hope they pulled the maps. I have no fucking idea how to get back to our route."

"Stand easy, mano. It's like when I was an advisor to the local forces in ..." Chivo looked around and shrugged. "... Guess it doesn't matter anymore. I was an advisor in Argentina. You've got to be cool; act cool. Act like you trust people, but have a plan to kill everyone you meet."

Terry stared at Chivo as he spoke into the headset; Chivo winked back at him and smiled, which seemed to upset the man. Chivo estimated him to be in his mid-twenties; he had the look of someone who used to be heavyset but had lost a lot of weight.

The bus rattled westward, farther from the Interstate and closer to the mountains.

In The Garage

Erin held up the hand-cranked shortwave radio, climbing out of the FJ. "What's this?"

"That's a radio."

"Does it work?"

"It did. Crank that handle around for a few minutes to charge it up. I'll try to find where I wrote down the frequency for the BBC, which was the last station we found still up."

Erin cranked the handle and looked at the radio, while Jessie dug around inside the FJ. Sarah walked over to her daughter. "Honey, try the emergency button or one of the weather buttons."

Erin stopped cranking and turned the radio on, which filled the metal building with static until she pushed the first weather channel button.

"... and remaining military personnel. The secure location is located at the following grid coordinates ..."

"Holy shit! Mom, it's a real person!"

"... civilians: We are a safe haven. If you have a working HAM radio you can contact us on the following frequencies ..."

"Jessie, you were right. There are people there!"

"... if confronted with a reanimated corpse, do not approach. Flee if possible. Striking the skull and destroying the creature's brain is the only known way to stop the threat. If traveling overland, be warned that the last known location of mass herds of undead were tracked on the following Interstates, cities and directions ..."

Jessie walked to where Erin sat with the radio in her lap; tears ran down Sarah's cheeks, and she saw the first smile on Erin's face since they had met the day before. "We should really be writing this down; some of the information might be important."

Sarah focused back on the radio. The broadcast was past the notifications of danger and was back to stating information for military personnel.

"I bet he repeats it."

Sarah quickly left and came back with a small grease-stained notebook and pen.

Cortez, CO

Cliff walked slowly in the middle of the large hallway. Normally, he would have been closer to a wall, but he was more worried about running into undead than cult members. So far, he estimated, he had cleared half the school. *People never change*, he thought, scanning rooms with bedding and items that obviously belonged to the survivors—the general life clutter that people accumulate even after the end of the world. The only useful items he had found so far were a couple bottles of water and some cans of dog food. The dog food would be his dinner.

The only thing he found that was wrong were the letters painted on the wall in blood in the first room. The chemistry labs looked untouched; Cliff checked the storeroom and found it locked. With three hard kicks the door broke free of the frame.

Looks like everything is still here .... Score one for the home team.

Cliff pulled the door shut and re-stacked the lab stools in front of it to hide the door and the damage from kicking it in. Exiting the lab, Cliff continued his self-guided tour of the middle school. Reaching the gym, he found the metal doors locked. The door frames were metal as well. *If I had my pick set this would be easy work ... but I don't have it, so get over it.*

Continuing on, he tried the rest of the gym doors and found them all to be secure. The women's locker room was unlocked, so he opened the door. This locker room didn't smell like he remembered his middle school locker room smelling. The mixture of shower room humidity and teenage sweat was missing; the pungent odor of death assaulted his senses. The beam coming from the combat light at the end of his rifle swept back and forth methodically as he checked every corner and crevice where someone or something could hide. The rows of lockers all stood open and empty. The hair on the back of his neck stood; his heart rate quickened when he neared the entrance to the showers. During his entire career, the one time he had ignored his own personal spidey sense was the only time he'd gotten shot. After that experience, Cliff had never ignored his intuition again. Sometimes it was wrong, but most of the time it was spot-on.

Cliff edged to the row of lockers next to the doorway and concentrated on his breathing, slowing his heart rate before taking a step. Planting his foot firmly, he launched into the dark showers, rifle sweeping left then right. He took another step to the right and tripped over something large on the floor.

The rifle clattered to the tile as he stumbled, rotating his body like a cat as he fell. His hands free of the rifle, Cliff drew the pistol on his right hip and flipped the tactical light on in one swift motion. The light found a body lying face down; or it would have been, if the body still had a head. The floor around it was thick with heavy pools of congealed blood. The body's skin rippled as maggots crawled just beneath the surface, eating the rotting flesh beneath. Cliff stood and retrieved his rifle, taking a moment to clip his one-point sling into the loop on the back of the lower receiver.

Searching the rest of the room with his rifle and attached light, Cliff found three more headless bodies to his right. They appeared to be men, but they were so bloated and discolored that it was hard to tell. The wall had big red letters spelling "SINNERS." This time, he didn't have to check to see if the letters were painted in blood. He knew it was blood.

These are some sick fucks. We'd all be better off if they would all just drink the Kool-Aid and take the big nap.

The heads were not in the shower nor the rest of the locker room—the women's locker room at least. He paused by the exit to the gymnasium, straining his ears to try to hear a sound that was just barely caught by his conscious mind. But the harder he listened, the more he only heard his own heartbeat.

Not able to hear anything clearly, he slowly crept into the open gym. The windows, high upon the roof, allowed enough sunlight for him to see. The bleachers were pushed closed, forming towering brown wooden walls on either side of the court. Blankets and bedding were piled in a corner; at center court stood a basketball rack.

Well, found the heads. Damn.

Eight heads sat in the rack in place of basketballs. Their teeth were snapping and gnashing at Cliff, unable to reach the flesh they so wanted.

How in the fuck ... how in fuck can they survive like that? Jesus.

Keeping to his noise discipline, Cliff quietly dispatched each of the heads using his knife, their dead faces wretched with horror and anger. Without having to check, he knew that the rest of the bodies would be in the men's locker room. Five minutes later, he confirmed his suspicion. After seeing their faces, he was sure that the bodies were the missing men.

That's eight of the other survivors, I think. Where are the other twelve ... where are the women and girls? This place is a tomb. I need to find the rest of them ... I need to check out that church. I need to end this bullshit so I can get back to the real mission. I need to get to the SSC!

In The Garage

Road atlases were spread across the dusty concrete floor as Jessie showed Sarah and Erin her planned route to Groom Lake. With a red pen, Sarah looked at the notebook and drew circles around the known locations of the large hordes of undead from the shortwave broadcast. They had no way to communicate with "Bill," who was the new voice of Groom Lake. Jessie guessed he was a civilian by the way he spoke, which was decidedly different than the manner in which Cliff had spoken.

"Flagstaff and Las Vegas are off limits, so is the southern route is on 40." Sarah drew big red X's in the circles around each.

Tracing routes through the mountains, Jessie and Sarah were confident they had a good route planned, but at best guess it was over seven hundred miles. Jack and Sandra's Toyota FJ45 was a big solid beast, even if it was sort of rare. The fold-down windshield made sense, especially with Erin's exceptional rifle skills, as long as they could stay warm. The problem still lay in the eighteen-gallon fuel tank; Jessie didn't have an exact number but was guessing they'd get about ten mpg. Before, her sole focus was just getting on the road and driving. But now that Sarah was helping her to plan, the details she had forgotten starting ringing in her mind. *Eighty gallons or more for the rest of the trip to be safe; that means stopping every one hundred fifty miles to top off to keep from running on fumes ... so roughly four and-a-half fuel stops. If we average fifty mph, we'll cover the route in fourteen hours. So, we will have to stop every three hours ... if everything goes right. If.*

"How many fuel cans do you think we can round up and top off over the next day or two?"

Sarah shrugged. "We haven't really been focusing on that lately. My old Jeep had five jerry cans, twenty-five gallons of extra fuel, but that Jeep and those cans are long gone. What are you thinking?"

"I'm guessing we'll need at least eighty gallons of fuel for the trip. With my three gas cans we have fifteen extra gallons. We have no way of knowing how many vehicles will be on the road for us to syphon gas from when we go through the mountains."

"We never had any problems with that, well, for the most part. But if we could round up another seven or so five-gallon cans, we would have a spare fifty gallons on the roof rack. That would give us a lot of wiggle room."

Erin shifted back and forth, trying to sit and listen to the two "olds" plan. When she couldn't take it anymore, she went and sat on the roof rack of the Land Cruiser and began playing with the shortwave radio.

The Compound

Bexar never saw a highway sign, but the road across the brush looked like a four-lane road with a median, probably a major road or highway. But the bus wasn't on that road. The bus rattled to a stop. Terry opened the back door and jumped to the ground. In short order, he had the padlock holding the chain that secured the gate opened and had pushed the gate wide. The bus coughed more black smoke and rolled up the driveway. The home seemed like it had been a nice one, with a three-car garage on a large lot. A row of tall privacy walls made of construction siding panels stood in front of a once-expensive ornamental iron fence. The adobe-style home next door was also fenced into the compound. Once the engine shut off and the group could speak without yelling, Terry called from the gate, "We're secure." Chivo watched Terry push the gate closed, securing it into the ground with a thick metal rod followed by a heavy pipe across the whole front, locking it tight against attack.

"OK, boys—let's keep your hands where we can see them."

Chivo and Bexar turned to see Jeff pointing a pistol at them, the smile gone from his face. Chivo nodded slightly to Bexar and raised his hands, leaving the M4 hanging across his chest by the sling. Bexar did the same, hoping his partner had a plan.

"Go ahead and climb out the back door there. Don't get stupid or you'll find T.D. happy to assist your stupidity."

Chivo walked to the open door at the rear of the bus and hopped to the blacktop driveway only to find Terry standing to the side with a pump shotgun, using the edge of the bus for cover. *These guys are smooth; got to give them credit for that.* Chivo winked and smiled at Terry again, who did not look amused.

Bexar followed Chivo out of the rear exit of the old bus. Jeff and the rest of the family walked out the regular side door and joined the group on the driveway. Chivo kept smiling; Bexar couldn't figure out why. He held his arms casually above his shoulders, his hands relaxed and closed slightly.

Growling brought Bexar's attention towards the house, where Amanda, T.D.'s wife, appeared with a quite large and angry-looking German shepherd.

"OK boys, now place your hands on top of your heads ... good. Now, on your knees, and cross your ankles. If you do what we say, you might live through this ... even you, spic. All we need is your gear and supplies. We have no use for you two, and we don't want to harm either of you. Once we're done here, we will drop you off away from this compound—but all of that depends on your cooperation."

Chivo kept smiling, turning his head slowly from one side to the other, scanning the group. T.D. held a pump shotgun. Both of the women had AR-style rifles, except that Amanda's rifle hung on a sling, the dog's leash in her hands. Jeff stood with his hands empty, the obvious leader of this small group. The boy, Danny, stood next to Jeff.

"Danny, fetch their rifles."

Danny drew a knife and walked behind Bexar and Chivo, where he cut the rifle slings, letting them clatter to the driveway, before walking in front of the two men in tactical gear, picking up the rifles, and laying them on the ground behind Jeff.

"OK boys. Now unfasten your helmets, and slowly place them on the ground in front of you."

Bexar took a sideways glance at Chivo, who nodded slightly, still smiling. He released the clasp on his helmet and set it in front of his knees on the pavement. Chivo slowly did the same.

Danny came around the two and retrieved their helmets, laying them next to the rifles.

"This won't take too much longer. Just keep playing along and you both live. Hands straight up above your heads, please."

T.D.'s gaze remained intense; the worn, pump shotgun was pressed into his shoulder in a stance of familiarity with the weapon. The long, tube barrel was kept pointed towards Chivo and Bexar. After their hands were straight up, Danny approached them both again, pulling the Velcro side panels open, unfastening the tactical carriers that they wore. He pulled each heavy carrier over their heads, taking them one at a time back to the growing pile of gear behind Jeff.

"Secure them, Danny. You boys play nice now, and we might let you live," he repeated.

Might? Bexar glanced around the yard, looking for an escape, but the fence looked about ten-feet high. *There's no way I can make it to the fence and over before that fucking dog chews my ass or I get shot.*

Chivo turned his gaze towards Danny, who walked forward with a pair of handcuffs ready. They looked ridiculously large in his small hands. Bexar glanced at Chivo with a look of concern, which only garnered him another slight nod for a reply. Chivo just smiled the entire time.

Danny slapped the cuffs hard against Bexar's wrist and pulled his right arm down behind his back, followed by the left. He slapped Bexar's left wrist into the cuffs, the muffled sound of the ratcheting lock barely heard above the growling dog. *Way to go dumbass. That's going to bruise. And you put my hands in facing each other instead of facing out. Amateur move, buddy. That at least tells me you aren't trained or weren't trained very well.*

The kid stepped away before double-locking the handcuffs and repeating the process on Chivo. Bexar glanced over and could see that the kid had put the cuffs on wrong with Chivo as well. *Too bad I can't do shit with this opportunity. How did those fucking meth-heads flip their cuffs in the back of my patrol car?*

Suddenly, any fear Bexar felt was replaced with rage. Anger burned in the pit of his stomach. *How fucking dare these fucktards take my stuff, take my friends' stuff? Fuck all of them.* His pistol was still in the holster on his right hip, but he knew Danny would probably take that away soon as well.

"... four, three, two ..." Bexar looked at Chivo in time to hear him yell "NOW" followed by a blinding explosion behind them. Bexar fell forward onto the driveway, but Chivo was standing, the handcuffs hanging from his left wrist, pistol in his hand, moving and shooting, double taps with each minor turn of the pistol. Bexar heard none of this; his ears were ringing in pain. One of the tactical carriers was on fire. By the time that he rolled back up onto his knees, feeling dizzy from the explosion, Chivo had released one of Bexar's handcuffs, leaned in front of his face, dropped a small plastic handcuff key on the ground, and flashed him a thumbs up. He then quickly jogged to the tactical carrier, ripped his shirt over his head, and beat the carrier with the shirt to put the fire out, leaving it smoking in the silent compound.

Bexar stood, still feeling dizzy, and looked around the driveway. The dog was dead. T.D. was dead; everyone was dead except him and Chivo. Bexar looked at Chivo, who was talking to him, but he still couldn't hear anything. He shook his head and pointed at his ears. Chivo flashed another thumbs up and pointed to Bexar's carrier and gear, motioning for him to put it on. Bexar nodded and did what he was told. *I'm not sure how in the fuck Chivo pulled that off, but fuck all of them anyway. There was no way they were going to let us live. And even if they did, even if they dropped us off in the city without any gear, what then? We'd still die.*

Chivo walked to his gear, pulled his damaged carrier over his head, and fastened it back up the best he could. One of the pouches was a ragged mess, as was much of the Cordura fabric near it, showing the scorched armor plate beneath. Chivo pulled each of the M4 magazines out of the pouches on his carrier, checking each one. Two of them were bent and badly damaged; he dropped them to the ground. Helmet on, Chivo turned to Bexar, patted the top of his own helmet, and pointed to the house. Bexar nodded and followed Chivo towards the house. The ringing in Bexar's ears was starting to dim, but he still couldn't hear anything.

They didn't know if there were any others inside the home, but Bexar figured they probably would have come outside or started firing at them by now if there were. Ten minutes later, the house was clear, the other adobe house was clear, and Bexar could hear again. He and Chivo stepped back into the sunlight and walked to the parked bus.

Undead rattled the metal siding fence and gate as they beat against it; their moans could be heard over the noise. Buzzards circled lazily and low overhead, some of them already picking at the German shepherd's dead form.

"Shit, man. Where did you have that handcuff key? And what the hell was that? A flash bang?"

"I had it taped behind my belt, small and plastic—undetectable. I've been carrying something like it for years but have never been in a spot to need it. And yes, that was a flash bang; one I modified at least. Two-minute fuse. When that kid pulled my carrier over my head, I let my hand pull the pin hanging just outside the pouch. Don't look at me like that, mano. I don't carry it like that, they're normally taped down. I set that up while riding in the bus to get here. Like I said, be cool, act cool; act like you trust, but have a plan to kill everyone you meet. My radio's fucked by the way. Let me see yours."

Chivo pulled the radio, the push to talk, and the control head out of Bexar's carrier. He took his own carrier off, pulled out the ruined gear, and replaced it with the working unit. Bexar didn't care; he didn't really know how to work it and it saved him weight off his kit, which was nice.

Bexar climbed into the bus and onto the roof to see over the fence. "Holy shit. That's a bunch of undead."

"Fuck those corpses, mano. One piece at a time. We're OK for now. First, we need to figure out our gear, dig through these homes to see what we can scavenge, and then figure out our wheels situation."

"We do have the bus."

"Sure, but that old piece of shit might not make it down the block, much less across the mountains."

CHAPTER 27

Diamond Valley Lake, CA
March 7, Year 1

By the time the full rest cycle for the men on security watch was complete, Aymond estimated it to be close to 9 a.m. The men would have pressed on without the complete rotation, but after what they found at Twentynine Palms, today's drive towards Camp Pendleton would probably be tough. He needed his men rested more than he needed an extra two hours of time.

After they woke at sunrise, the first-watch-rotated pair was sent on a foot patrol to recon the area and locate a fuel source. They traveled in the general forward direction of the convoy, and they found and secured what they were looking for at a construction site approximately two miles to the west. The large fuel bowser stood nearly ten feet in the air on a stand, the construction company's name painted in large bright letters on the side. The fuel was gravity fed; the padlocked nozzle would be quickly set free upon their arrival with the M-ATVs and the bolt cutters.

"The convoy rolls in two mikes. How copy?"

"Good copy, Chief. Still secure, and no activity."

A few minutes later, the convoy drove onto the construction site and the trucks each took turns being fueled. The new additions to the team took care of the fueling while the rest of the team held security.

Once full of fuel, the convoy drove west and quickly neared I-215. The tree-lined road to reach the Interstate, flanked on each side by housing developments, was in shambles. Aymond was stunned to see the destruction. Many of the homes were significantly damaged; it looked like a large fire had raged uncontrolled. Abandoned cars, disabled by the EMP, rotted into the pavement on flat tires; some of them involved in collisions. The convoy kept tight, but resorted to rolling around ten mph, driving across the curbed median and onto the sidewalks to avoid groups of shambling dead and choke points where the rotting vehicles made traveling on the road surface impossible.

"Chief, this isn't looking good."

Aymond frowned at the radio transmission. "Still better than Fallujah. Keep scanning, keep looking; there might be survivors."

They bounced across the median again, light work for the armored 4x4's sophisticated suspension. It took much longer than expected, but the lead M-ATV finally reached the intersection before the bridge over I-215. An eighteen-wheeler lay on its side across the bridge, the cab badly burned, at least a dozen other vehicles mangled in its wake, blocking the northbound feeder road and the bridge.

The truck stopped; Aymond pointed. "Take that gap; drive down the embankment."

"Aye, Chief." The driver squeezed between the eighteen-wheeler and another vehicle, nudging the car with the bumper as he pushed the truck through. The sandy grass surface of the manicured bridge embankment paled in comparison to what Aymond's team had driven through in northern Afghanistan on the last deployment. The M-ATV traversed it with ease. The Interstate below, choked with vehicles, looked nearly impassable.

The sergeant driving the big truck looked at Aymond, who responded, "Do the best you can, stay in the median if you have to."

The radio crackled in the cab of the truck. "Chief, we have a large group of tangos following. Confirm the ROE?"

"Twenty meters or closer, put them down."

The Rules of Engagement ... Aymond hadn't thought to lay out what those should be. He didn't have a transition, a real chance to plan and brief for this; he simply hadn't known it was this bad. Zig-zagging back and forth across the median, across the roadway to the center divider and back again, the convoy made slow progress; the rear M-ATV's 50-cal thumped in short bursts.

There's no way we can keep this up without getting resupplied, but we have no supply depot. I guess we'll have Camp Pendleton ... if we're lucky.

The Garage

Erin slowly rolled through the frequencies, hoping to hear more than just static as she went. More than a few times she could have sworn she heard voices in the static, but just as she seemed to hear them, they disappeared into the white noise and she wondered if she had really heard them at all. Still sitting on the roof rack of the Toyota, Erin looked at her mom and Jessie sitting on the floor, except that Jessie was lying on her side and rubbing her belly. She was starting to show, but not too badly yet. The map still sat between them, and her mom took notes on a notepad. They didn't plan like this when they left the first time, and Erin couldn't understand why her mom was acting like this now.

"... five, three, seven, nine, thirteen, one ..."

"Hey, I found something on the radio!"

Erin turned the volume up and a man's voice could be heard with a bit of an electronic hum in the background, clearly reading off a random list of numbers.

"What is this shit? It's really creepy!"

Sarah looked at Jessie, who slowly sat up and kind of shrugged before getting to her feet. "Bexar said something about 'number stations' before. I guess this is what he meant."

"What does it mean?"

"I don't know. Supposedly some sort of way to communicate with secret agents or some bullshit like that. It was one of the conspiracy theories Bexar had. I swear that man was one step away from wearing a goddamned tin foil hat."

The transmission faded in and out, eventually melting into static.

"Huh, weird." Erin went back to slowly changing the frequencies on the shortwave.

The SCC

"Clint, what is the cypher? How does it break down?"

"The series actually means nothing. It just announces to any surviving Lazarus operatives that a particular facility is up and operational. In this case, the numbers are all odd and they occur on a specific frequency, but the sequence itself is ordered randomly—that's a computer-generated recording. In twelve hours a second series goes out that uses a one-time pad."

"Out of everything you've told me, you've never fully explained Osiris and Lazarus."

"OK, Amanda ... each of us technically operated under the Office of the Direction of National Intelligence, but in reality, we were our own separate group with a totally black budget. There are twenty-four of us in all. You know Cliff and I and Chuck Johnson, and you know that those aren't our real names. With our group, we all assumed first names starting with a C, and a last name like Smith, Johnson, or something just as common, even the four women. We all had specific, assigned duties. Cliff was assigned to the Secretary of State, who was near Denver when notice of the attack was given. After Babylon Shield was set in motion, he took control of the SECSTATE and moved her whole security team to the facility under the Denver International Airport. That facility was overrun and lost; all persons there are presumed lost, except for Cliff. Once the SECSTATE died, Cliff's directive was to operate as a bit of a free agent to help the rest of the Osiris Project. *Lazarus* is what we were all currently coded as; the name was born from the Lazarus Project, in which we were 'killed' in our former lives, and then 'rose from the dead' as our current selves, starting from scratch with fresh identities. None of us had any living close family members; it served as a false flag to make our friends think we were dead. I have photos from my own memorial; it was touching."

Amanda looked at Clint with a bit of surprise and disgust.

"Don't look at me like that—like you've never entertained the thought of how well you were liked by your friends. It gave our friends closure and it gave us closure, and notice that we could never go back. We were eyes forward and mission driven from that point on. Well, these projects have been operating in some fashion and name since 1947. Originally, new members were being brought in one at a time, but early on, it was found that new recruits needed to be initiated together in groups to help with the solitude of being 'dead' and starting over. Primary training takes many forms. It starts at The Farm, which you're probably familiar with, if for no other reason than its reference in popular culture. The Farm members attend a laundry list of Special Forces schools and training, going through the selection process under their initial aliases. Afterwards, those identities are killed off in various training accidents post-graduation, and new ones are assumed. I've been through Airborne, Ranger Selection, and the Para-Rescue selection processes and training. Each of my new personal legends came with back stories and rank. Each time, we have to indoctrinate ourselves in that armed branch's culture, including jargon and lifestyle applicable for our age and rank. As we each grew older, the training cycles changed to schools and selections that would be appropriate for us, so recently it was the State Department's diplomatic protection training, the Secret Service's driving school, that sort of continued professional extension. Cake-walk training compared to what we had before."

"All you did was train?"

"No, we rotated in and out of training cycles. Out of our cycles, we operated as trainers at The Farm for the CIA's clandestine programs until we were complete.

There isn't any way to finish those early schools back to back; it takes too much time and it is just too hard on the body. We needed a month's downtime in between to recover from injuries and start the process of learning and living our new legends for the upcoming schools."

"Jesus! How long did this all take?"

"A bit over ten years."

"And you're OK with all of this?"

"Absolutely. A very small percentage of our service men and women get to attend even a single Special Forces program; I've been through more than a few."

"What happens after the training?"

"We're assigned our target. Say we're assigned someone in the Presidential line of succession. We move to where they are located and shadow their movements, traveling under various commercial and government means."

"So you lived in Arkansas?"

"Yes."

"And you followed me around?"

"Yes."

"Was Chuck with you during all of this?"

"No, Chuck just graduated from the initial process last year and was sent to shadow with me; I was his field training officer."

She did not look happy; Clint saw it on her face, but there was no other way to conduct the program. She might understand, or she might not.

Amanda took a deep breath before speaking. "So how closely did you follow me?"

"Close enough to know what was in your nightstand drawer and how often you used it."

Eyes wide, Amanda looked horrified. Her mouth hung open in complete shock.

Clint winked. "Don't worry. You're completely vanilla compared to my previous target. You are genuinely a good person; your sweet nature is the reason why I've fallen in love with you."

"Did you feel that way before you took me out of my home?"

"No, but I liked you; especially compared to the last guy. It was our time on the road, fighting to get here, that really did it. If that becomes known, by the way, I will be removed from the program, which would be ... bad for me."

Amanda pulled Clint's t-shirt over his head. "It doesn't matter. I'm in charge, and I say you stay with me."

The Compound

The bodies of the would-be capturers, including Danny and the dog, lay in the far corner of the property, inside the fence. Bexar tried not to look at them, but would glance over and see the buzzards picking at their flesh. He realized that he hadn't seen buzzards picking at the undead. They smelled bad enough that it seemed like it would have been an all-you-can-eat buzzard buffet, but they avoided the walking bodies for some reason. The flies and the stench were bad enough, and Bexar guessed that adding buzzards to the mix would probably make things worse. He wasn't sure how, but it seemed to feel worse just thinking about it.

The high desert sun hung low against the western sky. Piles of gear and supplies were grouped in the larger part of the three-car garage, with the door open. Surprisingly, most of the gear they had on the Defender had been recovered by the other group, even the radios, armor, and weapons from the bodies, which Chivo appreciated. He replaced his ruined carrier with his dead partner's gear. Bexar's radio components were supplemented with a mix of gear from Apollo and Lindsey, as some of it was damaged in the bridge collapse.

Bexar's gear and rifle lay on the pavement next to the bus. He lay under the decrepit yellow whale, crawling around and checking the tires, the drive train, and other components as he could. He knew how to wrench, but a diesel guy he was not, much less a school bus guy. He crawled out from under the chassis, arms covered in black grime and old oil; Chivo stood waiting.

"Will it work?"

"I don't know. It's fairly fucked, but it's better than walking for now."

"How much fuel does it hold, and how far can we travel before we need to top off?"

"I'm not sure, the manual is missing. But I measured the outside of the fuel tank, so everything I come up with is a smooth guess. I'm also going to guess that when healthy, the bus got maybe five to eight mpg on a good day; this bus is far from healthy."

The smudged and dirty notepad in his hand had a square drawn on it with measurements taken with a tape measure found in a tool box in the garage. Bexar worked the multiplication out by hand, a nearly forgotten skill he had relegated to a calculator on his cellphone.

"Best guess, about sixty gallons. Let's call it five miles per gallon for easy math, so three hundred miles of loud, black-smoke-belching travel before we need to find a significant amount of fuel."

Chivo held his hand to the western horizon. "Four fingers to sunset, mano. We need to wrap up, button up, and rest up. Tomorrow we roll, and I think it might just suck."

Nodding, Bexar walked into the surprisingly immaculate garage and sprayed carb cleaner on his arms, wiping most of the grime off on a dingy beach towel from the house. *I bet we top out at forty mph; we're a bit less than three hundred miles away, so it will take over seven hours to rattle the fuck into Cortez. Shit, I better find some ear plugs.*

The Garage

Jessie lifted the heavy box over her head and, standing on her toes, pushed it onto the roof rack. Sarah and Erin had been gone for close to two hours by Jessie's estimate; there hadn't been any gunfire that she could hear. She wanted to worry for her new friend and her daughter, but she couldn't; the worry would garner nothing in return but more stress. She absentmindedly rubbed her belly, which barely pushed against her shirt. *Whether they're back in the morning or not, I leave. I can't wait; I can't put my little guy in harm's way for faint hope, or for other people.* The windows high along the roofline glowed red with the setting sun; the interior of the garage darkened with the waning light.

They returned at length and, after some discussion, they decided the three of them would travel together in the FJ, leaving the old motorcycle behind. The gear and supplies they needed increased by a large magnitude. The big canvas wall tent stayed on the roof rack in its weather-sealed box, along with the EMT poles and other associated gear. Sarah wanted to ditch the tent, but Jessie couldn't let it go—maybe for practical purposes or maybe due to sentimental reasons after all the heartache and loss of the past few months.

All told, it would probably take a few more days of gathering supplies to be fully ready. Canned food and bottled water were high on the priority list. In terms of mileage, there was only a solid day's drive between their location and Groom Lake, but Sarah agreed that it would take longer, possibly even up to a week due to all the unknowns.

Waiting, sitting on the cold concrete floor, Jessie turned the hand crank of the shortwave for a few minutes before switching it on and tuning to the emergency station where they had found the radio traffic from Groom Lake. It was the same information; it sounded like they had recorded it and played it on a loop. *I hope that there are still people behind the loop and that it isn't just playing automatically with everyone dead.*

Scrolling through the frequencies, she stopped on a man's voice reading numbers, the same from before. Jessie took a notepad and wrote some of the numbers down. *All the numbers are odd numbers, but the order makes no sense.*

Jessie sat on the floor trying to figure out if the numbers lined up with the alphabet or if there was a pattern, but she was interrupted by the low popping exhaust of an approaching motorcycle. She picked up the rifle lying on the floor next to her, tossed the sling over her shoulder, and press-checked the bolt to verify a round was in the chamber. Jessie peered through a small hole in the metal siding next to the roll-up door and saw Sarah and Erin on the bike. She pulled the rolling chain loose and proceeded to raise the door for her friends. Once they were inside and the door was secure, there were more questions than answers to be had. Their clothes were splattered with blood, dusty, and covered with grime.

"You two look like shit! What happened?"

"Found a collapsed bridge north of here—some sort of SUV crushed in the rubble along with the bodies of a black guy and some white chick. Both of them had military-style clothing on, but no gear or weapons. They looked picked clean."

"That's it?"

"No. Huge damned herd of corpses came up on us. We had to shoot our way back to the bike and led them on a rounding chase away from here before circling back."

"How far away was all of this?"

Sarah looked at Erin, who shrugged. "I don't know, like, maybe a mile, mile and a half. It was a hell of a fight and we had to shag ass. We got nothing on our list today."

"Think we should take the FJ and all go together tomorrow?"

"No, keep that thing secure and hold the fort. We'll make another run tomorrow and another the one after that if we have to. Once we're really ready, we can roll. How many more weeks till you pop?"

"I don't know ... sometime in October most likely."

"Good, we have time; at least we have that on our side."

Cortez, CO

The western sky was that shade of dark blue just before the end of twilight; it was Cliff's time to move. The middle school had provided more questions than answers, except for the one that most likely accounted for some of the survivors. But there were still more people left to be found. If anything, he saw that this cult, or militia group, or whatever they wanted to call themselves, was a serious problem. *A bit more recon and then I'll start mixing up their Kool-Aid for their final journey home.*

His truck was close by and the school was a dead end, so it was time to go home, rest, and regroup. Cliff waited and watched, easing towards the open front of the school, and standing in the shadows of the doorway, M4 in his hands. He strained to hear any vehicles or movement of any kind.

Not much undead activity in the middle of town. The new town leaders probably took care of that; I can't count on it, though.

Cliff took a deep breath, sprinted out the door, and ran for the cover of the homes and yards across the parking lot and street from the middle school. Just as he reached the edge of the parking area, an old Jeep turned the corner, headlights illuminating his sprint for safety. Caught in the open, all Cliff could do was keep sprinting for cover, the large trees in the yards across his first chance at safety. A low, chain-link fence was the only obstacle in his path—a stutter step in the sprint and Cliff had just reached out to vault the fence when he felt a hard hit on his thigh, causing him to stumble and crash into the chain-link.

With no time to do anything else, Cliff rolled up onto a knee and began firing at the Jeep as it came to a stop. Three shots later and the headlights were out, allowing him to see the figures in the open top Jeep. *Three of them,* he noted quickly. The passenger stepped down from the lifted suspension to the pavement, and Cliff lined up the shot, concentrating on slowing his breathing. He fired twice, a double tap to the forehead of the passenger. The man in the back, wearing a heavy jacket, lifted a large rifle and laid it on the top of the roll cage. Cliff shot twice, both rounds impacting within a half-inch of each other. The man's skull shattered outward. The driver put the Jeep in gear and drove forward towards Cliff. Cliff fired six more times, shattering the windshield and striking the driver in the head and throat. Dead, the man's foot pinned the gas pedal to the floor. Cliff stood to run out of the path of the closing Jeep and fell to the ground, his right leg buckling under the pressure. Rolling onto his back, he flipped the selector switch all the way around and emptied the magazine into the front left tire of the quickly approaching vehicle. The tire shredded from the onslaught, causing the Jeep to pull hard left, passing just inches away from Cliff's prone body before slamming into a tree. The body of the driver launched through the shattered windshield and landed in the yard. The engine continued to rev at full throttle.

Cliff looked at his thigh; his pants leg was soaked in blood. *Shit. This is all I need.* Smoke began billowing from under the hood of the Jeep. With no time to waste, Cliff stood on his left leg and used the chain-link fence as a handrail to hold his weight as he limped around the corner of the low, square, adobe-style home. Hobbling as fast as he could, he made his way against the wall of the home just before flames leapt from the Jeep, flickering orange and black shadows into the street.

Before anything else, Cliff made a tactical reload of his rifle, dropping the partially spent magazine into his cargo pocket. Knife in hand, he cut off a long strip of wool from his blanket poncho, along with a few smaller pieces, before cutting the leg of his pants open. Using a scrap of the blanket, he applied pressure to the bullet wound in his thigh, finding that a chunk of flesh was missing from the bullet's destructive path. He pushed the other pieces of the blanket into the wound and used the strip of wool to tie a tight bandage. *I have to get to the truck, I have to get back to the house, and I have to disappear before any others arrive.*

Southern California

I-215 joined with I-15 and the convoy continued to make slow time, driving back and forth across the roadway, choked in perpetual rush hour. The homes and businesses sat ravaged by fire, many of the cars on the roadway burned into the pavement. The undead continued to tail them, following in greater numbers the farther they traveled. Night was quickly descending on the convoy, but Aymond did not want to attempt to bivouac in such a built-up area. The last M-ATV's fifty-caliber weapon's heavy, thumping, short bursts of automatic fire added punctuation to an already bad situation; Aymond needed to get the convoy away from the cities and back into the mountains where they belonged. Some of the signs were missing, but the one welcoming everyone to the town of Temecula still stood, darkened by the smoke and soot that seemed to cover everything.

"Take this road. Take the exit ... drive up the damned embankment, I don't care. We need to get west and into the mountains," Aymond said, pointing towards the horizon and the setting sun.

Still on the wrong side of the highway, the convoy threaded the needle between burnt-out vehicles and drove up the on-ramp to turn on Rancho California Road. The bridge stood high enough for the big trucks to drive back and forth through the traffic.

They were trained for urban warfare, and as operators they were good at it. But at the heart of every MSOT member is a Force Recon Marine. The natural habitat of a Marine in Force Recon is the woods, mountains, and faraway places where they can hide in cover, observe, report, and direct forward action.

The sprawling shopping and office complexes finally gave way to a simple two-lane road into the mountains. Aymond could feel the tension beginning to fade from the other Marines in the lead truck.

"Shake it loose back there. A few more mikes and we'll circle the wagons for the night. How are our following friends?"

"Still pursuing, Chief, but we've lost a few of them."

High ground is happy ground, and after a few turns driving higher into the mountains, a gravel road appeared to their left. A chain across the entrance held a sign warning that trespassers would be prosecuted.

"Just drive through it then follow the path. Let's see what we find."

The truck turned and drove through the chain, the tension against the front bumper causing it to snap and whip into the dirt. The convoy followed as the clearing gave way to a smaller gravel road pointing up from their position. Taking a left at the next "T" the convoy found themselves in a clearing above the road. What was left of the burned trees and desert shrub blocked the view from the road below.

"Davis, position to block the rear. Everyone else dismount and take defensive positions." The Marines climbed out of their vehicles, taking positions giving the group full 360-degree protection. The engines off, Aymond climbed onto the roof of his M-ATV and, with the binoculars to his face, watched their entourage of undead continue to follow the road, but they shambled past the turnoff.

At least they aren't that smart, but their being in front of us means that we'll run into them again.

For nearly ten minutes, the undead passed below their position, never aware that they were being watched from above. There was no other movement on the mountain; the smell and the flies were impressive, even to the Marines who'd had multiple deployments to Iraq and Afghanistan.

Aymond climbed off the truck and motioned for the Marines to circle up on him. "OK, I estimate that there were four to five hundred Zeds following. They passed by, so we at least know they're not thinkers. We can move off course and they'll keep following their current direction as long as they don't see us. The bad news is that they're still walking in the direction we're driving tomorrow. From now on, we're going to stay away from the Interstate. That was brutal, and we would have made better time without it. Tomorrow we reach Camp Pendleton, but this time we're going to set an FOB and run night patrols to recon the area before charging in like we did at The Palms. Set security, same rotation, eat and rest."

A series of quiet "Hoo-Rahs" and "kills" came from the small group as they set to work.

Cortez, CO

By his watch, it took Cliff four hours to stagger, limp, and crawl his way back to his truck, being forced to conceal himself and wait on more than a few occasions. During that time, the burning Jeep exploded behind him, causing a big increase in vehicle activity. First, a patrol showed up that he presumed went to the wreckage; the others he had to assume were looking for him. If the bodies survived the blast, the others would find that there were bullet holes in the skulls of their comrades. If they hadn't thought so before, they now knew that a saboteur was in their town. Cliff knew he needed to get back to the house, clean his wound, and have a couple of days to heal up a little and to let the cult settle back down into a routine. His worst problems were further detection and any infection, which could kill him now. Then he had to find the survivors and kill the cult members. After the fire call of slaughtered men and an explosion, his opportunity to take his time to recon other sights had now dwindled to nearly nothing.

The Compound

Bexar watched the buzzards continue to pick their captors clean. After a few minutes of heated discussions, Chivo relented that they should take another day or two to scavenge more supplies and test the bus's ability to run reliably, watching during that time for another vehicle that they could have more confidence in.

With their captors dead and no other activity in the area, they agreed upon a simple sleep and security rotation. At this point, neither of them believed anyone else would try to attack, especially with the number of undead milling around outside the gate. But Chivo didn't want to chance it. Bexar couldn't argue with him; Chivo had been in more shit storms than Bexar thought possible. In the morning, they would have to figure out a way to lure the undead away from the gate, but for now, Chivo slept in the house on the filthy couch while Bexar stood on the roof of the bus, watching the moon and the shadows of the corpses bouncing off each other and the fence below.

CHAPTER 28

Outside of Temecula, CA
March 8, Year 1

The sun illuminated the city below. A scout/sniper pair left before dawn to take position to scan the city for any signs of survivors. After a discussion with the team, it was decided they would remain in a defensive position for another day and run some recon outside their makeshift Forward Operating Base. With some Hesco, they could have turned their hilltop into a legitimate FOB, but they were still too far away from their first objective: Camp Pendleton.

Problem was that they were close enough that the PRC-150 radio in the trucks should be reaching Camp Pendleton by now. Ryan Hammer plugged through his last known freq list. SATCOMs appeared to be completely down, which really gave Aymond cause for concern. Once Snow and Davis returned from their observation post across the next ridge line east, he would at least have some Intel as to what lay in the town behind them. Gonzales, Happy, and Ski rolled west in one of the M-ATVs to scout the route ahead and the north end of Camp Pendleton. The scout/sniper pair simply checked in every half-hour with a click of the push-to-talk switch of their radio. On a separate frequency, Aymond had constant updates and communications with the mounted patrol. Kirk used the down-time to begin training their newly joined members from Twentynine Palms, Corporal Simmons and Corporal Jones. Every Marine is a rifleman, but not every Marine knows how to operate like Force Recon, much less an MSOT member. Both of them would have washed out of the process early on if things had been normal, but things were far from normal, and the two young Marines were making progress. Aymond was happy to have both of them, since outside of Ski's basic mechanical ability learned from his hobby of four-wheeling his built-up Jeep, the team had no way to repair, much less maintain, the big armored 4x4s.

Aymond glanced at his plain old windup watch, its nylon strap hanging from his LBE. It showed that Snow and Davis should have clicked in five minutes ago. No colored smoke on the horizon; no gunfire, so Aymond would wait another thirty mikes before breaking the radio silence on their frequency, followed by sending a Quick Reaction Force after them if necessary. Depending on where Happy and his patrol were, he might have to send Kirk and one of the corporals on their own. *Two people and a single vehicle ... not much of a QRF.*

The Compound

Bexar still had problems running; the wound in his leg was not fully healed. So after some discussion, Chivo suggested that he go up the fence line and fire a few rounds to get the undead motivated to move away from the gate. That would allow Bexar to start the bus, open the gate, and drive out. Neither thought it was a great plan, but it was the only plan they could agree on, so it was their plan of choice. Chivo stood on the fence frame and, after breaking the lock and removing the chain, he leaned over the top of the metal siding in front of the second house on the compound, east of the gate, and started yelling and firing his M4. Roughly fifty undead turned in unison towards the new stimulus and began shambling away from the gate. Bexar pulled the pin and lifted the cross bar off the gate and pushed it open before starting the bus.

The bus burped thick black smoke and a loud backfire as it started, but it ran. That was all they needed for now. It took four tries to get the shifter to hit first gear, but eventually the bus rolled slowly onward. Chivo ran the distance back to the gate, closed it, dropped the pin into the pavement, and jumped into the open back door, slamming it behind him. Bexar pulled against the large steering wheel and let the clutch out. The bus lurched hard and died.

"Smooth, punta," Chivo said, climbing up front.

Bexar worked the starter. On the third try, the motor finally caught and roared to life with another cloud of greasy exhaust.

"Fuck you and your bullshit polka music."

"It's not polka, pendejo, it's Tejano. You keep this up, I'm buying you some pointy toe boots and a deep, taco-shaped cowboy hat."

Both of them laughed as the bus slowly accelerated with each change of the gears. Seeing open road ahead of them, Bexar pressed the gas pedal to the floor to see what the bus would do. The needle stopped climbing just before fifty mph, and the bus shook like a cheap hotel mattress. Forty-five was about all it could do.

The unlikely duo drove south along the eastern edge of Albuquerque. It became progressively more apparent that the city had not fared well; there was significant fire damage

Yelling over the rattling old bus, Bexar looked over his shoulder at Chivo. "How is it that the only survivors we've met so far have tried to kill us, and we've ended up killing all of them?"

"Fucked if I know, mano. But even in the worst places I've gone, there were good people. I'm starting to worry none of them made it."

The Garage

Jessie had forgotten how terrible it was to be pregnant, since all of those bad memories had faded quickly from her mind the moment she'd held Keeley in her arms. Throwing up in the corner of the dusty old garage brought a flood of those bad memories back. At least she had her hair in a ponytail, otherwise there would be puke in it.

Breakfast being a lost cause, Jessie returned to loading the Toyota for their departure. Sarah wanted at least one more day to scavenge before leaving. From what she'd said, it sounded nearly pointless. Much of the city had burned, destroyed following the attack; the rest of the city was overrun with the dead. Regardless, Sarah wanted to get more fuel cans, more fuel on board, and as many baby supplies as she could find. Diapers and formula were going to be a bitch. Cloth diapers sounded great until Jessie thought about actually trying to wash them somehow. She hadn't had a shower since leaving Big Bend; how could she possibly wash dirty diapers?

Out of breath, Jessie sat on the floor with the shortwave radio, turning the handle to crank up enough juice for it to work. The numbers station was still there, but it was on a different frequency. The recorded broadcast from Groom Lake continued to repeat, fading in and out, seemingly at random. *Malachi would have known why, but I don't have any idea about the technical side of radios.*

Cortez, CO

Sitting on the cold concrete floor of the garage, Cliff cleaned his wound, slathered most of a tube of triple antibiotic ointment on the oozing flesh, and wrapped a fresh bandage on his thigh. If that didn't work, he would have to run a drug store raid and get his hands on real antibiotics. But for now, he went back in the house, ate a can of cold chili, and went upstairs to sleep. *Hydrate, elevate, sleep. If I can do those things, I have a good chance.*

Albuquerque, NM

Chivo and Bexar rattled along slowly southwards on Highway 556, bouncing the bus across the median at times to avoid abandoned cars and walking corpses.

"Where did all those deaders from two days ago wander off to?"

"Chivo, dude, I don't know, and frankly I don't give a shit. Just as long as they're not here now!"

After a half-hour of deafening, vibrating, bus enjoyment, Bexar slowed as they approached I-40. So far, all the neighborhoods and urban sprawl they had passed on the edge of town were mostly destroyed, burned-out shells of homes; even some of the vehicles in the roadway were burnt. Their plan was to scavenge for fuel and recon the city for a better vehicle. So far, they were possibly one up on the fuel situation, since they had come across an abandoned semi-truck that still had both saddle tanks full. Now all they needed was some hose to syphon with and something to put the fuel in. Bexar mentioned that they would have to fill the bus with five-gallon jugs to be able to carry it all.

Attempting to complete their lap around the eastern side of the city, Bexar took the turn to hit I-40 west and, dodging more vehicles, drove up the ramp. Behind them a growing gaggle of undead could be seen in the distance, steadily following the big smoking bus.

On the Interstate, it appeared that one of the roaming herds of undead had marched through; all the vehicles had been crushed and pushed to the sides of the road and off the pavement. The concrete barrier between the travel lanes had somehow remained intact. Even at their slow speed, they reached San Mateo Boulevard quickly and took the exit to travel north. Chivo kept track of miles and direction so they could locate the compound again. As of yet, they still weren't exactly sure where it was, but by making a big loop they were quickly narrowing down its location.

The surface street looked like an IED had gone off. Cars had been thrown off the roadway, and the light posts, signal lights, and trees were destroyed or flattened. The gas station was only recognizable because the awning over the pumps still showed a big yellow logo.

"Turn down one of the neighborhood streets; see if the undead clawed through there as well."

Bexar took the next right into what used to be a neighborhood. A few of the homes still stood seemingly unscathed, but many were very badly burned. The vehicles parked in the road sat where they were left, not pushed out of the way by the massive wave of undead that seemed to have conquered every large road in town.

Ignoring the stop sign, Bexar kept rolling, turning left to head back towards San Mateo before they got lost in the neighborhood streets. The sound of a horn caused him to instinctively slam both of his feet to the floor, clutch and brake, just in time to see a motorcycle roar past the front bumper of the bus, a girl on the back of the bike holding her middle finger in the air as they sped away.

"Who the fuck was that?"

"I don't know, mano, but she's got style."

"Want me to follow them?"

"No, mission first. Besides, everyone we've met we've had to kill, remember? Let's just assume they're cool and we shouldn't fuck with them. We need to figure out how to get that fuel; we've got to roll tomorrow if we're going to complete our mission. Looks like this fucked-up bus is our current ride, so roll on, mano."

Bexar drove on, turning onto San Mateo Drive to travel north again. Chivo sketched the map on his notepad as he observed the route in. A few more turns, and they were on Eubank Boulevard, where they found a pickup with three big fifty-five-gallon blue plastic water barrels in the bed. The barrels were empty, but now they had their fuel containers. Another turn onto Highway 423 and they were back to the compound for the night. Gate secured behind them and bus turned off, Chivo found a garden hose still wound up on a reel next to the house and brought it to the pile of gear. There was no way they could lift a fifty-five-gallon barrel of diesel fuel into the back of the bus, but they could load the barrel empty, syphon the fuel up, and syphon it back down into the bus's tank as needed. Their plans were in place: leave at sunrise, fuel the bus, fuel the barrels, and point towards Cortez. If Bexar's math was correct, they should be able to roll into Cortez in under eight hours and might only need to burn about sixty gallons of fuel ... but that was if there were no problems.

"So, you said you knew Cliff. How well do you know him? Do you trust him?"

"He's a fucking ghost, mano. I haven't decided about him yet. But like him or not, a rescue op is a rescue op; that's part of the code."

The Garage

Jessie rolled the door open; Sarah and Erin rode the motorcycle in and shut it off as the door closed behind them.

"Those prepper assholes are out again."

"Who?"

"Some family that's holed up out on the east side. They roll around in a fucked-up old school bus. They're weird. Met them once when we first got into town, about the only survivors we've found here. Like *really* weird; wanted to take me as a 'sister wife.' I don't have time for that shit. I have Erin, and we have to survive. They were really upset when we turned them down. That was about a month ago, and since then, I think they've been trying to figure out where we are."

"Could they have followed you here?"

"No way. Not how we rode away from them."

"Good. You're the first two survivors I've met that didn't try to kill me."

"And on the upside, we found two more gas cans, a box of diapers, and three cans of formula."

CHAPTER 29

The Garage
March 9, Year 1

The loaded FJ sat heavy on its rear springs. Besides the large box with the wall tent and all the supplies that Jessie had salvaged from their surviving prepper cache in Big Bend, Sarah and Erin had added a considerable amount of gear. Really, it was all useful, and it was better to have more gear than they needed to go over the mountains than to hope for places to resupply en route.

Sarah took the first shift driving, Jessie rode shotgun with her AR-15, and Erin sat in the back with her short M4 in her lap. The big fifty-caliber rifle rested in a case on the roof rack. Jessie rolled up the garage door and locked the chain in place to hold it open. This was it; this was their trip out, and they had no desire to turn back.

As they traveled down a small dirt road, Jessie realized that their garage sat very near I-40 and I-25, in the middle of a cemetery. She wasn't sure why she hadn't noticed before. In short order, the women were on the Interstate and traveling west. At Jessie's prompting, Sarah kept the FJ below sixty mph even though the road was clear. All the cars were pushed aside, crushed and tossed like a giant hand had swatted everything off the road.

"They start forming up into big herds and travel like a slow motion stampede—everything in their way is crushed, moved, or destroyed."

Jessie nodded in response to Sarah. She saw the dried blood and gore all over the crushed vehicles on the side of the road.

"If all of the vehicles are destroyed like this, we're not going to be able to syphon gas when we need it."

"We've only started seeing the stampedes in the past few weeks, and only on the big roads. It's like they're drawn to the wide open Interstates and wider roads; they bounce off the small roads, I can't really explain it, and I don't know why, but it's really weird."

"The vehicles look like they were pushed forward in the direction we're driving."

"Then if we catch up with the stampede we're hosed. We'll just have to take it slow and hope for the best. Worst case, we get off the Interstate and into the mountains, but those roads are sparse; who the hell knows how long that would take."

The Compound

One final check of the gear and they were complete. The garden hose was left intact for now; they knew that trying to syphon gas through a thirty-foot hose would be borderline impossible, but they didn't know exactly how much hose they needed to reach the semi's saddle tanks. After diverting the undead by the gate again, Bexar and Chivo were off, although in the wrong direction for a few miles, so they could start the fueling process.

Bexar stopped the bus in front of the semi-truck and backed slowly until the rear bumper of the bus hit the nose of the truck. With the bus idling, Chivo walked out the side door with hose in hand, and Bexar stood in the back of the bus by the large blue tanks. One end was in the top of the barrel, the other end eyeballed for length and cut. Once they got the fuel going, it would syphon on its own; the hard part was getting the fuel started. Bexar lost the rock-paper-scissors round, so he got to be the one who sucked on the hose.

Red in the face and feeling dizzy, Bexar spat diesel fuel out of his mouth. Having started the process, he stood in the bus, holding his rifle and monitoring the barrel. Guessing that the saddle tanks of the truck held around one hundred fifty gallons each, and being that they had three barrels, Bexar hoped to top all of them off with one tank so he only had to get fuel in his mouth once. He watched the tank fill slowly, ready to pass the hose to the next tank, hopefully without losing suction.

Chivo sat on the side step of the semi, holding the hose steady in the saddle tank, head down with his shemagh on his face, hiding from the black exhaust billowing out of the back of the running bus. Bexar watched the first barrel's level near the top and made ready to quickly move the hose, hoping not to spill too much fuel. The fumes of the exhaust, combined with the fumes of the fuel, were making him dizzy, but the transition went quickly with only a little bit of fuel splashing on his pants, boots, and floor. Making sure the hose wouldn't pull out, Bexar let go and looked up in time to see a corpse stumbling towards Chivo, who still had his head down from the fumes.

Bexar shouldered his AR, exhaled slowly, and smoothly pressed the trigger to the rear. Twelve inches from Chivo's face, the corpse's head ruptured, splattering black pus, skull fragments, and blood on Chivo, who leapt to his feet, rifle in hand. More undead continued to close in on the sound of the running bus. Chivo quickly began lining up his targets and pressing the trigger, his M4 barking rapidly as he walked quickly towards the open side door, leaving the hose hanging in the saddle tank. Bexar continued to fire on the undead as they approached Chivo from the rear. An errant round from Bexar's rifle skipped off the side of the saddle tank with a spark, and the mouth of the tank erupted in a four-foot tall spit of fire. Bexar held onto the hose while Chivo bounced into the driver's seat, grinding the selector into first. The bus lurched forward slowly as he changed gears. The cab of the semi-truck caught fire and was becoming engulfed. Bexar pulled the hose through the open window until reaching the blackened and melted end. *Two out of the three basically full—not bad. That's roughly one hundred gallons, and that might be enough.*

Bexar walked to the front of the bus. He heard the deep *thump* as the semi-truck's other saddle tank exploded, the sound reaching them four blocks away.

Yelling over the engine, Chivo said, "Thanks mano, I owe you now," and gave Bexar a fist bump.

"We have about a hundred gallons and one empty barrel. The fuel gauge shows three-quarters of a tank, so the next truck you see we should probably resupply, but I want to get out of this fucking town first."

"Me too, mano. Fuck this dead place."

Outside of Temecula, CA

Just as Aymond was readying his woefully small and undertrained QRF for his scout sniper pair, they walked back into the FOB. The batteries in their radios had died. Normally, multiple spares are carried on patrols, but this being the end of the world, they simply didn't have any extras. The mounted patrol set a safe rendezvous point on a truck trail that intersected near their current FOB and just north of Fallbrook. The M-ATVs and the lone Humvee set out following the waypoints provided, and were able to reach the rest of the team's location with little effort, since that was the sort of driving their vehicles were specifically designed for. The upside was that they were able to avoid other towns en route. The report back from the OP was that Temecula was destroyed, deserted, and populated only by Zeds. Aymond still hoped that there were survivors somewhere; everyone couldn't be dead. He wasn't sure how he could keep his team together and motivated if all they continued to find were walking corpses and burned-down cities.

Fallbrook was now the only obstacle between his team and Camp Pendleton North. He would be swift, silent, and deadly, not fast and careless like the way he'd approached Twentynine Palms. It had been over two months since the attack, and they had time; he had to be patient and safe or he would lose more teammates.

The new FOB overlooked the northern outskirts of Fallbrook to the south. Although they were too far away to see what condition the town was in, they were close enough to operate safely. Absentmindedly, Aymond wound the watch hanging from a MOLLE strap on his carrier and looked at the sun beginning its downward track towards the sea.

"Ski!"

Chuck Ski walked over to Aymond. "Yeah, Chief?"

"Put together a four-man patrol, prep for two nights, and roll out in ninety mikes. I want you to approach Fallbrook and make entry if safe, but stay low, stay silent, recon patrol."

"Anything particular you're looking for?"

"Any sign of survivors, any sign of large masses of Zeds; I don't want to be surprised like at The Palms."

"Got it, Chief."

Ski walked off to gather his team and provisions and set out. Aymond continued to look out over the ranchland and rolling hills. *All of this is irrigated; all of this will die and not come back unless society comes back to revive it. If California is now a state for the dead, where do I take my team? Where do my men survive?*

Cortez, CO

Cliff lay in bed. Every blanket in the house was on him, the windows shut and blinds drawn closed; he hid away, shivering and sweating. He was sure he had an infection. He knew he had a high fever, and he knew he was in trouble. All he could do was rest and hydrate. He couldn't risk leaving in the daylight to make a pharmacy run; he had to wait for the safety of darkness. Four generic acetaminophen pills washed down with a bottle of Gatorade; Cliff had been in worse condition before, but only once.

Groom Lake, NV

Two airmen stood with Bill in the cold wind on top of the mountain ridge to the southwest of the runways and lake bed. Fenced in on the flat-top ridge were all the antennas, the entire array for all the bands that were available to him. The SATCOMs he knew nothing about, but the high frequency array he recognized and understood, all a part of his lifelong hobby as a HAM operator, an amateur radio enthusiast. He had held an Advanced Class, which became an Amateur Extra Class after the license restructuring in 2000. He was familiar with the technology and the theory, although the technology available for communications in the radio hut was far beyond what he could have dreamed. When they lost connectivity to the satellites, most of that went to hell. The special internet that Wright and Cliff used to communicate with secret VoIP was new to him as well, although he had long suspected that there was a shadow internet not available to the public. The government doesn't give away technology to the general public unless there is something else in play already.

None of that mattered. If he was able to cobble together a high frequency rig, then other surviving HAMs could too—if there were any. All he needed was to have everything perfect on his end, and the right atmospheric conditions to get the right bounce, and he might be able to speak to someone across the country, or even further. There was a lot of chance involved. Before the attack, Bill used publicly available atmospheric and sun flare data to determine the best shots, but that information was gone too. On a lark, he tried reaching the International Space Station, but there was no response. One clear night, he had seen it streak across the sky, so it must still be up there. Of course he wasn't sure if the astronauts were alive or not. Just thinking about being trapped in space to die sent shivers down his spine.

Major Wright told him there were around a dozen USAF officers in orbit when the attack hit, but that they had the ability to de-orbit and land. Groom Lake was one of the landing sites, the other being Edwards AFB, but no one had yet landed. They had had no contact and heard no distress beacons. They just went off-line; just like the communications satellites and the imaging birds had. Now, that was something that impressed Bill. They still had to wait for the birds to pass certain locations, but the resolution was staggering. He bet he could read a newspaper from space with it ... if there had been one left to read.

"OK, guys. I think I've done what I can do. Let's head back to the facility."

The airmen didn't say a word, their breath hanging in the cold air. They climbed into the Humvee to drive back down the mountain road, the only Humvee at the installation they'd found that would still run.

SSC

The gym facilities in the underground base were impressive. Amanda kept leaner and stronger than she had ever been, even in her twenties, despite the lack of walking and fighting, and even with the addition of eating so well every day, especially when compared to her journey from Arkansas. Clint's level of physical fitness was staggering; the man could run miles and still have explosive lifting power at the end of it. During the last few days, Clint had taken Amanda on a tour outside the immediate center command structure and living quarters of the facility. The tunnel-boring machines sat idle at the long end of an eastbound tunnel, about two miles past the edge of the lake above them, forever doomed to rust into the dirt. The TBMs had been working on the original cover project for the Superconducting Super Collider. There was another six miles of open tunnel, concrete-lined, well-lit, and full of a strange array of hardware. The publicly known tunnel section had been backfilled and allowed to gradually fill with ground water, which became a backup source for the large stored water tanks below the main facility. But the concreted and preserved section of the secret tunnel held everything from military vehicles and weaponry, to what Clint described as local power generators. They looked like oversized semi-trucks, with over twenty wheels on the trailer alone; each was described as a portable nuclear-powered generating facility. There were, possibly still are, teams of technicians who were specially trained to isolate a small town from the larger power grid, and then power the entire town directly from the LPGs. Clint knew they existed; he knew the basics of how they operated, but he really didn't understand how to implement them. He explained to Amanda that besides the Osiris Project, there were other projects that were put in place specifically for technical people. He was an operator, and was in place to make sure leadership survived, or could be created from a surviving group. The rest of the people involved were for the other projects to rebuild.

Instead of plodding away on a treadmill, every morning Amanda jogged in the tunnel with Clint and every morning Amanda tried to invent solutions for protecting a city from the undead and for implementing an LPG. It would need to be a city with a climate suitable to sustain agriculture without serious irrigation needs, and it would need to be a city with the potential for manufacturing. Eventually, they would need things. They would need scrap metal melted down and made into new things; they would need to rebuild technology; they would need everything ... rebuilt.

Her heartbeat pounding in her ears, the sound of her breath overtaken by the echoing slaps of her running shoes on the spotlessly clean concrete floor, she passed the LPGs every day. Every day she became progressively more overwhelmed by the aspect of rebuilding a country.

Albuquerque, NM

The bus rattled up the on-ramp for I-40, the road cleared by the mass of undead that had passed through at some point before them. A sense of foreboding hung over Bexar. Even though their journey had begun with a close call that ended well, the empty Interstate worried him. All the cars were pushed forward, pushed the direction they were traveling, which meant they might catch up with the huge mass of undead. He'd seen what could happen; Apollo and Lindsey could attest to that. All he knew was that they had about six hours until sunset, and about seven hours of driving to get to Cortez. They had to drive with NODs, or with the headlights, or camp out on the road. None of those options sounded like much fun, but Chivo's dedication to the mission and his willingness to complete it using every ounce of his being was contagious. Bexar hadn't known any Special Forces people in his life, but now he could see what made them different. They simply wouldn't quit, no matter what. They were determined not to just finish, but to win. *I would never have made it through their selection process. There's no way.* Bexar thought about the SWAT officers he knew and wondered if they had met people like Chivo before. The highly trained SWAT cops looked like complete amateurs compared to Chivo, just in attitude alone. *He doesn't care. He doesn't feel like he has anything to prove to me, he's just doing his mission and he's going to win. If he's going to win, I'm going to win. I have to win ... or I could make him lose.*

The wind whipped through the missing windshield. At forty-five mph it looked like they were standing still, but the bus rattled and shook so badly it felt like they might as well been trying to go mach six in a Cessna. At least they were finally on the western edge of the city and getting into the open desert. Bexar unzipped his bag and removed a small bottle of Break Free and his cleaning kit. If he had to be bored rattling along in a slow-moving bus, he might as well clean his rifle and pistol.

Ten minutes later, Bexar's rifle and pistol were back together with a functionality check, loaded, and replaced. He took his heavy custom-made knife; blood was still crusted on the blade from fighting the bikers back in the park. He put a drop of Break Free on it and scrubbed the blade with the cuff of his pants. Satisfied, he checked the blade. *Still sharp; damn nice work. I hope CM Forge is still in business and Curtis is OK; I might need to order another one ... or maybe get one for Chivo.*

Smiling, Bexar stood, squinting his eyes in the desert wind that flowed through the bus. *Route 66 Motel? Oh shit, that's right, this used to be Route 66 ... well it used to be I-40 too; it's a wasteland now.*

The hotel stood like a white palace in the desert; windows dark, some broken, a handful of undead shambling through the parking lot. A sheet hung from the roof. Bexar dug in his bag and pulled out the small binoculars he had taken back in Terlingua. "HELP US" was painted on the sheet. He was going to say something to Chivo, but then he saw a dozen undead shamble to the edge of the roof, the sound of the passing bus getting them excited. One of them fell over the edge, the undead body dropping the long distance to the parking lot below. There was no scream. Even if he had been close enough to hear one, the undead didn't scream. There would be no voice, just the wet crunch of a body hitting the pavement. *The only time I've ever seen that before was a suicide, and she screamed the entire way down.*

Bexar took a deep breath. That was one of the worst calls he had been on in his entire career. The scream and the wet thump with a crunch that her body had made when it hit pavement after falling ten stories haunted him. He shook his head. The past was the past, and there was no use in trying to live it again.

The bus rocked as it drove around a small group of undead, the first they'd seen on the road since getting on I-40. Bexar looked out the back of the bus and saw they were walking along with the bus, but he wasn't sure if they had been moving in that direction before the bus had passed or only after. If it was before, then these stragglers might be flowing into the tail of the large herd. They had a long way to go on I-40 before turning north to get to Colorado, and if they hit the back of the herd, Bexar wasn't sure if they should slow and follow or try to detour around. The problem was there were a lack of roads that would make an easy detour.

Grants, NM

About an hour after leaving the garage, with Sarah keeping the speed close to sixty mph, they drove through the edge of Grants, New Mexico. The town had long since been bypassed by the Interstate. The roadside passed quickly by without presenting much of a glimpse into what the place had once been when Route 66 ran through the middle of town. The further they traveled, the more frequent and the larger the groups of undead they had to swerve around became. All of them were walking west, but as Erin noted, if they were seeing more and in larger groups, they were probably nearing the back of the huge mass of walking corpses. Jessie was uneasy about the chance of running into the back of that huge stampede, but more urgently, she had to pee. It felt like every twenty minutes she had to ask Sarah to stop so she could squat against the edge of the Toyota. *Yet another wonderful aspect of being pregnant that I had expunged from my memory.* She was at least thankful that Erin stood outside with her, the short M4 in her hands giving protection while she pissed on the road. It was one of those moments when she suddenly noticed how hairy her legs were. Her mind wandered. *When in history did women start shaving, and why on earth did they decide to?* She was getting used to seeing her legs hairy; it was quite nice not shaving them constantly. Without a word, Erin fired her M4 twice, shocking Jessie from her reverie. A corpse not fifteen feet behind the truck fell to the pavement, released from the walk of the damned.

She couldn't even get excited about it anymore. Erin's expression didn't change; it was as if she simply turned and flipped a light switch, using the same amount of emotion and effort involved for the switch as for killing an undead corpse with her rifle. Jessie stood and pulled her panties and jeans up, leaving the top button undone and the fly half-open, as it was beginning to feel uncomfortable against her growing belly. She looked at Erin and really wondered what sort of world she was bringing a new child into. *It doesn't matter; my child will have the best I can give her, the best protection, the best education I can provide, the best life—even if it is radically different than what we had a few months ago.*

Back on the road, Sarah gradually brought the FJ back to sixty, gas mileage being more important than time. They had time; they had a few more months until Jessie needed to be ready to give birth. But there was only so much gas available to them, which gave all three women concern.

"Hey! We're passing the Continental Divide, Erin."

Erin responded with a grunt, not unlike any other teenager would have. Jessie tried to remember why the Continental Divide was so neat. She had looked it up on a trip years ago with Bexar, but the memory seemed just out of reach. *Fucking mommy brain.*

With each passing minute, another mile ticked over on the odometer, and with each passing mile the number of undead on the road increased. Each was walking west, the stragglers of a stampeding herd, to be picked off by the predators; except there weren't any lions on the plains waiting to cull the slow. It was just the three of them in their SUV, and they didn't have nearly enough ammo to put them all down. So, gently swerving the FJ from shoulder to shoulder, Sarah picked her way through the groups as they came upon them. Luckily, the undead don't turn and move quickly like real people do, or someone might have stepped out into the path of the SUV. Taking a two-hundred-pound corpse to the grill would really hamper their efforts, even with the spare fan belts. The sun continued to drop in the western sky, filling the windshield with bright glare.

"Think we should drive through the night and trade off, or stop to sleep?"

Jessie pondered the question for a moment. "We should rest for a little bit, stretch our legs and eat, then push on. We'll just have to drive slower since the headlights don't reach very far, even with the brights on. Erin?"

"Whatever, I'm just riding in the back anyways."

"You know how to drive. Why don't you take the next shift, and when it gets dark, I'll take over for you—if that's OK, Sarah."

Entering the edge of Gallup, New Mexico, Sarah took an exit and pulled to the top of the hill at the edge of the overpass. There were four cars in the intersection, forever abandoned. Climbing on the back bumper, Jessie pulled down one of the five-gallon gas cans and a section of garden hose and topped off the SUV's tank. She walked to the nearest vehicle, a late model 4-door, and tried the doors, but they were locked. The next vehicle's doors were unlocked. Erin stood by her, guarding, but also wondering what she was doing. Jessie unlatched the seatbelt, removed the child safety seat, and set it on the ground. She then pulled up the back seat and banged on the plastic cover for the fuel tank. Knocking the cover loose, she twisted it and pulled it, along with the fuel pump, out of the gas tank. Moments later, she had syphoned enough gas to top off the gas can, which she replaced on the FJ's roof rack. Jessie stretched and took the opportunity to pee again, but before she climbed back into the FJ, she walked back to the car, retrieved the safety seat, and tossed it into the back of the FJ on top of all the gear.

"I might need that in a few months."

"Worried about getting a ticket now that the world has ended?"

"No, it's my husband's fault. He was a cop and he's seen some pretty bad wrecks. We were in a really bad one before ... Keeley ...." Jessie choked up, wiped her cheeks with the back of her sleeve, picked up her rifle, and climbed into the passenger seat in silence.

Erin looked at Sarah, who shook her head very slightly before motioning towards the FJ. Sarah climbed into the backseat, and Erin the driver's seat. After starting the truck, Erin deftly slid the shifter into first and operated the clutch like a seasoned pro.

"Stop!"

Erin slammed on the brakes. "What the hell, Mom?"

"Turn the motor off, get your foot off the brake, and get down."

Erin did as she was told. With the windows down, Jessie and Erin could hear it: an old diesel motor rattling down the Interstate, a black cloud of exhaust trailing it as it slowly approached. Barely peeking through the windows, they watched the old yellow school bus drive by slowly, unaware of the three of them on top of the overpass and off the Interstate.

The Bus

Bexar felt like he was on a really crappy motorcycle trip, the cold desert air grinding and burning at his face and beard; his eyes felt raw from the assault from nature as they drove with no windshield.

"We're getting close; we need to take the exit for US-491—that should be in the next mile or two."

"That's great, except there're no road signs left standing."

The two yelled back and forth over the wind and engine noise. Bexar wished he had ear plugs; he looked at Chivo and realized he had a 9mm round stuck in each ear. *Son of a bitch! Ammo ear plugs?*

"Just take the next one; we'll check the signs up top."

Chivo turned the wheel and slowed as they traveled to the top of the overpass and the intersection to see if any of the road signs were still standing. The signs were standing, and they had guessed at the correct exit. Chivo swerved around stalled vehicles in the intersection and turned north on 491. They were getting close, but they would have to drive into town at night. Gas stations, a car wash, fast food, and strip malls lined each side of the road. Chivo bounced the bus over the center median to clear a collision that blocked the road. Around each of the buildings, Bexar saw a growing number of undead staggering out of the shadows and into the afternoon sun, the bus instantly garnering their much unwanted attention.

"We should probably stop and fuel soon."

"Not yet, Chivo, the fucking dead are all around us. Keep rolling, and wait until we get up in the hills."

With each passing mile, the buildings would grow sparse, but then a new pocket of civilization would sprout up. Chivo looked at the fuel gauge, now under a quarter tank, and not known to be reliable. He just stopped and said, "Fuck it, mano. We've got to fuel up." He left the motor running and the shifter in neutral and pushed on the parking brake. As he let off the brake pedal, the bus began rolling backwards. "Fucking *pinche* bus."

Chivo looked around and saw a stalled car ahead of them. He put the bus in gear, drove in front of the car, and rolled the bus back against the abandoned Mercedes. It stopped the bus, proving once again that expensive German cars can be useful.

Bexar fed the hose out of the window by the fuel filler cap, then climbed onto the roof of the bus, his AR in his hand. An old barbed-wire fence separated the highway from the service road; a lonely convenience store stood in a cluster of buildings with manufactured homes behind it. As Bexar expected, undead shambled out of the mobile home park and out from behind the gas station towards their running bus. It was time to see if the old fence would hold.

Slowly, one by one, the undead bounced into the barbed-wire fence, catching clothing and flesh on the sharp points, tearing each away as they moved side to side trying to find a way at a fresh meal. More bodies pushed against the rusted wire, and the first strand broke.

"Care to hurry the fuck up down there, guy?"

"You want me to check the oil and clean the windshield for you too, Meester?"

"OK, ha-ha. Seriously, are you getting close?"

"Yeah, just tickle my balls and show me your tits."

Bexar shook his head and watched the second wire break. Bodies fell forward over the fence from the pressure, then climbed back up only to trip through the low desert shrubs. Standing on the roof of the bus, Bexar took aim at the closest corpse and fired before driving his rifle to the next and the next. Chivo left the hose to work on its own, turned, and began engaging the undead with his pistol.

"Hey Bexar, what would happen if we drove off while fuel was still syphoning?"

"Nothing, but we'd probably lose some fuel in the process, and we couldn't put the filler cap back on."

"Does that matter?"

"Fuck no. Let's roll!"

Bexar kept addressing threats as Chivo turned and sprinted to the side door, swinging the metal handle to close it. Seconds later, the bus lurched forward and ground through first gear. Bexar almost fell off the roof, but caught himself and climbed back down the hole to the interior.

"Well that was fun. Thanks for stopping, Dad."

"If I'm your dad, the first thing I'm going to do when I get home is slap your momma for having such an ugly baby."

Bexar laughed. It was the first time in a long time he'd had a good deep laugh, even having to wipe tears from his eyes.

Gallup, NM, the FJ

"Think we should wait longer, or do you think we could go?"

"If we go, we should drive slower."

"Or we can drive normal, and I'll shoot the driver as we pass. Shit on those guys."

Sarah and Erin both looked at Jessie.

"No seriously. It's like they were following us to get you two, that's sick. It's like the damn bikers before. Drive 60, and when we catch up, get next to them and I'll shoot the driver and the front tire."

Erin shrugged, started the FJ, and drove down the ramp onto the Interstate. A gaggle of undead walked west, possibly following the stampede, possibly following the bus that had passed. Either way, Erin drove around them and pushed on, getting excited to see Jessie put down the assholes that had caused them so much grief before.

The miles wore on and the sun glowed angrily against the edge of the western horizon, yet they saw no sign of the old yellow school bus. The excitement wore off, and all three of them began to feel drowsy from the letdown. The endless desert road was punctuated by a handful of small towns that had been bypassed when the Interstate was built. Straggling undead continued to punctuate the roadway, but the rest of the road was clear—pushed clear by the previous mass of bodies. They still worried that they would reach the actual back end of the massive stampede, but so far they had seen no sign of it. By Jessie's estimation, they had been on the road for six or seven hours. All of them were exhausted. After a quick discussion, they decided it would be best to stop and rest for the night, if they could find a safe place.

"Erin, just take the next exit. We'll see what we can find."

"What exit? There's nothing out here but empty and trees; even meth heads don't go out this fucking far to cook up their dope."

Jessie smirked. "Well, just slow down. Drive off the roadway and park against the fence line if we don't see something soon. We can sleep in shifts, or put the tent up on the other side of the fence, if you want."

As if on cue, an exit appeared, curving back around the trees to a small road that ended in a dirt lane on their left. Erin looked each way before deciding to go left and drive north along the dirt path, following it as it meandered through the trees before stopping. They were a good distance away from the highway, and Jessie knew Erin was right; there was nothing out here. Nothing is good; nothing means no threats. *No, it means a lower chance of threats. There is no such thing as "no threats."*

"Let's put up the tent. You'll like it."

Erin and Sarah pulled the heavy plastic box off the roof rack, along with the long canvas pouch holding the metal poles.

"These things are awesome. You're not going to hike with one, but they're awesome tents."

Jessie set out the tent poles and slid them into the angle adapters, making rafters like a house. She pulled the dyed canvas tent over the rafters, then raised a corner and placed the vertical poles, six in all. Once done, a ten foot by ten foot canvas wall tent stood next to the FJ. Jessie tucked the sod cloth under the poles to hold the bottom in place, and moved the FJ to where the driver's side was touching one end of the tent, the flaps tied closed. They tied the other side closed, and sat in silence, listening to the normal sounds of nature around them, while they ate cold MREs.

Jessie felt happy to be in her tent again, even if it was one of the group tents and not her normal camping tent. But, as she fell asleep, wrapped in a green wool blanket, and holding her rifle, through her mind flashed the faces and the deaths of Malachi, Amber, Jack and Sandra, Will, and Keeley. She could see Bexar running towards her, a crazed look in his eyes, rifle up, and firing as he ran. Keeley at least had a grave, and she had helped bury Malachi and Amber. Sandra, Jack, and Will's bodies were still in the Basin when the bikers brought her in. Bexar became a ghost. Her last thought as she drifted to sleep was that she would never give up hope until she found his body. Bexar was her man, the father of her unborn child, and she loved him so bad it hurt.

CHAPTER 30

Colorado, the Bus
March 8, Year 1

For Bexar, just using high end NODs was a novelty in and of itself, but driving a beat-up piece of shit bus while wearing one simply took the winning spot in random situations he'd been in. The slow drive had his nerves rattled; his face was raw from the wind even with his shemagh wrapped over his head and face, and his helmet pushed down on top of it, keeping everything in place against the constant onslaught. Somehow Chivo slept, leaning against the wall of the bus by the stairwell. Bexar couldn't sleep in this bus if he was tranquilized with a rhino dart.

The upside to exiting the Interstate was that the road signs still stood on the small U.S. highways. The downside was that cars and undead were scattered here and there, causing him to jerk the bus shoulder to shoulder as he navigated around them on the small, two-lane highway. According to the signs, he was very close to Cortez. The vast, empty green glow of nothing in his night vision was quickly being punctuated by farms, houses, and ranch land.

"Chivo," he said looking back over his shoulder. "CHIVO!"

Bexar threw his half-empty water bottle at his sleeping partner, hitting him in the groin. Chivo snapped awake and threw it back hard enough to knock Bexar's helmet and NODs askew. As he scrambled to straighten them, Chivo came over and stood next to him.

"What's up? Are we there?"

"Almost. Do you want to just roll in, or do you want to take it slow? You're the secret squirrel—what should we do?"

"What would you do?"

"Roll up the middle and hope for the best."

Chivo shrugged. "Sounds fair. As far as we know, Cliff has killed everyone and is only in need of a ride."

Bexar slowed and drove through a dark intersection. The traffic lights looked odd without being illuminated; they shown in a green glow through his goggles. The road split and divided into four lanes, and both of them could see the football stadium ahead on their right.

"Our guy is supposed to be north of the school a few blocks. Follow the road to a dead end in a neighborhood, by a field."

"Wow, Chivo, real helpful."

"I can see the map in my mind; I just don't know the road names. See if you can turn off near the middle school—that was one of my way points."

Both of their heads snapped right at a burst of light. Bexar had no idea what it was; Chivo yelled, "RPG!" and pushed the steering wheel hard left, away from the launch point.

Cortez, CO

Cliff, restless and unable to sleep, heard the explosion. It sounded like a light rocket or an IED; he knew that the cult had RPGs—he and his aircrew had been the victim of one. *Who would they be shooting at?* Cliff's mind was having trouble pulling focus; he didn't have a thermometer, but he was guessing his fever was dangerously high. Instead of being wrapped in blankets as before, he lay in his clothing on top of the bed with the bedroom window open, which was probably why he heard the explosion.

Could be the QRF, assuming Wright got my message. Shit.

Cliff stood. The room felt out of balance; he decided to break cover and take a more direct route. He put on his bag, carrier, and the blanket poncho, and grabbed his arms, press-checking his rifle and pistol. He carefully walked downstairs and rolled up the garage door. Lowering the door behind him, Cliff scanned the neighborhood and saw no movement. *All the patrols are probably converging on the blast.* Muffled rifle fire could be heard in the distance. He walked across the street to where his first truck sat hidden in the trees. Pulling the covering branches off the truck, he climbed in and was happy to find that it started on the first try. He backed out and spun around; the tires squealed as he sped towards the sound of an intense firefight.

The Bus

Bexar pulled Chivo through the hole in the roof of the bus, which now lay on its side. The RPG had struck the rear axle; the back of the bus exploded, along with the spare barrel of diesel fuel. Bexar's helmet took damage and was burning, but after taking it off and throwing it away, he was happy he'd had it on. Chivo slumped under the steering wheel once the bus came to a rest on its side; some of his utilities were blackened, but he wasn't on fire. He appeared to be mostly OK.

Clear of the bus, Bexar pulled Chivo by his chest carrier. His NODs now damaged and thrown away with the helmet, he could only return fire at muzzle flashes in the darkness. The bus was still burning, becoming more engulfed with each passing moment. Bexar was worried that the vapor in the fuel tank would combust and explode, if it hadn't already when the RPG struck. He had no idea. All he knew was that he was on the wrong side of a firefight, and standing near a burning vehicle didn't seem like all that great of an idea.

The bus had come to a rest against the outside wall of a car dealership, which was now catching fire as well. The muzzle flashes seemed to be coming from the hotel across the street; Bexar let his rifle hang on the sling, squatted, and picked up Chivo by his carrier and belt, nearly falling off balance as he put him across his shoulders. Bexar ran northeast through a parking lot as fast as he could, which was painfully slow, nearly stumbling several times. Finally, he got behind the business and finally had cover. He laid Chivo against the back of the building, propping him up against the cinderblock wall. Bexar pulled his Mechanix glove off, checked for a pulse, and found one, a strong one. He then ran his hand under the front and rear of Chivo's carrier and found no wounds or blood. *Unconscious or internal ... fuck if I know, but fuck all of these goddamned assclowns!*

Bexar looked at the building. The rifle fire came between the hotel and the building to one side, so he crept in a crouch around the north corner, pulling off the wall and cutting the pie with his rifle as he went, then taking a kneeling shooting position once he could see the muzzle flashes. The flashes stopped, but by the light of the raging fire he could see men climbing into two trucks, both of them driving towards him. Bexar knelt in the shadow and waited. The first truck stopped in the road, just past where he was kneeling; he fired at the driver. *Breath, aim, squeeze ... look, turn your head ... breath, aim, squeeze ...look ... breathaimsqueezelook ...*

Bexar had killed the three men in the truck in front of him before he realized he was taking fire from his right side. The cinder block wall of the business shattered in chunks, the concrete hitting him in the face, cutting his cheek and chin. Another truck drove from the south at a high rate of speed, and as Bexar pulled away from the corner of the building, he saw another truck coming in from the north.

Fuck. We've got to move; I have to get Chivo and move off the X.

Bexar ran around to the back of the building. Chivo was missing. Looking frantically in every direction, Bexar heard a soft whistle and looked up. Chivo was on the flat roof of the business. He pointed at Bexar and then to the south, then at himself, and towards the front. Bexar flashed thumbs up and crept to the right side of the building. Above him, he heard Chivo let loose with a full auto burst from his M4. All the men in the trucks turned towards him, including another guy with an RPG. Bexar knelt and shot the man with the RPG in the torso just as he fired the rocket, which skipped off the ground and slammed into the truck with the first people Bexar had shot. The truck exploded in a shower of hot burning metal. Bexar shot the man with the RPG again, to make sure he would stay down, before firing on the man next to him and the third.

It felt like an hour, but in the course of ninety seconds Chivo and Bexar had killed nearly a dozen men the main street of Cortez. The truck that had sped in from the north slid to a stop in the middle of the aftermath and a man stepped out, waving at Chivo to come with him.

"Bexar, come on, it's Cliff!" Chivo yelled.

Chivo climbed off the roof and ran to the truck. Bexar ran from the back of the building and dove into the bed just before Cliff slammed the truck in reverse, executed a fast J-turn, and sped off north.

Cortez, CO, Cliff's House

After some escape and evasion turns and double-backs, there were no signs of any other cult member patrols. Cliff parked the truck in the trees, stepped out, walked towards his house, and collapsed in the driveway. Chivo picked him up while Bexar tried and found the garage door unlocked. Once inside, Chivo lay Cliff on the living room floor and checked him for wounds. The bandaged thigh was quickly found. Removing the dressing, Chivo saw that infection was setting in, and that Cliff had a very high fever.

"We need to do a pharmacy run; my med kit went up with the fucking bus."

"Shouldn't someone stay here? Should I go?"

"I'm going to take a swing and say that my level of medical training is significantly higher than yours—unless you're a registered nurse and never told me."

"Nope, but I can do a really half-assed CPR and call for a medic."

"OK, then I'm staying here. You're going to have to do this on your own. Stealth, mano. You can't be drawn into a prolonged gun battle, and we have to assume two things: one, that every able body they have with a weapon is out tonight looking for us, and two, if they find us we're royally fucked. I don't know where they got an RPG, but I wouldn't be surprised if they have even more hardware. It's like being back in the fucking 'Stan; a Hilux truck with a 105-mm recoilless bolted in the back. Fucking people, it must have been like going to a hotrod shop, but they outfitted their shitty truck with hardcore weapons."

"Sure. But what do we need?"

"Antibiotics, IV bags ... shit, everything. Find a fire department. Raid the ambulance or the EMS gear in the station if you have to. IV bags—as many as you can find, and all the associated gear; get any of the script meds they have on board too. The insulin will be toast from age and temperature, but some of the other stuff should have survived. You might have to hit a pharmacy to get the antibiotics; I'm not going to suggest you go to the hospital. That place has probably already been picked clean if it isn't fucking overrun .... Oh! Fucking vets! Find an animal hospital, get anything labeled with these names." Chivo wrote a half-dozen medication names on his notepad, ripped out the page, and gave it to Bexar.

"Mag check—how are you topped off?"

"Nearly down two."

"Trade me. Take these." Chivo handed Bexar three full M4 magazines from his own carrier. "You've got about seven hours until sunrise, but you really need to be back in under two. Cliff is going to be iffy. Normally, this would be nothing—run a bag, a broad spectrum antibiotic, fever reducer, and keep him comfy ... a few days later and he would be mostly normal, except for trying to walk."

Bexar nodded, noticing the book bag on the floor. He picked it up and dumped the contents onto the bed. The spotting scope and the spare magazines were first to be noticed, but Bexar saw the folded map and pulled it open. It was a civilian map, but it gave him an idea of where things were in the town; he stuffed it behind his carrier to take with him. Bexar looked at his new watch from the storage lager at the SSC. "Be back in two hours."

"Good luck. Watch your six, and it would be better for you to ditch the truck somewhere and have to sneak back through yards and shit rather than drive back with a tail following, so pay attention out there."

Bexar nodded, press-checked his AR, and walked out of the room, down the stairs, and out the garage to the truck. He was surprised that he wasn't nervous; he didn't have any fear about driving into enemy territory. The strongest emotion Bexar had was anger. *How dare those motherfuckers fire a rocket at me?*

Groom Lake, NV

Bill wasn't sure if the adjusted HF antenna would work better or not. It *should* work better, but the only way he could tell would be to DX someone. That contact would require the other person to have the ability to respond in the HF band as well. The HAM community as a whole might be seen as odd, but they are a resourceful bunch. Bill was sure that if there were any other HAM survivors in the country, he would DX one at some point. It was the ultimate Field Day, and he even had hot coffee … no donuts, though.

SSC

"What do you think his chances are of contacting others with the modified equipment?"

"Quite good, babe. With SATCOMs down until further notice, HF is the only method we really have to reach over the horizon. It still doesn't solve our subfleet communications question, unless they surface close and start responding. But if any of the surface fleet has survived, that would give us a chance to contact them. My best guess is that they all started a mad dash back to CONUS, San Diego, and Norfolk when everything went to shit. We just don't know yet."

"What about the Chinese; what about North Korea?"

"We're going to be in the dark unless someone can figure out how to bring our birds back online. We don't even know why they went off-line as of right now, we're just guessing that the Chinese took them down. The last mission brief I had on the technology was almost two years ago, although those who study such things didn't believe that the Chinese had the assets in orbit that could hard-kill our birds; the tracks make that look to be wrong."

"So we sit, we wait, and we do nothing. I'm a President with nothing to do."

"You're not the first."

Amanda snorted and laughed at the remark.

Cortez, CO

Bexar crept through the shadows to the truck hidden in the trees. He checked, and the tail lights were already broken. His NODs had been trashed and thrown away at the bus, so he was truly in the dark. Even still, he wouldn't turn on the headlights unless something bad happened and he had to drive fast. After backing out and driving a few blocks south and east, he stopped and looked at the map. Originally, he had thought that the map wasn't marked up, but now he could see small pen marks on a few places around the town, including the middle school, some other school, and what was probably a church, guessing by the notation in the map legend. The fire department closest to him was on North Ash; the others were spread on the edges of the city, which made sense to Bexar, as a previous first-responder himself. Seven slowly driven blocks later, Bexar parked the truck in a driveway off an alleyway, across the street to the north of the fire station. He backed in so he could pull out in a hurry if he needed to; he also left the windows down and the keys in the ignition. He wasn't that far from Cliff's house, so if the truck turned up missing, he could walk back without any problems. He ran across the street and into the parking lot behind the small fire station. Bexar guessed there couldn't be more than a handful of apparatus in the small fire station.

The overhead doors were closed tight, and a tattered American flag hung from the front of the building. The side door was locked as well. Looking up, he saw a small fire escape to a second-story door. Bexar climbed the ladder and found it unlocked. Quietly, Bexar opened the door and held it with his foot. Surefire flashlight in his left hand, and his heavy CM Forge knife in his right, he stepped in, closed the door, and whistled into the darkened building. A handful of moans came from the interior.

Great. I hope they don't have their bunker gear on, or this might get sporty.

Bexar waited, hoping they would make their way to him instead of having to feel them out in a dark building he wasn't familiar with. He didn't have to wait long for his first customer of the evening, who had been fairly overweight in life and wore typical EMT pants and a t-shirt. Bexar pushed hard on the paramedic's shoulder before plunging the heavy blade of his knife into its temple. As the fat body fell to the floor, the knife jerked out of Bexar's hand, still stuck in the skull. Another younger and thinner corpse turned the corner and started towards the light. Bexar took two steps back and drew his pistol; the second undead fell over the body of the first, making for an easy single-shot kill with his pistol. The sound was deafening in the small hallway. Bexar wiggled his knife out of the oozing skull, wiped the blade off on the corpse's t-shirt, and stepped over the bodies. He continued into the building, banging the butt of his knife on door frames as he went.

No other moans came and no other undead were found in the building. Bexar made his way downstairs; there was no brass pole, to his disappointment. There he found the bunker gear laid out and ready to jump into, as is typical in most firehouses. An engine, two brush trucks, and a small ladder truck were shoved into the concrete bays. Behind them sat a lone ambulance; that was Bexar's first stop. Inside, he found the EMT bags, which included most everything on Chivo's list, except for the antibiotics. He zipped the bags up and shouldered both, which were much heavier than he would have thought.

Bexar walked around the ladder truck, unlocked the downstairs side door, and slowly opened it, peering into the night. No threats visible, he walked around the back of the station and across the street to his truck, placing the bags in the bed. Sitting in hiding, he consulted the tourism map once again. Veterinarians weren't marked on the map, and long gone were the days of being able to search the internet for an answer. A rare moment of clarity struck; Bexar looked at the home behind him. It looked like an old lady had lived there, judging by the clothesline and vintage lawn furniture. *Old ladies love phone books ... phone books have addresses.*

Bexar climbed out and kicked in the back door to the house. Inside there was no response to the noise, so knife and flashlight in hand, he walked through the home until he found the kitchen. A phone was mounted on the wall next to the cabinets. He checked the drawer closest to the phone and smiled when he saw last year's phone book and Yellow Pages for the surrounding area. The phone book went with him back to the truck.

Looks like the closest clinic is north on Alamosa; that doesn't look too far. Bexar folded the map to show the spot and marked it with his pen, then circled the fire department building. Some quick planning, and the truck was started, in gear, and Bexar was on his way. Driving faster this time, he turned north on Mildred and sped towards Alamosa, passing the local hospital along the way. The hospital was a mess, a complete disaster, as far as Bexar could tell in the darkness. Chivo was right; it looked bad enough that he wanted nothing to do with stopping and checking it out. A few moments later, the truck was parked around the back of the animal clinic and the back door was kicked in.

In the kennels lay the bodies of cats and dogs, rotting where they'd died, left trapped in their cages by the end of society. The sight of the animals that had starved to death in their cages, clawing desperately to get free, affected Bexar more than killing the undead firefighters had, and it took him a few moments to clear his head to look for the medicine stores.

The list of supplies needed in hand, Bexar took a plastic trash bag and dropped in every pill bottle and every vial he found that matched, or looked close to, what Chivo had written. He noticed the syringes and realized he wasn't sure if there were any in the EMT bags, so he grabbed a handful and dropped them in with the medications. In less than ten minutes Bexar was back in the truck and driving towards the house. All told, it took him ninety minutes to make his rounds, only to be greeted by a pistol in his face when he parked and rolled up the garage door.

"I guess next time we should work out some sort of code—a secret knock or something."

"Yeah. It sucks getting a pistol pointed at your head when you arrive home. Here are the bags; I hope I was able to get everything. How's Cliff?"

"Weak." Digging through the EMT bags and the trash bag full of medications from the animal clinic, Chivo nodded. "This will do, or at least it will get us started. Come upstairs and I'll teach you how to start an IV."

Bexar nodded and followed Chivo, happy to take the role of student for a skill set that he'd never had the opportunity to learn.

CHAPTER 31

The FJ, Campsite
March 9, Year 1

The three women woke with the rising sun. Erin, having last watch, had fallen asleep on the job, but it turned out OK, even if she was embarrassed for it. All three of them lay in the cool air of the tent, knowing that it was colder outside. Jessie stood and peeked through the front flap; nothing was moving near their campsite. They listened quietly and could hear only birds in the trees around them. Jessie untied the canvas strips that tied the flaps together and rolled the tent flaps up, tying them to the frame. The crisp morning air was dry but refreshing. A hawk flew lazily overhead in search of breakfast, and if not for each of them holding a rifle, this could have been a normal girls' weekend camping trip.

"God, I feel exhausted." Sarah stepped out into the morning sun, stretching. She was sure she smelled horrible; it had been a month since either she or Erin had showered or washed clothes. Jessie pulled another case down from the roof rack of the FJ, and after relieving herself by squatting against the back tire of the SUV, returned with an old Coleman stove and blue enamel percolating coffee pot. They didn't have any real coffee, but the MREs had instant coffee packs in them, and that was better than nothing. Jessie had refrained from coffee ever since she figured out she was pregnant, but she knew a little wouldn't hurt. *Everything in moderation.*

Ten minutes later the girls sat on the ground in front of the tent and sipped their coffee, steam rising out of their blue enamel camping mugs.

"Let's stay one more night."

Jessie and Sarah looked at Erin, Sarah speaking up first. "Why? Don't you want to get to the facility? They're supposed to have showers and hot food."

"Sure, they're *supposed* to, but what if they don't? This is nice, and it's the first time we've had a chance to relax ... to have some feeling of normalcy."

Sarah shrugged and looked at Jessie, who said, "If that's what you and your mom want to do, then we can stay another night. But Erin, we're going to need you to go about fifty feet over there and dig a slit trench, about twelve inches wide, twelve inches deep, and three feet long, I'll get my camp shovel."

"What's that for?"

"For us to shit in. I don't have any lye, but we'll just have to cover with dirt as needed."

Jessie stood and dug around in the back of the FJ, produced a three-piece collapsible military surplus shovel, and handed it to Erin, who took the shovel without a word and walked towards the spot Jessie had pointed to.

"If we're going to stay, we should make a quick patrol of the area to make sure there aren't any surprises. If we're lucky, maybe we'll find something we can cook for dinner tonight." Jessie nodded at Sarah's suggestion.

Sarah finished her coffee and stood, holding her AR. After telling Erin their plan, they walked north through the trees then turned east to begin their lap of the surrounding area.

CHAPTER 32

California
March 9, Year 1

While the patrol was out, checking in at regular intervals via their PRC-152 radios, Aymond had another member of his team working the VRC-104 mounted in the third M-ATV. The trucks were loaded and configured strangely, as they weren't a part of their original mission workup, but had been found at the MWTC after the attack. Normally, the equipment would have been standardized throughout each of the M-ATVs that his team operated for redundancy. Those checks and balances, always being prepared for the worst, were long gone now that the worst had happened. *I guess there could have been worse scenarios; all out nuclear war would have probably been worse, but this is definitely towards the top of my 'things are fucked' list.*

Happy was the backup communications guy. He was not as on-point with the radios as Garcia was, but Garcia played with radios as a hobby; he knew more about the radios, antennas, and all sorts of random things than some of the communications specialists. Regardless, Happy was in the truck with the HF capable radio trying to make contact with someone, anyone.

"Chief, get up here!"

Aymond climbed down from the roof of his M-ATV and stowed his binoculars before walking to where Happy had a handset pressed against his ear. He punched a couple of buttons and the external speaker crackled, fading in and out. "... Groom Lake, any surviving military personnel or civilians, return transmissions on ..." The transmission faded out and was garbled. "... safe and secure facility, on site contact via the speaker box located at ..." the transmission drowned in static and faded out.

"Who was that, and why did we lose the transmission?"

Happy pushed buttons on the digital display trying to bring the transmission back to life, but every channel was filled with static, the squelch turned low.

"That was on one of the civilian HF bands; I was trying to DX but couldn't get the frequency right and wasn't getting the right bounce."

"What is DX?"

"Make contact—it's HAM jargon. When you DX someone, you make contact with them, typically used for long distance communications in the HF bands, at least what Garcia says."

"What's bounce?"

"Bounce off the ionosphere ... HF transmissions are affected positively and negatively by everything from solar flares to atmospheric conditions. That's why we use SATCOM for the majority of our over-the-horizon transmissions."

"Good work, Gunny. Keep working on it. At least we know someone is out there ... Groom Lake ... do you think he meant *the* Groom Lake?"

"Yeah, Chief, I do. Or it's a prank, but if someone went to the trouble of rebuilding an HF rig, why would they use it to prank like that? Unless it is some sort of trap. Even then, a trap would be odd; society collapses, most of the population are now Zeds, why would someone fuck around like that? Seems unlikely. I think it's a legitimate thing."

The handheld radio on Aymond's armor carrier squawked to life. "Car Ramrod to Chief."

"Ramrod? You knuckleheads are using the call sign of Ramrod? Over."

"Chief, the town is dead, most of it destroyed, and it is overrun with Zeds. No friendlies found at all. Request permission for another day and to push to get aboard Camp Pendleton. Over."

"Request denied. Secure a new OP and the rest of the team will come to your location."

"Happy, spread the word. Wheels up in thirty mikes."

"Will do, Chief."

Happy left to walk around their small hillside, kicking loose the security teams and the other teammates on rest. Simmons and Jones were found under one of the M-ATVs, elbow deep in grease.

"Can you two be ready to roll in thirty?"

Both of them slid out from under the old truck. Simmons stood and spoke first. "Yes Gunny, but this truck is smoked; one of the coils is broken and we're surprised the motor hasn't imploded yet. It will, and soon.

"How soon?"

"Roll the dice, but it's not going to make it through the day."

"Shit. Start unloading gear, ammo, and anything else useful. Spread it around the other trucks."

Simmons looked at Jones, who shrugged with the kind of indifference only the intermediate-ranked enlisted Marine could achieve, typically reserved for those times during a deployment when nothing seems to go right.

The FJ

Sunrise brought another perfect morning. Jessie sat on the ground outside the tent warming coffee for the other two, who were still sleeping. Erin had just gone back to sleep when Jessie relieved her from the security watch earlier than expected. *This would be a great family camping trip; perfect morning to sit and drink coffee with Bexar while Keeley played, running around the trees, finding interesting leaves and flowers.*

Jessie wiped the tear off her cheek. *No more. I can't be sentimental any more, never again. I can't afford to be weak for my new baby.*

Sarah climbed out of the tent, waking a groggy Erin. Teenagers, no matter how hard core, no matter that the world had ended, still had problems waking up in the morning. Coffee and another breakfast of MREs finished, with only the crackers for Jessie—the smell of the food pouches turned her stomach—the three began to break camp. Jessie used, then filled in the slit latrine, and brought the shovel back to camp. By the time she returned, the tent was collapsed, folded, and back in the big plastic box it was stored in. The poles went back into their canvas bag, and all of it was being loaded into and onto the FJ.

The sun pierced the wispy morning clouds as they drove down the dirt road back to I-40, Jessie taking her turn behind the wheel. One of the fuel cans was now empty, but the FJ's fuel gauge showed a full tank, and they still had five more full gas cans on the roof rack, twenty-five gallons in all. After a bit of discussion they decided to wait until they were down to ten gallons to replenish the supply, otherwise they would be stopping every few hours to scavenge fuel. All of them were excited to get to Groom Lake and off the road.

The Interstate was still mostly clear, the stampede of undead having paved the way for easy travels before them, but the random groups of shambling dead were more numerous than they were the day before. Jessie wasn't sure if it was because the undead were excited by the noise of the truck as they passed, slowly marching out and onto the Interstate to find the source, or if these groups just formed the tail end of the stampede. Regardless, Jessie knew it didn't matter; she drove around each group as they appeared in the windshield, trying to keep the speedometer as close to sixty as she could.

Cortez, CO

"His blood pressure is finally up, closer to normal. His pulse is steady; I think he's going to make it." Chivo checked the IV bag that hung from a nail in the wall above the bed; the blood pressure cuff remained on Cliff's arm. Chivo stood up, stowing the stethoscope in the MOLLE webbing of his chest carrier in a manner that made Bexar think he had carried medical equipment in his gear before, probably more than a few times.

The one thing that they didn't have was a catheter, so they "solved" the problem with bath towels, which could be replaced and dried more easily than bedding. The room smelled like piss for their efforts.

"His temperature is 101, so he's much better in that regard; we've got that moving in the right direction." Chivo checked the bandage on Cliff's thigh, unwrapping it and inspecting the wound. The previous night, they had scrubbed it clean, applied antibiotic ointment, and re-bandaged the wound, using vet-wrap that Bexar brought back from the animal clinic. The syringes that Bexar grabbed turned out to be a good thought on his part; Chivo was able to draw from the glass vial with the antibiotics, unscrew the needle, screw the needle into the IV tubing, and inject the medication with ease.

"Where in the fuck did you come from?"

"My mother, so she claims."

"No asshole, how did you learn all of this?"

"The Army. Special Forces, specifically. Before Apollo and I both got out, got dipped, and went to work fighting our secret-but-important conflicts."

"What secret conflicts? Pakistan?"

"No, not Pakistan, although that conflict isn't much of a secret. The last few years we were in southern Mexico and Central America mostly, fighting a war against the cartels, mainly the Zetas. Before that, we rotated through Afghanistan a few times. I ended up spending a total of four hundred seventy-five days in country with that."

"I'm guessing you weren't married then."

"Ha—no. My first and only marriage fell apart fifteen years ago when I first made The Unit."

"What unit?"

"Delta."

"What are we going to do here?"

"Once Cliff is mobile, we're taking our new truck and heading back to the SSC."

"Did you know him or something?"

"Yeah, well sort of, he was a training officer at The Farm when Apollo and I were dipped. He taught a lot of our transition school."

"You were already a Special Forces guy; what else did you need to know?"

"All the spy stuff—communications, encryption, dead drops, nothing too James Bond, just standard working knowledge stuff."

"What's his background?"

"I have no idea. Talking about anything 'real' was highly discouraged. Best I can figure is that he had been a part of the SpecOp community at some point; he knew the right things. To be fair, I don't even know if 'Cliff' is his real name. The cloak and dagger shit is very real to guys like him. Me, I'm just a knuckle dragger putting bullets into bad guys."

"How long until we can get driving again?"

"I don't know ... maybe a day, maybe a few days. I'd say we should be ready to sit in place for a week to be safe."

"But you trust him?"

"I'm not sure."

The FJ

Bored, Erin played with the shortwave radio in the back seat of the FJ. She slowly flipped through the frequencies, moving the antenna around and trying to get the best signal if she thought she heard something. She stopped on the repeating message from Groom Lake.

"... upon arriving, if you have no means of communicating on the return frequency, locate hanger seven, near the dry lake bed on the southwest corner of the lake bed. Enter the hangar and dial 973555. You will be greeted by one of the civilian residents ..."

With a marker from her bag, Erin wrote 973555 on her arm before moving up frequencies. She stopped on a frequency that had a computer-generated voice reading a series of numbers again. Erin looked at the frequency and noticed it was different than before. Listening closely, she realized that the numbers were no longer only odd numbers. She turned the hand crank and left the station playing when it was interrupted by a loud cartoon voice: "I'll get you, you varmint!"

Everyone in the SUV jumped at the sudden change, which was followed by a series of tones and then more numbers.

Erin stared at the radio, as if waiting for an explanation. Jessie shook her head and took a deep breath, trying to slow down her breathing after being startled.

"What do you think that was about?"

"I don't know, Mom, but that was weird."

Fallbrook, CA

The convoy, short one M-ATV, drove near the town of Fallbrook, which appeared to be mostly destroyed by fire and owned only by the dead, before driving off the paved road, following the directions that Ski had given them. The GPS wasn't working either. It was like everything in space had failed.

The drive straight through the town should have taken less than half an hour in traffic, but it took three hours due to dodging Zeds and making an attempt to drive the walking corpses in a direction away from where they were going to be operating from. *What I wouldn't give to have some engineers, heavy equipment, and some Hesco. We could build a real FOB and have a place to truly base operations.*

On the military crest of a ridge line between Fallbrook and Camp Pendleton, Aymond and what was left of his MSOT set camp. It was close enough that recon patrols could run into Pendleton and still return, but far enough away that their chances of being overrun were low. At least they had escape routes available if things went sideways. At this point, Aymond's primary concern wasn't trying to resupply the team; they were still set well for provisions, except for diesel fuel, which they would have to gather while on patrol. The main priority was trying to locate any command structure that remained, or any surviving Marines. For all he knew, he was now the Sergeant Major of the Marine Corps, whatever that was worth anymore. *My luck the only surviving officer is some new kid fresh out of the fucking Academy ... fuck'm. I'm in charge.*

Holding his hand to the horizon, he estimated another two hours until sunset. He told the team to set watch and stand down for rest, which meant most of the team wouldn't really rest, they would just get to switch-off for a bit while they cleaned their M4s and the rest of their gear. Marines, especially Recon Marines, were never really "off"—they just slowed down for a little while to clean gear, PT, or train.

An hour later, security elements lay on the roofs of the trucks watching for any approaching threats, while in the wagon circle, some of his Marines were doing push-ups and buddy squats: squats for reps with their buddy on their shoulders for weight. If they'd had a legitimate FOB, someone would have fashioned a bench and made a barbell out of something, sand-filled gas cans, or water cans ... or something. *Never underestimate a Marine's resourcefulness as well as his need to PT.*

Realizing that he had been awake for nearly thirty-six hours, Aymond climbed into the back of his M-ATV and fell asleep, using the gear bags for a bed and pillow.

I-40

Only a few hours went by before the women passed the entrance for the Petrified Forest National Park. That was one park that Jessie and Bexar had never visited, but always wanted to. Even though it killed the small towns along the way, it was helpful for Jessie and her group that I-40 bypassed the hamlets. In each town they entered they found nothing but walking corpses, no survivors, nothing. Despair began to set in each of them. They had assumed that they would have found other survivors as they drove across a good chunk of the western United States, but so far, nothing turned up. *Maybe they're not by the Interstate. I know if I had been by the Interstate when the stampede came through, I would have run for the hills. Hell, I did run for the hills with Bexar. We would still be living safely in The Basin if it wasn't for that damned biker gang.*

Jessie took a few deep breaths and worked to get her thoughts under control as she drove onto the shoulder to pass another group of shambling dead. *On the upside, if we ever defeat the dead, this Interstate is clear.* Jessie looked at the map and the marks she'd made on it for their route. Even with their early start, she wasn't sure they could make Groom Lake today; they would need to stop and camp again. Each of the larger towns was circled on the roadmap. Flagstaff, Arizona was the next big hurdle to cross, but that was also the waypoint where they would turn north. Otherwise, they would have to drive through Las Vegas, and as much fun as a gambling fling with the girls sounded, this would not be that kind of trip. At least Erin had quit messing with the shortwave radio; the "numbers" station was creeping her out. Even at the end of the world there were spies and governments doing secret things and it made her feel like someone was watching her. Looking side to side out the windows, she knew that the only eyes following her were already dead, but those eyes didn't creep her out anymore. They were a nuisance to be dealt with, an aggravation, like fire ants in her yard. No, Jessie had quit worrying about the dead after meeting up with Sarah and Erin. Her only fear was of other people, the school bus being the new threat. With an extra day of camping to rest up, she hoped that the school bus and the crazy family that Sarah described would be long gone and that they wouldn't meet up with them again.

Jessie glanced at the atlas and the circle around Flagstaff. She saw where the Petrified Forest National Park was noted on the map, so she at least knew where she was; she just wasn't very sure about how far away the park was or how long it would take to get there.

We can't do Flagstaff in the dark. We shouldn't do any large city in the dark, or any small town for that matter; it is just too dangerous. Jessie decided that if they hit the edge of Flagstaff and it was still within a couple hours of sunset, they would backtrack and find a safe place to sleep for the night. Otherwise, they could find a spot on the highway northbound.

Cortez, CO

Cliff woke up with a start, but after years of training and conditioning he was unlike most people. He could control it. With his eyes closed, he took stock of what his body felt like, knowing something was different. Slowly, he opened his eyes and scanned the room. There was an IV in his arm, and his head hurt, but not as badly as his leg, which throbbed with each beat of his heart.

Two men in the room with me, both wearing tactical gear, one white, one Hispanic, both with heavy beards and rifles. The Hispanic man stood near the window, staring outside but standing back from the window so he couldn't be seen from below. *Smart man; he's been trained.* The other man sat in a chair against the wall, dozing, his rifle propped up against the wall. *That guy isn't trained right.* Taking stock of his body, Cliff realized that he wasn't wearing pants or a shirt and that his weapons were nowhere near him. The Hispanic man by the window turned and looked at Cliff, which caused Cliff to smile.

"Chivo, you fucking wetback, what are you doing this far north? There's no taqueria up here!"

Chivo laughed. "Fuck you WASP. I came up here because I heard you needed help with your golf game. All your friends from the country club were making fun of you for your small putter."

The laughter woke Bexar. The laughter also made Cliff's head and leg hurt worse, but he was happy to see a familiar face. Slowly, the memory of the burning bus and driving out to the firefight came back into focus, but Cliff couldn't remember how he'd gotten back to the house or how he'd ended up naked with an IV.

"You were in a bad way, mano, but we were lucky to have you come pull our asses out of that fire. Once we got back here, I sent Bexar on a supply run. If you feel like eating some hay it's probably from the vet clinic meds we gave you."

Cliff moo'ed and laughed. It had been years since Chivo showed up to The Farm and years since Cliff took Chivo out on his first OGA operations, which ran differently than he was used to with The Unit.

"Where's Odin? Who's this guy?"

"Valhalla—guarding the gates. Same with Apollo and Zennie. This is Bexar."

Bexar stared at Cliff. "So you're the asshole in Groom Lake."

"Yup ... at least I was, until I was stranded in this shithole. Why are you here with this short asshole? Shouldn't you be with your family and at the SSC?"

Bexar stared at Cliff and walked out of the room. Chivo tossed Cliff his clothing as he pulled the IV out of his arm.

"He's all that's left, mano; bikers killed his daughter and his wife. When we plucked his ass out of south Texas, he was in a hell of a battle with them. An IED went off and leveled the place; all we found was him, and he nearly died too. Drove him to the SSC where he recovered. Apollo and his chick, Lindsey, formed the rest of the team that left to come get you. In Albuquerque, a fucking massive herd of undead blew through and knocked a bridge out from under us, killed Apollo and Lindsey. Zennie was killed leaving Mexico, Odin died in El Paso. It's been a complete shit storm, a damned clusterfuck from the beginning."

"So how does he do?"

"Bexar? He's solid. Needs more training, but he's got it and doesn't hesitate to get in the shit. He pulled my ass out of the bus. They ambushed us with an RPG. Who are these people?"

"Some sort of cult—a very well-armed cult—mostly hopped up on meth. We rescued a group of survivors who'd been living in the middle school; they were on the run from these cultists. They're sick fucks; they decapitated bodies and left the reanimated heads in a basketball rack. The Herc we were on was put down by an RPG as well. I'm not sure what else they have, but every member has been armed with an M4 and I've seen some M2s in trucks. After I took shelter, I started running recon ops, but so far I only have a couple of places marked and I don't even have them figured out yet."

"So cut and run or what?"

"No, we need to find the rest of the survivor group if we can. Fuck this cult. We get our people and we get out of here. With you two here we can do it better. You guys got commo?"

"Sort of. Bexar's headset was destroyed with his bump helmet, but the rest of his gear looks to be fine; my gear is fine. Also, SATCOM is down."

"Huh. OK, so no commo. We'll have to adapt and overcome ... where's my map and my notebook? There's a church we need to check first."

Near Fallbrook, CA

Aymond woke and wiped the drool off his face. The sun was down, and the moon shone brightly against the hillside. He checked the windup watch hanging from his gear and it showed eleven p.m. Winding it, he climbed out of the back of the truck to check on the security team.

"All quiet, Chief. We haven't had anything moving near us all afternoon."

"OK. Tomorrow we start sending patrols."

Aymond walked around the perimeter of his camp; the darkness was incredible. There should be lights from the town, lights from the installation, light pollution everywhere, but there wasn't. There was no artificial light to be seen in any direction; only the moonlight brought the hills to life. It reminded him of northern Afghanistan, except that the hills in California were much smaller, and there weren't any cooking fires that he could see. The star-filled sky was just as staggering and impressive, quickly making a thinking man feel small and insignificant to the universe.

Maybe this is man's extinction event; maybe our turn is over. No, this isn't nature. This isn't the natural course; this is an attack. We failed to protect our own home soil, and now we have to take it back. Aymond looked at the trucks around him. *There is no way I can do it with so few, but we'll have to try. If we find nothing, no other survivors, we'll start clearing towns, using every last piece of weaponry we can scavenge. When the last round on earth is fired, we'll use machetes; when the machetes are gone, we will use rocks; when the rocks are gone, we will use our hands. We will win. We have to win.*

I-40, the FJ

The sun fell lower and lower against the horizon. Jessie was still behind the wheel, and she was enjoying the time more so than if she had been just sitting. At least she had the driving to keep her occupied. Erin slept out of boredom, which was understandable—no radio, no books, nothing to keep you occupied as you sit in the back of an old SUV rolling across the great American West. For a while, they all played a game of trying to label some of the walking corpses they passed with what they did before they died. Some were easy; police uniforms for example, sort of gave it away. Others, such as the severely obese and nude, were harder but often gave funny results. One man had a long, inexplicably neon pink beard and hair that led to a wild speculative discussion lasting at least twenty minutes. Erin referred to the popular buffet-based restaurants as "Golden Trough," and the larger the person, the more likely they would be labeled as the "live-in roll tester," or the perpetual "white trash mobility scooter racing driver." At times it was hilarious, but others, like the woman who carried her reanimated infant in a backpack, were far from funny.

The road signs were still flattened, so finding the turn-off for Highway 89 was going to be difficult. Looking at the atlas, it appeared that the turnoff was just before the heart of the city. Large billboards in fields well off the road became more numerous and were referencing hotels and restaurants in Flagstaff at distances between fifteen and twenty miles. Jessie held her hand up to the horizon, moving it up and down. *Eight fingers until sunset. Two hours.*

"We have about two hours until sunset. Want to shut it down early, or do you want to try to make 89 first?"

"I say we go for it, get north of town. Things are already becoming too populated for my tastes."

Jessie couldn't disagree. More homes, ranches, shops, and businesses were appearing on the roadside. They drove past an exit, seeing an increase in businesses off the road. Jessie slowed as they approached an overpass. Sarah strained to read the signs on the road overhead, but the signs were still missing from the highway, flattened by the stampede.

"We missed it!"

Jessie stopped the FJ in the middle of the Interstate.

"The bridge above us has a sign pointing north for 89. We should have gotten off back there," Sarah said, pointing behind them.

Both of them looked in the side mirrors at the approaching undead behind them. The groups they had passed had grown in frequency and number as they got closer to Flagstaff. They all continued to follow and were shambling towards the idling SUV.

"Think I can get around them?"

"I think you should go up *there* and drive the wrong way up the ramp."

Jessie nodded, letting the clutch out and making the sharp turn to go up onto the overpass. Even now, months after the end of the world, she still thought in terms of past traffic laws while driving. Bexar was a hardass about driving correctly; his idea of correctly meant legally as much as it meant safely.

At the intersection, cars were abandoned in every direction. Blood and gore was smeared on the outsides of the cars. Following the road signs, they traveled north until reaching the intersection for 89, then turned right to follow. The abandoned cars were thick in the roadway; a mall lay next to the road. Jessie slowly navigated around each vehicle, undead bouncing off the FJ's fenders as she drove. The view would have been staggeringly beautiful if not for all the carnage. Jessie sped up, the FJ rocked hard side to side with each sweeping turn of the steering wheel. Trying to escape the mass of cars and bodies before they were swarmed, Jessie did what she could. Erin woke up from all the movement. She rolled her window down and leaned out with her short M4.

"Settle it the fuck down so I can actually hit something!"

Jessie tried her best to drive smoothly. The sound of the M4 barked sharply, a tongue of fire flashing against Sarah's window with every press of the trigger.

"Hang on. I'm climbing on top."

"What?"

Before an answer could be returned to her mother, Erin had climbed out of her window and onto the roof rack, her feet dangling over the middle of the windshield, the M4 in her hands barking rapidly, the undead in front of them dropping after each shot.

"Mom, mag change!" Erin yelled, slapping the passenger side window with an empty magazine. Sarah rolled down her window, took the empty magazine, and passed up a fully loaded Pmag.

As quickly as it had started, they were past the worst of it all, the number of undead in front of them dwindling to manageable and navigable numbers. The trail of destruction in their wake from the hands of little Erin looked like a battalion of troops had rolled through. Jessie began slowing to let Erin off the top of the FJ, but she climbed back through her open window before Jessie could stop.

"Erin, what the hell?"

"Chill, Mom, it worked, didn't it? Better than losing this ride like we lost our Jeep."

Sarah looked at Jessie, who had no comeback. Keeley had been a sweet little girl, not the strong, spirited teenager that Erin was. Jessie wondered if Erin was like this before the end of the world or if she had grown into her new lifestyle.

The sun was falling behind the mountains; it was time to find a spot to stop for the night.

Cortez, CO

Around the kitchen table, Cliff, now fully clothed, held an intel briefing for Chivo and Bexar, making marks and notations on the map.

"After nearly a week of recon, all I have is that this church is somehow important, the cult is probably operating out of this elementary school, and the middle school was turned into a shrine or altar or serves as some sort of fucked-up payback. Honestly, I have no idea. These guys are well-armed and way off the reservation. I don't even know how many members we're dealing with exactly, but I guess there were around thirty before the fight at the bus. Between the ones I've killed and the group you killed when you rolled into town, we're dealing with about a dozen people or so left. That could be their entire group minus some leadership, or that could be just the beginning."

"I haven't seen any patrols come by the house, nor have I heard any gunfire or any other activity," Chivo offered.

Bexar shook his head. "Turds. They're like turds. You can't use normal military logic; think like a meth-headed gangbanger. The middle school was a rival gang's hangout; they shut it down and made sure that if anyone showed up again they had a vibrant example of what would happen to them. The church is storage or possibly a hangout. The other school is their mom's house; it's where they quietly operate from. If they had bigger weapons we would have seen them. Twice we've seen them with RPGs; that's the best they got. Otherwise, they would roll with the scariest thing they owned. Fucking bangers are like that. If they have a $50 ghetto blaster, that is what they carry. If they have a Desert Eagle or a sawed-off pump, that's what they bring when they go to war with a rival or if they want to do their stupid alpha wolf bullshit."

Chivo nodded. "That's what it was like growing up. This isn't the Stan. Maybe we're looking at this the wrong way, treating them like tribes with elders and a complex social structure."

"Don't get me wrong—they have structure, but it's short. There is a leader; there is a trusted lieutenant, and then there are the rest. Amongst all of that are their women, the chosen ones who are property of the leadership, and then the whores that sucked their dicks on the side. The whores were the ones fucking the regular members."

Cliff had spent months in war zones, guerrilla wars against narcos and terrorists, but he hadn't thought of this angle before. "Let's say you're right, Bexar. What's our first step?"

"Same that you thought. We go to the church to see what they're doing with it. If we really want to fuck with them, we tag it with spray paint or burn it down or something to let them know we're still here and we're hunting them. They'll circle the wagons, and believe me, it'll be obvious. Then we figure out how to burn their fucking wagons down."

"What about the survivors?"

"They're dead."

"How can you be sure?"

"In police work, if someone went missing who didn't mean to go missing, like it wasn't a wife skipping out on a bad marriage or something, they would typically be used for whatever purpose the turd wanted and then killed. If this cult already has their own women, if they already have their members, they're not going to keep people in cells or pens where they could rise up, escape, or fight."

"So you think we should just leave?"

"No, let's check the church first, and then we leave."

Cliff looked at Chivo who nodded. "Fine. After sunset, we go to the church."

Groom Lake, NV

"Send the SSC a message. Have them tune their HF comms to this frequency and let's see if we can make contact with them."

"Alright, Bill, but what makes you think it will work?"

"I don't, but we have to start testing and adapting. If the SATCOMs are down, if all the space-based equipment is down, we have to assume that this electronic link will go down as well. We need to get a solution in place so we can communicate."

The airman shrugged and typed the message, copying the frequency off the scrap of paper that Bill wrote on.

SSC

"Clint, do you know what this means?"

Clint walked to the console where Amanda sat. "Yeah, Bill is the civilian commo guy; he wants to try to make over-the-horizon contact using our HF radios."

"What makes you think that will work any better?"

"Well, High Frequency works differently. It can reach a long way, halfway around the earth, if conditions are right. The problem is that it isn't consistent; solar flares, atmospheric conditions, strong smells, birds flying, all sorts of shit makes it fail."

"Strong smells?"

"Not really," Clint smiled. "But the point is that it isn't reliable. That's why SATCOM technology was developed in the first place. Then the secure VoIP and the secure Internet Relay Chat were built using the government's own shadow internet."

"Well, give it a try. Even if it works only sometimes, we might reach a point where it's all we have."

Clint switched to a different console, punched in the numbers that were sent over the secure IRC, and waited. "Tell them I'm listening."

Groom Lake, NV

"Alright, Bill. They're ready."

Bill smiled and keyed the PTT. "WC5GLA calling WC5SSC ..."

"What are those call signs?"

"A variation of old RACES licenses."

"What's RACES?"

Bill smiled. "When we're done here I'll see if the library has an ARRL Operating Manual you can read."

SSC

"Well, I heard something, faintly, but I couldn't make it out." Amanda typed in what Clint said and hit return.

Groom Lake, NV

"Bill, it looks like they picked you up, but it was so faint that they couldn't make any of it out."

"Damn. OK, I wish we had more information about the meteorological conditions ... tell them I want to try again tomorrow at 1400."

Flagstaff, AZ

The city was replaced by trees and the countryside, which quickly gave way to suburban neighborhoods before going back to trees again. Every time Jessie thought they were out of the danger area, they fell right back into it again. The sun was now completely behind the mountains, the sky barely glowing orange. The trees, full of darkness and shadows, moved in the wind. Jessie wasn't sure what was just a shadow or what was going to shamble out into the beams of her headlights.

Amongst the trees, two signs on the side of the road flashed, reflecting the headlights. The brown sign stated: "Forest Access," and the blue sign had the tent symbol, universal for camping.

"This better work out, or we might as well drive on till daylight."

Sarah was exhausted from the emotional roller coaster and from riding in a vehicle all day, and could only manage a grunt. Jessie took the turnoff to the left and followed it across the other side of the highway. The road crossed a metal cattle guard and was no longer paved. She drove a few hundred yards off the road, drove into a copse of trees, turned off the lights and the motor, and cracked the windows. There would be no tent tonight, so they took turns making use of the rugged facilities against a nearby tree while the other two held security. They climbed back into the FJ, locked the doors, and ate their MREs in silence. The fun of camping the previous two nights was gone, if for no other reason than their day on the road had been long. Pulling through the mass of undead in Flagstaff had left all three of them frazzled.

No words were exchanged before one-by-one, each of them drifted off to a restless sleep, curled up as best they could on the vinyl seats.

Cortez, CO

With the cover of darkness, the intrepid group of three made their way to the truck stashed in the trees near the house. Cliff walked stiffly, limping with each step, but he insisted he would be OK. Bexar wasn't sold on him coming, having been so close to death only hours earlier. Chivo assured him that if Cliff said he was good to go, then he was. Bexar hadn't been exposed to the "mission first" dedication of special operators before; that level of mental toughness and ability to focus on a task simply didn't exist in the civilian world.

Bexar opted to ride in the bed of the truck, leaving the two old friends to drive, headlights off. The cold air suited him and he was happy to have the elbow room, room to bring his rifle into a fight. The ambush in the bus the previous day had flipped a switch in his mind. Like thousands of men throughout the ages, when they went to war they hoped for the best, but once combat started, the primal switch of a warrior flipped and it would never fully turn off again, even if it could be learned to be controlled.

Bexar was angry, but unlike back in The Basin, he wasn't out of control. It helped that he wasn't half-drunk, nearly hung over, and in full berserk mode. No, this anger was focused, like a spotlight aiming out of the bed of the truck. He wanted a fight.

Cliff, behind the wheel, opted for the direct approach, driving by the church and parking in the driveway of a three-unit apartment close by. They saw no movement; the bus wasn't anywhere near the church, and in fact, Cliff realized he hadn't seen it for a few days.

The double red doors at the front of the church were locked; Chivo went to work on them while Cliff stood back against the wall, facing the main street to the north. Bexar looked at the small windows of the entryway and saw flies on the inside of the windows.

Whispering to Chivo, he said, "Dude, flies inside the windows."

"Damn."

"Yeah, that's a giveaway that there's a body inside. Typical of the decomps that I dealt with as a cop."

Chivo shrugged just as the last cylinder clicked out of the way and he turned the deadbolt over. Bexar turned and took the first-in-line spot against the other door, ready to make a fast entry into the church. Cliff took the last spot just because he was moving slower than usual. Chivo ripped the door open, Bexar planted his right foot in the door frame, the light on his rifle flipped on. He pushed left into the vestibule of the church, Chivo followed fast to the right and Cliff to the left, each holding a slice of the pie inside the building to engage any threats.

They stopped in the vestibule. Bexar lowered his rifle, removing the Surefire from the pouch on his carrier. None of them were prepared for what they found. At about head level hung dozens of feet and legs, twitching and swaying. At the altar of the small church was the body of a young girl, no more than five or six years old. She lay on her back on a table, the cloth underneath her stained deep red. She was tied down; her dead eyes staring at the three intruders, teeth snapping as she twisted against the ropes. Blood had puddled below each of the hanging undead feet, staining the carpet down the steps and under the pews.

Bexar walked forward, shining his light up at the vaulted ceiling. Nearly twenty bodies hung from ropes strung across the rafters, their weight gruesomely stretching their necks out of proportion in death. Their hands were tied behind their backs, their feet bound together, and they writhed against the restraints. Their blackened teeth snapped hungrily at the fresh meat standing below them, frustratingly out of reach. Some of the bodies were very small; children. They hung from longer ropes, presumably so their feet would dangle at the same level as the adults.'

Chivo crossed himself.

Cliff scanned the room. "They all have crosses cut into their chests."

Bexar dropped to his knees, overwhelmed at what he saw, and asked Cliff, "Are these the survivors?"

Barely heard above the gnashing teeth was the soft answer, "Yes."

"But yet this, which ought to have been done long since, I have good reason for not doing as yet; I will put you to death, then, when there shall be not one person possible to be found so wicked, so abandoned, as like yourself, as not to allow that it has been rightly done."

"What?"

Bexar wiped tears from his face. "Marcus Cicero. These people need to die. We have to kill them ... we must kill all of them."

CHAPTER 33

Fallbrook, CA
March 10, Year 1

The first recon patrol checked in, Aymond requiring hourly radio checks from his teams. They were stationary overlooking the airfield, and the only thing they had found moving were a lot of Marines in utilities. The problem was that they were already dead. The team wanted to move in and check building to building, but after the ambush at Twentynine Palms, Aymond denied their request and sent them to the second objective. There was too much ground, too many people, too many buildings, and just too much to cover with any sort of detail for such a small unit. Even with air support, they would never attempt penetrating an enemy-held military installation of this size. They would complete their current mission, centered on the one thing that the MSOT members knew well: reconnaissance.

Between the north side and the south side of Camp Pendleton stretched numerous fire roads, dirt trails, and hills. This was terrain the M-ATVs were specifically designed for, so besides taking time, Aymond wasn't worried about his guys making the drive. The rest of the team tasked themselves with maintenance of their weapons and rested, rotating an on/off schedule. They had to remain ready to be a ragtag QRF for the recon team if need be. Aymond debated keeping them all together for support and conducting the recon as a whole team, but given the layout of Pendleton, he was mostly OK with just the small recon element while giving the rest of the team some much needed rest.

Ski spent hours scanning the nets with the mounted radio in one of the M-ATVs, but with no positive news. Nearing 1400 hours, he thought he'd found a transmission on the HF band, but couldn't get a good signal. He did note the frequency in his notepad to check again later; if it was a real transmission, and maybe if they could get on a higher piece of ground, he might be able to make contact then.

Flagstaff, AZ

Morning came with little fanfare, although the interior of the FJ smelled strongly of body odor and general uncleanliness. Groom Lake said they had showers. God, how I could use a shower ... maybe they have a bathtub ... to be able to soak in a tub, ahhh, what dreams may come. After a round of morning necessities at a nearby tree, the trio pulled off the dirt road and back onto Highway 89 north, eating their MRE breakfasts as they drove. Towns so small that Jessie was surprised they even had names passed by the windshield. Jessie opted to drive again. Already feeling nauseous from her breakfast, she couldn't think of sitting as a passenger; she wouldn't be able to keep her meal down. With each passing day, she seemed to show more and more; women had always told her that second babies showed earlier in the pregnancy, but she hadn't experienced it before. Her jeans unbuttoned and unzipped, a piece of 550-cord used as a belt was about the only thing holding them up when she stood. She doubted that maternity pants would be easy to come by, but maybe she could at least find something more comfortable soon.

They were in Grand Canyon country, the wide open great American nothing for miles and miles on end. The upside was that with nothing came nobody, and nobody resulted in no undead, and also no cars in the road. So, the needle pegged at sixty, Jessie hoped to make Groom Lake by sunset. Her best estimate, looking at the atlas, was that they were in for an eight-hour drive. However, at the first car they saw, they would need to stop and syphon gas to top off the dwindling supply in the cans lashed to the roof rack.

Nearing lunch, the trio crossed the Navajo Bridge and found three vehicles abandoned in the parking lot of the overview. Erin volunteered to be the unlucky one, syphoning gas while the other two held security. A half-hour later, they set out with a full tank of gas, full cans on the rack, and Erin trying to rinse the taste of gasoline out of her mouth. Jessie had never seen the Grand Canyon in person before, but the terrain they passed reminded her a lot of Palo Duro Canyon in Texas, where she and Bexar had camped a few years ago. The tiny highway gave way from the desert canyons to the mountains with their majestic trees once again. The two-lane road was barely painted, the yellow line cracked and faded. In the road were a number of large RVs, seemingly abandoned, but after what Bexar and Jack told her about the RV park in Big Bend, she wanted nothing to do with them. They could have held scavenged treasure, for all she cared; right now her laser focus was pointing to Groom Lake. She absentmindedly rubbed her belly between gear shifts, her AR set across her lap for the probable need to use it.

Time ticked by, noticed only by the gradual dance of the sun across the cold blue sky as the mountains and trees gave way again to desert. She slowed to pass through the tiny town of Fredonia, which looked abandoned and untouched, as if every person had simply packed their bags and left. Jessie's mind turned to finding maternity pants once again, but she dismissed the thought as the farming community barely had a gas station, much less a women's maternity clothing shop. More importantly, it was a marked waypoint on the atlas to take the next road on their grand tour across America.

Cortez, CO

Bexar couldn't sleep after returning from the church. Every time he began to drift off, his dreams fell back to the little girl sacrificed on the altar like some animal. Sometimes Keeley's sweet face appeared, sometimes it didn't. In less than three months, Bexar had gone from the comfortable life of a city cop riding a motorcycle, to having lost his daughter, his wife, and everything he knew. He had been confronted with evil at a level he had never imagined could exist. The strangeness of some culturally significant cults that touched the newsfeeds every few years paled compared to the savagery he'd seen here. Even in Jonestown there was just death, not the inhuman violence and disregard for life he saw last night.

Cliff and Chivo somehow slept. Conditioned to combat, they could switch off and shut down quickly. Bexar gave up on sleep and sat looking at the map of the town with the notes and information that Cliff gave him, formulating a plan. First, they had to burn the church down. He couldn't set foot in there again, and he couldn't leave all of those people doomed to hang and struggle against their bonds as reanimated corpses. Cliff had told Bexar about the middle school and the chemistry lab, but Bexar had failed middle school, high school, and college chemistry, so the closest he came to an understanding was how to use a field tester for the presence of narcotics. Cliff listed off what was in the storage closet; Chivo smiled and told Bexar not to worry about it, that they could make something special. Chivo didn't elaborate and Bexar really didn't care. He saw three simple steps: Burn the church, burn the elementary school, and kill everyone that came out from positions of cover.

It was well past noon; the other two men still slept. Bexar, wired, sat in the living room on the first floor and stared at the black screen of a blank TV that would never work again. *Burn them down; shoot the runners. Like killing fire ants.*

Camp Pendleton, CA

The reports were not good. All of Camp Pendleton that could be observed was heavily damaged and overrun with the dead. Aymond thought about pointing the convoy east and never looking back, but he wanted to check the Recruit Depot. Even between training cycles, some of the cadre might have survived. However, that was secondary; he wanted to get to The Center. If anyone would have survived, it would be his rival brothers in the SEAL teams at Coronado. It would be foolish to give up now and turn east without at least checking those places. The first task was to get his team back together at a rendezvous point located near Bonsall, and then actually make it to San Diego. There were many densely populated areas between here and there. It was important to keep his team together; if they were overrun, then they would be overrun together—no more recon patrols for now. I-15 to I-5 was their most direct route without driving straight down the coast. *If there are any SEALs left in Coronado, at least that is a semi-defendable location ... blow the bridges and only worry about the southern approach.*

Groom Lake, NV

With this attempt, Bill had success. The transmissions back and forth weren't very good, fading in and out, but he would take it. He had at least created a backup communications platform in case the shadow internet failed, or for any other reason. Bill trusted his radios more than he trusted fiber optics. After all, his radio technology had worked for over a hundred years; it was proven.

Now if he could set up self-reliant repeaters at specific intervals throughout the nation, he could have a coast-to-coast radio net. He would place them on the highest points, mountain tops, buildings, making it easier to get the radio waves from point to point. As it stood, however, Bill might as well have been trying to land on the moon. *Telegraph line ... if only the lines still were up, a little juice and some tin tapping for communications. All we need is wire, miles and miles of wire.* The burst of excitement fell to feeling overwhelmed at the totality of the situation they were all in. They all realized that it would be the complete luck of the draw to live long enough to see the start of a project that ambitious, much less see it completed ... or to have enough people left in the world to even need it.

Bonsall, CA

The convoy once again together as a team, they pointed east through the edge of town, back towards I-15, away from the mountaintops and dirt roads of safety, and into the asphalt jungle. Pervading all was the weary feeling of combat troops headed into a mission that has bad intel and a high likelihood of enemy contact. It felt heavy in the vehicle, and Aymond wasn't sure if it was just him or if everyone felt that way. His two new corporals and their Humvee were sandwiched in between the first and second M-ATV in the convoy, so if they had a failure, the trailing truck could push them to safety. After his years in the Marines, Aymond just didn't trust the Humvees to perform; they seemed to always break down, specifically when you needed them the most. However, it was all they had so it was what they would use. The number of vehicles and Zeds on the road as of yet was light, but Escondido would be their first test, the first larger city, and they would be there very soon.

The FJ

The three of them stopped long enough for Jessie to pee and to top off the fuel tank from a gas can before hitting the edge of Colorado City. The barren world, punctuated with hills and homesteads, passed by them mind-numbingly dull, but broken by Erin voicing her opinion that she would actually like to encounter some of the dead so she would have something to shoot at for a little while. The statement earned a scorning look from her mother. Arizona gave way to Utah, followed by more unending road. The town of Hurricane came and went with only a few undead bouncing around the streets, turning to follow the SUV, nearly unnoticed by the women as they passed.

Like a shot of caffeine, making the turn onto the ramp for I-15 changed the mood in the FJ instantly. Long gone was the grey boredom of a road trip through the middle of nowhere; back was Erin press-checking her M4 and Sarah sitting up in her seat, ready to do something. She didn't know what, but she was ready. Jessie shifted gears and had to slow coming into St. George, the largest town they had seen since Flagstaff. The vehicles on the road were densely packed, once again causing Jessie to drive shoulder to shoulder, threading the needle through the small gaps, catching the front bumper on the edges of vehicles only a couple of times. Jessie drove in first gear, painfully slow; the undead approached the FJ only to bounce off the fenders as it passed by just slightly faster than their walking speed.

"Just keep your window up, Erin; we don't need one of those hands reaching in here."

Erin just grunted in response to her mother.

The number of vehicles slowly dwindled, as did the number of undead, until they neared the southern edge of the town, Jessie was able to shift through the gears and gradually get back to a respectable traveling speed. Mountains to the east, the sun blazed angrily into the windows of the passenger's side windows of the FJ. Sarah estimated that they had about three hours until sunset. Jessie glanced at the map and guessed they had about three hours until they reached Groom Lake. As full of nothing as this part of the country was, Jessie just didn't care anymore. She was tired of driving, her back hurt, and she still felt nauseous. She was going to make it to Groom Lake; she wasn't sleeping another night in the FJ.

Cortez, CO

The sun sat low on the horizon. Cliff and Chivo were up and joined a sleep-deprived Bexar at the kitchen table, the city map laid out in front of him. Cliff liked the idea of burning down the church; if they did it right, it would give them a place to set an ambush. First, they needed darkness, then they needed to go to the middle school and the chemistry lab.

"I don't know. Will they respond to the fire? If so, how many? How many total people are we dealing with here?"

"That's an unknown, Chivo. I haven't had the time or resources to accurately account for all the people, much less what sort of weaponry they have. We have a rough idea of how many of their numbers we've killed between the three of us, and a guess as to how many they had before, based on same. We can suspect that the patrols haven't been as heavy as they were before, from what you two tell me, so I think we've put a significant dent in their numbers. As for weapons, well, we know they have RPGs. Jake stated that they had crew-served weapons as well, but I haven't seen any of those in play."

Chivo said, "We'll have to assume that they will be employed in a defensive position to their HQ."

Bexar nodded. "First we need to get to the middle school and pull supplies from the chemistry lab."

"And I still have the instructions from a guy named Bill who was in your facility about a high frequency radio setup." Chivo looked at Cliff.

"Not yet. I don't want to break the news of all the deaths until I can say we carried out justice and that we're headed to the SSC."

"Why not back to Groom Lake?" Bexar asked.

"Clint needs help. Wright will be able to keep Groom Lake running just fine; between him and the civilians they should be able to continue to pull in survivors as they're contacted. We, however, have a more important mission. With a sitting President, we need to try to get any remaining elements of the military organized and centralized. We start by clearing out small pockets of area, creating safe zones, then slowly work our way across the country. The large masses, the Zs, those are going to be a problem. We're going to need serious hardware, maybe even some of our suitcase nukes to make a dent in those."

"Suitcase nukes? I thought that was just a bullshit story."

"Did you believe in Area 51 before now, Bexar? How about the underground at Denver International Airport, the SSC, Chemtrail?"

"Well, kind of."

"As a general rule, a conspiracy theory starts when some grain of truth sneaks out. We then work hard to wrap that grain of truth in a huge shell of crazy so people are aware it exists, but believe it is bullshit being spewed by an unstable person."

"Makes sense."

"Regardless, we've got to take care of our immediate problem. Chivo and I can make the IEDs. Bexar, you're going to be our security at the middle school while we work, keeping watch towards the main street and watching for patrols."

"I don't get to watch the magic happen?"

"Nope. Magicians never reveal their secrets," Cliff said with a wink.

The FJ

Small towns came and went without much fanfare. The few undead on the Interstate bounced off the fenders as Jessie threaded the needle between them and the handful of abandoned vehicles. North of Las Vegas, through the tiny town of Moapa, and across a few more desolate small highways, they turned onto the colorfully named "Extraterrestrial Highway," Highway 375, and drove into the mountains.

"How will we know where to turn off? This is a secret base, right? I doubt they have signs."

"Sarah, I don't know. Bexar just said we'd know it when we got there and to look for 'the black mailbox,' although I have no idea what that is. There are supposed to be large 'No Trespassing' signs along the dirt roads into the base, so I guess that's what we look for."

The sun was below the horizon now. Driving using the headlights, they approached a turn off to an unmarked dirt road. Parked next to it was a plywood sign with an arrow pointing up the dirt road with "Safety" painted in red spray paint.

"What do you think?"

"I don't know; there's no mailbox."

"Jessie, I'd say take it. Worst case, we turn around and come back. Quite frankly, as desolate as it is out here, I'd be surprised if we actually saw another walking corpse."

Erin slept curled up against the gear in the backseat. The headlights barely lit the dirt road, but Jessie drove along the bumpy route slowly, hoping that it was the correct way and also hoping that she didn't break the FJ out here in the middle of nothing.

I-15

The drive on I-15 wasn't bad, better than typical rush hour traffic by a long shot. That was until they reached the edge of the city of Escondido. At that junction, the lead M-ATV's remotely operated M2 fifty-caliber machine gun sprayed burst after burst of fire in front of the convoy, while the driver had to make sweeping maneuvers side to side, around disabled vehicles. The trucks were strong enough to push vehicles out of the way, but there was no way Aymond could risk disabling one of their vehicles with aggressive actions.

Aymond stared out the windshield. *My God, it looks like a nuke went off here. Everything is destroyed, burned; there's no way anyone could have survived all of this. This is so fucked.* He keyed the mic for the intra-team radios. "Guys, the Recruit Depot is between cycles; we're in heavy trouble. I'm actually going to ask for opinions on this one. So ... who wants to just push on to Coronado? If anyone else could have survived, it would be someone from The Teams."

In each of the vehicles, a quick debate was held, yelling over the engine noise and weapons fire. Each of the MSOT members wanted to push on to Coronado, so the plan was set into action. Aymond had driven from Camp Pendleton to

Coronado on more than a few occasions. The route was familiar; the unknown was if the Coronado Bridge was still standing, if it was blocked, and if they would have to take the convoy all the way south to Imperial Beach and back up.

What should have been about an hour's drive took the convoy nearly three hours, Aymond's M-ATV having to take the rear position due to running out of ammo for the truck's primary weapon. He hoped the bridge would be standing and they could cut the drive short. They could use the beach as a buffer and set a solid perimeter to keep the Zeds off of them if need be, but what they needed most now was more ammo and more friends with rifles. At least one of the two would be found on the island housing The Naval Amphibious Base, home of the West Coast SEAL teams.

The bridge still stood. There were many vehicles on it, but the convoy found it passible—no worse than the drive through the greater San Diego area. Peering over the edge of the bridge as they passed by, the docks and shipyards stood open for them to see in the later afternoon light. Zeds swarmed like ants. It would be a long time until someone was able to offload any cargo or work on any ships. *There's no way we have enough ammo in the U.S. to kill every single Zed. This is so fucked.*

Groom Lake, NV

Surprisingly, the winding dirt road turned to asphalt as they climbed higher into the mountains. They came to a stop at a gate with signs warning of the use of deadly force; a metal building served as a guard shack. Attached to the guard shack was a note: "Go inside, lift receiver, and dial 973555 to gain access."

Erin, now fully awake after bouncing along the dirt road for the past hour, climbed out and offered to clear the building for them. Jessie declined, asking her to keep watch over the FJ while she and her mom took care of it. Jessie left the engine running. Rifle in hand, she opened the door to the metal building, banging on it several times, waiting for a response from any undead. When nothing happened, they went inside and found a single table with an old, heavy, touch-tone telephone sitting in the middle next to a notepad and a pen.

Jessie picked up the receiver, heard a dial tone, and pressed 973555. Three rings later, a man answered the phone.

"Groom Lake Operations, how may I assist you?"

"We are survivors from Texas who were told by Cliff to come here for safety."

"Yes ma'am, welcome to Groom Lake. If you'll use the notepad and pen, I will give you the combination to the lock on the gate. Please make sure to secure and lock the gate after entering; we are trying to keep out the migrating undead population." The male voice read off three numbers, which Jessie wrote on the paper and repeated back to him. He gave instructions as to where to go once entering the base, and thanked them for coming.

"That is possibly the kindest person I've spoken with, besides you two, since the shit all went down."

"Don't get soft on me now, Jessie. Keep cool. You've got us, but we don't know about these people yet."

Once unlocked, Jessie drove the FJ through the gate and waited for Sarah to close and lock it behind them. Continuing on their journey, they followed the road as it descended from the mountains onto the edge of a dry lake bed. Resisting the temptation to drive off the road and onto it, as the man had warned against, Jessie stuck to the paved road, which continued around the western side of the lake bed until reaching a turn-off with a series of large hangars. The rest of the buildings looked downright shabby, which was disappointing to the three of them. They expected the secret base to be high-tech-looking, alien-like. All three of them stared out the windows. Lights on the buildings glowed brightly, lighting up the world around them in a way they hadn't seen since the attack in December. Reaching the end of the hangars, Jessie turned left towards the last large hangar, as instructed. The big hangar door slid partially open, revealing a small collection of ragged old vehicles parked in a neat row along the side wall. Jessie parked the FJ and turned the motor off. They were here, finally here.

The three of them climbed out and stretched, each holding their rifle, when a young man with shaggy hair and a thin beard walked out of a door and waved. He wore camouflaged pants and a green t-shirt, a pistol holstered on his hip. Another young man, this one wearing combat gear and holding a rifle, stood alongside of him.

"Hiya. I'm Jason. Welcome to Groom Lake." Jason waved again as he walked closer. The other man with the rifle stayed farther back, looking alert, but relaxed, as if this process was routine for him.

"Welcome. I'm glad you three made it," Jason said, shaking each of their hands, except Erin, who simply held her rifle and glared at him.

"OK, well, there is a process as we go underground. First of all, some of our women will conduct a strip search for any signs of bites or scratches. None of you are bit, are you?" When the three of them shook their heads "no," he continued. "Good. Well, like I said, the women will be conducting a strip search. You can leave your gear up here if you would like, but please bring your weapons and your ammo;

you are required to be armed at all times. After your inspection you will have a chance to shower and clean up, and given clean clothes ... they're military surplus, but they work OK ... then a general checkup. For the safety of our citizens, there will be a quarantine period for observation of any manifestations of the Yama Strain."

"What is the Yama Strain?"

"That's what makes the dead reanimate. We'll explain the whole back story later, if you're interested ... most people want to know. The citizens also have some theories as to why we were attacked. The military personnel, mainly Air Force, treats us very well and with a lot of respect ... strictly careful to adhere to the Constitution ... anyone have any medical conditions we need to know about?"

"I'm pregnant."

Jason smiled wearily, his lips quivering slightly. "Congrats," he mumbled, his mind going back to the day they had arrived at the base, his young wife killed and reanimating in the big cargo plane. She had wanted children so badly, pestering him non-stop, but he had been scared to make the leap.

"Well, grab what you want to bring with you and come with us below."

CHAPTER 34

Coronado, CA
March 10, Year 1

The scene on the other side of the bridge stood in stark contrast to what the mainland held. Mostly untouched by the fires, the palm trees stood tall and green, giving way to memories of friends, meetings, and training held on the base. The well-manicured lawns in the medians of Orange Avenue needed to be mowed, badly. But tall grass was of no concern to the convoy as they bounced back and forth over the median, dodging abandoned vehicles and the undead. With Aymond in rear position now, it left the lead vehicle the only one with any amount of stored ammo ready. However, the grenade launcher was really something Aymond wanted to save; it seemed like extreme overkill for the groups of undead in their path, and would create other problems, like fires, things they wanted to hold off on dealing with until absolutely needed.

The beachfront resort looked like it'd served as a temporary shelter; sheets were stretched across the exterior wall and hung from shattered windows with "HELP" spray-painted on them. Scanning the buildings with his binoculars, Jerry saw they were much too late to give any help. Zeds fell from the open windows as the convoy rattled past, attracted by the rumbling diesel motors. The two corporals in the Humvee had been a concern, but they reported they were fine at every radio check-in request. The soft body of the old truck couldn't take the abuse, compared to the armored M-ATVs, but hopefully their journey would be over soon and the truck could be left behind. However, the more he saw, the more hope drained from his thoughts. Aymond grew angry at the wanton death, the brutal destruction—all brought upon his country by foreign forces.

The yachts and sailboats sat in their slips, most of them looking to be in decent condition; assuming that the owners had maintained them, they had only been abandoned for a few months. *I imagine that they'll start to fail and sink, but for now they sit, bobbing in the waves ... if we could find two with good sails we could sail to North Carolina ... but that would suck. The Panama Canal can't be still operational; that would be a long, open ocean voyage. Fuck.*

The convoy rolled to a stop at Rendova Road, the brick and rod iron fencing still strongly intact.

"Ski, Hammer, see what you can do about the gate. We want to be able to secure it after we enter."

The lead M-ATV pulled alongside the fence, and his two Marines climbed out of the back hatch and over the brick pillars next to the gate, bolt cutters in hand. A few moments later, the pins were pulled out of the concrete and the gates swung open. The convoy drove beyond the fence and reset the gate behind them. They were now protected from the civilian side of the island, between the fence and the beach, assuming the entire fence was still intact.

Rotating through various frequencies, Aymond tried to establish contact with any remaining military personnel in the area using both UHF and VHF channels, but with no luck. Around the buildings and onto Trident Way, the convoy stopped again. All the Marines dismounted near a series of buildings enclosed within another fence and set a security perimeter while Aymond gave a quick mission plan, although they already knew what it was.

"Clear the buildings, secure everything inside the fence, get the trucks inside. Immediate mission objective is finding survivors and rearming the M2. Further resupply will be evaluated once our FOB is established."

A series of low "Hoorahs" was the response, and the team got to work. The two maintenance corporals were tasked with convoy security, each of them standing on the roof of an M-ATV, picking off Zeds as they shambled near the team.

The MSOT Marines split into two, four-man teams to begin clearing the buildings; as large and as many rooms as there were, it would take some time for primary and secondary searches. This wasn't a fast-moving movie version of a tactical entry; the Marines moved with purpose, but methodically and carefully.

Two hours later, the sun setting over the ocean, the buildings were declared clear and safe. A total of thirty-seven Zeds had been put down, but no remaining survivors were located. There was evidence of a standoff in which some survivors were likely overrun, judging by the presence of spent brass casings and the large pile of permanently dead Zeds outside a conference room. Inside the room were cases of MREs and dozens of empty green ammo cans.

The MREs were carried out to the trucks. The Zeds, all Navy men from The Teams, were placed in the conference room of their last stand. A small American flag stapled to the outside of the door was the only token of respect the Marines were able to give to their brothers.

In the storage units of the fenced area were mission prep containers, containing each SEAL team's members' individual go-bags for different missions. All the gear had been meticulously maintained and carefully stored for a rapid departure. Each of the teams had been responsible for urban environments for operating, but each of the four Teams housed here was assigned to different areas of the globe, their gear reflecting those needs. Aymond doubted they would need the arctic gear of SEAL Team 5, but all the gear that had been used up, lost, destroyed, or simply not on hand when the attack came while they were on the mountain at the MWTC, they now had access to once again. This included ammo, dive gear, and demolition supplies. The HALO gear was probably destined to remain in its boxes for all of eternity; they hadn't seen a single aircraft since the second day. Also, Aymond couldn't imagine a need for them to skydive into a location for tactical purposes now.

The low rumble of heavy marine diesel motors stopped all the Marines in their tasks in the yard. Being on the ocean side of Coronado, the beach was only a few hundred yards away. The same infamous beach used in the BUD/S Navy Seal indoctrination training.

"Gonzales, Hammer, Happy, Ski, get to the beach, and find out what they are."

The four Marines jogged to the gate and out towards the beach. Explosions rumbled from the east.

"Simmons, Jones, you two stay here, keep security, keep hidden. I don't like what's going on and we need to remain invisible until we figure out what the fuck this is all about."

"Aye, Chief."

"Snow, Davis, Kirk, with me."

Aymond keyed his intra-team radio. "COMSEC, hour checks, two clicks to return, four clicks for QRF, how copy?"

A single click of the radio was the answer given and the one that Aymond wanted.

The Beach

Ski held his hands low, squatting, a practiced team movement. Happy, Gonzales and Hammer each took quick action to be boosted up for the climb onto the roof of one of the training buildings along the edge of the beach. Hammer reached over the edge and helped Ski onto the roof. Staying flat, they inched towards the ridgeline. Happy took first watch, pulled the shemagh off from around his neck, and draped it over his head and face, holding the binoculars to his eyes, using the dirty brown scarf as an impromptu blind. Normally, they would have dug in and covered on the beach, but they had to secure themselves from the Zeds, so the roof was their refuge.

Four large Panamax container ships rumbled towards the mouth of the harbor north of where they held watch. Ski whispered the descriptions and markings as he could read them, identifying each ship as a Chinese flag carrier. Not military vessels; the sight of the four ships was very peculiar. The trip for a container ship to traverse the Pacific Ocean typically took about a month, tops, sometimes much quicker than that. The captains would therefore have left long after the attack on the United States; they would have known about it before they sailed.

In the waning light, and possibly due to the absence of tugs and harbor pilots, the four large ships stopped short of entering the harbor, and secured at anchorage.

The Harbor

Aymond and his team jogged south around the buildings, along Trident Way, dodging Zeds as they passed, sometimes simply pushing them down on the run before one could take a bite. Leaving the pavement and running out onto the beach, the Marines passed the training stations in place on the sand for the BUD/S classes: the pull-up bars, ropes, and the obstacle course. They ran out onto the narrow southern section of Coronado before crossing the roadway to crawl out onto the eastern beach. The four of them formed a loose circle, each of the members facing outward, lying flat on the sand so they could hold security and stay hidden, then began figuring out where the explosions came from and what they were for. The binoculars that Aymond had weren't a strong enough magnification for this purpose, but he could see smoke and debris in the air across the harbor on the mainland side, north of their position, on the other side of the Coronado Bridge.

Explosions erupted northeast of Aymond's location. He rolled to his back and saw an aircraft passing high overhead, the contrails giving away the location. Even with the binoculars, it was hard to tell what sort of aircraft it was; twin engine with swept wings, very large, most likely a heavy bomber. The rolodex of aircrafts in Aymond's mind flipped through hazy images of aircraft that matched a similar model, part of his long ago Force Recon training workup. He couldn't remember the name of the aircraft, but was sure it was an old Soviet design, or maybe Chinese.

The Beach

The explosions surprised all four of the Marines on the roof of the small building. The air-grinding sound of large, turbo-prop aircraft engines replaced the rolling sound of the bombing run. Into their view came a tight formation of what looked to be strangely shaped C-130s. They approached from the west at a low altitude, passing north of the watch. Happy rolled to his back, keeping the aircraft in his binoculars as they flew past the harbor. Barely visible in the setting sun, round canopies sprouted by the hundreds in the air behind the aircraft. Happy keyed his radio twice, clicking on the frequency the "return to FOB" signal. It was answered with two clicks; they were in trouble, serious trouble.

The Compound

Ski and his team made it inside the fence and under cover before Aymond returned. Within half an hour, two of the team members lay under tarps to keep them hidden while giving security from the rooftop of the main building.

Sporadic gunfire could be heard in the distance, barely audible across the harbor. Aymond rallied his team together to compare notes of their very quick recon patrol. The sound of large jet aircraft turning "base to final" for landing whined loudly overhead as they passed.

"Things we know: One, we suffered a major attack on CONUS. Two, the spraying aircraft appeared to be Russian or Chinese. Three, the bombing runs were made by Russian or Chinese heavy bombers. Four, there are four Panamax container ships flying Chinese flags in anchorage at the entrance to the harbor. Five, paratrooper mass drop happened across the harbor, most likely at the civilian airfield, and six, my guess is the heavy jet traffic overhead is strategic airlift.

"Things we don't know: Everything. Right now, I'm assuming that this is a hostile invasion force and we are vastly outnumbered. Give me your thoughts, guys."

"Chief. Use darkness tonight to traverse the harbor and conduct recon on the airfield."

"My thoughts too, Hammer. Anyone else?"

"We mine the Panamax ships now, before they have a chance to enter the harbor and offload what is likely the invading force's long term resupply ... probably more ships en route already. Isolate their supply chain and end it."

"Good, Kirk. I want you to prep that mission with your fire team. Hold off on launch until we verify hostile intent with reconnaissance across the bay."

"Chief, we need to tell someone about this."

"Who, Ski?"

"I don't know, Chief, but we need to figure out a way to contact someone."

"Yes, I agree. Start coming up with something that will work, but for now, we need to focus on our immediate threat."

"Kirk, prep your mission to the freighters. They'll most likely sail into the harbor after dawn, but instead of leaving a deep water harbor open for their use, I want to shut them down at the mouth, by North Island. If it is an invading force, we can't just annoy them, we have to fuck them and take away supply access."

"Aye, Chief." Kirk walked off to the containers holding all the gear boxes.

"Hammer, put together your fire team. Put your mission together; at this point we have to assume it is just us and only us on this one ... check the gear. If the MK 25s are in working order, use the rebreathers and a CRRC, if any of the motors still work on those rubber boats. Worst case, get one of the fucking BUD/S Zodiacs and paddles and make it happen tonight."

"Hoorah, Chief." Hammer and the rest of the team members jogged to the gear storage to start testing the Draeger rebreathers, to find one of the Combat Rubber Raiding Craft, and hopefully one of the SEAL training cadre's side-by-side ATVs to pull it to the water. Referred to as the MK 25 by the Navy, Force Recon and MARSOC used them extensively as well as the SEAL Teams. Like SCUBA, they gave operators underwater operational capabilities, but unlike SCUBA, they were closed-circuit and made no bubbles in the water to give away a team's position. The problem was their limitations for time and depth.

Cortez, CO

Three hours after sunset, Bexar stood in the shadows of the open glass doors of the middle school, watching the road. One patrol had already driven by, but didn't stop. It was an ancient-looking Ford truck with three men in it, a large machine gun that Bexar didn't recognize mounted in the bed. Cliff's truck was parked in the courtyard between the back of the building and the baseball field, well-hidden from the passing patrols.

Pushing a cart with a box full of glass bottles from the lab, each wrapped in a towel and filled halfway with liquid, and another sealed glass vial sitting in a glass bottle, Cliff and Chivo waved at Bexar to follow, and out the back doors to their truck they went.

"So what's the deal with the bottles in the bottles?"

"Bexar, ever see a video where someone drops Mentos into a diet cola before?"

"Yeah."

"It's like that, but with more fizz, oh, and fires, except our Mentos are sealed in glass that will break when we throw it ... or shoot it."

Bexar nodded at Cliff's explanation. He still had no idea exactly what the special cocktail was, but they had ten bottles of it. Chivo sat in the bed of the truck with the box of explosives, Bexar sat in the cab with Cliff, and they left, slowly rounding the corner of the school, towards the church of bodies.

"What's the deal with this town? There aren't any walking corpses wandering around."

"My best guess is the cult spent a considerable amount of time eradicating the majority of them, at least the ones not trapped in homes."

A few minutes later, the truck stopped at the front of the church. Bexar started to climb out, but Cliff stopped him. "Hang on a minute; Chivo will do this and then we move."

Chivo climbed out with one of the glass bottles, opened the door to the church, and pitched it underhand into the sanctuary, where the outer bottle and inner vial broke with a crash, followed by a loud pop and flames lapping the side of a blood-stained wooden pew. Chivo propped the front door open with a rock from the parking lot so the fire could breath and climbed back into the bed of the truck. Cliff drove across the street and parked the truck in a driveway two houses away from the main road. The three of them climbed out of the truck and used the shadows to walk to the manufactured home sitting across the street from the church. With some hushed words and subtle pointing, Chivo explained how an L-ambush was set and worked, before running across the street to set the other side of the trap.

Ten minutes later, the heat from the fully engulfed church warmed the cold spring air, and felt hot on Bexar's face. He lay prone across his rifle, behind a tree in the yard. The first patrol showed up to the church, the same that Bexar had seen passing the middle school. They stopped for a moment then sped away. Looking right and across the yard at Cliff, he raised a finger to imply: "Wait a minute."

They didn't have to wait long. Three trucks arrived, nine men total, each of them armed. They stood in the street, talking while looking at the church. Bexar couldn't hear what they were saying, but he guessed the conversation followed the lines of, "How did this happen?" and "What do we do now?" Following the animated conversation between the men, the one whom appeared to be the leader, (although it would be hard to tell from their matching uniforms of white button-down shirts, black ties, and camouflage field jackets), pointed to the homes around the church. The men fanned out from the church in four pairs, each heading towards a different home to search for the saboteurs they believed they had in their midst.

Chivo took the first shot, his metered firing tempo taking careful aim with each shot. Cliff and Bexar immediately joined, each taking shots in their assigned fields of fire. The targets tried to return fire and retreat, letting loose with full-auto bursts with their M4 rifles, emptying entire magazines of ammo into nothing as they died. The leader dropped to the ground and began crawling towards the closest truck; his eight comrades had been quickly killed before they could return any accurate fire. He was not entirely sure where the ambush was coming from. Chivo fired, striking the man in the leg. His knee erupted in a shower of blood, stopping the man just feet from the side of the closest truck. Chivo fired again, striking the man in the shoulder—deliberately aimed shots that would eventually kill the man, but hopefully hold him to the ground in pain for a few moments first. Cliff and Bexar jogged from their positions across the street, Chivo holding cover as they approached the fallen man, writhing in pain on the pavement, shattered bone and blood on the road around him.

The strong heat of the fire burned against Bexar's skin. A bright orange glow illuminated the man as the blood and fat of the undead survivors popped and smoked in the fire behind them.

"How many more of you are left?"

The man shook his head. Cliff put his foot on the man's ruined knee and applied pressure. "Tell me how many more of you are left!"

"Three—including The Prophet."

"Are they in the elementary school?"

Gasping, he cried, "YES! God help me!"

Cliff raised his rifle slightly to kill the man, but Bexar swatted the barrel away. Before Cliff could respond, Bexar pointed behind them. Most of the dead cult members were reanimating and beginning to stand. "Fuck this guy, let his brothers have him."

Bexar drew his pistol and shot the man in the other knee and shoulder, rendering him unable to move or defend himself, and walked away, around the approaching dead and back towards their own truck. Cliff watched him striding off before walking over to join him.

Chivo jogged from his spot to Bexar. "What was that, mano?"

"He didn't deserve a mercy kill; he deserves his brothers' hunger."

"That's fucked up."

"Yeah, well, so are they. Fucking 8-ball is neutral, buddy. If you're going to play it, be prepared to lose. They don't get to sacrifice innocent people for their own shitty religious beliefs, then get to play the shot they left on the table. Now we fucking end this and go home."

Cliff joined Chivo, who stopped walking to allow Bexar to go ahead. He climbed into the passenger seat of the truck and shut the door.

"Dude, what the hell is wrong with your friend? He's unhinged."

"No, I think he gets it. They flipped his switch. He didn't even know he *had* a switch, but now it's flipped, and we just have to keep him alive long enough to teach him what we know, how to control it."

Cliff shrugged and climbed into the truck. Chivo jumped into the bed and they drove east, towards the school.

Groom Lake, NV

Bill had taken to sleeping on a cot in the radio hut. Civilians, other HAMs, had cobbled together HF radios out of their resourcefulness and tenacity, so survivor first-contacts were becoming more frequent, adding more pins to the map. But he also figured that they should have heard from the mission group that left the SSC for Cortez. Specific instructions had been passed on how to operate his own HF radio left behind in the middle school, if their other communications failed. The team should know that the SATCOM was down, and they should have checked in on the radio upon arriving. He didn't know what was wrong, since by his estimate, they should have arrived by yesterday.

At least for now, the secure IRC connection between Groom Lake and the SSC was operating. Jake checked in every hour or more, anxious to hear news of the rest of his group, including his wife. Also, being the elected "Mayor of Groom Lake" for the civilian population, it was his duty to check in. He'd just returned from the quarantine and his interview with the new arrivals. Everyone's past skills and assets were noted, as well as details about their overland routes and the countryside. That helped Jake plan where people could best fit in the civilian population and what jobs they could help with. It also helped Wright and his team plan safer routes for other survivors trying to make the journey. One important note he'd made from his interview with Jessie, the pregnant woman from Texas, was that the signs on the highway were too vague. He would have to talk to Wright about that in the morning. Now well past midnight, he sat in the radio hut with Bill, drinking coffee, unable to sleep, anxious for a report from Cortez.

Cortez, CO

Parking the truck between mobile homes on Washington Street, the team climbed over the low fence into the schoolyard, creeping through the shadows towards the back of the school. They could set fire to the school and wait for people to come out, but there were only three of them; the remaining cult members could exit in a direction they couldn't see and then disappear. The decision was made early on that if able, they would make quiet entry into the school and slowly search for the rest of the members.

The firebombs were left in the bed of the truck, too dangerous to carry on an operation like this. They planned to return and retrieve them if needed. Chivo picked the lock to the door on the south end of the building, pulled it open, and then picked the padlock holding the chain between the crash bars of the doors. Five minutes after walking to the door, they quietly crept inside, moving in a three-man formation that was similar to what Bexar had learned as a cop in active shooter training scenarios. His nightmare was always that he would be doing this for real in an elementary school, but he'd never guessed it would be with people like Chivo and Cliff, or in a situation even remotely like this. He imagined the scenario as rushing towards the sound of gunfire in the school, a hard lesson from Columbine, now taught to law enforcement across the country.

The classroom doors were propped open; some of the rooms were obviously used as living quarters, others arranged in a strange manner for purposes unknown. Each one they passed was quietly checked and found empty. Farther down the hall, the dancing flicker of candlelight skipped across the floor and walls, a dim beacon calling to the three men in the darkness. Their approach slowed as they neared the final corner, and the source of the light. Chivo knelt and cautiously peeked around the corner. He gave hand signals to his team, holding up his right hand, four fingers up: *four people*. He pointed right, one finger, and left, one finger: *a man to the right, and to the left.* Finally, he pointed forward, two fingers: *and two in the middle, then covered his eyes to indicate he couldn't see everything.*

Chivo pulled back slowly from the corner, standing, first in the chalk. Bexar, in the middle position, duplicated Chivo's hand signals to Cliff, who had been holding rear security and facing away. Cliff nodded and put his left hand on Bexar's right shoulder. Bexar put his left hand on Chivo's left shoulder. Cliff squeezed Bexar's shoulder. *Ready* ... Bexar squeezed Chivo's shoulder ... *ready* ... Chivo lifted his head back ... *set,* then nodded sharply—*GO!*

Chivo stepped through the door, turning left to cover his slice of the room, the cafeteria. The man in front of him started to raise his rifle—Chivo fired twice, both rounds striking the man in the forehead. Chivo's muzzle was already sweeping right before the man's body landed on the ground. Bexar stepped straight through the doorway to the right. The man in front of him also raised his rifle. Bexar fired six times, hitting the man in the chest and neck twice. The man fell to the floor, dropping the rifle to clutch his neck, already gurgling blood. He would die soon. Almost a dozen men stood in the room, all facing one man standing at an altar. The three of them fired and moved rapidly, striking each of the worshipers either center mass or in the head. One by one, in a blink of an eye, all the men except the priest were down or dead.

All three of them turned, rifles pointing at the last man standing in the room. Wearing white robes, a table in front of him with a small body tied to it, he dipped a gold chalice into the body cavity, lifted it over his head, and poured the contents on his head. Blood.

"You men will repent, for my prophecy is true; judgment has come, in the ancient heart of man blood flows of ancestor warriors of God ..."

A single shot echoed in the room, Bexar firing once, his round striking the prophet in the head, a single hole just above the left eye. The man fell to the floor dead. The child's body on the table writhed against the ropes, dead eyes staring at them, teeth snapping, hoping to find living flesh. Chivo fired once and ended the little girl's fate of living death.

Searching the rest of the school, they found the cult's arms cache, an incredible amount of ammo, wrapped pallets of MREs, and a dozen wooden cases of rockets for the RPGs. Silently they walked out of the school the way they'd come, back to the truck, which they drove to the front of the school, carrying the box with the rest of the firebombs. After loading the bed of the truck with as much ammo and MREs as they dared to weigh the old suspension with, they tossed the firebombs in the hallways and the cafeteria.

"Once the fire reaches those crates of RPGs they should go up spectacularly. We probably don't want to be standing around for this one. Cliff, I still have Bill's instructions. We need to check in before leaving."

"You're right, Jake has a right to know. We go there first, then back to the house. At first light we leave for the SSC."

Chivo nodded. Bexar ignored the conversation and sat in the truck's passenger seat, lost in his thoughts. A short drive later and the three of them climbed out of the truck. Bexar helped Chivo take the battery out from under the hood and carried it into the middle school. Following the directions in his notepad, Chivo hooked up the radio and tuned it to the correct frequency.

CHAPTER 35

The first fire team—wearing wetsuits from the SEAL Teams' gear lockers, their tactical gear over the wetsuits, holding rifles, their swim fins, masks, and with the Draeger systems already on—drove the only working side-by-side ATV they could find. They pulled a trailer holding the only CRRC with a working motor they could find through the gate and across the wide roadway and east towards Glorietta Bay. This mission was cutting it close for gear, but all of them knew they would not fail; they *could* not fail. Clouds obscured the moon, making for a dark night, but also making for conditions the MARSOC Marines were happy to have. Riding the ATV through a small park and past an empty children's play place, they drove the ATV, the trailer, and the CRRC to the water's edge. Slipping silently into the dark water, the CRCC's motor coughed quickly to life and the team was off, lying on the gunwales as they sped across the water.

Hammer piloted the CRRC across the harbor and past the Coronado Bridge, gliding quickly across the water to the USS Midway. The aircraft-carrier-turned-floating-museum was as close as they dared bring their craft. Mooring the rubber boat to the rudder on the southern side of the ship, the team slipped over the gunwales and into the still water. Swim fins kicking, they kept in formation and followed the compass heading on their dive boards. Swimming under the anchored and abandoned sailboats in the harbor, they quickly found the rock edge of the harbor. Slowly the team broke the surface of the water, the suppressors on the end of their M4 rifles leading their progress. Passing the moored sailing boats, the team silently made their way out of the water and across North Harbor Drive to the overgrown triangle of a median, using the grass and palm trees as cover. This time, equipped with night-vision-equipped spotting scopes from the gear lockers, the team was able to make better use of their reconnaissance time.

With one man on the scope, and the other three holding a defensive perimeter, no one said a word. Maintaining their highly trained discipline, the team held still, secreted in the tall grass as clusters of undead shambled by. Although suppressed, the rifles still made a lot of noise and the muzzle flash would give their position away. Contact with the enemy, living or undead, was to be avoided at all costs. This was the sort of operation that the men had cut their teeth on in Force Recon before rotating into their positions in MARSOC.

Happy, propped up slightly to peer through the spotting scope, made mental notes as they waited. Hammer kept an eye on the dive watch attached to his board. They needed to be back at the compound by sunrise, and they had two more hours before they had to leave to make the swim back to their boat in time.

Through the scope, Happy watched as a large tactical airlift jet was unloaded. Around the flight line were the paratroops; at least he assumed they were the paratroops. *If we'd stopped at the Recruit Depot we would be in the middle of that shit right now.*

The troops had improved their emplacements, but in addition to what looked like crew-served weapons were what appeared to be large radar panels, sweeping in short arcs back and forth. There were ten of them arranged in a semi-circle facing away from the offloading cargo aircraft. The equipment looked vaguely familiar, probably Russian, but the men didn't look Russian. They looked Asian.

Fuck. Chinese, the PLA.

Slowly adjusting the scope's view back towards the radar panels, Happy watched the crew manning it. Beside each was a cart that looked to be a generator for power. The panels were mounted on trailers, and each had an operator manning a control panel on the outside of the trailer. Scanning slowly outward, he saw undead shambling towards the improved positions from the flight line and terminal, approximately thirty yards from the emplacements. As the panel swept across the Zeds' path, the damned things fell to the ground, unmoving.

Holy shit, they're zapping the Zeds with that thing.

Happy tapped Hammer's leg with his foot to gain his attention. Slowly turning his head, Hammer looked at Happy, who made a small circular motion with his finger. *Time to go.* Hammer nodded slightly and passed the signal to the others. Slowly Happy stowed the advanced spotting scope in his waterproof pack, and the four of them slowly made their way to the water, slipping beneath the inky surface for their journey back to their improvised FOB.

Groom Lake, NV

"Bill, wake up!"

Bill sat up on the cot, blinked, and looked at the airman.

"Bill, it's Cliff. HHe's made contact, it's spotty but it's up right now."

"OK, would you get Jake for me, and the major? I'll take the radio."

Bill spoke with Cliff and asked him to stand by for Wright and Jake. Ten minutes later, both of them entered the room and Wright spoke into the radio mic. "OK Lazarus 1, I guess our rescue team made it to your location since you're making contact. What's your situation, over."

"Part of the team, Chivo and Bexar made it. The others were KIA en route. Is Jake in the room, over?"

"Yes, we have a full house, over."

"There were no survivors. The cult killed all of them. We neutralized the cult, and Wright, you have command. We are returning to the SSC per my mission protocols, over."

"Acknowledged Lazarus 1, safe journey, out."

Jake hung his head in his hands. His people, his wife, they were all dead. Bill gave him a hug.

Then Jake leaped to his feet. "Holy shit, Jessie! Bexar! Wright, get Bexar on the radio!" Bill nearly fell over, startled by Jake's outburst.

"Lazarus 1, Lazarus 1, respond."

Cortez, CO

"Well, that's the end there, I wouldn't want to be Jake right now."

"Who's Jake?"

"He's the leader of the group that was here. His wife was one of those left behind in the original rescue mission, one of the ones killed by the cult."

Bexar ignored the conversation as he reached to unhook the truck's battery from the radio so they could drive to the safe house and get ready to leave, stopping when the speaker barked to life again.

Cliff walked back to the desk and keyed the mic. "Go ahead Groom Lake, over."

"Is Bexar with you? Put him on the radio, over."

Looking annoyed, Cliff said, "Stand by, over." Then he turned to Bexar. "They want to talk to you." He handed the mic to Bexar, who looked perplexed.

"This is Bexar."

"Bexar, Jessie is here, she made it from Texas, she is safe ... she's pregnant!"

Bexar dropped the mic and sat on the floor, the room spinning around him.

"He copies, Groom Lake, anything else, over?"

"No, Groom Lake out."

Bexar sat on the floor while Cliff unhooked the car battery.

"I have to ... we have to go there." Bexar looked up at him.

"No, my mission, my rules, we go to the SSC."

Bexar stood. "Fuck you, fuck your mission, fuck you for telling us to go to Groom Lake in the first place." He punched Cliff in the face.

Cliff stumbled back and swept Bexar's leg out from under him, then drew his pistol and pointed it at Bexar, who was lying on his back, facing the pistol.

"This mission, this country, this is more important than you! You hit me again and you won't live to see my pistol, you will just die."

"No, Cliff."

Cliff looked up at Chivo, who held his rifle pointing toward his former trainer officer and his friend.

"Not this time, Cliff, you're wrong."

"So this is how it's going to be?"

"I ride with Bexar."

Groom Lake, NV

Jake, after the outburst of good news for Bexar, sat on Bill's cot, his old friend sitting beside him. Wright looked at the clock on the wall. *0400, guess I'm up for the day now.*

The airman at the console cycled through the HF frequency ranges again, now that the waiting game for Cliff was over. That guy had always creeped him out. It was just as well he was going to Texas instead of coming back. This was *their* facility now.

Coronado, CA

Aymond smiled at Ski and the corporals. "Gentlemen, if I had the authority all three of you would be promoted on the spot."

. 219 .

"Thanks Chief, I expect it to reflect in my pay stub at the end of the month," someone catcalled from the group.

"Now we have to do something about it. If we can't make contact with anyone we have to assume we're on our own and we have to fight the Chinese ... those bastards attacked us, now they've invaded. We will go on to the end. We will fight them on the seas and harbor, we will defend our land whatever the cost may be. We will fight in the streets, in the city and on the beach ... we will not surrender, we will carry on the struggle until the last of us is dead or we have beaten the enemy from our land."

WINCHESTER: RUE

PROLOGUE

March 15, Year 1

Peaceful dust floated in the air as time stopped around them. First, nothing to see except the sky through the windshield, the truck's engine growling in protest as the horizon rose into view to be replaced by roadway below. The truck shook. Bexar could see each piece of gravel in the median in finite detail, the cracks in the pavement, the sun-baked lane markings. Everything in bright vivid colors. The world around him paused. Jessie, Keeley, Malachi, Jack ... all of their faces flashed in front of him, a sped-up movie, the good times and the bad, his wedding, digging Keeley's grave, it all raced through his mind. The serene peace burned away with hot anger, anger that he couldn't catch a break, that every time he made any progress he was slapped down by the world in which they now lived. Jessie was alive, she was going to have his child, their second ... their only, and now it was all taken away from him ... again.

The long brown hood of the truck inched towards the pavement. In the distance Bexar heard yelling; at the last second he realized that it was his voice before time violently snapped forward with a hard scream of twisting metal and shattering glass. Everything went black.

CHAPTER 1

Cortez, CO
March 12, Year 1

"December 26th changed everything. Everyone had plans, everyone had a future, and all of that was ripped from us by assholes like you! I don't give a fuck about you. I don't give a fuck about this country; the fucking dead own it all now. All I want is to get to my wife and try to do right by my family this time." Bexar glared at Cliff.

"What about you, Chivo, after everything you're going to ride off with this cop for his family?" Cliff turned from Bexar to Chivo.

"My family was my teammates, Cliff. They're at the gates waiting for me. Think about it as paying up karma for the two decades of duty served."

"Fine, you guys met the President, you know with our help she can rebuild what's left. She needs our help, though. Groom Lake is a damned zoo. The Osiris operation plan was to put up the big beacon of hope and I realize now that was wrong. I've had to clear that dammed hole in the ground of the dead twice now, and if you go then you'll have to do it again as well. The problem is that more and more people are showing up. Clint is right, and that's why the SCC underground complex in Texas is where we go. Locate, organize, and deploy what is possibly left of the military, take the country back one town at a time. Just like Denver, the bunker in Groom Lake is a mausoleum of politics and bullshit, a secure place to house your corpse as it bumps into the walls for the rest of eternity."

"Look mano, I'm not saying you're wrong, just that you're an asshole. Getting Bexar to his pregnant wife is the *right* thing to do."

Bexar peeked out the slit of a window visible from the fortifications Cliff had made to the house. "Guys, the sun is already getting low. The debate is useless. We have two trucks, we have two directions. Split it and get."

Cliff nodded, staring at Bexar. "Just like that? Fine, but slow it down. We leave at first light. Traveling at night is stupid. We'll have time to split the gear and prep the trucks ... Chivo, you're making a mistake, you know. Let the cop drive to his family and share their tomb in Groom Lake. Come with me, we can use a guy like you."

"You've known me for a long time. Hell, you fucking taught me, but I'm telling you that we need to make things right for Bexar and his family. We do one then do the other. What's the rush? Why one or the other? The country is already dead, and a few extra days won't change that."

Cliff turned and walked out of the room without another word.

Coronado, CA

Michael Happy, Chuck Ski, and Peter Snow lay prone in a defensive position in the tall brush of the overgrown golf course. Happy faced towards the interior of the island, face painted and strips of ratty burlap hanging off the suppressor of the M4 SOPMOD rifle. He watched carefully, breathing slowly, ears straining to hear the first snap of a twig, swish of grass or any other indication that danger approached. Ski and Snow faced towards the mouth of the bay, suppressed M4 rifles ready to be deployed. Their primary weapons were the two spotting scopes mounted on low tripods and draped with the handmade ghillie suit each wore. The three of them were part of the remaining members of the Marine Special Operations Team, or MSOT, which fought their way across California to San Diego to find ruins overrun by the dead and their country being invaded by Chinese and Korean forces.

Off shore, four large Panamax ships sat in anchorage, the Chinese flags fluttering lazily at each of their sterns.

"Are there even cranes for the CONEXes in the harbor?" Ski spoke in a hushed whisper, not so much a spoken phrase as much as a really loud thought.

"Maybe one or two. I thought this was where new cars were driven off the ship, that they used Long Beach or somewhere else for ships like those."

Not even ten feet away, Happy couldn't hear the conversation; the shadows grew long across his back as the sun set out to sea. An hour after sunset the three of them would slither back to the wrought-iron fence that separated the naval base from the public beach, where their unconventional transportation, three bicycles, awaited. *Assuming some punk hasn't stolen them.* Happy's mind flashed to the image of a Zed riding a bicycle, which was both hilarious and, for some reason, terrifying.

"Maybe they have some sort of other plan to unload the containers?"

"I doubt it, those cranes are fucking huge." Snow used his spotting scope to watch the decks and bridges of the anchored ships; he couldn't see what Ski was viewing, but on a small waterproof notebook he made quick notes about the number of men and what they were doing.

The sun slid into the ocean, the sky glowing red as if in protest to the night. The ear pieces each man wore for their radios clicked once. Ski keyed his mic twice as a silent response. *We're still alive, we'll be home soon, have dinner waiting for me, dear.*

Dinner. Another night, another MRE, bang out a couple hours of sleep and rotate into site security while another patrol heads out for the night shift. Ski sighed.

Another heavy jet roared low over the mainland, landing to off-load at San Diego International Airport. More jet engines spooled up as an empty jet bounced down the runway and back towards China, they assumed, to return with more men, materials, and all the things they needed to stop.

"Why the civilian airport. Why not the Naval Air Station?"

"Fuck if I know, Ski."

SSC, Ennis, TX

"Clint, honey, I understand, but we can't live underground forever. We're going to need to establish safe areas, places for agriculture, industry ... it won't be overnight. Hell, we're basically back to hoping a blacksmith is still alive, but those are the things this nation needs if we're going to reclaim it for the living."

"I don't disagree, but that isn't your job, Madam President ..."

"Oh now I'm 'Madam President'? Perhaps I should go put a bra on."

"No, Amanda, Christ, that's not what ... Damnit, look, I love you, but you *are* the President of the United States. You don't go establish safe zones, you go visit the safe zones after we have them established."

"We who, Clint? Who is left? We have one little enclave of people out in Nevada; they have contact with what, a few hundred people? How many people are left to do the job for us? They don't exist anymore. They are up there on the surface, doomed to a fate worse than death, because at least in death it is over."

"Fine, but not yet. Wright said they established contact. Cliff and what is left of the rescue team will be back soon. That's their job. Your job is to lead, my job is to help you do it and keep you ... keep your sexy ass safe so you can lead."

CHAPTER 2

Groom Lake, NV
March 13, Year 1

"Bexar, *my* Bexar is alive?"

"Yes, but he's in Colorado."

Jessie sat on the cot, tears streaming down her face. She was still in the new arrival quarantine area, where she had to remain until she was allowed into the main section of the compound. During that transition, a woman who introduced herself as "Brit Sanchez from *the* Mayor's office" came to visit with her, explaining how the facility worked and gently finding out what skills Jessie had and could contribute. She'd also brought the good news.

Jessie wanted to believe Bexar had to be alive. She'd never wanted to stop believing and now it was true, her Bexar was coming home. "When will he arrive here?"

"I don't know. They made contact with us and we have no way to communicate with him or his team."

"His team?"

Brit nodded. "He was attached to a Special Forces team sent to rescue Cliff after he was shot down in Colorado."

"Shot down, like in a plane?"

"Yes."

"But how …"

She held up her hand, stopping Jessie. "I really don't know. The operations side of the facility keeps to themselves and we only know what Jake or Bill tells us. The Air Force guys are nice, but they keep to themselves ... you said you were a teacher before?"

Jessie wiped her face with the back of her hand. "Yes, I taught Algebra and Calculus at the high school."

The woman smiled. "That is great. We don't really have many children who fit that age group or need right now, but could you teach adult education courses in the subjects? Jake, and the major agrees, that all of us should take time to learn as much as we can, that we're responsible for passing along all our knowledge to the next generation."

"Sure, yes, well that makes sense."

Sarah sat on the cot across from Jessie, watching the conversation and smiling. Her friend had finally been given the good news she deserved. Sarah looked over at her daughter, Erin, who sulked in her spot across the room. Sarah wasn't sure why the change, but Erin hadn't been herself since they arrived, not that she had really been her old self before they arrived either. Her little girl's eyes were cold, sharp like a cobra's, guarded. She looked like a hardened combat vet even though she wasn't even old enough to get a driver's license.

Coronado, CA

"Chief, we don't know why those big container ships are even here, but Ski brought up a good point: I don't think they have the right kind of cranes to offload a ship like that here."

Master Gunnery Sergeant Jerry Aymond, referred to as Chief by his team, sat at the table cleaning his M4 while listening to the patrol report, the sound of cargo jets landing and taking off a constant in the distance. Snow flipped through his small green notepad, and then looked up. "Not a single man was armed."

Aymond looked up. "What?"

"On the container ships, none of the men I saw were armed. They had no guards posted, nothing. From what we could tell they were just Merchant Marine. If they're PLA they weren't even in uniform. Don't they have a dock here?"

"Several, including the berths for cruise ships."

Snow looked at Ski. "A dock for the cruise ships? Shit if I know, I was never able to get enough time off to go on a cruise." He smirked at Aymond.

Aymond ignored the jab. "Assume they have a way to offload those ships. What are we going to do to deny it access to the harbor? And gentlemen, let me remind you that every one of those planes is full of people with gear who want to take our country from us. Sure, it's full of Zeds, but fuck'em, it's still ours to have."

CHAPTER 3

Cortez, CO
March 13, Year 1

Snow dusted the town overnight. Bexar stamped his feet, cold. He longed for Texas. No, not Texas, but the life we had before in Texas ... I need my wife, I need to hold her in my arms and ask for forgiveness. If I had planned better, if we'd had a better bug-out plan Keeley would be alive. So would Malachi and Amber, Jack, Sandra, ... no, damnit, you don't know that. Breath, focus.

Two houses down from Cliff's makeshift fortress, Bexar walked up to the front door and absentmindedly pushed the doorbell, turning to stand at the side of the doorframe, his finger covering the peep hole. He stood for a moment before realizing how ridiculous this all was. Like he was still a cop doing a knock and talk at a drug house. Bexar shook his head and checked the door handle. It turned and the door opened easily. The flat scent of stale death oozed out of the cold house. Pistol holstered and rifle slung, Bexar held his heavy hand-made CM Forge blade and decided to take Cliff's advice.

Cliff. Fuck that guy. If we hadn't talked to him on the radio, if we didn't try to flee we might all still be in The Basin and living the good life eating javelina and mule deer. The last guy who pointed a weapon at me is still in prison ... maybe. Bexar thought about how bad it would have been locked in a prison when the EMP hit followed by the virus. Using the butt of the knife handle, he tapped solidly on the open front door and took three steps off the porch, waiting past the broken and missing porch railing.

Eh, screw'em all. Catch and release, the turds go to prison then come out and go back to slinging dope, stealing shit, to their old gangs with new skills learned from the other turds in prison ...

Bexar's focus was ripped forward by the child that stumbled out of the house and fell off the porch face-first into the yard. Without a word he plunged the heavy blade into the back of her skull. Dark, pus-filled blood seeped out from the girl's ruined skull, staining the snow. Bexar rocked the knife back and forth to get it loose and turned in time to see big brother come off the porch. Turning quickly, Bexar straight-armed the teenager in the chest and away from him, took two steps and planted the knife into the flat, unfocused right eye, cratering the socket, and popping the eyeball like a large zit.

Wiping the blade off on the teenager's filthy jeans, Bexar stepped back onto the porch and tapped on the door again, waiting and listening with focus this time, but nothing stirred. Slowly stepping into the house, Bexar swept the dark corners in the house with his small flashlight. The dried-out remains of what was probably a large dog greeted him in the middle of the living room, the carpet stained dark with blood. It was hard to tell what it had been, but the kids' last meal appeared to have been their friendly family pet.

Turning right, Bexar opened the interior door to the garage, stepped through all the piled, boxed, and random storage of knick-knacks that families everywhere relegate to the garage instead of throwing away, pulled the release and lifted the garage door. The kids still lay motionless in the snow, the radius of dark clotted blood expanding from their heads.

Light filtered through the open garage door, and the search for a gas can was on. No mower, no shovels, no nothing ... Bexar glanced through the window on the back wall and into the backyard where a shed stood open, lawn mower visible in the shadows. Tilting his head back, Bexar looked at the ceiling, closed his eyes, and took a deep breath. Stupid mistakes are found in the details and those details will kill you. Chivo's words rang in his head. Bexar knew Chivo was right, and if he was going to live long enough to scoop up his wife into his arms and disappear to somewhere safe with his family, the details mattered. He headed out to the shed that he should have looked for before going in the house.

A few minutes later, Bexar placed a big plastic fuel can down at the end of the driveway. His goal was to gather enough for thirty gallons per truck, what he guessed would be a full tank of gas for each. This can contained five gallons out of the sixty he needed to account for. Trudging across the snow-covered lawn to the next house, this time Bexar walked through the backyard to check for a shed.

No joy. With a deep breath, he walked around the low brick wall on the porch of the patio-style home, pulled the screen door open and checked the door handle.

Coronado, CA

"Chief, we have a plan, well, two plans really." Kirk looked at Davis, who produced a piece of copy paper with a crude sketch on it.

"Sorry Chief, I tried calling Battalion I.T., but apparently PowerPoint won't run on these computers the Navy use."

Aymond stared at Davis, expression flat. It was funny; he knew it was funny, and if the situation wasn't as bad as it was he probably would have laughed, quietly.

Davis nudged Kirk, who continued, "Anyways, it isn't enough that we scuttle the ships, we have to deny any further access for any possible ships in the future. We have to run two of them into the channel by the sub docks, get them turned and down them right at the narrowest point. Like a blockade that can't move until the hulls are cut for scrap."

"OK, not a bad idea, but an op like that would take two full teams, plus support. Maybe launch from the lockout of a converted missile submarine or a team insertion with a flight of Little Birds. How do you accomplish this task with no support, not enough men, and without getting our Chinese neighbors up our ass?"

Kirk flipped the piece of paper over. "That is where things get a little sporty, Chief. This op is going to be run sort of loose, but we'll wear our PT belts so you can promise the colonel we'll all be safe."

That drew a smirk from Aymond. The reflective PT belt, a glowing safety-band of freedom and safety, was loved by all with a rank of O-5 or higher, and hated by everyone who pulled a trigger for a living. "OK Kirk, break it down and tell me how you're going to achieve the impossible."

"We're Marines, Chief, we *are* the impossible."

"Fucking Rah, Chief."

The smirk was gone. Aymond was back to business, and the other two members of the team knew it. Kirk produced a notebook and started walking Aymond through each step and detail of the operation plan.

Cortez, CO

"This is it; all that I could scrape together, even what was left from our ambushed school bus."

While Chivo was out scrounging for ammo, and Cliff had done whatever it was that super-spooks did, Bexar had unhappily spent the morning kicking in doors of the houses in the neighborhood to pull together enough plastic fuel cans to give each truck thirty extra gallons, which he'd syphoned out of the abandoned vehicles ruined by the EMP. It was still better than dealing with Cliff.

Bexar looked at the plastic tote of ammo on the floor of the cold garage. He knew that Chivo would have found more if there was more, but the pickings looked slim when dividing it between three people for two separate journeys. Now returned from his morning-long scavenging expedition through the town, it was time to prep the truck he would use for the long journey ahead.

According to Cliff, they were roughly five hundred miles from Groom Lake, and over nine hundred miles from the SSC. The irony that each were paths the other had taken was not lost on the group. After the dust-up two days prior, which Cliff seemed to shrug off with no emotional attachment, the atmosphere was serious but nearly giddy.

"We have the shorter route; we can split it in a way to help you out. I have to warn you, Albuquerque is a cast-iron bitch." Chivo was completely serious; a massive swarm of the undead had collapsed a bridge out from under their group, killing Apollo and Lindsey in the process. Even thinking about that day and their "visit" to the strip club made Bexar feel a little hungover. Like the few times he'd visited strip clubs before the EMP hit, he'd immediately regretted the decision. The undead stripper had wanted a piece of him, and he and Chivo had drank too much. *Nothing all that different from the old days, except the stripper was a reanimate and wanted me for more than crispy twenties.*

Bexar grunted and walked to the door. "You two figure it out; I'm going to get the trucks ready."

They had two trucks, both of them ragged-out pieces of crap, and only one of them with a windshield. *I bet the jackass will take the truck with the windshield, after we came up here and saved his ass.* Bexar took another deep breath; he had to control his emotions. It was amazing that Chivo did it so well; it was like there was a light switch in his brain. *Emotions on, emotions off, emotions on, emotions off, wipe on, wipe off ...* "You're losing your damned mind, Bexar," he whispered to himself.

Kneeling down, he checked the tire pressure in the first tire before wondering how he would put air in the tires if they were low. He couldn't fathom trying to pump a tire up with a bicycle pump. Maybe they could find some of those CO2-cartridge-fired air pumps or a bunch of cans of fix-a-flat, but Bexar had always used the air compressor in his garage or at a service station to air up tires. His Wagoneer had a small air compressor that ran off of leads to the vehicle's battery, but that truck was destroyed and gone forever.

Bexar raised the hood, giving up on the internal debate about tires for the time being to check the oil and radiator fluid. While going door to door for fuel a few hours prior, Bexar had had the foresight to snag a few quarts of oil from one of the garages. Soon each truck was topped off, fueled, and had spare fuel cans in the beds of the trucks with sections of garden hose for syphoning tied to them.

The rag-tag war-wagons are ready. Now for ammo, food, water, and blankets ... an extra few of them if we end up with the wonder truck with no windshield. Bexar kicked the snow off his boots and walked back into the garage to find Chivo sitting on the floor, filling magazines for their M4s one round at a time.

"Where's Cliff?"

"Upstairs mano, packing for his cruise I guess."

SSC, Ennis, TX

Bra firmly in place, hair pulled back into a tight pony tail and sunglasses pushed up on her forehead, Amanda stood alone in the dim tunnel and pulled the bungee holder over the last M4 magazine on her chest rig. Along the outside wall of the outrageously large concrete-lined tunnel stood silent the equipment she knew would be needed to accomplish her plan. She was determined to fight and establish a toe-hold, however tiny, on the surface, knowing the acres and acres of farmland around and near the lake could be brought back into production. First with stable feed crops to help bring the cattle back into action, if there were any still left alive, then seasonal crops to feed the survivors she knew existed and had to help.

She estimated that her battle rattle weighed in at over fifty pounds, most of it consisting of loaded magazines for her rifle and pistol. This was a quick day trip, a patrol outside the protection of her underground fortress. The first task was to walk the park's fenceline, making notes of needed repairs. Once the small lakeside park was secure, then she could start branching out and expanding the perimeter in larger and larger concentric rings, leaving in place the barriers that would be multiple layers of protection. Even without the semi-trailer-mounted nuclear power stations, the SSC facility generated enough power from its own nuclear reactor to power a small city. The SSC would serve a purpose, even if it wasn't what Clint thought the purpose should be.

Amanda stopped at the metal rungs leading upward and topside. The facility diagrams and overhead map of the surface showed the emergency hatch overhead would open near the southern boat ramp. Before mounting the ladder, Amanda jumped up and down to check for any loose gear that might make noise. Satisfied she could maintain stealth, she twisted the lock of the suppressor on the end of the short-barreled M4 to check it was attached and pulled the charging handle back slightly to press-check that a round was in the chamber. The bolt carrier slid forward and, after a couple of taps on the assist, Amanda took a deep breath, let the rifle hang on the sling, and began the climb upwards.

The metal wheel on the hatch turned smoothly and, with a hydraulic hiss, the hatch rose upward and tilted to the side, the cold crisp March morning sunlight assaulting her eyes. Amanda pulled the sunglasses down and pulled herself out of the vertical tunnel and onto the surface.

The brown grass crunched quietly beneath her boots while she turned in place and scanned for any undead that posed an immediate threat. Satisfied she was alone and hidden in the trees for the moment, Amanda inhaled deeply and took in the smell of the lake, the trees, and the cold. The sun was beginning to warm the day. She hadn't been underground for all that long, but her mood instantly lifted with the sunlight and fresh air. Not completely confident that she could open the hatch if she closed it from the outside, Amanda left it open, chancing that a walking corpse could accidently fall in. If it did she would take care of it when she returned.

Amanda walked north to the short sandy shoreline and started towards the east. The highway bridge could be seen spanning the end of the lake ahead of her. She knew that she would eventually reach the pumping station, which was what controlled the holding pressure of nitrogen before Clint activated the facility. She could then follow the fenceline back north and along the edge of the farmland to the west. Amanda figured she had about an hour before Clint realized she was gone and might come looking for her, so she had no time to waste.

Groom Lake, NV

Jessie sat nude in a plastic chair she had brought into the women's shower room, which reminded her of a high school locker room shower, or like those she had seen on prison TV shows. No stalls, no privacy, just dozens of showerheads around the room and on pillars in the middle. With the chair positioned in the water flow, she never thought she would be so happy to shave her legs again. Her tummy was already starting to show a little; in a few short months she would have problems even reaching her calves. Never in her life had her leg hair grown to this length, but having experienced the far end of the women's rights movement over the last few months, it was really calming to take some time for herself. Jessie kept telling herself that she wasn't primping for Bexar's return like some high school sweetheart, but still, with everything she had been through, with all the fighting, the road-weary battle-hardened protective shell she had constructed to make it this far, she couldn't help it that her heart fluttered a little thinking of wrapping her arms around her husband, her lover again.

Sarah hung her towel on the rack and joined Jessie in the shower room, turning on the spigot next to her. "Getting all dolled up to see Bexar again?"

"Is it that obvious?"

"Honey, you haven't stopped smiling since you heard he was alive, and I don't blame you, but since we've met I don't think I really saw you smile."

"What about you? What are you going to do when we get out of quarantine, see about meeting a nice Air Force boy? God, I feel like we're about to get released from jail or something, talking about when we get out."

"No, Erin first. I've got to try getting my little girl back ... I don't know if that's possible."

"She loves you. I'm sure you can."

Sarah stopped washing and turned to face Jessie, "And she idolizes you, but you can see it in her eyes, like a switch flipped. My little deer hunter in pink, I'm afraid that girl is gone forever and the woman that replaced her is cold. No joy left, not since her father died, not since we had to fight our way across the country ... not after what she's seen and how many of those God-damned walking corpses she's put down."

Jessie stood to rinse off, looking down with her hand on the small growing baby bump. One tear escaped down her cheek before she flashed hot with anger. *Not for you, my little pea in the pod. I don't know how, but you're not going to grow up in a world of death, without joy or compassion.*

SSC, Ennis, TX

Amanda stood at the fenceline, looking at the open backyards of a small country neighborhood. A dozen reanimated corpses stumbled across the road and into the yard in front of her. Glancing around to make sure she didn't have any surprises, she took a kneeling position, propped her elbow on her leg, flipped the selector to single fire. A muffled crack broke the morning air, the closest undead's face exploding towards her in a black mist.

Surprised, she dropped into a prone shooting position. Amanda moved her rifle to find where the unexpected shot came from, only to see Clint walking down the narrow neighborhood street with his rifle up, death leaving the end of the rifle's suppressor with each careful squeeze of the trigger, each shot falling in cadence with each rolling footstep, each round finding its macabre target in a shower of shattered bone and dark rotten brain matter.

Amanda flipped the selector on the M4 to safe and rose to her feet, letting the rifle hang on the sling. She watched Clint down the last walking corpse before he walked to the fenceline where she stood.

"I told you not to come up here."

"And I told you that we have to start somewhere. Our nation's survival depends on the farms and farmers. The military can't give us crops of cotton to spin into new thread; they can't grow feed corn for our cattle ..."

Clint kissed her on the cheek. "I know, babe, but my mission is to protect you and coordinate the survival of our nation, not plow a field. Same for you."

"You're not going to stop me. You can keep working on your mission, but first the farmers fight, then the farmers farm. All of civilization was built on the back of agriculture and that is how it will be rebuilt. How about I make that my first Executive Order, what would you do then?"

"Your order would be law unless overturned by the Supreme Court."

"So be it, and take it up with them, after I find and appoint new people to the Court."

"Yes ma'am."

"Well, now that you're here, help me walk the fenceline. We start taking back our country by taking back this park. We'll take it step by step from there."

CHAPTER 4

Cliff stowed the small shortwave radio in his backpack. He couldn't transmit, he couldn't talk to anyone, but messages could be sent to him, if indirectly. The secondary number station was up and broadcasting. The first day of broadcasts gave the letter designator for the memorized pad cypher to be used the following day. The transcribed message was short, but it didn't need to be long. He didn't think it would come to this, but missions have to adapt as new intelligence is gathered, deciphered and analyzed. This mission, the new mission, he had to complete alone. He couldn't be followed, had to make sure he wasn't followed. Some state secrets had to be kept, even after the collapse of society just in case society rose again.

I could kill them ... but Chivo is right; Bexar should have the chance to get back to his wife. Besides, I never enjoyed putting down my own recruits. So distraction, something that will keep the two of them occupied but that they can work through. Something just enough to give me time and distance ... he unlocked the bedroom door and headed downstairs.

Cliff walked into the garage. "After all the help we gave the 'prophet' to see the light and then scrounging all we could find, we've got thirty fully topped-off magazines for the M4s and a small handful of loose rounds." Chivo started to interrupt but Cliff held up his hand, "To keep things aboveboard, we split things evenly. Each of us can have ten mags, you two can even keep the pocket change of ammo. Everyone has a topped-off pistol and complement of magazines, but that's all we had, right on the dot."

Chivo nodded and looked at Bexar, who looked at Cliff. "How are we going to split the trucks up?"

A slight glint of contempt flashed in Cliff's eyes. "I have the longer journey, so I'll take the one with the windshield, and you guys will have reached Groom Lake before I've even made it halfway. Chivo has the Berretta. How are you set for ammo with that big bitch?"

"I have about two dozen rounds left for it." The ridiculously large 50-caliber long-range sniper rifle had served Chivo well in The Basin, as similar rifles had in a number of clandestine missions during the past twenty years.

"Good, I have one of the Nikon spotting scopes, you guys take the other. The food we split three ways." Cliff pointed to the three duffle bags lumpy with canned goods and other non-perishable food stuffs. He glanced at his watch. "If you two leave now and shag ass you might make it halfway before sunset, but Yo-Yo motherfuckers."

Cliff picked up one of the bags of food and walked out of the garage, shutting the door behind him. Outside they heard one of the trucks start and idle for a moment in the driveway before two shots could be heard over the engine, followed by what sounded like an air horn.

"What the shit?" Bexar said to an empty garage, Chivo already running through the door with his rifle raised. Bexar followed quickly. There was a muffled shot and the air horn stopped, the silence now feeling louder than the horn blast had been.

Reaching the driveway, Bexar saw Chivo standing at the curb, rifle up and slowly turning in place, scanning every open direction. Their truck, the one with no windshield, sat with two flat tires, a punctured air horn in a can obvious in the snow of the front lawn.

"On your left," Bexar called as he raised his rifle and took a position next to Chivo, not knowing what threat his friend had seen, but without having to say so, taking his slice of the pie, his portion of the area to scan for threats. Bexar held his rifle at the low ready and slowly scanned left to right. "Seriously, fuck that guy, what is his problem?"

"Guess I should have shot him when I had the chance. His outlook is very simple; it's binary, on or off, one or zero. In his mind we weren't for him, following his plan, so we were now against him."

"Really? He's that simple? I thought you super-spooks were more intelligent than that."

"He's not a super-spook, he's a conditioned machine. If A then B, then C, otherwise go to plan E and F, it's very linear and that's how guys like him are trained."

"But he trained you."

"Sure, but I was Special Forces first, taught to be creative and adapt, be flexible to achieve a mission and that with new intel sometimes missions can change. That's why we were tasked with difference missions out there in the real world. He would never have been able to befriend the village elders in the 'Stan."

"Then what is your mission?"

"First to live long enough to find new wheels, and then it's to live long enough to make sure you make it back to your wife."

"After that?"

"Don't know yet, mano, but I'm sure we'll figure something out."

"Shit, got a dead one." Bexar raised his rifle.

"Same here, actually quite a few."

"Stay or go?"

"Go. I'll keep things fluid out here, go inside and grab the food bags, toss them in the bed of the truck."

"But ..."

Dozens of dead streamed into the open from between homes.

"Go mano, go fast!"

Bexar turned and ran into the house and to the garage, shouldered the bags, grabbed the big case with Chivo's sniper rifle, Chivo's other bag and his bag, before trotting outside in more of a heavy waddle as Chivo, now standing in the bed of the truck, began opening fire on the closest approaching undead. At a quick glance, Bexar guessed there were at least fifty stumbling to the siren call of the air horn that Cliff had left for them.

"OK dude, you drive."

Bexar looked at Chivo a bit sideways. Anticipating the look, Chivo interrupted Bexar's unspoken statement. "Fuck the tires, mano, pop smoke and extract. Head to the school we burned down."

Bexar turned the ignition over, and to his surprise it started. He'd assumed Cliff would have pulled the distributor wires or something else like that. Chivo slid into the passenger seat, riding rifle as it were, took advantage of the missing windshield and helped clear a path as Bexar drove as fast as he could with the two passenger-side tires shot out and flat.

Within a block, large chunks of the ruined tires were being thrown from the wheels, the rims sparking on the asphalt as they drove, but even though the amassing herd of undead turned to follow, they were quickly gaining safety in the increased distance.

Radio Hut, Groom Lake, NV

Headphones plugged into a radio panel, Bill sat, listening intently and writing quickly, filling page after page on his yellow pad of paper. Flipping back to the first page, he used the tip of his pen, ticking off each character in rhythm as he listened. He pulled the headphones off his ears and called out, "Hey Major Wright, check this out."

Wright slid the proffered headphones over his ears and listened, brow furrowing. Bill handed him his notes, which he followed in rhythm to what he heard. Wright removed the headphones and handed them back to Bill.

"OK, but what is it, who is it? What does it mean?"

Bill chuckled. "You're supposed to tell me what it means, and it's a numbers station."

"What's a numbers station?"

"They've been around since the Cold War started; they're transmissions on shortwave bands that read letters, numbers, sometimes both. A lot of conspiracy theories in place as to what they were or what they meant, but before the attack there were a number of people who spent a lot of time trying to figure that out. My best guess is that they meant nothing at all and were in place to obfuscate real communication channels, or were one-time cyphers for spies, secret agent types."

"Besides being creepy, how is it that it's still going on? There isn't much of a world left to need black-cloaked spies and such."

"Major Wright, your guess is good as mine. All I know is that this wasn't being broadcast before and now it is, so either some secured system woke up and began an automated run, or someone turned it back on."

"Is it ours? Where is it being transmitted from?"

"Major, I have no idea, and to geolocate the signal it would take more than we have here, multiple sites, people ... basically the short answer is that we can't."

"What about the SSC?"

"Haven't asked them yet. The last message that came across the computer screen from them said that they would be off the net for about two hours this morning, and they haven't checked back in yet."

"How long has it been?"

"Almost two hours."

"Well, send a request and wait. Let me know if they don't respond in the next two hours or so, but spend that time verifying that our connection still works. As many problems as we've had recently, I'm not sure how long we'll even be able to do that."

The room went dark, the hum of computers stopping instantly. Digital displays blank, radios silent, complete darkness engulfed the room before the eerie glow of the emergency lighting clicked on. Wright cursed and walked out the door, pulling a small tactical flashlight out of the breast pocket of his old-style woodland-patterned BDUs. Flickering twice, the main lights came on for a few seconds and went dark again. Airmen, flashlights in hand, were under the consoles pulling the power plugs from their sensitive equipment and computers, wary of a surge destroying the electronics when the electrical system restarted.

Civilian Berth, Groom Lake, NV

"This is the women's dormitory. Sarah and Erin, you are welcome to stay here. Jessie, you are welcome to stay here until Bexar returns and then you can move to the married couple's housing."

Erin looked at the woman giving the tour. "What's the difference?"

The women smiled. "The male and female dormitories are basically open squad bays with rows of bunk beds; the married couples' housing is basically the same except that there are curtain partitions between each of the berths. That and most married couples push two of the bunk beds together to form a sort of full-sized bed."

Sarah looked at Erin and shrugged with a crooked smile, as if to say, "It's just me and you, kid, no special housing for us."

Erin looked blankly at her mother, then at Jessie, Jessie's stomach, and back to the woman. "Good, then we can help take care of Jessie as that baby gets closer to coming." A thin smile escaped to her lips for a microsecond.

The woman opened the door to the women's dormitory, explaining the artwork on the wall as the "town's logo" and how each of the dorms had split into towns, each with an elected leader, Jake being the overall civilian leader elected by all who lived in Groom Lake at the time. "There are no taxes, no crime, and the neighborhoods are friendly, if close together," the woman remarked jokingly. Bathed in harsh overhead lighting like a Fortune-500 partition farm, the rows of dark metal bunk beds seemed to extend forever. In the next instant the room went pitch black, the gentle hiss of air moving through the HVAC and filtration system becoming noticeable in its absence. In the darkness they heard a few women curse, a couple laughed, and one by one little beams of light pierced the darkness, islands of glowing electric life.

Brit grimaced. "This just started happening in the past few days. So far they've been temporary. Should be no more than ten minutes before the electrical system restarts and everything comes back online. When we leave here I'll get you all some of those LED flashlights and spare batteries."

The emergency lighting flickered on just as the overhead lights powered on then off, on and then off again. None of the women moved, although they could see the flashlights moving in the darkness of the dorm. Erin, weary of the situation, raised her rifle, Jessie drew her handgun, holding it in the SUL position, and Sarah raised her rifle, the three of them turning away from each other, standing back to back. Their tour guide, left out of their circle, looked at them in a mix of surprise and horror as the lights came back on and stayed on.

"You don't have anything to worry about; we are all perfectly safe down here."

Barely audibly, Erin hissed, "Then why can't you keep the fucking lights on?"

The woman laughed nervously. "Tell you what, let's take you down to the storage floor, get you some of those flashlights and see if we can find something that might make you all feel a little safer."

Jessie looked at Sarah, who looked at Erin and back to Jessie. Without a word spoken, Jessie holstered her pistol, Erin thumb-flipped the selector on her rifle back to "SAFE," and the three of them let their tour guide step through the door first, either oblivious to the danger, unwilling to accept that there could be danger, or just that confident that there wouldn't be any danger.

Over her shoulder, Jessie whispered to Erin, "Think she gets a commission on the sale?"

"No, but I bet her business card has her fucking picture on it."

"Shush you two," Sarah hissed back. "Besides, she would have told us about the great schools and shopping in the area."

Jessie snorted, stifling a laugh as she stepped through the door, the woman standing in the hall looking a little suspiciously at the three new arrivals.

"Uh, sorry, I think my allergies are acting up 'cause of all the perfectly filtered air," Jessie managed to say with a straight face as their tour guide walked down the hall towards the stairwell. Erin playfully kicked Jessie in the back of the calf, Jessie stopping in place momentarily, causing Erin to walk into her. They both giggled.

"Children, behave," Sarah whispered. Their friendly post-apocalyptic realtor didn't seem amused; she walked through the metal door to the stairwell without waiting for the three, who hurried to catch up, curious what the storage floor entailed.

SSC, Ennis, TX

Clint and Amanda walked side by side northward along the park's main road, back towards the front gate, which they'd ruined by crashing it the day they arrived. Not much was said between the two. Other than the reanimated dead they had to put down in the neighborhood, the park was relatively quiet, although Amanda had nearly shot a dog as it came crashing out of the brush and stopped to look at the new intruders. It sniffed the air and its tail wagged slightly before it turned and ran back into the woods.

"Pour guy. Man's best friend is eaten by the man after death, but it looked like he knew we weren't dead." Amanda thought about her dogs that she'd unwittingly abandoned in her Arkansas home, before taking a deep breath and screwing down the lid on her memories and emotions.

"You know, Amanda, during all the briefings we had on the Yama strain we discussed civilian populations and we never thought that any significant number of household pets would survive. The analysts believed that either the animals would die of exposure and starvation in their pens, homes or yards, or they would be eaten by the reanimates. Looking back, we should have brought in an expert in animal behavior to study how the survivors would adapt and if they could be a help or hindrance to the survivors. For now, I would assume that any animal we encounter is no longer friendly to anything still on two legs, and will most likely run away, but I wouldn't test my theory for fear of getting mauled."

As they approached the front gate on their left, Amanda glanced at the first building, which was an office. Across from the office, under an awning, stood an RV which the park host would stay in. The three main lanes of travel in and out of the park were deserted. The gates stood open, not that it mattered, and the exit roadway was a bit of a throwback design with directional spikes to deflate the tires of anyone attempting to drive the wrong direction. Great against a vehicle, not so much against reanimates stumbling through the open area.

"Clint, we never cleared these buildings."

"I did."

"What, when?"

"Right after we first arrived. I've already made the same loop we're taking now."

"You bastard, why didn't you tell me?"

"You didn't ask."

"Really? We're going to play that game now? You're like a malfunctioning robot, specific voice commands only and then the response is truthful only if you feel like it."

"That's not fair; I've never lied to you."

"Not telling me is the same as lying. You're the secret agent, I'm the President, regardless of our involvement, and we have to be on the same page of the same book for the same mission. When we go back down below we are going to have a very long and detailed talk."

"Fine ... yes ma'am."

"For now, tell me about the rest of your tour of the grounds up here. What do we have to do to secure it?"

"We either have to run all new fences or we can fill the gaps with some HESCO, but we don't really have the man power to do either."

"What is HESCO?"

"They're like giant moving boxes with a wire frame on the outside; fill them full of dirt and they're nearly a solid wall ... think of them like big sandbags that you fill and stack."

"Do we have any?"

"Yeah, I don't recall the exact number but we have a significant amount. Quite a lot of them actually."

"How do we fill them?"

"Usually we would use a front-end loader."

Quickly becoming more annoyed at Clint, Amanda snapped, "And do we *have* a front-end loader?"

"We do, we have three of them in the motor pool storage area."

"How long would it take us to secure our gaps with the HESCO setups?"

"Probably just a couple of days at most, but it would make us a target. Anyone who sees them would know that something is up at the park. Part of the reason for my resistance is that we have to remain invisible, a secret; we can't have survivors coming here for help or a handout, and we can't support them."

"We *can't* support them or you don't *want* to support them?"

"We *can't* because it compromises your safety. Groom Lake is swarming with people now, hundreds of them, and they already had an uncontrolled outbreak in their facility. I promise you it will happen again. We can't take that chance with you.

The other six facilities are dead, full of the dead. As far as Cliff and I have been able to find out, our two facilities are the only two left. He opened his up for business; with you here we have to keep this one closed to the public. Period. After he gets here then we might be able to work on establishing a secure area near here for survivors, but not until then."

"Wait, Cliff is coming here? What about the group we sent to save him?"

"They're supposed to be coming back with him. Only Bexar and Chivo survived, but that'll be two more people we can put to work, but two people who are trained but expendable is better than the unwashed masses descending on our facility and jeopardizing everything!"

"Expendable! What do you mean ..." Amanda's raised voice was silenced by the unmistakable feeding call of the dead, the rasped moans announcing to all that a live meal was to be had.

Emerging out of the woods to the north on their side of the park's fence were a dozen undead. They crashed through the brush in a stumbling march, determined to feed.

Clint spun towards the threat. Hunched back, rifle up and feet rolling gently with each step, he made way towards the approaching dead, taking them out one by one, each shot muffled by the suppressor. Amanda moved quickly to the right and forward to take a firing position that didn't have Clint in her line of fire. As mad as she was at him at the moment, she wasn't going to kill the only man she knew who could run the facility, the only one who, at the moment, could help her achieve what she had decided her *real* mission was to be.

Not able to shoot while moving like Clint, Amanda knelt and supported her rifle on her raised knee. Breathing steadily, she quickly fired, giving cover to Clint who, while faster than seemed humanly possible, rotated his rifle, finger-pressing the magazine release while his left hand ripped a fresh magazine out of the pouch on his carrier, thumb striking the bolt release as the rifle came back into action and instantly firing. Although only seen out of the corner of her eye, Amanda was shocked at how quickly Clint worked through a simple bolt-back magazine change, making a mental note to spend time working on reload drills in the tunnels.

As quickly as the threat emerged, it was neutralized and the two dozen dead lay truly dead in the brown grass around the park host's shelter.

"See, this is why we need to keep you safe and in the facility."

"No, this is why we need to secure our little pioneer homestead and make it a safe place for others."

The ten minutes it took to walk to the main entrance to the facility on the north side of the park was made in silence, and with no further undead surprises. Both Clint and Amanda were thinking about how to make the other see the virtue of their own plan, which seemed insurmountable.

Cortez, CO

Sparks followed the truck as it leaned toward the passenger side, driving on the steel rims, shuddering and shaking at thirty miles per hour, the fastest Bexar dared to push the old truck. Even so, it vibrated as if it was the truck's death rattle and last breath.

Chivo looked behind them for any stragglers, each block seemingly having more and more undead shambling through the streets than before.

"Dammit!"

"What?"

"Mano, that asshole took our fuel cans!"

Bexar looked over his shoulder and swore, looking forward against just in time to swerve, mostly retaining control of the truck, around a small gaggle of undead that turned to follow the smoking, sparking, rattling death trap of a truck.

Continuing south, Bexar had a very basic idea of the layout of the town. If he kept driving south he would hit 4th Street, and a right turn would take him to where they'd killed the remaining cult members.

"Chivo, do you remember any vehicles at the headquarters, their school?"

Chivo thought for a moment. "No, no vehicles, just a small cache of weapons and food and such; basically we took all they had."

"Cliff talked about a school bus, a jeep, and some other vehicles. Where are they?"

"No idea, mano."

"So far these assholes liked schools and churches, so we look for either; maybe we'll get lucky and find a new ride."

"God, I hope it isn't another fucking school bus."

The engine began making a hard metallic clacking sound before steam started pouring out from under the hood, followed by a hard *thunk*. The engine locked up, stopping the transmission; the rear wheels locked up before Bexar could slam the clutch pedal to the floor and slam on the brakes. The truck spun off the road, bounced off the traffic light pole and stopped, wedged against a low brick wall and a tree.

"Shit, Chivo, you OK, man?" Bexar shook his head a couple of times to clear it before trying to open his door, which was jammed shut. Chivo pulled himself through the hole where the windshield would have been before spinning to sit on the dash, facing the back of the truck and the intersection, his rifle barking sharply in the cold air.

"Bexar, shake it loose guy, we've got to un-ass this mess fast, like now ... MOVE!"

Following Chivo's lead, Bexar climbed through the windshield and onto the hood of the truck. By the time Bexar put his feet on the pavement, Chivo stood next to the truck, still firing and in the middle of a magazine change.

Shouting over the rifle fire, Bexar gestured at Chivo. "What now?"

Chivo stopped firing for a moment. "We walk."

"Walk?"

"Yeah mano, we walk. If we walk we won't get as tired. We don't have to be fast, just faster than those undead assholes."

Bexar couldn't argue that logic, as with a few more shots to put down the closest of the approaching dead, Chivo turned to walk south.

"What about our bags, the food?"

"Leave it for now. First we neutralize the immediate threat, then we can come back for it. Why, do ya think we'll get towed for leaving our truck there?"

Bexar shook his head and started walking south. He didn't know how Chivo kept making jokes when everything went to shit. They walked a few feet apart in the middle of the road. A dangerous tactic when dealing with people, but the only safe tactic when dealing with the possibility of an undead surprise springing out from around a blind corner. Southward they walked, quickly, with purpose, careful to conserve their energy, for they had a gaggle of undead following that would never tire or stop.

Bexar sighed as flakes began to drift lazily from the sky and they crossed the intersection for 1st Street. "Just three more blocks and we can head east; should be just a few blocks up 4th Street."

"See mano, nothing to worry about! Adapt and overcome, and all the stressing does is fuck up your thinking," Chivo yelled over the sound of his rifle firing rapidly.

Coronado, CA

"Guys, that's ballsy, but how are we going to maintain security while the entire team is out?"

"Simmons and Jones can maintain it while we're outside the wire."

"Kirk, why them?"

"Chief, they're motor pool. They can't dive, they can't swim, they can't pilot a fucking Zodiac, but they're Marines! They're riflemen and can hold a damn post until relieved."

Aymond couldn't argue with those points. Last year, while deployed, if he had presented this plan to his team commander he would have been thought a lunatic. If that commander had presented it up the chain of command, the plan was so under-staffed, ill-conceived and broke so much doctrine that the commander's career could have been in jeopardy. Special Operations Command, SOCOM, might be the tip of the spear in the fight on terror around the globe, but there were certain short cuts that weren't taken unless under dire circumstances. Those rules were written into the book of policy by the blood of other special operators before him. Even in the A Shau Valley in the late '60s such lunacy wasn't tolerated. However, he had no choice.

There was no support, no command structure for approval and no command structure to slap him down if something failed. No, Aymond knew the punishment would be the loss of his men, a punishment far worse than an Article 15 could ever be.

"Put the gear together, get the boat teams together, and run practice as best you can." Aymond looked out the window facing the courtyard at all the containers holding various mission profile gear boxes for the SEAL teams that had previously occupied the building. "Do it fast, but fuck the Chinese. Everyone comes back even if it means the mission fails. We are too few and we will be completely ineffective if we lose anyone else."

"Especially me, Chief?"

"No Kirk, that might actually increase our effectiveness if you didn't come back. Now get moving and send Simmons and Jones in here."

"Aye Chief!"

Groom Lake, NV

"Wow. Just wow. This is like preppers-in-wonderland, we went down the rabbit hole and have found another world fully stocked for any and all." Jessie stood in the middle of the aircraft-hangar-sized room with Sarah, Erin, and Brit, their intrepid tour guide, as she slowly turned in place, staring in disbelief.

"You could damn near outfit a war with everything that's here. Do we get to have our pick or are things assigned to us? Bexar won't believe it ... how do we get access to the gear here?"

The tour guide turned to answer Jessie's question. "You will be given an allowance of basic items, toiletriés and the like, but clothing outside of your issued gear will have to be requisitioned through your 'town' representative. Anything else, any special requests can be sent through your 'town' representative as well. This isn't Santa's workshop, there aren't little elves making new stuff every night."

"How much ammo do you have and what calibers?"

"Honey, why would a sweet young thing like yourself need to ask a question like that?"

Erin frowned at the woman, Jessie speaking up before Erin could say what was on all of their minds. "I don't know your story, but the three of us have been on the road and in a daily fight crossing the country since December 26th. I don't know if you noticed but the dead rule most of the country and the filth of society rule the rest. How long have you been safe here underground?"

"I was a part of the first civilian group to arrive after the early shortwave broadcasts."

Erin muttered something that sounded exceptionally offensive, then turned and walked back the way they'd come. The woman looked at Sarah, whose hard eyes betrayed her thoughts. "She has a point. You can't even keep the lights on; we have to be ready for this facility to fail or to be overrun or both. We are all low on ammo after the fight we endured to make it this far, and we could use some better gear to carry all the ammo we can."

"You three are going to be trouble."

"No, we just want to be prepared. That's the point, isn't it? Prep for destruction, train for the worst, and hope for the best ... now more importantly, besides ammo, what are the chances there are either some maternity pants in this giant cache site or some spandura or something I can use to modify pants to fit? I'm not very far along and these BDU trousers are already uncomfortable."

Cortez, CO

Even with the freezing temperatures, the brisk movement, although only a walking pace, caused sweat to drip from Bexar's brow. While wiping his face with the back of his sleeve, Chivo stopped suddenly and caught him by surprise.

Standing in the middle of the road, halfway between intersections, Chivo turned in place, rifle raised slightly, careful not to flag Bexar with his muzzle as he turned. "Did you hear that?"

Trying to hide how hard he was breathing, Bexar took two deep breaths before answering, "Hear what?"

"What did it sound like?"

"Shush dude, give me a sec."

Bexar turned in place, scanning around him, rifle tucked tight into the SUL position. The harder he strained to hear, the more all he could hear was his own heartbeat banging in his ears.

A few seconds passed, the following undead closing the gap to Bexar and Chivo with each step they weren't taking.

"I don't know, Bexar, I thought I heard ... something, but I can't hear anything but the dead now. We better get moving."

The next intersection was 4th Street. Chivo started to turn left to head to the destroyed cult headquarters, but Bexar held up his hand to stop him. "School zone sign another block up. We burned the school they were using practically to the ground, and we know nothing is left in the other school that had the radio. Cliff said the cult was using schools, so I say we check this one out en route; it's only a couple of blocks."

Chivo nodded and the two continued south before stepping over a low gate and into an empty parking lot. The single-story building's windows appeared to be intact, the blinds closed, so they were unable to see inside.

"Why do schools always seem to look like a cross between an office park and a prison?"

Bexar didn't even have a response, only a shrug.

Both men spun in place at the sound of a head slapping the frozen asphalt, like a watermelon falling to the pavement. The following parade of death had caught up to them. The chain-link fence was erected on only a portion of the parking lot perimeter and not the whole length, for some reason unknown to Bexar. Although his attention was momentarily drawn to the strange security measure, the dead lacked the cognitive ability to recognize the lack of fence, but they also lacked the mobility to step over the small pipe gate across the drive.

Both men, growing accustomed to the dead's constant threat, were beyond being nonplussed by the shambling corpses. Chivo tilted his head towards the gathering numbers at the fence, and Bexar nodded in response. Silently they understood the plan; Bexar would hold rear guard while Chivo picked the lock on the heavy metal doors. The reinforced glass in the upper half of the doors would be a non-starter, the wire mesh able to withstand a lot of abuse.

Bexar knelt to brace his support arm, his AR-15 raised, the tip of the triangle-shaped reticle in the combat optic holding steady on the tip of the closest skull. The rifle was sighted for two hundred yards. At one time Bexar would have had to calculate the hold over distance based on how far away his target was, but weeks and weeks after the world ended, the adaptation wasn't even a conscious thought any longer.

Instead Bexar concentrated on his breathing before reminding himself to scan. Lifting his head slightly off the rifle, he looked left then right, breaking the rule to follow his eyes with the muzzle of his weapon.

"Shit!"

Bexar fell backwards, trying to move out of the kneeling position. On his back and driving his rifle as quickly as he could, he jerked back on the trigger three times before making contact with the corpse less than ten feet away.

"Talk to me, mano."

"I'm good, we're good, keep working."

Bexar clambered to his feet, angry at his lack of attention and quickly engaged the rest of the trailing dead gathering in number. Bexar quickly cycled through a full thirty-round magazine until two dozen dead lay motionless in final death, pools of dark blood surrounding them.

Fresh magazine in his hand, Bexar ripped the empty magazine from his rifle, slapped the loaded magazine into place, his thumb skipping across the bolt release as he stowed the empty magazine. A few weeks ago he would have let the empty magazine fall and not worry about it, but magazines were rarer than ammo now, and he had to keep the ones he had.

The nearest walking corpse was a mere five feet away, most of the macabre face covered by the glowing red triangle in his optic. Bexar squeezed the trigger and nothing happened.

"Ugh!"

Bexar let go of his rifle, jammed his left palm into the chest of the dead woman and knocking her back. The rifle swung by the sling across his body while his right hand fell to the pistol on his hip; the pistol out and up, Bexar began pulling on the trigger while the pistol was still at hip level, stitching rounds up the woman's torso with no effect until he grasped and supported with his left hand, driving the muzzle of the pistol forward. All Bexar could see was the faint glow of the green dot on the front sight as he pulled the trigger twice, one round entering the woman's left eye. The back of her skull exploded, the blow back covering Bexar in rotting, pus-filled brain matter. Adjusting slightly, Bexar took aim at the next closest corpse, nearly in hand's reach, and pulled the trigger. Nothing happened.

Too late he realized that the slide of the pistol was locked back on an empty magazine.

"Fuck, Chivo, tag in!" Bexar slapped the skull of the reanimated elderly man with his pistol, which did nothing to help his situation. The man didn't stagger or react, merely wrapped his hands around Bexar's arm when suddenly his head erupted. Chivo had fired his pistol right next to Bexar's head, and now all Bexar could hear was a loud ringing sound. Chivo tugged on the back of his carrier. Essentially deaf for the moment, Bexar turned and saw his friend climbing through a broken window, ripping through the blinds in the process, the attempt to unlock the door abandoned. He followed his comrade swiftly and they stepped into a classroom, desks askew. Bexar quickly changed magazines on his pistol, still not sure what the stoppage was in his rifle and with no time, cover or concealment nearby to dick with it. The pistol was going to be it for the moment.

Through the window, Bexar saw the parking lot was now teeming with the dead, as if he had stepped in an ant hill. More and more dead seemed to appear out of nowhere, and some were falling through the broken window and into the classroom with them. Quickly they exited the classroom and shut the door behind them. In the hallway, Bexar saw Chivo's lips moving, but his ears still rung. Realizing that Chivo was probably talking at normal volume, Bexar didn't attempt to talk for fear of yelling; he simply pointed to his ear and shook his head. Chivo nodded, pointed at Bexar, pointed at himself, patted the top of his head and then pointed towards the interior of the school.

You follow me; we are going to clear the school to make sure we're safe.

Bexar held up a finger and pointed to his rifle. Chivo nodded.

After holstering the pistol, Bexar looked at the ejection port on the AR and saw he had a bolt over; the round hadn't ramped out of the magazine correctly and had become lodged between the bolt carrier and the inside of the upper receiver.

A few moments later, the malfunction was corrected, the round caught by the bolt discarded on the floor with a badly dented casing. Now Bexar was back in service.

He looked at Chivo, using his fingers to mime someone running and then someone walking. *Fast search or slow search?*

Chivo shrugged and tilted his hand back and forth. Bexar guessed that meant half and half or somewhere in between. If there was some universal hand signal chart out there for Special Forces types, he didn't know it. Bexar flashed back on when he used to make fun of his department's SWAT guys; he'd made up all sorts of ludicrously complicated and outrageous hand signals to communicate the information that was of the upmost importance to a Texas motorcop, like which taqueria they'd grab breakfast at after morning school zones.

At a moderate pace, Chivo and Bexar made their way through most of the school, taking about a half hour to search. There was no one living and the only dead they found were completely dead. The gym was another story, though. In the gym they found three women, their legs tied, hanging from their ankles from the ceiling just over center court; Bexar swore as he saw an alter similar to the one in the school they'd destroyed a few days prior.

Surprise wasn't the first emotion that Bexar felt, nor was disgust. Anger burned deep in the pit of his stomach. *If we hadn't killed them all, these sick fucks would have to die.* Bexar realized he was angry he couldn't kill the prophet and his followers again.

Chivo bumped his shoulder to catch his attention, jerking his head towards the front of the school. Peering out of the front glass of the front doors, and seeing the dead filling the street, Chivo pushed on the doors gently and found them unlocked.

"Damn."

"I heard that, but my ears are still ringing."

"Yeah, it happens. You'll be getting over it soon ... usually."

Bexar looked at Chivo, realizing he most likely had more than a single experience with the issue of ringing ears from gunfire.

"What now?"

"We wait. We have nothing but time. If we have to we'll gather and melt some snow to drink, but otherwise we give our going away party time to go away."

"We barely saw any dead at all in this damn place until today. What's up with that?"

"I don't know, mano, my guess is that the cult members did a decent job of keeping their areas clean and free of the dead ... well, of the reanimated dead outside at least."

"Your buddy sure as fuck didn't do us any favors."

"Can't focus on that now. If we see him again I'll kill him, you can kill him, we can take turns killing him, but for now that is a nonstarter. We have to focus on our immediate situation and work the problem step by step. Adapt and overcome. If you think too much about the past, if you dwell on what should have been, then you will never come to see what will become, and you will die."

Chivo had a point and Bexar knew it.

Cortez, CO

Cliff drove slowly through the middle of town, scanning for the school bus he had seen the cult using before; now that they were neutralized he wasn't worried about being stealthy. He also figured Chivo and Bexar would have their hands full for a few hours, barricaded in the house waiting for the undead to get distracted and disperse. He didn't want to kill them, but he needed a chance to get out of town without raising suspicion or being followed. Where he was going, he couldn't have anyone follow. End of the world or not, some secrets had to be kept.

So he had time to cruise and look; where the school bus was, so should be more supplies. At least if his assumption about the cult members was correct.

"Well ain't that some shit?"

The other truck lay wedged between a tree and the brick façade of a bank, a large puddle of oil covering the ground around it. Shambling dead began to zero in on Cliff, stopped in the middle of the street, engine running.

"Chivo's a big boy; he can babysit Bexar. If not, then not my problem. Mission first."

Cliff sped up and made a few turns to leave his trailing army of death behind before reaching Highway 491 and turning north. He was going to Texas and the SSC, but first there was a mountain in Utah that he had to visit.

Coronado, CA

Aymond, the remaining men of his Marine Special Operations Team, and the two motor pool corporals they'd acquired at Twentynine Palms all stood in the conference room, the only light that streaming through the windows from the afternoon sun.

Kirk and Davis stood at the front of the room. The dry erase board, having suffered no ill effects from the end of the world, stood in for the typical PowerPoint presentation of an Operations Plan, or Op Plan. Art was not a subject either of the men would have scored well in, but the point was coming across.

"It's just that simple."

"Kirk, you asshole, that's about as simple as a twelve-sided Rubik's cube."

"It wouldn't be a cube with twelve sides, Ski, you dumbass."

"Gentlemen ..."

The bickering stopped on Aymond's first word. "If we could do the operation the right way, we would have two full teams, air support, drone coverage, satellite imagery, and a dozen other assets in place before we would be allowed to even take a piss. But we don't have any of that, we can't even wish for any of that. It is up to us, and if you have a better plan to deny access, I want to hear it."

A helicopter roared over the top of the building, low and fast. It sounded like it nearly dragged the landing gear on the roof. All the men instinctively ducked, even though they were inside. The men closest to the windows all edged towards them, careful to stay in the shadows and hidden from view while peering outside.

"Holy shit, Chief, armored personnel carriers."

"How many, Hammer?"

"Eight ... looks similar to the Type 92s the Pakis use. Six by six. Can they airlift those or did they already off-load a ship?"

"Are they stopping?"

"Negative, Chief, they're rolling north, towards Halsey Field."

Another helicopter roared past the building.

"Damn, that guy's running a tree trimming service!"

Aymond walked around the edge of the table and looked over Hammer's shoulder at the back of the APCs as they lumbered down the narrow bike lane, which was mostly free of abandoned vehicles. Frowning at the window, Aymond took a deep breath.

"Well Kirk, as much as I wanted to do your op, things have changed slightly ... Hammer, Gonzo, pack out for a three-day. You two head to the mainland, give the airport room, but report how far the Chinese lines have expanded, if there are patrols, what their area of operations is ... well, you know the drill. Don't get friendly with the natives."

"ROE?"

"Rules of engagement are to not be stupid. I need you to make it back, I need you to gather Intel. You're Critical Skills Operators, use your heads. Kirk, Davis, and Snow, you're tasked with North Island; figure out what the new Chinatown expansion involves at the Naval Air Station, also plan for three days. Happy and Chuck, you're with me. We're taking Hammer and Gonzales across the harbor, using the bridge for some cover. After insertion the three of us will run up the shoreline in the Zodiac to check the commercial ports. If any of their ships are in berth we need to disable it. Happy, see if our hooyah buddies left anything useful in their mission boxes. If you can't find a limpet mine, make something, make anything, I don't care, just make something that'll work. Ski, comms, get the net set up, test them out and get Simmons and Jones up to speed."

Turning to the two corporals, he continued. "You two guys are now in charge of staying low and making sure our little Forward Operating Base still belongs to us when we return. Questions?"

The seven men of the MSOT looked determined; Simmons and Jones looked a little wary.

"Good, make it happen. Wheels up in three hours, team meeting in two."

Everyone started towards the door. "Simmons, Jones, stand by for a sec."

The two Marines stopped and faced Aymond. "You don't get to sit on your asses while we're gone. Sit down and grab a pen, you're going to need to take some notes. First, pick your favorite M-ATV of the group; you're going to be our Quick Reaction Force, ready to roll if someone has a call-out. You'll want to load it with the following items ..."

Colorado and Utah border

Cliff looked at the sun edging towards the mountains in the west, the direction highway 491 was now facing. The tiny town of Dove Creek, Colorado lay in ruins behind him, not from his own doing, nor from any living person he saw. The town was owned by the dead and would be for some time, not that there was much of anything left that anyone would want to save. The town was obliterated by fire and who knew what else. It seemed unlikely that the cult had traveled this far. They appeared to have worked hard to keep the center of Cortez clear of the undead, even though the stores on the east side of town were still completely overrun. Cliff would never know and he didn't care. His simple mission continued to evolve as new information and intelligence was gathered, but he had to act fast or the small groups of what remained of society would be lost. Nothing else mattered.

The piece of paper that he used to work out the encrypted message using the one-time pad cypher was long gone; burned, the ashes scattered. Not that Cliff seriously thought anyone would find a scrap piece of paper amongst the death and destruction, but state secrets are just that and they only remain secrets through diligence.

Cliff checked his watch and looked at the sun. He had no map, but he had a basic idea of how to get to where he needed to go. At some point he would probably have to scavenge a gas station for a map, but for now he could simply follow the signs for Salt Lake City. Granite Mountain wouldn't be too hard to find from there; he had visited once a number of years ago. The archive was real; that much was public knowledge. What was housed far deeper into the mountain beyond the archive was a closely guarded secret. The facility didn't appear to be up and running according to Clint's message, so Cliff had to assume he would have to fight his way into another damned hole in the ground against the army of death.

Maybe some of the Mormons in the archive survived; they could help ... if anyone could survive this shit storm it would have been the Mormon people.

Will they actually help ... will they believe me?

When he'd visited the facility before, he'd been in civilian clothing, as were the others in the archive. To all the people working with the microfilm and computers he'd been just another archivist. There were a series of secured areas that separated the white from the dark worlds that lurked in the heart of the mountain. A digital empire of caffeine, cigarette smoke filling dimly lit rooms full of monitors, and the most rag-tag-looking group of elite government operatives that the new era had ever seen, fighting many enemies. Like the Lernaean Hydra, all from the same body, all with the same mission, but every time an attack was foiled, two more took its place. The People's Liberation Army of China had, *or has,* Cliff corrected himself, an advanced cyber warfare unit, and deep inside Granite Mountain were the college dropouts, dorks and digital savants that were the best the United States had to offer. They fought a war unseen, against the ones and zeros of the new age, a keyboard the sword of the modern warrior.

Cliff shook his head. *Maybe it would make more sense if it really was aliens for once ... just once.*

The sign gave a distance to Moab, Utah. The distance didn't mean much except to help Cliff gauge the time it would take for him to travel. The speedometer and the odometer in the truck didn't work, although the fuel gauge appeared to function, but Cliff doubted its accuracy.

He stole a glance at his watch again before driving onto the shoulder and around an overturned RV.

I'll stop on the edge of town, find a gas station, find a map, and fill up the tank ...

Cliff jerked the wheel to the left and across the dotted yellow line of the two-lane highway. A group of dead were clustered, feeding on what appeared to have been a deer in the middle of the road, and he hadn't even seen them until he came around the edge of the RV.

I better not drive through the night.

With a slight frown at the thought, Cliff knew he would have to take the usual elaborate steps of finding a place he could secure, clearing it of any threats, then reversing the process in the morning. The entire process was growing tiresomely annoying.

CHAPTER 5

Coronado, CA
March 13, Year 1

Aymond knelt on the roof next to the big HVAC unit to hide from view. Using binoculars, he scanned the bay and Silver Strand Boulevard, which traveled towards the base at North Island. Clouds blocked the twinkling stars and the moon hadn't risen yet. Aymond frowned at the thought of the moon. He had no idea what phase the moon was in currently, nor when it raised or set. He didn't even know what time sunrise and sunset were. These were all details of mission planning that he took great care in acknowledging for an operation, but he'd never worried about the actual data before. It was so easily looked up via the Navy's weather reporting database, which contained teams and reams of data for any point on the globe. Today he simply had to wait impatiently for the sun to set before beginning his survey of the surrounding area.

Below decks, on the ground floor, his men were finishing their mission preparations. Their weapons were clean, locked, loaded, and verified ready, face paint was being applied, medium-sized rucks were loaded with the basics that each team believed they would need. Aymond was anxious, not for himself, but for his men. Even in Afghanistan he'd entered their missions with the quiet confidence of a trained professional, but everything about their situation pushed against the grain of that professionalism. They were taking chances ... he was taking chances against the hope that they could remain like the Raiders of World War II: quiet, stealthy, observe, report and leave a destroyed and confused enemy in their wake.

A gentle tap on the shoulder brought Aymond's attention around to see Ski, his face and body a dark mass in the shadows of the roof. Face, ears, hands, and neck, any skin that might show and glow against a dark background was painted, but the shaggy bush appearance was from the ghillie suit he wore. Ski tapped his wrist like he was tapping a watch, and then gave a thumbs up. Aymond nodded. *Time to go.*

Quietly they climbed through the roof hatch, closing it behind them. If the overhead flights were taking notice of such details, they couldn't let it be seen. Right now they were comfortable operating from the complex that housed the Teams, but if they had to go to ground again they might be in a bad way with so many PLA and Zeds in the area.

Aymond joined the men under the covered area in the rear courtyard. Kirk, Davis and Snow each wore some combination of ghillie suit. Happy, Ski, and Aymond wore their standard combat load-out, with wetsuits under their utilities. The bay was cold, and they might end up in the water for some time.

Simmons and Jones stood ready, loaded with a full combat load; each appeared nervous but resolute in their task. Hammer and Gonzo wore the dark blue camouflage pattern of the Navy's utility uniform.

"Switching sides on us, gentlemen?"

"No Chief, we figured we had a lot of concrete and not many trees on the mainland along the bay."

Aymond nodded with approval. They were right.

"What about you three? Going for the only three bushes on the runways at NAS Halsey Field?"

Kirk, Davis, and Snow all looked at Aymond expressionlessly, his lame attempt at some pre-operation humor falling flat.

Kirk spoke up for the group. "We're going to sneak and peek along the shoreline, use the golf course for cover, and make our way across base towards the carrier berths. Snow had a good idea about that."

Aymond looked at Snow, who explained without being asked. "The attack was well-coordinated: EMP, the virus spray flyover; everything makes sense except for the Panamax ships anchored at the mouth of the bay. So I believe either the PLA has already off-loaded at other facilities like Long Beach, or they got fucked and this is a backup location. There's a lack of multiple cranes on the civilian side of the bay, and what are left are the Navy's cranes. They move on rails and could handle a Conex, no problem."

Nodding, Aymond agreed. "You have a good point, Snow. If that is the case then we need to deny them access, if at all possible."

"It's only about a three-mile hump to the golf course, so it shouldn't take us too long ..."

"Master Guns, maybe we're approaching this the wrong way."

Aymond looked at Jones, a little surprised by his interruption. "Chief, just call me Chief, and how is that?"

"Uh, Chief, you ... we, well. We're approaching this like a conventional force. Observe, plan, act then repeat. There ain't enough of us to do that, maybe if we had a battalion, but not with less than a dozen guys. Why not treat this like the goat fuckers in the 'Stan? IEDs, booby traps, destroy supplies, harassment stuff, you know?"

Looking at Jones, Aymond stood quietly.

"You know, uh Chief ..."

Aymond held up his hand to interrupt Jones. "I'm not saying you're wrong. Guys?"

One by one, each of the MSOT expressed their opinions. Generally most agreed with Jones, with some minor tweaks and suggestions. Aymond listened to each man intently.

"OK, I like it, what about tonight?"

"We still do it; we need the intel, but also be on the watch for unconventional approaches, tactics and locations we can use against those assholes."

"Well there you go, gentlemen, The Gonzo has spoken and I agree."

On The Beach

Ten minutes later, Kirk, Davis, and Snow slinked out onto the edge of the beach, moving slowly and deliberately in the darkness, using every shadow they found to their advantage. From the towering resort windows high above them, dull thuds fell against their ears. The trapped dead were hitting the glass, trying to reach them as they moved past, Snow slowly moved his head from side to side. Kirk and Davis were barely a shadow of darkness gliding silently past on the beach.

How could the dead possibly see or hear us.? I can't even see or hear us.

Movement caught the corner of Snow's eye. His eyes trained on Kirk, who was about twenty-five yards ahead of him and had his right hand raised in a fist next to his head, before flattening his palm and pushing downward slightly. In unison the three of them sank onto the beach, appearing nothing more than pieces of vegetation against the large rocks in the break of the beach next to the resort.

Lights!

Snow moved his rifle slightly, using the powerful optic to peer out at the water and the boat approaching the shoreline to the north of their position.

Patrol boat. Looks like it came from around the edge of the bay or one of the ships.

A powerful spotlight blasted from the bow of the boat, which was over a mile to their north. The boat slowed and trolled slowly southward along the shore, shining the spotlight on the beach along the perimeter of the naval base.

A hard concussion radiated out of the dark blob that was Kirk ahead of him; the suppressed sound of a ridiculously large .50BMG round wasn't, in reality, very quiet. It just wasn't as loud as it would have been. Snow watched the boat in his scope as the powerful spotlight exploded in a shower of shattered glass, draping darkness across the beach as a shadow fell from the bow of the boat into the water. It was hard to tell, but Snow believed it to be the man that had been operating the spotlight. The boat drifted towards the shore with the waves for a moment before the sound of the motors spinning up could be heard echoing across the water. Paralleling the shore, the boat rocketed towards where they lay. Snow tracked the boat with his rifle, moving ever so slightly to maintain his aim. He expected the vessel to look like what the U.S. Navy used, but this ship was smaller, much smaller, possibly something designed for rapid deployment and shore patrol. It all seemed surreal to Snow, in that the order was wrong. The container ships shouldn't be anchored without a naval escort. At the least some sort of Corvette-class ship should be maintaining a patrol, with groupings of landing ships to offload men and material. The aerial lift campaign that they'd observed didn't fit a normal operation for an invasion force.

Maybe it's all they had left to secure this bay? Maybe they fucked up and the virus got loose over there too?

On the bow of the boat, as it quickly grew in the view of Snow's scope, he could see a man standing behind some sort of heavy machine gun as they bounced across the incoming tide. The pilot house appeared to be unarmored. Snow placed the reticle of his optic just over the base of the man's neck when he saw his head explode. Quickly shifting his point of aim to the pilot house, he could make out a shadow of the man at the controls as he heard the sound of the diesel motors screaming, pushed to full throttle. Snow fired and watched the figure disappear and heard the engines cut to idle. The boat continued in a long arc towards the beach, slowing as it drifted into the shallower water.

The boat drifted towards the beach, being pushed by the tide inland; it appeared it would run aground about three-quarters of a mile north of their position. Kirk leapt to his feet and began a fast jog, as fast as his pack, large rifle, and ghillie suit would realistically allow him to run, trying to reach the boat. Snow followed quickly and Davis stayed in position, scanning their gloriously funny-looking run up the beach towards the approaching boat. Scanning the boat for survivors or any other personnel, Davis saw a figure climb into the pilot house; a gentle press of the trigger, and that dark figure fell out of view and the boat continued to drift towards shore.

Davis scanned back and saw that Kirk and Snow were stripping out of their ghillie suits on the beach for the short swim to the boat. The swim against the tide took longer than the run, but he watched his teammates board the vessel. With pistols in hand, they cleared the boat quickly. It turned towards shore, and one of his teammates waved towards Davis to come to the boat before jumping over the gunwale into the chest-deep water. By the time Davis made the run up the shore, Kirk had gathered the ghillie suites, rifles, and rucks, acting as sherpa and carrying them out to the boat. Davis waded through the water, opting to leave his ghillie suit on, and a few minutes later was helped aboard by Kirk, Snow having taken the pilot's position in the wheel house.

Kirk quickly dressed and took the controls while Snow, shivering in the cold air, put his ghillie suit back on. Kirk guided the vessel gently northward along the shoreline, as if the patrol boat was continuing its previous search along the naval base. The discussion became lively, the remaining three dead bodies pooling blood on the rough deck.

"Where do you think we should moor it on this side? Run it aground by our building?"

"No Snow, that's not what I'm saying, I'm just not sure we should go into the bay."

"Why the fuck not, Kirk? This is their boat, those are their own ships, and this is the first water-borne patrol we've seen. Not a single helicopter has flown overhead since dark and no planes are taking off or landing. This seems like the perfect time to steal a fucking boat and take it into the bay."

"Where do we put it?"

"Tie it up in one of the civilian docks, dump the bodies overboard and take the keys."

"What keys?"

"Dammit Kirk, I was speaking figuratively. Point being we would have an enemy patrol boat we could use. We just have to dock the damn thing somewhere that would lead them away from us if they find it." He paused. "I have an idea, but first,

Davis and Kirk, why don't you get behind the gunwales so you won't be seen. Let's slow-roll the ships at anchor, then take the chance to check North Shore and the bay on the way by. Davis, hit the comms and tell Chief we're coming around the bay in a patrol boat."

CHAPTER 6

Coronado, CA
March 14, Year 1

Long before first light glowed across the eastern sky, the patrol boat that Kirk, Davis, and Snow had liberated was tied in a slip, hidden between two impressively sized yachts in Glorietta Bay. The patrol boat's new parking spot was nearly a direct shot across the narrow part of Coronado from where they had swum out to the boat, less than half a mile, but in terms of over water they were miles away.

The radio traffic on the boat's lone radio was constant; none of it sounded too excited, but the three of them had no idea what was being said. The special language courses all of them attended would have been useful if a northern tribe from Afghanistan had decided to invade, but training in Mandarin hadn't been offered. Chief was excited to have the boat, as he said he had a special plan in mind for it, but they kept radio transmissions short. The team members weren't sure if the PLA were employing signal intelligence devices or trying to fixate on any radio transmissions. Fixing a location on the transmission wasn't a problem, but what would be a problem was if the enemy realized that the MSOT was in the area at all.

Snow keyed the radio. "Chief, screw'em, let them know, let them be scared, make them divert men and time to trying to find us. That will at least slow down their mission, over."

"Snow, I agree. Complete this operation and we'll plan it out. Chief out."

Before departing from their new boat in the marina, the three of them had already decided to break the mission profile and work across the eastern side of the island towards the NAS. There was more cover, and with daylight approaching with each passing minute, they could set an observation post in one of the parks or the golf course across the bay from where they all guessed a cargo offload would occur.

"Kirk, I think you're right, but we have to convince Chief."

Davis nodded at Snow's statement.

The three of them broke cover from the overgrown landscaping next to the marina's edge and began a slow patrol walk to the north along Strand Way. Zeds shambled between the homes on their right; as the men walked about twenty-five yards apart from each other, the three of them looked more like walking shrubbery with the ghillie suits diffusing their form. The undead saw them, but only a few took any interest and tried to follow. The rest seemed to ignore them as the three-man team moved silently along the roadway.

Kirk raised his right hand with a fist before slowly lowering it with his palm flat. All three of them melted into the shaggy grass next to a tree on the side of the road. Kirk, walking point, took the tactical area of responsibility to the front, Davis angled towards the homes on their left and Snow held tactical security to the rear. Their right flank was covered by way of the shaggy trees and fences separating the sidewalk from the tennis courts.

Headlights bounced across the face of the houses ahead of them to the north. The headlights continued around the corner and soon were visible and approaching quickly. The vehicle turned right and stopped in the middle of the intersection, engine running, headlights still on, but facing away from the Marines. It was a four-door ruck that looked vaguely like a Jeep. Davis resisted the urge to sweep the muzzle of his big rifle to the right, instead daring to only move his eyes. Kirk keyed the radio four times without saying a word. *Four men.* Davis and Snow both keyed once in succession to acknowledge the transmission.

Kirk watched as the four men got out of the truck, leaving it idling in the middle of the intersection, while they lit cigarettes and pointed to the tennis courts and then to the homes. Their voices could faintly be heard.

Well whatever, assholes, at least you don't know we're here, and if you're stupid enough to stand in the middle of a road to smoke you don't deserve the opportunity. Kirk slowed his breathing and lined up the first shot, the man who appeared to be in charge. He was the only one of the four without a rifle, only a pistol holstered on his right hip. Letting out his breath slowly, Kirk slowly pressed the rifle trigger to the rear. Just as he fired the impossibly large 50BMG round, decapitating the officer, one of the other men's head exploded. A follow-up shot from Davis left a fist-sized hole in the third man's chest, and Kirk's last shot resulted in the last man's head vaporizing into a fine mist. Less than one hundred yards away, the huge, nearly six-inch-long round's fourteen-thousand-foot-pounds of force was designed to punch through armored plating. Against four men the results were nearly comical, if especially violent.

The three of them stood and sprinted towards the still-running vehicle, Davis shouldering his short-barreled M4, Kirk and Snow both with pistols out, their four-foot-long Barrett-made rifles left behind temporarily.

"Turn the lights off."

"Sure Snow, I'm trying to but I can't read this damned shit."

Davis, ignoring both of them, went to the front of the vehicle and smashed in the glass headlights with the butt of his M4.

Kirk laughed. "This thing looks like the bastard love child of a Jeep, a Humvee, and a Land Rover!"

"Whatever, clean the scene and exfil ... let's take our new transportation on a tour of the island."

With Davis' suggestion, they each dragged a body out of the road and hid them behind a low railing on the front porch of a home on the corner. The only body of the four with a head received a pistol round to the skull to keep it from walking back later. The three Marines checked in the cargo area of the vehicle and climbed into the Chinese-made Jeep-truck thing, not knowing or caring what it was really called.

Looking around the dash, the labels on all the switches and gauges might as well have not been there for all the help they gave Davis, but fortunately the numbers on the gauges were regular numbers. After a few moments the vehicle was in drive and the team continued on their journey in the second commandeered vehicle of the evening.

"Shit, guys, if this keeps up we'll be able to open up a used car and boat lot in a few days. We could offer financing in-house, like you pay three chickens a month for thirty-six months and this beauty could be yours."

Davis and Snow both looked at Kirk and shook their heads. Choosing to ignore the bad joke, Snow said, "Headlights, no operational security, no tactics, I think that tells us a lot about what our invaders think."

Glancing at Snow, Davis asked, "Like what?"

"First of all, if a patrol was worried about an oppositional force they would have been traveling dark, using NODs, and they sure as shit wouldn't have dismounted to smoke in the middle of the damn road."

Kirk shrugged, unnoticeable in the heavy ghillie suit. "Who knows, maybe they have night vision and weren't using them? Maybe the air patrols already called this area clear?"

"Speaking of which, they haven't been flying at night."

"You know what that means, Davis; they don't have shit for night vision gear."

"Then fuck'em, we own the night; let's gate crash the NAS and see what we can find."

The other two nodded. Davis turned left onto Third Street and drove at a steady fifty kph, remembering that was near thirty mph.

San Diego Harbor

The Zodiac slowed at the edge of the wall along the walkway of the bay side of the Hilton Hotel. Rows and rows of Dole tractor trailers sat in the shipping yard next to the hotel, and the smell of rotting bananas was surprisingly strong. Hammer and Gonzo climbed out of the boat and onto the large concrete walkway. Moving slowly and methodically towards the hotel's parking garage, they would take the next to highest level to give them overhead coverage, using the shadows to observe the commercial pier to their left.

Over the sound of the water lapping against the built-up shoreline, thumps of Zeds against the windows of the high-rise hotel could be heard. Aymond shook his head. *Seems like an impossible task. Millions of Zeds, trapped, walking, waiting ... all it takes is one bite, one fucking bite ...*

The original recon boat patrol that Happy, Chuck, and Aymond had planned was essentially accomplished by Kirk, Davis, and Snow after they stole the Chinese patrol boat. Adapting the mission, Aymond and his crew now had time left to wrap around North Island and check Point Loma, specifically the Naval Base and submarine berths there. Even if the Naval Base was home to the dead, on the point near the historic lighthouse they would have a good vantage point to observe the big Panamax ships at anchor. First they had to get around the bay, land and stash the Zodiac.

Cortez, CO

"Dude, there are a shit ton of them out there still. Seems like the whole town went on vacation and then came back to say hi to us! So we're stuck in here, no wheels, surrounded by the dead ..."

"Bexar, you worry too much. Adapt and overcome, remember? All we have to do is work the problem one step at a time. Besides, we still have those giant cans of refried beans we found in the cafeteria; that'll feed us for a couple of weeks."

"As bad as you smell already I don't want to be around you for two weeks of nothing but refried beans."

Chivo continued, unphased. "What do we have we can use for a diversion? Something simple but something that will be big."

"You could whip up your secret squirrel solution in glass jars like before, but we didn't find any glass jars. Think you could do it with a lifetime supply of Styrofoam cups from the cafeteria?"

Smiling, Chivo said, "That's it, mang. Styrofoam. How much fuel did you find over in the athletic faculty's storage?"

"About ten gallons between three cans and a UTV."

"Go get it and meet me in the cafeteria. Also, we need bungee cords or surgical tubing or something, but that's for later; see what you can get."

Before Bexar could ask what the deal was, Chivo was already headed down the hall towards the cafeteria, singing "Napalm sticks to little children, all the children of the world ..."

"Seriously, something is wrong with that guy," Bexar muttered to himself.

He walked through the locker room and weight room towards the football faculty's storage they had found the previous night, but stopped at a squat rack. Hanging on the wall were large silicone bands that were used in weight training. Different colors for different band resistances. He grabbed all of them and stuffed them between his ammo carrier and his shirt. In the faculty's storage Bexar picked up the two plastic gas cans and shook them. They were both practically full, so if Chivo needed more than this he would have to return and syphon gas out of the UTV.

Ten minutes later, Bexar walked into the cafeteria to find Chivo standing over four large stainless pots; each of them so large they had to be measured by gallons and not by quarts. Two boxes of Styrofoam cups were open next to him. Pulling groups of cups out of the boxes, Chivo crumbled them into one of the pots.

"Come give me a hand with this; we need to crumble all of the cups into this pot before we pour the gas into the other pots. Then we slowly stir in the Styrofoam."

"What then?"

"Didn't you ever read the Anarchist Cookbook? Napalm, mano, well, not real napalm, but not a bad substitute for our needs considering the circumstances."

"Great, then what?"

"Did you find any bungee cords?"

"I have these."

"Perfect. We pour this shit back into the cans, light 'em with a rag and launch them like a fucking water balloon into the singlewides across the street. Maybe fire a few rounds off and let the flames bring the fucking dead to the fire like bugs to the zapper. We sneak out the back and hop the fence into the neighborhood to the north. We still don't have wheels, but have faith. We work the problem one step at a time."

Bexar shrugged and crumbled a handful of cups into the large pot.

Groom Lake, NV

"Bill, I appreciate what you're doing. So many survivors are still out there, and the fact that they're coming here and we've started a new community is really all your doing. I'm impressed."

"Thank you, Jake. My concern is that we're only reaching out via different radio frequency broadcasts. I wish there was a way we could reach more people. How many people can the facility hold at maximum capacity?"

"Wright says twenty-five hundred, but I'm not sure that people would like to be packed in here like that. Right now we have a certain level of comfort and privacy, which would be lost. What do you think about establishing aboveground "towns"? There are supposedly thirty dormitories aboveground here."

"If we could power them ... perhaps with power from this facility, or maybe they have their own power source that we don't even know about ... and if we can establish security aboveground, then it would be a good idea. Power might be the easiest hurdle to overcome; I know that we still have undead meandering in over the mountains somehow. I know some of our residents are glad they don't have to worry about surviving, but are unhappy about being forced to live underground. They want sunsets and rain."

"Rain they probably won't see much of, but I'm sure we could get some people together to make sure a sunset happens every evening," Jake said laughingly.

The lights in the radio hut flickered then went dark, the constant swishing hum of the air system falling silent.

"Damnit, this is a problem. If we can't get this figured out then we will have to live aboveground again and power may actually be the biggest problem."

The lights snapped back on, the air system again moved air, and the computers in the room booted back up.

"This is wreaking havoc on my computer systems in here, not to mention the surges aren't good for the radios."

"Well Bill, as long as we've been here, and with the many changes we've made, we've never taken the time to systematically search each of the buildings in our secret world aboveground."

"What will Wright say? Think he'll be worried about classified information in those buildings?"

"Bill, I don't think he knows what is in those buildings; I'm not sure even Cliff knew. At this point I really wouldn't care if there are dead alien bodies and spacecraft, just as long as it isn't zombies."

"How are you going to do it?"

"We'll need special people. People who have tactical training or a small group of people who can help train others."

"That's not these airmen. They're exceptionally intelligent but they're not really the type to go kicking in doors for fun, not like the PJs were. They loathe having to pull aboveground guard duty for arrivals and general security patrols."

"I'll get with Brit and come up with a list, and then we'll simply have to ask those people."

"What if you made an announcement over the system?"

"Sure, what would I say? 'Uh, this is your mayor speaking, do any of you know how to shoot people, we could use some help up here ... and thank you for flying Janet Airlines.' No, we need to do this discreetly at first, figure out what we have to work with and how we're going to do it. I need maybe a dozen people who can make it happen."

"Well, good luck then, I'm going to stick here with my radios and see if I can get good skip on the HF bands and QTH some more folks."

"Do what?"

"I'm hoping for good ionosphere conditions to bounce my radio signals over the horizon to find new people. QTH is a Q-code; it's a question that means 'what is your location?'"

"OK, well, whatever it is, Samuel Morse, good luck with what God has wrought. I'll check back in with you tomorrow unless you come across something I need to know about."

"Roger that. Good night, buddy."

Cortez, CO

"What the fuck, man." Bexar coughed while stirring to mix the dissolving Styrofoam into the gasoline, Chivo breaking up cup after cup into little pieces. "Why can't you just dump them all in here? This is taking forever and it smells like ass!"

"It won't dissolve as well, mano, and we want it to work. Besides, if you do anything you do it right and you do it all the way, there's no half-assed effort on my watch. Did you find the janitor's supply room?"

"Yeah, down the hall on the left."

"Did you get what I asked for?"

"One mop, three rags, three spray bottles, which I emptied as instructed, and all the toilet cleaner in the closet. It's all in the mop bucket over there." Bexar pointed by way of tilting his head.

"Keep stirring, it'll start to firm up like hair gel." Chivo walked to the bucket and pulled out all the supplies; he set each bottle on the table next to the bucket, placed a rag in front of each, and left the gallon-sized jug of toilet cleaner sitting there, before walking into the kitchen area of the cafeteria only to return with an industrial-sized roll of aluminum foil.

"This is starting to get sort of, um, gooey, but there's a bunch of shit on the surface."

"Scoop the scum off the top, leave the rest in the pot, and start on the next one. I've got to run down the hall for a minute. I just thought of something."

A few minutes later Chivo returned with three large, brightly painted, lumpy ball-shaped jugs. "Art class, I remembered seeing them. I guess they were making some fucked-up pottery or something."

"Yeah, something to smoke their dope in."

"Dude, no reason to be mean, some zombie kids worked really hard on these, probably got an A for it too. Tell you what, fuck the second batch; it's time to fill these up. I can't take much more of this smell."

Carefully, ladle by ladle, each of the three ceramic art class creations was filled with the gasoline mixture. Chivo tore large pieces of aluminum foil off the big roll and stuffed them inside the plastic spray bottles, then taped the bottles to the sides of the clay art jugs. A rag went into the top of each clay jug.

"Grab all your shit, toss the workout bands into the mop bucket and bring it with you, and bring that jug of toilet cleaner. I'll carry our babies."

Bexar had no shit to grab, as his rifle was still slung across his chest and all he owned was either in his pockets or presumably in the bed of the abandoned truck near Main Street. Pushing the mop bucket by the mop handle, he hustled after Chivo, the wheels squeaked softly as they walked to the front of the school.

Once at the front of the school and standing in the shadows, they saw the schoolyard was overrun by the dead, which were ambling to and fro, bumping into each other, not chasing anything but not leaving either.

"Bexar, how far away do you think those singlewides are?"

"Eh, call it fifty yards?"

"I'd believe that." Chivo carefully set the jugs down one by one, then picked each back up and examined it carefully. He then picked up the different-colored workout bands, stretching them between his hands.

"I'd say we use the orange and grey bands together."

Bexar shrugged; he still didn't really understand what Chivo's plan was.

Chivo stuffed the rags deeper into the thick gas mixture in the jugs and unscrewed the caps of the spray bottles, setting the caps next to its companion.

"Bexar, I'm going to get this ready. I need you to go find something we can use to prop the doors open."

Bexar nodded and walked towards what he assumed was the main office.

A few minutes later he returned, holding a gold-painted brick and a large dead potted plant. Chivo had each door ajar, the bands looped around the door hinges and tied to the sides of the mop bucket.

"The first one will be a bitch. If everything goes to plan then these fuckers should be distracted by the time the second and third volley are launched. "

"What are we doing exactly?"

"We light our homemade napalm via the rag, we then pour toilet cleaner into the bottle with the foil and screw on the caps. Then very quickly we use our industrial-sized water balloon launcher to hurl these damn things across the street. The spray bottles should explode, spreading the ignited gas mix across those trees and mobile homes, which should draw our town greeting party here towards the flames. We then run out the back, hop the fence, and figure out what to do after that when we get that far."

"OK MacGyver, minus a fucking ball point pen to make your complicated plan work, what's the deal with the mop?"

"Oh, I just wanted you to have it. We're going to clean up this town and you're leading the charge." Chivo started laughing; Bexar swung the mop and hit Chivo in the shin.

"Aye chinga you punta!"

"Yeah fuck you too, you and your stupid mop ... fast or slow with the doors?"

"I'd say fast. Once this shit is lit you're going to want those doors open. I'll pick off the leaders while you do your thing with your magical brick and plant."

Chivo produced a cheap gas station lighter from his pocket, and after a few tries finally got it to hold a flame. One at a time he lit the rags; once the gas mix started to catch the hallway began to choke with thick black smoke as he unscrewed the lid to the toilet cleaner.

"Do it, mano!"

Bexar threw open the first door and dragged the plant into place; he could hear the crack of the rifle rounds snapping through the air as they passed by him.

"Moving!"

"Move!"

Chivo held fire for a breath as Bexar turned for the second door, throwing it open and kicking the brick into the door.

"Rifle up, Bexar!"

Bexar turned and began firing, dropping the closest undead to the door; a dozen already lay sprawled out on the concrete walkway, heads ruined by Chivo's fast aim.

"Get back!"

Bexar ducked under the silicone bands, Chivo pulling the mop bucket back and down as far as the bands would stretch. Without pausing he let the bucket go. The clay jug rocketed out of the door and caught a walking corpse in the face about fifty feet from the door, knocking the undead woman off her feet in an exploding rainbow of flames, the ten or so other dead shambling near her covered in the burning homemade napalm.

"Holy shit, they're on goddamned fire!"

"No time, mano, adjust up ten and fire for effect!" Chivo grunted as he pulled the bucket back, this time laying on his back and holding the bucket nearly to the floor. Once released some unknown kid's art project sailed through the air, exploding in a slimy rain of fire above the trees and mobile homes across the street, the night sky glowing in orange flames.

"Wow," was all Bexar could say as the third jug flew slightly right from the other, exploding over another group of trees and mobile homes. The undead still stumbled into each other on the large walkway in front of the school; the ones that were on fire, catching more walking corpses ablaze. Chivo kicked the brick and potted plant out of the way, pulling the doors closed, which wouldn't latch because of the bands in the hinges.

"Bexar, grab the mop."

"Sure, now you want my fucking mop."

Bexar handed it to Chivo, who slid it through the crash bars on the back of the doors, barring them closed.

"Dude, out of everything that's happened since Christmas, this has to be one of the more fucked-up things I've seen; she caught it right in the damn face!"

"You should have been in El Salvador when the shit hit the fan ..." Chivo shook his head.

The dead slowly succumbed to the flames, flesh melting into the pavement as they fell and burned. The mobile homes across the street were fully engulfed, the fire continuing to spread. The rest of the undead within view were beginning to make their way towards the flames.

"Looks like your plan worked. Are you going to smoke a cigar now, Colonel Hannibal?"

Chivo only nodded, turned and walked towards the back of the school, waving at Bexar to follow through the dark school hallway.

Near Monticello, Utah

Cliff woke with the eastern horizon's morning glow, the sun not quite up yet. The small home on US-491 had a wood-burning stove, which he'd decided to light after sunset with the impressive stack of firewood stacked neatly in the living room next to the stove. The smoke would be visible, but not as obvious during the night. Besides, mid-March in Utah was still cold. The previous occupants of the home had been happy to greet him the previous evening, but having learned his lesson from the apartment-turned-observation-post in Cortez, he let the undead man and woman shamble through the back door before center-punching their skulls with skillfully placed shots from his rifle.

The day was young and if he pushed hard he would make it to Granite Mountain by the afternoon, although the trip would have been much faster before the end of civilization. Using the growing daylight, Cliff searched the home for anything useful. The lawn equipment and ATVs in the metal out-building had enough gas to top off his fuel tank and fuel cans, but the home was devoid of any food. The most exciting find was a Utah road atlas in the glove box of a beat-up old VW Rabbit in the metal building. The map was at least ten years old, but it didn't really matter; where he was going was older than that and the atlas would be accurate enough.

Vienna sausages weren't the most gourmet breakfast Cliff had ever eaten, but they were far from the worst. Although the fire in the wood-burning stove was out, the residual heat was comforting and anyone less mission-driven would have had a hard time leaving the relative safety of a warm house. With two trips, Cliff loaded the firewood from the living room into the bed of the truck; he wasn't sure if he would use it or how, but cut firewood was a nice commodity in the supply locker for any of the cold March Utah nights that probably lay ahead.

The truck took a little coaxing in the cold morning, but the engine finally stuttered to life; the heater worked, but Cliff turned it on low. He would be far more comfortable outside the truck by adjusting to a cooler temperature in the truck than stepping out of a blazing furnace into the freezing air. While waiting a few moments for the truck to warm up, Cliff looked at the road atlas. The fastest route would take him through some of the more populated areas in Utah, including Salt Lake. If at all possible Cliff wanted to avoid population centers. Avoiding large numbers of undead would increase his chances of survival.

Dead roamed the streets of the small town, some turning to follow from the old one-story motel as the truck rolled by. The green sign's arrow pointed right with "MOAB" printed on it. Having referenced the atlas before leaving, Cliff followed the arrow and turned north on US-191.

Too bad I can't take a couple of days to hike around Canyonlands National Park. For once I bet there wouldn't be anyone on the trails ... but I'd probably have to shoot the ones I found.

CHAPTER 7

Cortez, CO
March 14, Year 1

Bexar followed Chivo as they walked out of the back of the school. The urgency in their movements was temporarily missing, as behind them the sky was awash with the crackling orange glow of a mobile home park burning uncontrollably. Reaching the low chain-link fence, the pair took care to be quiet instead of quick as they climbed over and into the dead-end street between the back of a church and an empty lot. Walking slowly, Bexar followed Chivo, trailing by ten paces, every few steps turning to look behind them. Bexar worried about undead appearing from behind trees, abandoned cars and home, but he still had concerns that Cliff might not have left town.

Frowning at the thought, Bexar hoped to see Cliff again so he could kill him. *I had a chance to kill him in the garage yesterday and I didn't take it. If it wasn't for that asshole I would be in Big Bend with Jessie, Sandra, Jack ... Will would be alive and my precious little Keeley would still be chasing deer in The Basin. Fuck. We should have stayed off the radio and hunkered down. We were idiots. We gave away our position, we chased his dream. I have to make it to Groom Lake. I'm taking Jessie and we're dropping off the grid. We'll raise our new baby alone, somewhere we make safe, far away from dead civilization, far away from survivors ...*

His lack of attention caused Bexar to walk into Chivo, who had stopped abruptly. Chivo cast an angry look at him and pointed left. Parked on the street in front of the church was a small yellow school bus. Bexar shook his head in disbelief and with a hint of dread at what the church might hold.

Chivo darted silently into the yard of the church, careful not to be seen by anyone looking out of the windows. At the corner of the first building Chivo found a set of wooden doors. Gently he turned the door knob, which turned. Bexar resisted the urge to watch, instead facing outward from the building, flexing his fingers against the stock of his AR, trying to calm his breathing. The scene inside the previous church flashed through his mind: blood dripping from bare feet as the bodies squirmed, jaws snapping at them although death had found them. Bexar closed his eyes, shaking his head from side to side and trying to clear the image from his mind. Chivo nudged him.

Looking over his shoulder, he saw the wooden door stood open in front of Chivo. No flies rushed out, no death, no bodies, only the smell of stale air and a hint of mildew. Bexar turned around and squeezed Chivo's shoulder, who slid into the dark hall like a ghost, the light on his M4 snapping on once he was inside. Bexar followed and pulled the door closed behind him, twisting the latch for the deadbolt. No one would follow them inside.

One by one they slowly checked each small room. One appeared to have been a day-care-type room, the others probably where the church held Sunday School, all of them empty of anything but stacked chairs and folding tables. The hall opened into a small foyer ahead of them, glass doors separating the sanctuary from the entryway. Bexar steeled himself against the worst, but was surprised to see that the pews had been pushed to the walls, a large bed positioned where the pulpit would have been, and hundreds of burned candles surrounding the bed on the raised platform. No signs of death, no signs of life, just a bizarre scene out of a twisted fantasy.

"Well mano, looks like nothing but a place for an orgy."

"I doubt it was a happy one."

"Yeah, I doubt that too. Out we go, our big yellow chariot awaits."

"I'm starting to hate school buses."

"Yeah, well, Bexar, I hated them until they became all we had."

Exiting through a side door behind the stage and baptismal, they saw the sky had turned grey with the approach of sunrise. They were happily surprised to see the rear of a two-toned brown pickup truck. The old square-bodied GMC sat on oversized off-road tires and had a chrome light bar, four large lights mounted on the bar.

"Wow, well that's not a school bus, Bexar."

Bexar smiled. The driver's door was unlocked, keys in the ignition, door chime dinging in protest as the door opened.

"That's a good sign."

The front of the hood popped loose with a pull of the lever. Standing at the front of the truck, Chivo unlatched the hood and held it open, the chrome top of a large circular air cleaner reflecting their faces. Bexar popped the rotor off the distributor with the blade of his knife and smiled.

"There you go, Chivo, carburetor, no fuel rails, points, and no electronics. We have seriously cool wheels for once."

Distributor snapped back together, Chivo closed the hood and held his hand out towards the driver's door. "After you, Lee Majors."

Bexar snorted. "I didn't know they dubbed that old show into Spanish."

"Shit man, I've never been with less than an ocho or nueve, so fine."

The truck roared to life with a couple pumps of the gas pedal and a turn of the key. The deep rumble of the V-8 vibrated the truck.

Chivo leaned in to look at the dash. "How's the gas?"

"Three-quarters ... wait." Bexar pushed the button to select the left-hand tank, which showed full. "I forgot about that, these things had the saddle tanks."

"Hell yeah! First we get our bags from the other truck, then we get the hell out of here. Fuck this town; we'll put together our fuel needs on the outskirts of this shithole. I've had enough of it."

"My thoughts exactly, brother."

Chivo stared at the tank selector switch. "Doesn't that have circuit boards in it or behind it or something?"

Bexar looked at the dash and the switches. "Yeah, probably."

"You're the end of the world super prepper, why does it still work after the EMP?"

"I have no idea and right now I really give zero fucks about that."

Bexar glanced to make sure the button for two-wheel drive was pushed, pulled the selector to Drive, and pushed on the gas, gravel spitting out from under the back tires as the truck bounced over the curb and into the street.

US-191, Utah

Cliff kept a steady pace of fifty mph as the old truck lumbered and rattled along the edges of the smaller towns before reaching Moab. Moab was a different story. Small gaggles of undead filtered past his windows; abandoned cars, many of them large SUVs and 4x4s, littered the roadway, causing him to slow as he drove through the middle of town. There just wasn't an easy route to miss the town and stay on schedule.

The sight of death and destruction in a town, undead trapped in hotel rooms and cars, bodies lying in the open, blood smeared along the cars and fronts of business had become unremarkable. Sweeping his head side to side in a controlled and trained manner, Cliff scanned for other threats, more important threats. He watched for any survivors that might have an ambush in mind, or ill intent. At this point his previous quest to rally survivors had long passed; specifically when his C-130 was brought to a violent end from an RPG. It passed with the church full of bodies. It passed when he decoded the message from Clint. Serious issues were at hand, more serious than just survival; this was a continued attack, a renewed attack, and this could be the prelude to invasion of the United States.

The Colorado River looked like it always had. The sign for Arches National Park flew by his window as he gently accelerated the truck back to his highway speed, and for a moment he considered walking away, disappearing and just wandering out into the wilderness he loved. It wouldn't be hard to survive, scavenging as he drove to and fro finding the perfect secluded place to live out the rest of his days like a fur trapping mountain man of old. But his training was too engrained, his mission too valuable to simply walk away. No, first he had to verify what Clint believed and, if true, shut everything down. Every piece of it would have to come apart.

Cliff looked at his watch and to his right at the sun; he would arrive today. If the facility was still up by some chance, then his task would be easy. If it was overrun then it might take him a couple of days to get his mission done.

The turn onto I-70 was anticlimactic. However, with interstate roads come rest stops, and on the eastbound side of the road was a rest area. Cliff had no need to rest, he could rest after taking care of the problems in Granite Mountain, but this would be a good place to top off fuel before getting closer to any of the larger towns.

The sign implied that it would not be legal to cross the median on the improved surface, but then again he probably wasn't supposed to drive the wrong way on the Interstate either. Passingly taking note of the quirks of the new world, Cliff drove through the cross over, continuing against the flow of traffic, had there been any, and driving into the rest area through the exit ramp.

A dozen cars sat in the rest area; Cliff stopped in the middle of the parking area, away from the closest vehicles, and stepped out of his truck. Rifle slung across his chest, he raised it slightly as he approached the first four-door rental car near the restrooms, ignoring the big Ford diesel truck, which was of no use for his gasoline needs. Cliff punched the flash suppressor on the end of his rifle against the glass a few times before it broke. After pushing the broken glass out of the way, he unlocked the door, pulled the bottom of the rear seat out of the car, and tossed it on the asphalt next to the car. A couple of quick taps and the fuel pump in the center of the fuel tank unscrewed to be tossed into the floorboard.

Ten minutes later the truck's fuel tank was full, the fuel cans were topped back off, and Cliff was about to leave when the sound of rocks dragging across the pavement resonated in his ears. From around the back of a large RV staggered a woman. Dried blood on her bare chest matched the blood on her skirt and the dark, rotting dead skin of her face and body. Cliff shook his head slightly before firing a single round, brain matter exploding out of the back of her skull as she slumped to the ground. A pool of blackish-purple pus spread slowly from beneath her head.

Moans echoed from the only building in the rest area, the restrooms, as one after another the dead shambled out. Cliff sighed, climbed into the truck, which started with a loud backfire, and drove away from the two dozen undead futilely stumbling after.

Each little town along the drive was the same as the last. They represented little hope, and Cliff gave them little care; he mostly disregarded anything but the mission. The only challenge presented was to remember that he had to take US-6 instead of following the signs to Salt Lake City. Just sounded like a bad idea to go anywhere near the towns leading up to Salt Lake and then have to skirt the city itself to get to the mountain. Glancing to the bed of the truck and the fuel cans therein, he calculated he could drive straight to the mountain without having to syphon any more gas. There was treated gas in large tanks on site, and he could top off with as much as he could carry when he arrived, or before he left.

The mountains were gorgeous, and every time Cliff looked up to admire them he would inevitably have to swerve around another abandoned vehicle or a corpse or something that had the potential of ending his journey. A single lapse of concentration had caused him to crash the old VW bus and that nearly killed him. So methodically he drove, forcing his focus to stay on the road, on his mission, continually scanning for any threats along the way. The discipline wasn't hard to keep, his training at The Farm had made sure of that. Besides, this was a simple drive in the mountains compared to what he had been through before. He hit the tiny town of Duchesne, which looked like all the rest, and after about a dozen blocks and left turns he was out of the town and back into the mountains.

Herber City gave more cause for concern; it was one of the larger cities he'd driven into so far that morning, and the Walmart parking lot was overrun with the dead.

What is it with Walmart and the dead. It's like everyone in town went to there to die ... they went to Walmart because they weren't prepared, found it overrun with people, someone was killed, and then it spread like wildfire. Classified documents from the USAMRIID predicted it would be this bad, but no one wanted to believe them. The US Army Medical Research Institute of Infectious Diseases ... seems like they could have come up with a shorter name or a better acronym ... too bad no one in the administration believed their report.

Driving north through the middle of town, Cliff was amazed to see that everything else looked fairly normal and clean, just deserted as if everyone had walked out of town together. Cars had been pushed out of the roadway, and he saw what appeared to be chimney smoke rising from homes of survivors well beyond the strip centers and stores on the highway. All the traffic lights were dark, and Cliff continued through town at a steady pace before breaking free of civilization on the north end of town.

After turning onto I-80 and heading west, the signs and his atlas showed he was quickly approaching Salt Lake City, which was exactly where he did not want to go. At least the Interstate would keep him to the eastern edge of town and it would only be for a short distance. He snacked on a cold can of stew as he drove.

Interstate 215 was practically choked with abandoned vehicles, but the number of undead on the road and in Cliff's way was light. He wove through the vehicles, the divided freeway making it harder to get around some of the vehicles and a few wrecks, but slowly one by one, Cliff passed through and continued towards his turnoff for 190 and then 210. On the Interstate, large developed tracks of homes were visible. Once again some chimneys showed smoke rising in stark defiance to the ruin of the outside world.

I knew that if there would be anyone who could weather the storm of the end of the world it would be the Latter Day Saints, some of the more practical preppers in the entire country.

Just a few short miles was all it took for Cliff to get some distance from the thick suburban sprawl and closer to his destination. The small yellow sign showing the address and an unmarked drive to his left announced his arrival. The yellow metal gate stood closed and locked with a chain. Cliff set the parking brake, left the truck's engine running, and walked up to the gate. The chain had two padlocks, and one took a key. The other, a specially made combination lock designed to outwardly look like a standard hardened combination lock, was what Cliff needed. Flipping the padlock over and removing the rubber weather protector from the bottom, he quickly rolled each of the number dials into the correct position. Seven in all instead of the usual four; once set, two quick tugs on the lock was all it needed to open. Cliff swung the metal pipe gates open, hanging the chain on one. The fiberglass pole entry gate beyond the metal gate wasn't something he had a key for or even needed a key for; retrieving the truck, Cliff drove into the post, the fiberglass shattering away from the attachment. Once through, like a cattle rancher, Cliff stepped out of the truck and closed the metal gate behind him. This time he used a shorter section of chain, locking his padlock as the only lock that could now open the gate. He had business to attend to and he didn't need anyone else coming in to "help."

Cortez, CO

"Dude, that fire is really going now, you're like some sort of evil Mr. Wizard!"

Chivo looked through the back glass of the truck, the flames almost visible above the buildings and homes between them, the morning sky filling with a thick dark plume of smoke.

"Mano, that's a beacon for the dead and for the living. The quicker we get our shit and bug out, the better off we'll be."

Bexar stopped the new truck next to the destroyed old truck that they'd wrecked out on Main Street. Their bags and Chivo's big sniper rifle were quickly moved from one truck bed to the next, and soon a left turn and west was their new direction. West towards the highway, west towards where the bus ambush had occurred just a few days before, west towards the road they needed to reach Groom Lake.

"Wasn't there a parts store near where the bus was destroyed?"

"My bell was rung. You had to pull me out of the bus; I don't remember much besides the fight and Cliff roaring in as a one man QRF."

"I still don't get it. We came up here to rescue him, he then rescues us from an ambush, we destroy the cult and then he fucks us. I mean, I used to jack up gang bangers who made more sense."

"People don't matter to him, it's just the mission. If you're for his mission then you're on his team; if you falter away from that mission or stray from what he thinks is the process, then you're now against him. His type have no friends, no family, no personal connection, no emotion ... they're just machines. Any emotion they may have once had is trained out of them. Even the guys I used to be in The Unit with weren't like that. They had passion and a love for each other. Those bonds mattered, you fought for your brothers. The warrior's code exists and Cliff lives outside of it. He's ronin."

"Say what now?"

"Ronin: a samurai with no master. His thought process, his means, his actions, they're all with no regard to a code, no honor, no brotherhood, only singular devotion to his task at the time. He could be on a mission to help a group of people defeat a group of rebels one moment and re-tasked to help the rebels defeat the first people the next. If his commanding officer said he had to switch for the sake of the mission, then he would switch without a thought or a second's remorse."

"That's fucked up."

"It is, and there's a whole group of guys like him. Cliff isn't his real name; whatever identity he had in his life was wiped clean, same with Clint. That person was killed, and any evidence that he existed is only a whisper of fog in a forest, fleeting and gone. It's fucking spooky, man."

Bexar followed Main Street as it wrapped to the left and onto the highway, before stopping in the parking lot of an auto parts store; the charred remains of their bus sat in the road, and the building's exterior was pockmarked from all the rifle fire.

"What's up with the parts store. Looking for some sweet mud flaps or maybe some flame decals for the hood?"

"No Chivo, we're going to start this journey right. We're going to get tire plugs, fix-a-flat, oil, fan belts, hell, we'll even get some window cleaner, anything we can think of that we could use to make sure we get to Groom Lake."

Bexar shut off the truck, climbed out, and looked at the VIN plate on the front of the dash. Counting the digits, he stopped on the year location, but it took a couple of moments to remember what the designator meant.

"1979, so that'll make things a little easier."

Chivo walked through the gaping hole in the front of the business, his boots crunching on the broken glass. He pointed at Bexar and then to the right, and Bexar nodded.

Bexar followed the inside front wall towards the right corner of the store, clearing the aisles as he went. Chivo mirrored him on the left side of the store, both with rifles up and weapon lights on, beams of light cutting through the darkness. The store looked intact, which struck Bexar as weird; if he had been one of the survivors or a part of the cult he would have picked this store clean by now. A few moments passed before the back of the store was checked and they were confident that they were alone.

"Chivo, grab a cart, get a case of 10W-30, a name brand synthetic. Get all the fix-a-flat they have on the shelf, WD-40, and anything else that catches your eye."

Chivo nodded, and Bexar went behind the parts counter. The computer terminals were dark, the keys covered with years of grime and grease. Kneeling, he scanned a lower shelf before pulling out a well-worn catalogue and opening it on the counter. The catalogue listed the numbers for each of the parts he might need to and could fix while on the road. Bexar jotted notes on a notepad before walking through the parts shelves in the back.

Next to the door was a stack of shopping handbaskets. Chivo had an idea. He put the entire stack into the cart and pushed the exit door, finding it unlocked. In the parking lot, Chivo placed like items in the baskets and put the baskets in the bed of the truck to keep the items from rolling around.

Two trips later, Chivo was done and leaning against the truck. Bexar walked out pushing two carts, one full of things like fan belts, radiator hose, oil hose, a fuel pump, a set of sockets and wrenches, the other cart stacked full with a half-dozen red plastic gas cans.

Chivo helped load the bed of the truck, which was quickly getting full, and smiled while holding up his prized find for the day, a hand-cranked fuel transfer pump with a five-foot-length of tubing on each end.

"No more spitting gas out of your mouth, mano, this is primo."

"Awesome, and next door we go to put it to use," Bexar said, pointing at the used car lot fifty yards to the north.

"You load your loot, I'm going to walk over and start ripping out seats and fuel pumps to get ready."

After Bexar climbed into the truck, he couldn't help but laugh. On the center of the dash was a plastic Jesus with about a dozen tree-shaped air fresheners hanging from the rearview mirror. He was still laughing when he pulled up alongside Chivo in the used car lot.

Chivo smiled. "The Jesus is for me so I don't care if it rains or freezes, and the forest of air freshener is for you, 'cause you smell like ass. I would have done more but apparently in Colorado the taste in vehicle accessories isn't as varied as it is down on the border."

Taking turns cranking the fuel transfer pump while the other held security, soon they had the fuel in the truck topped off and all six gas cans were full. The sun stood angrily overhead, their adventures in shopping excursion having taken up most of the morning. Both men were sweating heavily as they climbed back in the truck. Bexar steered across the lawn in front of the dealership, and the truck bounded off the curb and north on the highway. Chivo reached over and tried to turn on the radio, which didn't work.

"Hey mano, can't fault a guy for trying. Next thing I know you're going to be telling me some bullshit story about how you arrested a guy driving a truck like this once."

"This truck, no, but the felony forest is usually a solid clue."

Chivo looked over quizzically, and Bexar's reply was to point at the air fresheners. "There's a rule of thumb: three or more cheap tree-shaped air fresheners and they probably have a suspended license; you start getting into a whole damn forest like this and I promise you nine times out of ten they've got dope in the car."

"Huh. The more you know, right?"

"Yup, and knowing is half the battle."

Chivo smirked. "The other half is violence!"

CHAPTER 8

Coronado, CA
March 14, Year 1

Daybreak brought a new flurry of activity from the PLA, helicopters overhead roaring past the compound. Simmons and Jones took turns napping while the other monitored the radio. Chief, Happy, and Chuck were back and taking a combat nap, and Hammer and Gonzo were on the mainland, clicking the transmit button every hour, a non-verbal check-in to verify they were still alive and OK. Kirk, Davis, and Snow were somewhere in or around Halsey Field. With daylight, they should be hunkered down in a good position where they couldn't be seen, nor could their newly acquired vehicle.

Simmons sat in the first M-ATV, the engine off with the radio on, volume turned up just loud enough to hear. He checked the time with his new watch. The metal containers that held the SEAL Team's mission profile gear had apparently protected some of the gear from the EMP. He wasn't sure how much a watch like this would cost at the Exchange, but Simmons knew it wasn't the sort of thing that the chain of command just gave out to random motor pool Marines.

Nearly 1300, should be checking in soon.

As if on cue, the radio hissed with two short clicks of a transmission followed by a long then short click of another transmission. Both deployed teams checked in on time and were OK. Another thirty minutes and it would be his turn to rest while Jones came on the watch. Simmons held his breath every time a helicopter roared past. On the other side of the building it sounded like small convoys of vehicles were passing and headed towards Halsey Field.

The distant rumble of heavy jet transporters landing then taking off seemed to be nearly constant. *I never knew the Chinese had this sort of capability; how could we not see this coming?* Simmons shook his head. There wasn't anything he could do about the past now, he had to focus on the now and hope for the future.

The radio's speaker clicked on. "Dagger-Actual, stand by for SITREP."

Simmons shook his head to clear the drowsiness and responded with a single click of the transmit button on the radio, pad of paper and pen in his hand. The next transmission was short, but important. Simmons woke up Jones early to man the radio post while he left to wake up Aymond, who was sleeping in the back of the second M-ATV. Once awake, Simmons handed the short note to him.

"Well shit."

With the curse, Aymond stood and walked inside the building. After checking back with Jones, who was fine with an early shift, Simmons lay down in the back of the lead M-ATV to sleep. He knew he needed to bank as much sleep now as he could; sleep might be a hard commodity in the very near future.

Granite Mountain, Utah

Cliff approached the loading docks. By all outward appearances the mountain was dead: no facility activity, no power, nothing. He knew better. Behind a group of large storage pods in front of the right-most entryway, a digital keypad was concealed in a metal box that looked, and was marked, like a telephone junction box. A quarter-turn to the left on the bolt head in the middle of the box, followed by a half-turn to the left while pressing into the bolt, and the whole box lifted up off the rock face. The touch-screen panel behind the box was lit, the numbers appearing on the screen. Cliff punched in a twenty-four-character numeric code before the screen went blank and he pressed his right thumb firmly against the panel. The panel flashed red twice then green before the heavy metal security gate rolled upward into the mountain. Cliff walked into the loading dock area and stood in front of the heavy blast door at the rear of the entry tunnel. The tunnel was shut, secure and locked. With the keypad mounted on the side of the door, Cliff entered another, but different, twenty-four-digit code followed by the thumbprint routine. This time the door hissed with a click before Cliff could open it. He walked into the security area of the first floor and to the secured metal door at the back of the room. Repeating the process with another digital pad and yet another twenty-four-digit code, he opened the door into the archives. Before him were rows upon rows of microfiche catalogued and ready to be scanned for millions of people to use.

The Latter Day Saints archives had been used by thousands to build their family tree history. What those people didn't know was that they were also building their own family tree and history; while interconnecting with distant relatives that some didn't know they had, the church was retaining all the data, all the family tree information, all the genealogical information that people had researched for free. Even if everyone knew, Cliff assumed no one would really care; there had been far more heinous data-mining operations going on ... *or there still was.*

An unmarked door sat on the back right wall of the third vault, with another digital keypad. The entire routine was repeated with yet another unique twenty-four-count set of numbers before that door's lock clicked open.

So far Cliff hadn't encountered a single person, living or otherwise. Where he was headed always smelled a little bit anyways, due to how this group lived, but mixed in with the smell of stale pizza, cigarette smoke, and body odor was the sharp smell of death and rotting flesh.

Frowning slightly, Cliff stepped into the hallway, the automatic lights turning on with his presence. The electrical system was operated by its own generated power, so if there was anything that should have survived the EMP it was this facility. Cliff was puzzled as to the lack of people in the semi-public front end of the Granite Mountain Records Vault. His M4 rose slightly, ready for what the smell of death held in wait for him. Cliff moved in complete silence from one room to the next. The dormitories were disgusting; he had seen cleaner huts in the middle of Third World slum areas. Some of the beds appeared to have large lumps under the covers. Reaffirming his suspicion, Cliff found different young men lying dead in their beds. Some of them with visible bite marks, all of them shot through the head either through aggressive means or by a self-inflicted wound.

Straining, Cliff tried to remember how many hackers were a part of this unit and the facility. He couldn't remember exactly, but thirty was the number that kept coming to mind, so Cliff would keep with that until proven otherwise.

One by one, room by room, all he found were bodies.

Finally, the main room, like a cross between QuakeCon and Mission Control. It was a jumbled mix of top of the line computer hardware, much of it running custom-coded software that the group had modified from a standard distribution of Linux. In the middle of the room sat a man, rail thin, his head thrashing from side to side. Nearing the man, Cliff saw on the desk next to him two large prescription pill bottles, both which were empty. A notepad had a half-page of instructions scrawled on it. The man sat, ankles and wrists handcuffed to his chair, having died in place then turned after death. His left bicep was wrapped in heavy bandages;

blood had soaked through, but now all that was left was final rest for the electronic warrior. With a single shot from his rifle, Cliff gave the man what the first item listed in his note asked for: rest.

With the note in hand, Cliff sat at station four as instructed. The monitor lit up with a tap of the space bar and, careful to follow the scribbled instructions, he signed in. Passingly familiar with Unix- and Linux-based systems, Cliff understood enough to correctly enter simple commands without much error. Carefully typing, he double-checked the characters on the screen against the note before tapping Enter.

The screen blurred in a rapid series of commands, a program loading before the screen flickered to show a video, the undead hacker he'd just shot coming to life on the screen. His eyes appeared unfocused, he was very pale, and his arm was already bandaged.

"Today is March 1st, and if you are watching this then congratulations on living. Chris, Clint, Carl, Agent Johnson, Smith, or whatever name you shady fucks made up for yourself may be ... as you can see things went wrong, very wrong. We learned of the attack on December 26th only ten minutes before it was launched. Our theory is that the DPRK didn't use any of their computer systems during the buildup and they were assisted by the Chinese. Three days before the missile launch we had ... well, the entire electronic infrastructure of the U.S. military was attacked. It was very sophisticated, much more than the Koreans have shown in the past. We've had their systems fully penetrated for five years, and quite frankly they don't have the skill or technology to pull off what was going on. It was probably Unit 61398, the Chinese, the PLA. Besides the Russians they're really the only ones that could do it. I ... we are nearly sure that it wasn't the Russians. Russia is dead, most of Europe is dead, middle Africa and Australia seem to be amongst some of the living, but it appears the submarine cables were sabotaged. All we're getting from Australia is RF picked up by the orbiting Sauron birds. The radio transmissions are what you would expect, but the country is in crisis. Our estimation is that *if* the Australians come to help, when they're able to, there is a good chance everyone in North America will be dead. It's almost there; we're getting pockets of RF ... fucking Groom Lake is pumping out enough Radio Frequency to cause cancer. The PLA are moving, they know ... they know where the facilities are. I've ... we monitored the communications between Nevada and Texas, I get it, but go dark, man ... China cyber-offensive against the underground bases, man, we've completely disconnected the systems here so we can hide."

On the video the hacker appeared to flirt with the edge of consciousness and he was becoming more incoherent.

"Fuck. China tried to appear overrun for the first thirty days after the attack. From the systems we have gained access to, apparently they were willing to kill off up to seventy-five percent of their own people to make their fucked-up plan work. Im—imaginary ... fucking photos from space last week show massive activity, clearing the major ... army ... the dead, using big radar trucks ... we ... the last ninety-six hours we tried to get into one of their systems ... this damned thing, but it was only Dickhead, Sauron, and me alive. Now it's just me. Since you're watching me now you have the note ... I was bit twelve hours ago, my fever ... one oh five ... fucking Yama got me. I've already had about four mills of Z-bars to calm the fuck down, a handful of Zofran, and now this large bottle of children's chewable morphine I've been eating ... heh, no, this is the real shit, but I'm going out on my own damn terms. I hope I don't bite you!"

The video ended, the screen returning to a command line.

Cliff looked at the hacker's body, his ruined skull pooling blood on the floor, his body still handcuffed to the chair, and frowned.

"You did well there, guy, but if you were listening to us you should have sent us a message and now I can't send one either because you pulled everything off line."

If the SSC and Groom Lake are the only two facilities left, then that's what we've got. Keep the SSC for command and to isolate POTUS from any further danger; use Groom Lake as a cattle lot for survivors ... but if the PLA is still active then the original intelligence assessment might be right, they might be coming to the U.S. ... how do I stop an invasion by myself? How do I fight a war by myself?

A few things were now clear to Cliff. First he had to see the rest of the information and files listed on the handwritten note, maybe the answers to his questions would be found there, but regardless he knew his task was monumental.

Cortez, CO

"I'm looking, but the routes I'm finding all involve an Interstate."

Bexar's routes to Groom Lake were traced in yellow highlighter across the pages of the thick road atlas. The truck sat idle in the middle of the highway outside of Monticello, Utah. Chivo flipped through the atlas, looking for another route when he realized that Bexar was driving north.

"I know, but that's all I could find. Look, everything due west is a National Park, a recreation area, or similar."

"Look here, if we go south on 191, go through ... Bluff, hit 163 and ... well, there's a lot of smaller highways, it looks like we pop out on I-15 near some town called St. George. That leaves us with a lot less time on the Interstate; the towns are smaller too."

"You don't know that."

"Well, we can assume they would be."

Bexar shrugged. "We're not in Texas anymore, so I'm flying blind. Whatever you think will work. We've just got to get going." He pointed over his shoulder with his thumb.

Chivo looked out the back glass of the pickup truck and saw at least a dozen undead slowly making their way towards the sound of the idling engine in the highway. The truck drove away from the approaching group and westbound into the center of Monticello, Utah. Dead stood in the middle of the road, some moving through the trees and buildings around them as Bexar turned left to drive south on Main Street. Gently pushing the truck left and right, Bexar drove around the dead as he got close to each. He was in a hurry to get to Groom Lake and Jessie's embrace, but not in a hurry to drive into a shambling dead body that could damage the truck.

Once clear of the town, the truck slowly increased speed until the speedometer showed fifty mph. Besides wrecking the truck, Bexar worried about the fuel consumption and tried to drive as conservatively as he could. What few vehicles were abandoned on the road were easily dodged with smooth driving inputs.

Both men tired from the constant fight of the post-apocalyptic world, neither spoke the half-hour it took to reach the next town along Highway 191.

"Who would name their town Bland?"

"Blanding, and who could blame 'em mano, look around."

Bexar took a left in the middle of town, following the road signs for the highway.

"Maybe it was someone's name?"

"Like what, Richard Bland? Hi, I'm Dick Bland and I want you to enjoy my wonderful Blanding."

"Well when you say it like that it sounds dirty, but still. Annnnd now we're out of the town."

"And if everyone would look to their right, you'll see Blanding International Airport and Used Tire Center."

"Look kids, Big Bend, Parliament."

Both of them smirked.

"Chivo, have you been to Groom Lake before? How safe do you think it will be inside?"

"Contrary to what you may believe, even though I worked for a three-letter agency I didn't get to go to all the cool places. I have no idea, but if it's like the one in Texas I think it'll be quite the resort compared to this bullshit."

"I'm going to sleep for days after we get there."

Chivo shook his head. "You won't, trust me I know. When you spend too much time outside the wire your sleep gets jacked. I bet it takes you two weeks to relax enough to sleep more than a couple of hours at a time, and even then you'll still be half-awake listening for danger."

"I'm still going to try, I'm exhausted."

"I get it mano, believe me I do. The difference between me and the other guys in the Army that didn't end up with the SF tab is all right here." Chivo tapped the side of his head. "There will always be guys who are stronger, faster, more talented, better at everything but this. The best, the pipe hitters out there giving away freedom one round at a time, they are tough here. Not that movie machismo bullshit, but being able to focus on a task, function at a high level no matter if they're hung out, hung over or have been awake for seventy-two hours straight and never quit."

"There's no way I would have made it."

"You're making it now, mano, and this is some of the hardest shit I've ever done. It's constant, there is no safe house, there's no cavalry, no air support, no reaction force. It's just you and me, one mistake and then it'll be one of us or none of us."

White Mesa, Utah came and went in a blink of an eye. No dead in sight, barely big enough to be labeled as a town. The green sign on the highway gave warning that the pair was quickly approaching Bluff, Utah.

"I wonder why they named it Cow Canyon?"

"Another one of your names, Chivo? I'm Richard Cow but everyone calls me Dick Cattle."

Chivo shook his head and another small town passed outside the truck windows with only a few undead showing up to greet them as they passed. Outside of town the small sign pointed south at a small road indicating another airport.

"While you were learning all your Special Forces stuff did you ever learn how to fly?"

"Nope, how about you?"

"Never have. That's too bad because how much better would it be to ditch the truck and fly cross-country to Groom Lake?"

"That's what got Cliff into that bind in Cortez."

"That's what saved those people too, well, except for the others."

"Well mano, we can't wish for what we can't have, so we keep on with what we've got."

"At least we're making good time, maybe we'll make it there by tomorrow."

"Well shit, you had to say it out loud, didn't you."

Groom Lake, NV

Jessie sat at the table in the cafeteria. Sarah and Erin sat with her, the flat colorless world of corporate America transplanted underground. On the walls were a half-dozen poster-sized photographs, all of them patriotic scenes of epic proportions. The Lincoln Memorial, the raising of the flag at Iwo Jima, a majestic bald eagle with large snowcapped mountains in the background. The only two colors added to the white-roomed world were red and blue.

Erin poked her spoon at the stew. Jessie and Sarah ate happily; even though the stew was bland it was hot, it had some sort of meat in it, and it was better than they'd had before.

Sarah looked at her daughter. So far there had been no other boys or girls her age, at least that they had seen. Erin's world had been ripped apart, her father was gone, and now she sat in a sterile world full of strangers far underground. Football games, fall weather, parks, quiet mornings in the deer stand with her father; all of those were gone forever. One tear and then another streaked across Sarah's face. She dropped her spoon into the half-empty bowl of stew and wiped the tears with her palms, taking some deep breaths. Jessie walked around the table to sit next to Sarah and wrapped her arms around her.

Erin looked at her mother and Jessie, her mind awash with a changing kaleidoscope of emotions starting with being embarrassed that they were in front of so many strangers. Dark sadness drew across her face like the approaching shadows of nightfall.

"Hi ladies." Brit stood by the table, looking down her nose at Jessie and Sarah. "Since you both haven't signed up for any jobs yet, maybe when you're done you could help clean up in the kitchen."

A burning hot wave of anger swept through Erin's body before she jumped to her feet, her plastic chair falling over.

"Fuck you Brit, fuck you and your stupid bitch attitude. You think you're special? You wouldn't last more than ten fucking minutes of what we've been through! You leave us the fuck alone I might let you live!"

Erin pushed Brit to the floor and walked out of the cafeteria, door slamming in protest to the silent stares. Brit sat on the floor, mouth open before she saw that every head was facing her. Her face flushed a dark crimson before she leapt to her feet and tried to walk out of the door with the false attitude of indifference.

Jake sat across the cafeteria, a spoonful of his lunch hovering between his bowl and his mouth, eyebrows raised. No one in the cafeteria moved; it seemed as though every person was holding their breath waiting for the next something, although what that something was they had no idea.

"Tell you what, everyone. We've all had a rough few days. Why don't we ask our friends working hard to feed us if they have any of those wonderful chocolate chip cookies left," Jake said as he walked to the front of the cafeteria by the serving lines. The survivors working in the kitchen looked at him and nodded, returning with two large trays of cookies wrapped in cellophane. Slowly conversation filled the room, mixed with the sounds of chairs scooting back from the tables, everyone excited to have a cookie, a rare treat after the end of the world.

Everyone except Jessie and Sarah. "Want me to go talk to her?"

"No, give her some time. She's been on high alert for weeks; it's going to take her some time before she relaxes enough to calm down."

"We've all been on high alert for too long, I think it will ..."

"Excuse me, Jessie and Erin, right?"

"Sarah."

"Mind if I sit for a minute?" Jake asked as he sat down in Erin's vacant. He pushed her nearly full bowl of stew away.

"If we could get enough salt stores that the logistics people felt comfortable using it for seasoning then we would have better stew."

Jessie kept her arm around Sarah; both of them just looked at Jake.

"Sarah, Jessie, don't worry about Brit. She, we, well you can imagine that everyone feels a lot of strain. We've all survived the end of the world thus far and are trying to do the same for the future. I'll speak to Brit about maybe having a little more tact. Frankly I think she probably deserved to be reminded that everyone here is a team member and that no one is more important than the next. If we're going to succeed then all of us are needed. Bill, the civilian in charge of communications, has made contact with many more survivors from all around the U.S. and we're trying to bring them here so we have the best chance of restarting our great country."

The lights flickered and went out, darkness pierced by emergency lighting over the doors, green exit signs glowing in between the battery-powered flood lights. Jake took a deep breath and frowned at the darkness.

"This is our problem. We haven't found the source to these outages. The housing facility, the operations facility, all of it is nuclear-powered; all of it is a closed system like on a submarine. Cliff's explanation is that everything should run automatically without any problems for at least twenty years."

Jessie and Sarah sat in the dark room wondering what they were supposed to be doing during an outage. Most of the people in the cafeteria sat cheerfully, eating their cookies. Jake continued. "We haven't explored the facility on the surface more than just passingly. Some of us think that for our survival we need to lay claim to the topside, like the pioneers of old: use the facility as our home base but create a homestead, a town of survivors on the surface. Before we can do any of that we have to clear and secure the topside, something we haven't been able to do. I think both of your experiences and skills would be wasted with one of Brit's housekeeping jobs, not that people to clean the kitchen isn't important, it is, but I think you two have special talents. Skills that would be perfect to help teach others how to help establish that homestead, the topside town."

"What exactly are you asking?" Jessie ventured.

"How far along are you?"

"I'm about six weeks, best I can tell."

"That's just fantastic. We, my wife and I, we were never able to have any children ... she didn't make it here. She was killed by a fanatical cult in Colorado. Cliff rescued us and brought the survivors we had here. Well, we've all lost loved ones. I'm sorry. Just think about what I asked. If you want to help then it would be appreciated."

Jake stood and walked off, the lights flickering back on as he left through one of the exits.

"What do you think?"

"I don't know, Sarah. It would be better than the damn kitchen."

"Let's see if we can find Erin and see what she thinks. Think we would train underground or go aboveground for it?"

"No idea, but I assume that we would have to go up top at some point."

"I'm worried that if we stay down here too long my little girl will explode worse or implode on herself."

Coronado, CA

The sun drifted over the ocean waves, sparkling yellow and red as it fell into the sea. Aymond stood next to the lead M-ATV, safe from view due to the open-air overhead shelter. Happy, Chuck, Simmons, and Jones stood in a loose circle around him. A siren wailed in the distance.

"As you know, as of their last communication Kirk, Davis, and Snow are on the northern end of the base, near where the carriers would be berthed. The PLA is systematically clearing the facility. The siren attracts the Zeds; a team of the radar trucks kill them. At some point we are going to need to get our hands on one of those trucks and figure out what it really is. Or at the least put it to use. Once the sun sets, their plan is to make their way to the south, to the hardened bunkers. They are going to take what they can and demo the rest."

Simmons and Jones fidgeted in their tactical kit. The MSOT members stood warily, taking notes on pocket-sized green waterproof notepads.

"The heavy-lift operations seem to have slowed in tempo. Our best guess is that the PLA is clearing Halsey Field to add another air facility into the mix. We're not sure what the plan is after that, but with the PANAMAX fleet sitting at the mouth of the harbor, we can assume they mean to move in. Tonight's operation is to support Kirk's team in munitions extraction from the southern point of Halsey Field ..."

An explosion ripped through the air. The siren cut off, leaving the sound of small arms fire chattering in the distance.

"Dagger-One, troops in contact, troops in contact, contact south and west, no, east ..."

"Well shit. Simmons, Jones, crank'em up. Stand by to go get them."

"Aye, Master-Guns," they both said in unison, climbing into the M-ATVs.

"Dagger-Actual, Dagger-One, SITREP, over."

Aymond looked at Happy. "What I wouldn't give for a VideoScout feed."

Happy shrugged. "Want in one hand, Chief."

"Dagger-One, sporadic small arms fire to the south and east, one PANAMAX hard-kill, stand by, over."

"Dagger-Two, Dagger-Actual, eyes on Dagger-One, PLA QRF approaching from the west, get small or get gone, Gonzo, over."

A helicopter roared overhead past the M-ATVs, headed towards the mainland.

Hilton Parking Garage

Hammer stood behind a stack of pallets, his poncho draped over the front of the rough-cut pine, the big .50 caliber Beretta shouldered and steadied on the top of the pallet stack. Slowly breathing in, he scanned the scene in front of him through the powerful optic. In the shadows against the back wall, Hammer and Gonzo were all but invisible to the PLA five stories below and almost nine hundred yards to the southeast.

"Command vehicle approaching from the north."

"I see'em, Gonzo."

The four-wheeled armored carrier drove quickly across the railroad tracks and towards the slip. The PANAMAX ship's bow crashed into the concrete, listing hard to port, crooked in the slip; some of the containers fell to the concrete below. Crushed against the large cargo ship and the side of the pier were two tug boats, one of which was now on fire. The lone heavy-lift crane rested against the top of the containers still on the ship, the foundation bent by the crash of the ship. Although moving slowly when Hammer took the shots, a ship with that much momentum has a stopping distance referenced in hundreds of yards.

When the command vehicle stopped, a radar truck drove to it and parked, facing the front of the transmitter towards the north, away from the water and towards any approaching Zeds from the mainland.

Hammer's chest barely moving with each metered breath, his finger firmly pressed the trigger to the rear before the hard concussion from the muzzle of the suppressed rifle thumped dust into the air around them. The large round traveled over nine hundred yards before impacting the center of the radar transmitter. Two men with rifles climbed out of the patrol vehicle before another man, who did not carry a rifle, climbed out with them.

Gonzo made notes on what he was watching through the spotting scope. The man without a rifle pointed and appeared to be yelling, which he couldn't hear over all the rifle fire. One by one the PLA troopers' SKS rifles fell silent. The commander pointed and issued orders before he turned around to look at the wrecked cargo ship and began to raise a radio handset to his head.

"I see him ..." the dust around the rifle bounced into the air from the concussion. A moment later the commander's body rotated to the ground in a spiral of blood, his head vaporized from the 50-caliber impact.

"Dagger-Two, Dagger-One, water patrol approaching fast from the north-west, over, about two clicks out, over."

"Dagger-One, copy."

Gonzo set the spotting scope on the ground and walked the few yards to the pallet stack and his large Barrett rifle, shifted his aim and followed the boat's wake to find a patrol boat approaching at a high rate of speed. Through the powerful optic Gonzo saw the silhouette of the boat's pilot in the wheelhouse, adjusted for the tracking movement, and fired. Watching through the scope a few seconds later, he saw the pilot knocked out of view like an amusement park popup game. The boat continued on its path, turning left slightly as the rudder trailed without a pilot to control it. On the bow a man stood behind a mounted machine gun. Gonzo tracked him, thought about taking the shot, but instead watched in amazement at how long it took the man to realize that his boat mate was dead and they were now out of control. Estimating that the boat was traveling at close to forty knots, Gonzo brought his head off the rifle to track the boat in the twilight as it raced across the harbor. The boat neared the harbor edge of the pier before catching the edge and rotating hard, throwing the machine gunner to the pavement, boat rolling into the stern of the cargo ship in a ball of fire. The thrown machine gunner was out of view for Gonzo, but he seriously doubted the guy would walk again as the living.

Walking next to Hammer, Gonzo picked up the spotting scope and scanned the scene towards the crashed ship. Whispered, "what do you think?"

"I say we stay put and see what happens for another ten mikes or so, then haul ass north."

"OK, where?"

"That park." Gonzo pointed to the marina park next to the Hilton, just a few hundred yards away and jutting out into the water.

"Sure. I'll call it in."

M-ATVs

"Roger that, Dagger-Actual out."

"OK guys, shut'em down. We're back to the planned operation, except now we're going to extract Hammer and Gonzo as well."

CHAPTER 9

Near Kanab, Utah
March 14, Year 1

"Look Bexar, I know you want to keep driving, but I'm telling you it's a bad idea. It's bad enough dodging the walking corpses in the daylight, but it's going to be much worse at night. You need to sleep; sleep is the most important commodity when you're outside the wire ... besides ammo."

"Why don't you drive while I sleep?"

"No. We'll find a place here to secure up for the night and roll at first light. I know you want to get to Jessie, but she's going to want you to actually make it. You have to make smart choices, choices with your head, not heart choices."

Bexar grunted and frowned at the sunset. Glancing at the atlas, he knew that ahead he would need to turn left to stay on Highway 89. The town looked vacant; only a few dead roamed freely. "Look at that," he said, pointing at the overhead sign. "I haven't been to the Grand Canyon or Zion; I bet the crowds wouldn't be bad this time of year."

"Everyone dying to go, mano."

The pun did get a half-assed smile, but Bexar was annoyed that they were going to have to stop for the night and rest. Although it would be nice to stop and rest without someone trying to kill them, without being overrun by the dead or worrying about some half-cocked secret agent strangling him in his sleep. He didn't see that happening anytime soon.

The truck slowed as it approached the only stoplight in town.

"Something is creeping me out; something's wrong and I don't know what."

Chivo nodded. "Me too. Everything is too clear, no movement ... the only dead we've seen were back on the edge of town...something else too, I'm not sure."

"Cars."

"You're right mano, no cars. There aren't even any cars in the parking lots."

"Fucking weird, dude."

Bexar turned left to follow the highway, driving slowly, scanning though the windshield for any threats. Chivo looked out of his window at the glowing remains of daylight over the low mountains.

"We shouldn't go too much longer, maybe five minutes or so, but I wouldn't mind putting the center of this town behind us. Weird things going on and I don't want to know what."

Accelerating gently, Bexar continued southbound on the small highway, passing ranch land and tractors parked in fields. The center turn lane ended and the countryside became more and more sparse.

"Dude, airport." Bexar pointed.

"So?"

"So? Airport means open area, hangars we can use for shelter, something we can hide the truck in with us, and fuel."

"Fuel?"

"Av-Gas. The truck should run on it, especially if we mix it with the automotive gas we already have."

Chivo shrugged. "If you say so."

Bexar turned into the drive for the small airport and they saw small clumps of hangars jutting out of the landscape like big rocks, aircraft sitting on the ramp, tie-downs in place, tires flat and abandoned to melt into the tarmac over the coming eons.

Driving past the main office, Bexar stopped at the gate, blocking access to the ramp. Chivo climbed out of the truck and walked to the person access gate near the large vehicle gate. The person gate was unlocked, so Chivo walked through and opened the control box for the mechanically opened gate and flipped the safety lever. Now released from the mechanical opener, Chivo pulled the gate open and Bexar drove onto the ramp. Chivo closed the gate and flipped the safety switch to lock the gate closed once again. It wouldn't stop much, but it was all they had.

Chivo tapped the side of the truck and walked northeast, tapping the top of his head and pointing left before practically disappearing like a ghost into the long evening shadows of the small hangars.

"I've seriously got to tell him I don't know what the fuck he means with those hand signals."

Bexar drove away from the gate and near the tie-downs between the hangars, turning off the truck's lights before putting it into park, conscious of the red glow from the brake lights. He had no idea where Chivo had gone, so all he could do was wait and haul ass if he heard gunfire.

A few moments later Chivo tapped on the side glass of the truck, startling Bexar.

"You going to sleep out here in the truck or you want to get in the hangar?"

Chivo walked in front of the truck to the second hangar on the right. A Cessna 182 sat inside, but the doors were open. The tires were flat, just like the aircraft's cousins on the ramp.

"Back up to the nose, I've got an idea."

Bexar did as he was told and backed up to the nose of the small aircraft. Chivo wrapped a ratchet strap he'd found inside the hangar around the nose gear and around the truck's hitch.

"OK, pull it out and stop where the other planes are parked."

Bexar pulled forward, the plane bouncing against the ratchet strap, the main gear's wheels sliding instead of rolling. A few moments later he stopped, Chivo retrieved the ratchet strap and walked back to the open hangar as Bexar backed the truck in. They pulled the hangar doors closed and dropped the door pin into the concrete to keep the doors from being pulled open from the outside. Chivo rolled up the ratchet strap and put it in the bed of the truck, knowing that a useful tool like that shouldn't go to waste, especially now that they had one.

Flipping on a flashlight, Chivo dug through a tool chest at the far end of the hangar before finding what he was looking for.

"Here ya go, mano, now you can fix your lights," Chivo said, handing Bexar a Phillips-head screwdriver.

Granite Mountain, Utah

Cliff looked at his watch. *Six hours until sunrise.*

The command line interface was becoming easier now that Cliff was using it; some of the training on it was starting to come back to him. Toggling through overheads stored on the computer, he followed the West Coast from Washington State southward, checking every deep water port that would be able to handle the types of vessels that the intelligence estimate stated China could or would use.

North Korea had nothing in the way of shipping or naval assets that were of that size, so all estimates had the NKP working with the PLA.

One by one, each of the cities appeared on his monitor; he zoomed in to view the port facilities for any activity or to discern what the remaining capability might be. One by one, he found the cities partially destroyed, burned, and overrun by the dead, and the port facilities and the gantry cranes all appeared damaged beyond repair. This was the first time Cliff had been able to see the West Coast after the apocalypse, the EMP attack that started it all. Previously, while reviewing overhead imagery, the view had been obscured by massive fires and smoke. The infrared view had shown the fires, but had been useless to find much else due to the thermal blooming. The results of the end of the world as we know it were painfully obvious now.

The Port of Los Angeles and Long Beach, two of the busiest ports in the world, looked partially intact; it would take an analyst hours to pore over each detail to make a judgment on the remaining functionality, but the channels were blocked by capsized vessels so it really didn't matter right now. The lone remaining port was San Diego; with a few keystrokes the screen resolved to show a high overhead view of the entire bay. Three dark spots to the south of the harbor entrance grabbed his attention. Zooming in, Cliff saw a group of container ships in anchorage. Moving the slider to the left, the view transitioned between time stamps, going backward in time slowly. The latest imagery stored on the computer was old, but his wonderful hacker friends had disconnected the systems and for all the training Cliff had, he was not a network engineer.

Each image took a little time to fully resolve and show clearly. Cliff frowned at how long the task was taking. Although the actual time elapsing wasn't that much, he had no patience for it right now. Suddenly he stopped. The last ship of the group was out of place, approaching the others in anchorage from the west.

Cliff brought the view in closer, viewing Halsey Field from the time the ship arrived to the last captured time stamp. The last two views showed some activity, vehicle movement on the facility, vehicles that Cliff recognized as a mix of Chinese and North Korean types. Point Loma had had no activity, but the San Diego International Airport had a massive amount. The surrounding city was owned by the dead, but the PLA and NKP had a toehold; Cliff could see that they were moving out slowly. Each moment in time on the imagery closer to real time showing a wider and wider area of operations, trucks and men moving out further away from the airport. Set on the perimeter of the PLA operations were mobile radar units with oddly shaped transmitters. Piles of dead made a thick wall around the front of each of the trucks, clearly killed by the trucks or something the trucks carried.

So that's it, that's how they do it. Radar, microwave, something they transmit killed the dead. That isn't what the analysts predicted, but we knew they would have something. Dammit. The dead gives me some time, but once they have the chance to secure enough area to begin offloading the container ships then we're going to be in trouble. That's going to be soon with the mobile radars.

This was a scenario that wasn't supposed to happen. Some portion of the United States' Naval Force was supposed to survive, but so far every indication pointed to the fleets being lost for unknown reasons.

If they were issued orders like the fuckup directives the President was issuing which resulted in the Denver facility being lost, then he might have had them working humanitarian missions. Trying to rescue American citizens trapped abroad instead of launching nuclear assets against China and North Korea.

Cliff tapped his pen against the screen and began to work the problem. He needed to destroy an invading force, he was on his own, and what he needed was the firepower of a national level asset. Overall he wasn't sure any were left; the bomber force was presumed lost with the loss of the physical facilities, the Navy was presumed lost ... *but there should be over four hundred Minuteman-III Intercontinental Ballistic Missiles sitting safely in their silos.*

Cliff put his head in his hands, a headache starting to throb behind his eyes. He took a few breaths and tried to remember what his access with the ICBMs was.

Even if I did have any sort of outside connectivity from here, I still couldn't access the ICBM systems. Those systems are ancient and kept isolated on purpose. I have to get to Wyoming ... North Dakota or Montana ... no, I only have to get to northern Colorado, there are missile flights there.

A few keystrokes later, the overhead view outside of Cheyenne, Wyoming came into view, the stark landscape dotted with numerous missile silos that were visible to the trained eye. Ten of the silos were clustered around a launch command center, which was underground, each flight of missiles able to be independently fired from the other flights.

San Diego or Colorado, fucking Colorado ... every time I leave, I'm whipped back. The mobile radar truck, if that's what it is, that is a key piece of technology we had no idea about. If I decimate San Diego with an ICBM then the technology is lost. If I go to San Diego the Chinese might be able to establish more of a beachhead and take control of more land. San Diego, that's almost a thousand miles from here. I could do it in less than a week, maybe even two days each way if I don't sleep and move quickly. Call it three days there, three days back, six days total, leave the radar truck at Groom Lake. If I leave for northeast Colorado, I could be at the ICBM LCC in less than a day, but that leaves a whole country of dead to put down.

Cliff took a deep breath and shook his head, looking at the hacker he'd put down, the same one from the video. "Dammit guy, you really fucked me by pulling this facility off-line."

Coronado, CA

The cover of night brought a blessing and a curse for Hammer and Gonzo. They could move with stealth in the night, the night was their friend for movement, but the massive Barrett 50-caliber rifles, even with suppressors, were very loud when fired. It was in no way discreet.

The large rifles secured and slung, their rucks on, M4 rifles in hand, the pair slowly made their way down the parking garage ramp. The dead they encountered on the way in the night before still lay motionless on the concrete where they'd been left, skulls ruined by their knives. The truck they'd pushed against the bottom of the ramp was keeping the rest of the dead from meandering upwards, but now they had to get past the truck, the dead, and out to the walkway below.

Climbing over the wall one after the other, they dropped to the patio below, the entombed guests thumping against the window glass of the resort hotel towering above them. Before anymore dead could make their way to them, the pair jogged to the fence separating the pool from the large public walkway and climbed over. Once on the walkway they moved slowly, deliberately. The PLA activity significantly reduced after nightfall, but they were still wary of being observed. Even though they'd handily killed a number of PLA that day, including the tug and ship pilots resulting in the destruction of the container vessel, they didn't want to be caught in the open. With the massive convention center on their right, and the large yachts of the fabulously wealthy on their left, Hammer and Gonzo used the shadows and moved to the road leading out to the marina park. The trees lining the roadway gave some comfort to both of them. The trees gave concealment and cover, a welcome friend in urban operations. They made it to the southern corner of the park before lying near some trees in the overgrown lawn. The NVGs gave Hammer a bright green bay to look across, the night vision goggles giving the park an eerie but familiar glow to Gonzo, who lay prone with his M4, holding rear guard for the pair. Some Zeds shambled through the park, but Gonzo would try not to fire his M4 if at all possible, even though it was suppressed. He wanted nothing more than to climb aboard the Zodiac with Chief without having the park erupt in gunfire.

Hammer's foot tapped against Gonzo's leg twice. *Extract approaching.*

The faint hum of the Zodiac's specially muffled outboard motor evaporated into the air, as the motor was shut off while the rubber boat drifted into position near the shore. Hammer knelt, watching the boat approach, grabbed his ruck and big Barrett rifle and ran to the boat, setting both in the boat as he climbed in, the other teammates holding cover with low firing positions against the gunwales. A few seconds later Gonzo joined them and, with five critical skills operator Marines aboard, the Zodiac came to life, powering south and towards Glorietta Bay where the team had put in.

Happy ran the boat onto the beach, the team barreling out before grabbing a handhold and pulling the boat onto the sand.

Simmons met them at the shoreline with the UTV and trailer. The boat weighed close to seven hundred pounds with the fuel and the motor; they could have carried it, but since they had the resources to use, Simmons and the UTV came to help. Once on the trailer and secured with a single ratchet strap thrown across the boat, the team grabbed a spot either in the UTV or in the boat while Simmons drove them out of the park, bouncing across curbs, through the gate by their team building and out onto the beach on the west side, the ocean side of Coronado. The team put the boat in and followed it into the water, climbing aboard as the waves jostled them around. The motor came to life and the five of them headed out, moving quickly towards the mouth of the bay. Simmons drove the UTV and trailer to a position alongside the beach facilities, using the buildings to avoid being seen. As per the plan, he left the UTV in place and jogged back into the team area where the M-ATVs were sitting at the ready. Jones sat in the lead truck, radio on and ready to roll for a heavy extract if needed.

Halsey Field, Coronado, CA

Davis and Snow loaded the back of the strange Chinese-made Jeep with every block of C4 they could find in the bunkers, along with spools of det cord. Kirk was set up in the bunker next to them with two large Mark 84 bombs on a cart. He had two mechanical fuses he was modifying for their needs before they could leave the airfield. Sweat dripped off Kirk's forehead; a small Surefire flashlight clamped in his teeth, he wiped his face with the dark shemagh wrapped around his neck. Working quickly but carefully, his modification would set both of the two-thousand-pound bombs off ten minutes after being set, which was outside of the normal operation of the fuse system.

The radio crackled in all three of their ears. "Five mikes." Snow appeared in the open door of the hardened bunker with his hand up, fingers spread to show a big five. Kirk gave a thumbs up and continued to work.

A few minutes later the heavy four-wheeled bomb cart's ring was locked in the Chinese Jeep's pintle hitch, and the team drove carefully out from the bunkers and towards the runways. The C4 and det cord they weren't worried about; they were shockproof, heat-resistant and proven reliable. The four thousand pounds of explosives bouncing along on the cart behind them was a different story. The Mark 84 bomb was an old design that kept getting upgraded with new guidance systems, and the system itself was reliable, but Kirk's hacked-together fuse system was an unknown.

"If they go off early we'll never know."

"I'll know, I'll find the little pieces of your body scattered across the airfield and I'll haunt the shit out of you, Kirk."

Snow shook his head. Kirk and Davis could joke, but they weren't the one driving the damn Jeep. Once on the runway the surface was smooth and Snow accelerated sharply, racing against the open expanse to park their trailer in the center where the two runways crossed. It would still be possible to land some aircraft on the ramp or on one of the shortened sections, but this was the best they could do in a short time and it should cause the PLA a lot of grief. The Jeep stopped, and Kirk and Davis jumped out to unhitch the trailer and to arm the timer. They piled back in and Snow wasted no time pushing the accelerator pedal all the way to the floor, driving back the direction they had come, towards the beach. As they bounded over the rocks and onto the sand, the Zodiac slid onto the beach. Their teammates exited the boat quickly, running to the Jeep to unload all the explosives they had retrieved. Kirk looked at the timer, counting down on his watch before holding up his hand with two fingers raised. *Two minutes.*

Snow drove the empty Jeep up the sand and towards the rocky seawall a short distance to the west. He shifted into neutral and jumped out of the Jeep onto the hard dirt as it bounced across the rough terrain and fell over the rocks into the deep channel. As much as they wanted to keep the Jeep, they weren't sure if there was a tracking device on it; they couldn't chance it being located anywhere near them. *At least this way if someone finds the Jeep they might think the saboteurs went across the channel to Point Loma.*

Snow ran as fast as he could towards the Zodiac which was already pushed off from the beach and holding enough throttle to keep it motionless against the approaching waves. Once he reached the boat his teammates pulled him onto it, where he fell atop the ruck sacks and explosives piled in the hull. Happy poured the coals to it, the nose of the Zodiac standing out of the water as the boat pushed hard in the water under maximum power. Forty-five seconds later the pressure wave washed over the team, followed almost immediately by the sound of the massive explosion.

Snow gave Kirk a fist bump, Kirk having trouble hiding a smile beneath all the dark face paint. Once the boat ran upon the beach only three miles away, the team bounded out of the boat while Gonzo ran to get the UTV and trailer. They didn't bother unloading the explosives, leaving the rucks, explosives, and other gear in the boat; it went on the trailer and Gonzo hauled ass to get it all under cover before any patrols flew overhead. The rest of the team followed the UTV's tracks in the sand, kicking the sand over the tracks and covering their paths. A few minutes later the entire team was together under cover by the M-ATVs, carefully unloading and cataloging the explosive ordinance they had just retrieved, the eastern horizon beginning to glow with the coming of dawn. They had plans for their newly acquired tools of war and it was going to be the story of legend, if anyone lived long enough for it to be told.

CHAPTER 10

Kanab Municipal Airport, Kanab, Utah
March 15, Year 1

Chivo was up before dawn, Bexar snoring loudly in the cab of the truck with the windows rolled up. After kicking him awake after midnight to get him to climb into the truck, Chivo slipped outside for a quick patrol of the airport to make sure the monstrous snoring hadn't brought any of the awoken dead. Now the hangar door stood partially open, mostly hidden from view from the passing highway. Chivo had tried to make the doors look like they were accidently left open and not purposefully opened for use while he fueled the truck from the plastic gas cans. Half of the cans were used to top off the tank, which worked perfectly for Chivo. With the hand-cranked fuel transfer hose they'd taken from the parts store, Chivo left for the planes tied down on the ramp in front of the hangar. Twenty minutes later Bexar stood outside and pissed on the side of the hangar, steam rising from his face after waking up warm and cozy in the truck cab, and Chivo had fuel cans full of Av-Gas. A roll of blue painter's tape in the tool box was used to mark the cans with Av-Gas; they would have to mix them in the truck's fuel tanks later and this would help keep the fuel types identified.

Loaded up, they were quickly on their way, Chivo taking the driving duties while they both ate cold stew out of a can. The countryside passed by outside of their truck in silence, including the small town of Fredonia, Arizona and their turn onto Highway 389. If not for the low vegetation and powerlines the highway might as well been on Mars. The highway dipped south before turning north again, skirting around the southern edge of the mountains on the border between Arizona and

Utah and towards Colorado City. The highway crossed the town, which for being so small had an amazing number of undead turning northbound to shamble after the truck rolling through town like a fifty-mile-per-hour flash. The stark landscape reminded Bexar a little of Big Bend country, although it was different. The number on the highway sign changed with the passing of the Utah border, but neither of them cared. As long as they kept this pace and didn't get lost, they would be in Groom Lake before dinner.

Granite Mountain, Utah

Cliff had his plan. Speed run to San Diego. He could spare a week and still be able to stop the Chinese invasion with an ICBM strike, although by his guess he would have to use two of them, striking further inland too. On the way back north he would leave the radar truck in Groom Lake and take whatever vehicle a survivor had left sitting topside. He could send a message to Clint with an update as well. Walking out of the mountain and into the cold March air, Cliff started the old truck and drove out of the complex. He would be happy to never return. All he had to do was clear the middle of the city between him and Utah Lake, then he could take Highway 68 and rocket south outside of the major cities, eventually cutting over to I-15 which would hopefully be clear enough so he could drive as hard as the truck would handle. After reviewing the stored overhead imagery, and measuring the distance with scaled overhead imagery and checking the major cities, he'd decided to break from I-15 in Las Vegas and shoot down Highway 95 until hitting I-8. If his plan worked, he should be able to arrive in about thirteen hours. Chasing the sunset he would get there just after dark, which should make acquiring the PLA equipment easier. The return trip might be longer, not knowing if the truck was governed, but the distance was shorter. Depending on what he found in San Diego he might even have the chance for a nap and a shower in Groom Lake before heading north again.

The road was barely visible in the pre-dawn light, but it was enough for Cliff to drive. He started the timer on his watch and accelerated; he had a schedule to keep.

Colorado City, AZ

The two of them sat in silence, the occasional fart breaking up the monotony of driving across the desert in a truck with no working radio, not that any radio stations would be playing music now anyways. Chivo rolled down his window, the cold air whipping through the cab, a loose wrapper flipping out of the window onto the highway.

"That's littering."

"We're not even in your state, so try to write me the ticket."

Bexar smirked, enjoying his turn in the passenger's seat for once. According to the map, they were approaching the town of Hurricane, but they could only catch glimpses of it from the rolling roadway. Highway 59 looped up and around, following a pass through the hills before dropping into the town and Highway 9.

"The sign said fourteen thousand people and I think every damned one of them died, came back and is here to greet us."

"Playing it cool, mano, but I'm wanting to clear this death hole quick; there's no way we can fight this many, we don't have the ammo for it."

"Or the time."

Chivo nodded.

The truck rocked hard side to side as Chivo steered around the staggering dead milling about in the street. Holding his speed as high as he dared, shambling dead bouncing off the quarter-panels, they broke out of the first town and into the next. They were near the Interstate and hopefully it would be clear, hopefully they could use it to speed away from the massing horde. Swinging the truck left and right, from shoulder to shoulder, Chivo fought to keep the truck on the road without running down a walking corpse. With each passing second it seemed as if the number of dead doubled, then doubled again, a riot of gore marching against their very existence. If the truck was damaged, if they lost a tire, if anything happened they might not be able to escape the flood of bodies coming out of the desert and from the surrounding neighborhoods; chasing them, swarming, and surrounded they would die.

Cars and trucks, heavy tractor-trailers and anything else in their path had been pushed off the road before they arrived, over the guardrails and down to the desert floor. The road would be clear if the thousands of dead would vanish, the journey easy if the path opened. The overpass ahead of them was Interstate 15; they'd take that then head south before they could turn west, where they'd nearly be to Groom Lake. Chivo turned the steering wheel hard to the left, bodies thumping against the side glass, the mirrors ripping free from the doors, dark smears of blood across the glass. The flies above the horde blocking the sun, the windshield wipers worked to keep the blood streaked across the glass from blocking their view ahead.

Bexar took his seatbelt off, heart racing and ready to jump, ready to fight. He press-checked his rifle—*loaded, ready*—and tapped each one of his remaining magazines. Focused intently, he scanned the area, looking for shelter, looking for a break, looking for their escape. The town behind them, nothing but the Interstate, mountains and the rolling desert could be seen through the gore-smeared windows. Chivo turned to drive the wrong way up the exit from the Interstate, trying to get to the high ground, trying to get to the hope the Interstate represented, if it even existed. He missed the ramp, tires sliding as they fell off the pavement and into the gravel roadbed; he pushed the accelerator pedal, further, further, nearly to the floor. The big V8 roared in protest, back tires spinning, caught in the gravel.

"Get off the gas; shift to neutral then shift back and then fucking gun it!" Bexar pushed the button for four-wheel high.

Chivo shifted to neutral, the transfer case shifting into gear with a hard thunk that was felt more than heard over the clawing moans of the dead.

"GO, GO, GO, GO!"

Frowning with the hard intensity of a man fighting losing odds having bet his life, Chivo pulled the selector to drive and slammed his foot to the floor. Dirt, gravel, and dust shot into the air from all four tires, spinning for purchase. The truck launched up the embankment, jumping over the edge of the exit ramp, the guard rails missing from the forced march of the army of death. The truck bounced hard as the tires found the pavement again, Chivo struggling to control their vehicle as it rocketed through the flat median and onto the southbound lanes of I-15.

The road ahead was clear. Behind them a dark cloud of flies flowed like smoke just off the ground and towards I-15. Chivo took a deep breath and started laughing. Bexar gasped, not realizing that he'd been holding his breath, and slumped into the bench seat, putting his seatbelt back on.

From the neighborhoods on their left, one-story homes along the Interstate emptied their dead to join Death's army's call, flooding along the desert floor towards the pavement. Chivo kept the speed of the truck high, the off-road tires humming on the clear pavement, sunlight glowing dark red against the rotten blood drying on the windows.

"Holy shit, do you think there's any paint left on the truck?"

"Fuck mano, I'm just glad the windows didn't break."

Each passing second, each breath, every click of every minute that elapsed was that much more distance between them and the following horde. Neither knew how long or how far the undead would follow; they hadn't seen them follow for more than short distances, but every time they could they turned or moved or went a different direction at a point where the dead couldn't see them and couldn't hear them.

The Interstate descended towards another town, the signs missing along the road, but the atlas identified the town as St. George. Bexar glanced at the speedometer and noted that the needle showed fifty-five miles per hour, which seemed like a reasonable speed to him, even if he secretly wished they would go faster and get to Groom Lake sooner. Slowly approaching the town, they saw the road became more cluttered with vehicles. Outside of town the dead had pushed the road clear, but getting closer to the center of town the dead hadn't.

Chivo once again forced pushed the truck from shoulder to shoulder, driving around the abandoned vehicles, their speed slowing from fifty-five to fifty, then forty as he struggled to keep his momentum with each swooping pass of another abandoned vehicle.

Typical strip-center big box stores lined the left side of the Interstate, all the recognizable names accounted for, interspersed with gas stations, restaurants, and other suburban clutter. In the median stood the safety wires, protecting oncoming traffic from a head-on collision, but now it limited Chivo from using both sides of the road. He picked up speed, a dark cloud of flies growing in their view, over another horde of dead perhaps, or the one they'd just escaped was much larger than they thought. The hurricane's eye, a moment's reprieve before storms raged around them once again; whichever it might be, it didn't matter. The dead pulsed towards the road from the shopping centers and from the road ahead.

"Shit mano, we've got problems."

The air around them turned dark from the swarm of flies. In an instant the dead were so thick if they slowed the mass of bodies might stop the truck completely. If they stopped they could be crushed in the truck, just like how the dead crushed the bridge in New Mexico. Chivo pushed the truck hard, the only option to charge straight ahead. Bexar braced himself against the dash and focused on remembering to breathe; he tried desperately to keep his heart rate down. Chivo drove into the median, the roadway reflectors clicking against the bumper as they sped by, the wire barrier blurring to his left as they drove. Seeing a gap in the crowd and swinging right to miss a shambling body, Chivo pushed the truck left and into what little median they had to pass a burned-out SUV, only to see a semi-truck lying on its side across the median, the wire barricade ripped from the foundations, the trailer blocking their path. Chivo ripped the steering wheel to the right, the truck bouncing back onto the pavement and around a moving trailer only to hit nose first into a churning knot of the dead.

A half-dozen bodies crashed against the bumper and the grill, some of them bouncing over the hood and slamming into the windshield, glass shattering inwards, showering Bexar and Chivo with small fragments, the safety glaze barely holding the bodies out of the cab. Others were ripped under the truck by the tires churning, all four spinning under power; the corpses were ripped apart, splintered ribs tearing the sidewall out of a front tire and then a rear. The truck lurched hard to the passenger side, both tires disintegrating from the damage, both axles spinning under the torque of the heavy V8 engine. Large chunks of rubber, pieces of the tires, were thrown into the air. The truck shot across the right lane to the shoulder and crashed through the top of the concrete barrier, the high suspension giving the front bumper barely enough room to clear.

The truck now in the air, a body came loose from the windshield, bounced off the hood and fell with them. The fuel cans, tools, supplies, spare parts, everything in the back of the truck floated out of the bed in the same ballistic trajectory as the truck, in painfully slow motion to the occupants. Bexar watched the ballet of destruction in awe and anger at his impending fate.

The nose of the truck hit first, slamming into the gravel of the ramp median nearly thirty feet below the top of the bridge. The gravel exploded outward from the impact, all moving so slowly, so perfectly in time with each small piece of rock.

Harrison Junction, Utah

Cliff saw the massive herd on the small highway below. The Interstate ahead was clear of any obstacles as far as the next ridge which blocked his view in the distance, so he continued his speed run. The route so far had basically been clear, easy sailing southbound, although he feared that he would find the back of one of the large groups of undead on the Interstate. The back of one wouldn't be as bad as charging headlong into the front of one.

The mass of dead to his left stretched on as far as he could see. Cliff shook his head. This was the moment he knew that racing to San Diego was the right decision. There was no way that all of the dead could be exterminated without the Chinese's new technology. There just weren't enough survivors, not enough ammo in all of the country. Not without massive bombing campaigns or destroying the entire country, a fire-borne suicide from nuclear detonations. Even if it killed every single reanimate the fallout and nuclear winter to follow could be the end of it all.

The Interstate pitched forward, and he raced towards St. George out of the mountains from the north, the roadway descending along the Interstate towards the town. As he approached the edge of the urban sprawl an explosion echoed in the distance. Ahead of him on the Interstate a fireball rolled upwards, engulfed in thick black smoke.

"Well shit," Cliff couldn't help but to utter out loud.

The roadway became more dense with the abandoned vehicles, Cliff slowing to ease past each carefully. He needed to be fast, but he needed to be careful; the dead were thick between each of the vehicles. As he approached the dark plume of smoke, it billowed and churned, the fire raging hard beneath it. Nearing, he saw limbs and torsos of reanimates torn and scattered across the roadway, and a semi-truck blocking the inside lane. He drove cautiously around each, worrying about puncturing a tire. The dead poured from the shopping centers to the south, along the roadway under the bridge, passing under the bridge, under Cliff in his truck, and towards the burning shell of another vehicle. The swarming herd pushed against his truck, a thick cloud of flies a dark fog blocking his view. The broken concrete, dark marks and burning truck made it obvious to Cliff that someone had launched their vehicle off the bridge and the remnants of the dead probably had something to do with it. Shaking his head slightly, Cliff kept driving, taking one last glance down the on ramp towards the burning truck, curious what the dead would do about the massive flames.

The dead gathered too close to the truck's bonfire, bumping one another into the gas-fed fire, each of them catching ablaze and turning to walk off into the crowd, spreading the flames to more walking dead. Cliff was surprised to see that there were at least three dozen that were on fire, bouncing into more, shambling up the ramp towards the Interstate towards his truck. Their flesh, rotted fat, and tissue melted into the pavement with each step; with every passing moment they burned to their destruction. Cliff cursed, pushing the accelerator down; the truck shuddered, and the engine stumbled for a moment before catching and propelling him forward. Cliff made a mental note that I-15 might not be the best return route if the herd kept along their current path; also that fire would work to kill the dead, although slowly.

He looked left and saw even more dead shambling out of the suburban sprawl, reaching the Interstate and funneling to each side against the hillside. The fence on the right kept most of the dead at bay, but all of them were headed towards the Interstate and all of them were headed the same direction he was. Cliff drove around another semi, this one jackknifed across the pavement, and slammed on the brakes.

Ahead of him in the distance, barely visible through the flies and bodies, was Bexar. He looked dead, lifeless and limp. Chivo held a pistol in his right hand dangling at his side, his left grasping the recovery handle on the back of Bexar's tactical gear. He dragged Bexar along the dirt in the median. Staggering with each step, as a new corpse approached Chivo would jerk the pistol up and fire a single shot, blood and skull exploding out the back of the corpse's head.

One by one, Chivo made every shot, never stopping, never faltering, and dragging Bexar with him. The slide locked back on the pistol; an empty chamber, Chivo thumbed the release, the empty magazine clattering to the pavement, never stopping, one foot falling in front of the other, barely keeping his balance as he pulled Bexar behind him. He jammed the pistol into his waistband, then another magazine from the carrier into the magazine well. Chivo grabbed the pistol, thumbed the slide release, his pistol loaded and back in battery just in time for the next shot. Cliff drove as fast as he could, Chivo taking shot after shot, each round finding another skull and each step one more that he lived, one more step that he protected his brother, one more chance to make it.

The engine shuddered again; a sharp knock rattled from under the hood, and oil sprayed across the windshield. Barely able to see Chivo through the glass, Cliff pushed the pedal to the floor, trying to gain enough momentum and enough speed to get to Chivo before the truck failed. He knew the truck's mission was over and it would give out soon.

Once the engine locked up, it would hold the transmission and wheels in place; the truck had to keep rolling or he wouldn't make it to Chivo. Swarmed, he needed Chivo and Chivo needed him. There was no emotion in Cliff's eyes, only determination and anger raging behind the veil of calm. He jammed the selector into neutral, the oil spraying across the smoking engine, flames beginning to bounce across the bottom of the dash. This was the end of the truck, the speed run was over, but the mission would continue. First he had to help Chivo; he couldn't let his former trainee die like this. Bexar looked dead and probably was.

For all the grief that he'd given Chivo and Bexar in Colorado it was only to one end, the mission. Nothing else mattered to Cliff; friendships and compassion were something that he did not have or would ever have. No comradery, no brothers in arms, only the mission and that dedication. Still, Chivo was an operator, one he'd personally trained, one of *his* rookies.

The truck blasted through a group of dead shambling towards the two men in the median. Cliff leaped out of the truck while it was still rolling and looked at Chivo. His face slack, eyes blank, his face showed no recognition. Blood soaked his shirt and covered his face, blood-matted hair stuck up from his head, and blood streamed out of his nose. Steam rose from his body, the exertion burning in protest against the cold air. Trickles of crimson froth fell from the corners of his mouth. Step by staggering step, Chivo shot another corpse as it closed in for the kill, took another step, another shot.

Cliff's truck caught in the median ahead of them, the wire barrier trapping it, the oil fire spreading from the engine to the rest of the truck. Cliff stood and fired his M4, facing Chivo as he shot, the rounds snapped in the air as they passed by Chivo's bloody face. Firing quickly, he created a buffer, a cushion that gave Chivo some safety as they made their way. Off to each side of the Interstate were homes and shopping centers, more urban sprawl, more approaching dead offering no shelter to the battered warriors.

"Drop Bexar and move it, Chivo!"

Chivo gave no response, showed no recognition that he heard Cliff or had even seen him.

Cliff turned his attention to the way ahead, firing rapidly, changing magazines as he went, walking slowly, and trying to match Chivo's slowing pace. The dead swarmed; the veil of flies overhead turned the sky gray, vibrating with the buzzing, covering the feeding moans of the dead. Cliff fired and fired again, quickly changing out an M4 magazine for another thirty rounds, then another before the bolt on his rifle locked back on an empty chamber, his hand finding nothing in the magazine pouches on his carrier. He turned as his hand ripped the pistol from the holster on his thigh to see Chivo face down in the median, blood pooling around him, Bexar sprawled in the dirt behind him, not moving, dirt-caked blood covering his body.

Cliff stepped towards them, his feet kicking the empty magazines from his rifle as he fired while walking, rolling his feet gently across the pavement, the front sight of the pistol floating steadily through the air, muzzle driving from rotting face to rotting face, not waiting to see if the shot found its home, confident that it did. Cliff moved to the next and the next. The first pistol magazine was chased by a second and then by the third and final magazine. Slide locked back on an empty chamber, Cliff swung the pistol, hitting the dead in the face as he moved. Wave after wave of death came at him, body after body, with no end in sight. Cliff stood over Bexar's body, ripping pistol magazines from his carrier, feeding his pistol first before using up what was left, then transitioning back to his M4, the pistol dropped in the dirt in the transition, smoke billowing out of the barrel.

With each thirty-round magazine torn from Bexar's body, one by one Cliff shot the approaching dead, his rifle reaching further and further out, slowly building another buffer between him and the dead, room to move. He only needed a few more minutes then he could pull Chivo to his shoulders and walk away from the ambushing swarm.

Flies buzzed into his mouth as he panted each breath, the exertion extreme; sweat-drenched, Cliff fired until the bolt locked back on an empty rifle once again, a pile of M4 and pistol magazines at his feet. The rifle fell to the sling as he reached down to pull Chivo's body up to his shoulders before he was pulled backwards off his feet.

Pain shot through his body, reverberating from his shoulder and back again. The rotted face came into focus as he fell, trying to reach a knife with his right hand, but his arm refused to work. Now on his back, pain burned through his right calf and another corpse came in view, pieces of his flesh and pants hanging out of its mouth. No lips left to hold his flesh, it ground its rotted jaws together. Pain washed over his body, white spots flashed before his eyes; all he felt was anger for failing the mission. The dark curtains of consciousness fell away, bringing peace before death. Cliff thought he heard firecrackers. They sounded very far away and then he saw a man on a horse, the sun glowing around him like a halo.

CHAPTER 11

The sun blazed overhead in the early afternoon. The Marines continued to sleep and rest in shifts, only after having cleaned their weapons, readied the Zodiac, and made sure that all of their gear was ready to go at a moment's notice. For each of them, except for Simmons and Jones, it was like one of their tours in Afghanistan. As for the motor pool corporals, they had both spent a year in Iraq, but their mission profile during deployment was different than the special operations Marines living and fighting in the remote provinces of tribal Afghanistan. When not on watch or not taking care of an assigned duty, the members of the MSOT slept easily, ready to jump up and fight. Button-down pajamas and fluffy slippers were not the uniform of the day; the Marines slept in their uniforms, combat gear at the ready.

Simmons and Jones attempted to sleep and eventually gave up to sit in the dark lounge on one of the sofas where they chatted quietly, each holding his breath when a helicopter roared past overhead. Since the previous afternoon's attack in the harbor and the subsequent raid that destroyed the runways at Halsey Field, the PLA's patrols seemed to have increased significantly. Far beyond what anyone had seen so far.

The daylight hours were too dangerous for any of the Marines to take a position on the roof as an observation post; it was also far too dangerous to venture outside of the building. The number of the odd-looking Chinese-made Jeeps speeding by just yards away from the front of the building was too great. They saw fewer and fewer of the armored APCs, mainly only the odd-looking Jeeps driving by now.

The constant overflights by helicopters made any sort of activity in the enclosed courtyard too dangerous as well. Luckily the M-ATVs were under the large covered parking areas, which were like oversized military car ports. The fire watch—Marines awake in shifts to observe and alert the rest of any security issues or attacks—took station in dark rooms on the top floor, window blinds turned just enough to give them a vantage point to see the outside world, but not enough to be seen or noticed. Each of them kept a log of what they saw: the number of men, types of weapons, direction of travel and other details in notebooks so that the team could compile an accurate count for what they faced.

Aymond sat at the large cherry-wood-finished desk in one of the larger offices. The previous occupant had been a high-ranking officer, but that man was gone and Aymond enjoyed the sunlight streaming in through the partially open window blinds. Across the desk was a map of Coronado and San Diego.

"We have to disable and deny access to any other deep water cargo craft to the bay. They could still use the facilities at Halsey Field to off-load. So we can start with the cranes or we can start with the ships. Which do you two think?"

Happy looked at the map closely. "The ships would be easier to disable or sink; hit them with charges on the screws or a few charges below the waterline."

Gonzo frowned at the map, putting his finger on the northern end of Halsey Field. "All we have to do is disable two cranes along the northern dock side, maybe go as far as destroy the sections of track near the cranes so they can't be moved either. It would take less time and less C4. We have a lot right now, but that's all we've got, Chief; we should try to conserve it as much as possible."

Aymond nodded and sat quietly, looking at the map. Finally he said, "We're going to do both, starting with the cranes."

"Chief, if the response is anything like it has been today, I don't think we'll get but one shot at this."

"I agree, Gonzo. We do both in one night, but this time we do it right; we go as a full team. Shake everyone loose to meet at 1500 in the conference room. Simmons and Jones can hold the watch while we meet, then I'll brief them as well. We're going to need them."

"Aye, Chief," was said in unison before they walked out of the office.

SSC, Ennis, TX

Amanda wiped the sweat from her face, her gloved hands tingling from the heat and vibration. The massive armored backhoe loader was called something that consisted of a bunch of random letters, or so it seemed to Amanda, but it was quite the piece of equipment. Clint gave her a crash course in how it was operated while still belowground in the tunnel, and it had taken most of the morning to really start to get comfortable with how it operated, although trying to be precise with the limited visibility out of the armored plated cab was hard. So far Amanda had caused considerable damage to a house near the park's fence, but the loader wasn't damaged. According to Clint the armor would protect her from small arms fire or an IED, which in turn would protect her from the undead, which was great, except that the air conditioner wasn't working as well as it should be and she couldn't exactly roll down a window. The best she was able to do while driving back to the farmer's field across from the main gate was crack the door open to get some fresh air in the cab. If Clint saw her with the door open he would be really upset, but he was around the corner setting and erecting HESCO barriers for her to fill with dirt and rock. Although the work was monotonous—driving the big armored backhoe loader back and forth, getting the dirt poured into the barriers one load at a time—it sure beat being stuck belowground. Finally Amanda was working in a direction she knew would be productive.

At least we're not having to fill those things by hand with shovels, that would take forever and be impossibly hard work.

A lone shambling corpse made its way down Bozek Lane towards Amanda as she was about to push the loader into the dirt for another load for the HESCOs. Amanda saw him limping towards the tractor, probably attracted by the noise of the engine and the movement. Turning, she drove slowly towards the corpse, raising the loader front bucket, the jagged teeth of the digging edge hovering in the air about head height for the corpse. Oblivious to his impending doom, the corpse kept limping towards the charging military grade construction tractor before being ripped off his feet by the bucket. Amanda slowed and lowered the bucket to the ground, crushing the man's head and chest against the roadway.

With an annoyed grunt, she backed the loader away from the corpse squished into the road like roadkill, turned and drove back to the edge of the field for another large scoop of dirt into the bucket.

Groom Lake, NV

Erin answered Sarah's question with only a noncommittal shrug. "Sure, whatever, Mom."

Sarah looked at her daughter and let the attitude slide, more concerned about the reason the attitude was there in the first place. The new world, trying to be born out of the death of the old, was destroying her daughter and there was nothing she could do about it.

Jessie, who sat on the end of the bed, stood. "Erin, we love you and it would be a chance to get aboveground for a while. Maybe during the classes you'll meet someone you might like, maybe a new friend."

Erin shrugged again.

"Well, Jessie and I want to do it, so we're going to tell Jake that we're on board. I have a feeling that if you don't come along with us that Brit will try to have you doing dishes or vacuuming floors or doing something else mindless just as a way for her to try to get you back. Instead of that, come and teach others your awesome skill."

"OK Mom, but next time that bitch tries to talk to one of you that way I'm going to kick her ass."

Sarah gave a half-hearted smile before walking away from their bunks in the open area dorm, Jessie and Erin following her. They had to tell Jake they were on board and then they had to come up with a lesson plan before doing anything else.

CHAPTER 12

The Zodiac ripped through the choppy waters of the Pacific, the eight remaining members of the MSOT each in their position on the gunwales. The cloudy night was a blessing, the cloak of inky darkness bleeding across the shadows around them. In the distance loomed the remaining large PANAMAX container ships stacked high with shipping containers. They had no way to know what was actually on those ships, packed in the containers, but all of them were quite sure that it wasn't counterfeit Air Jordan's.

They took a long arc out into the Pacific to approach the ships from a quartering direction towards the stern. The teams had two objectives and only six hours to pull it off before sunrise. Happy and Ski wore wetsuits and rebreathers, their task for the operation both harder and easier than the others; it really depended on whether the ships were holding position with their screws turning. The consensus was that the ships were simply holding anchor, but without sonar intelligence it would be impossible to tell until they were there. If the screws were turning then their secondary task would become their primary. As usual, they must adapt and overcome.

Aymond looked at his teammates, his family, around him and knew that they wouldn't fail. They might die but they would never fail. It was a proud moment. Every single time he had gone outside the wire while in Afghanistan he'd had the same feeling when looking at his teammates, his brothers. This was what he was born to do and, seeing how there wasn't much else to do in their brave new world, this was what he would be doing until the end.

Gonzo pointed to Happy and Ski and held up his fist giving the sign: *Two minutes!* Circling his hand at the rest of the group, he held up five fingers: *Five minutes!*

It wasn't that Gonzo wouldn't have been able to say that out loud and be heard; the sounds caused by the wind, water, and their movement wasn't that bad, and the ultra-quiet engine on the Zodiac, specially made for SOCOM, wasn't louder than a mouse fart. They were in full mission profile, which meant no talking until the shooting started. Stealth above all, until there was no more stealth to be had, then firepower would win the day.

Happy and Ski pulled their masks on followed by each piece of gear they needed for the rebreathers; each went through their pre-launch check of the wrist-mounted gauges, verifying their gear was in place and secure, touching each piece like a pilot inspecting his airplane before taking flight.

Gonzo pointed at them and pumped his fist up and down. Happy and Ski gave each other a quick fist bump and rolled off the gunwale backwards into the choppy dark abyss. Hammer, manning the outboard engine and thus the direction the rubber boat was headed, began steering their craft right, bringing to an end the arc through the ocean to approach the lumbering container ships that seemed to blossom and grown in size through the darkness as they approached. From the middle of the rubber boat, sections of poles were being interlocked together. It looked like a long handle for a pool-cleaning brush, but on either side of the pole were alternating footholds, the end of the pole section having a heavy duty aluminum hook. As they approached the ship, Chuck took a heavy plate with felt padding on one side and a handle tied to a rope on the other. The felt side went against the ship's steel hull and was held strongly in place by the strong magnetic plate, the felt used to keep the heavy duty magnet from making a loud thud against the ship's hull when it was placed. The rope was tied to the Zodiac, anchoring them in place.

The water below them was calm, which meant the screws were not turning; that was a good thing for the team since if this ship was sitting idle in anchor, then the two others next to it probably were too. If that was the case then Happy and Ski would have an easy swim.

The pole sections snapped together and quickly the hook was over the edge of the transom and the team quickly ascended onto the ship, the superstructure looming overhead, just barely visible from the towering containers. If they were going to fully take the ship, the search would take hours, systematically moving from section to section. Every nook and cranny would have to be searched. They didn't have hours though, and they really weren't concerned with finding anyone on the ship as long as the team could account for the people they encountered while reaching the bridge.

A waterborne ship take-down was something they had trained for before, but it wasn't a part of the normal training cycle for the team; terrorists in the Middle East weren't really big on operating large shipping vessels. This was traditionally more of a Navy SEAL job. Aymond looked around, scanning the shadows for any threats while maintaining a secure perimeter for the two more team members who weren't on board yet. *Adapt and overcome, that is what we're good at.*

PANAMAX Ships

Once on deck, the metal decking rolled gently under Aymond's feet. Rifle up and more quiet than a shadow, he led the other five men him up the gangway and towards the bridge high on the superstructure. Although fat suppressors were attached to the ends of the M4s they carried, the rifles would not sound like those one heard in the movies. There would be no quiet whisper with a rifle and regular ammo; no, the suppressors helped with the noise but there would still be a lot of it. The moment they fired a shot would be the moment they lost the element of surprise, then they would need to lay down overwhelming firepower. With only six of them trying to take a ship this size, surprise was all they had.

Slowly, one by one, the team ascended the metal steps, the soft rubber-soled boots they wore making no sound from their practiced steps. The ship rumbled softly, the generators in the engine room running to provide electrical power while the massive main engines sat dormant to conserve fuel.

The black balaclava Aymond wore steamed in the cool air, the black wrap soaked with sweat, a mixture of exertion and extreme concentration. They stopped at the metal door, the reinforced glass pane spilling light into the darkened passageway from the bridge. A small telescoping mirror was passed up to Aymond, who used it to assess what they faced in the bright room.

A quick series of small hand gestures explained the situation and the plan to the team. Aymond stood slowly, just on the outside of the door frame, as far as the passageway would allow. One by one each man squeezed the shoulder of the man in front of him, until finally Chuck squeezed Aymond's shoulder. *All ready.*

Aymond nodded then stood perfectly still, Chuck's right hand grasping the latch, ready to open the hatch on command. Aymond moved his head out, in, out. *Ready, set, GO!* The hatch ripped open to his right by Chuck's powerful arm, Aymond stepped over the hatchway and into the room, sweeping right, Chuck behind him sweeping left, each successive teammate through the hatch taking a slice of the pie out of the middle until Snow stepped in and shut the latch behind him.

After dogging the hatch and clipping a snap link through the external lock, Snow turned to see their six captives. They didn't look Chinese.

Underwater, PANAMAX Ships

Happy and Ski swam under the deep keel of the ship adjacent to the one their teammates were assaulting at the moment. Lacking limpet mines, the proper equipment for the task, the pair had come ready to adapt and overcome to make their portion of the operation a success. The enormous screw shaft had a specially shaped donut of explosives wrapped around it and against the edge of the hull. Luckily for both of them the screws were motionless, the large ships sitting in anchorage, tugging against the heavy chains in the flowing tide.

The inky black water held secrets of the deep, but the secrets were not theirs to be found this evening. After the first ship's screws were rigged, a series of charges were placed on the stern side of the ship just below the waterline, held in place by waterproof vinyl tape that was typically used for quick repair jobs while on mission. The tape reminded Happy of a super form of duct tape; it wouldn't survive a voyage, but it should hold underwater for an hour, and an hour was all they needed.

The second ship in the row had the same explosive treatment applied to its massive screw shaft, but they didn't bother with the charges along the hull. If their plan worked right then they wouldn't have to.

On Board The PANAMAX

"Uh, Chief, I don't think these guys are Chinese."

The half-dozen prisoners taken on the bridge sat against the rear bulkhead, their hands zip-tied behind their backs, their ankles zip-tied together.

"No Gonzo, they're Korean."

"What the hell, Chief, I thought the Chinese were behind this."

"I think they are, I think they both are. Too bad none of you slap dicks know any Korean or Mandarin."

"I know a few curse words in Korean."

"Thanks Hammer, you're a real help here. Screw it, let's get to work."

Chuck and Gonzo stood at the computerized console. Long gone were the days of bells to the engine room or even a full ship's wheel. The maneuvering thrusters were controlled by joystick, the main screw by a tiny wheel to set bearing, and the computer screen in the console showed the engine status and all a captain needed to know. Although written in a language neither understood, the diagrams showing the system status next to each made it easier for Gonzo and Chuck to get the main engines on line.

Once the enormous engines were online and had run long enough to reach a running temperature, Gonzo tapped a button. The engine power indicated on the screen raising steadily, the ship slowly pushed forward, pulling against the anchor chains. Chuck tapped through some menu options on his screen before finding the right selection. The winches pulled the heavy chain and anchors up, out of the water, the ship steadily gaining speed with each passing moment.

The rest of the team searched each crew member's pockets, the drawers and cabinets on the bridge for any piece of intel that they could find, stuffing what looked remotely important into waterproof bags that were clipped onto their combat gear when full.

Gonzo continued until the engine showed to be operating at just above one hundred percent of ability.

Aymond whistled and circled his hand over his head. Gonzo used the muzzle of his M4 to smash in the monitor at the engine control and helm before following his team through the open hatch, the Korean crew members yelling after them, flopping on the floor of the bridge like fish, unable to move their feet or hands.

With lightning speed the team ran down the gangways, deck by deck, before reaching the main cargo deck. Looking over the edge and at the passing shore, it appeared that the ship had already reached five knots. Five knots didn't sound like much until one considered all the kinetic energy the fully loaded cargo ship held at that speed, and it was pointed straight towards Shelter Island and the big right turn to the harbor.

One by one his team members leapt from the side of the ship, falling forty feet to the water below, feet crossed, hands holding their rifle in place as they hit the water hard. If they could hit and roll on the water they would have, but instead each of them punched through the dark surface and sank before pulling on the handle that inflated their survival gear from a cartridge of compressed gas. Shooting up to the surface, the team bobbed in the wake of the big cargo ship leaving them behind. Aymond paddled in place, counting dark spots on the waves. Happy to see all of his team in the water and above the water, he turned and watched the ship lumber at greater and greater speed towards land.

M-ATV 1, Coronado, CA

Simmons and Jones roared south towards Imperial Beach in one of the M-ATVs. As Aymond had predicted, the overflights ceased shortly after nightfall and they should be able to maneuver without too much issue. So far he'd been right, except that the Zeds seemed to be out and in a partying mood, Jones rocking the heavy armored truck through the traffic of death.

They weren't lucky enough to have any Mark 84s to rig as explosives, and in reality Simmons considered themselves lucky for not having any. Neither he nor Jones knew the first thing about those bombs; their expertise lay in being a rifleman first and a highly trained diesel mechanic second. In the back of the truck was a full ten pounds of the putty-like explosive, plus detonation cord, blasting caps, and a timer that was supposed to work. Imperial Beach was just one more airfield they had to destroy. As of yet the Chinese didn't appear to be using the airport, but after the previous night's excitement on Halsey Field, who knew what the Chinese could do.

Jones' map of the area was an overhead photo that they had taken out of a picture frame in one of the offices of their building. It was the best they had, even though neither had been to Coronado before and the photograph didn't have any street names. One of the other Marines had labeled the major roads with a Sharpie, but even then the surface streets were a jumbled maze of homes and businesses.

The short section of desolate highway along 75 gave way to a mass of homes and businesses in strip centers. All of the homes glowed different shades of green in the NVGs both men wore.

"Are you counting streets?"

"Yeah Jones, second right at a real street. I think we're almost there."

The sign indicated that it was 7th Street, but neither of them cared.

"At the dogleg go one more block, take a right, go to the second street, then a left."

"Got it." Simmons concentrated; driving with night vision goggles was a different experience, one he hadn't had before.

"Are you seeing what I'm seeing?"

"No, I'm looking at this damn photo."

"Good, you probably shouldn't look up then."

Jones looked up and out the windows. "Holy shit!"

"Dude, I told you not to look. You're like a fucking child, now you saw the scary part and you're going to have nightmares."

"Fuck you and damn, what are we going to do about all of this?"

"Nothing, there's nothing we can do."

Simmons kept the big armored truck rolling close to fifty mph, ignoring the stop sign for Imperial Beach Boulevard. Homes surrounded them, hundreds of homes in every direction. And flooding from each yard, coming out from each abandoned car, turning to follow at every side street, were the dead.

A body flipped over the front bumper, hitting the windshield with a hard wet thump; no damage to the thick armored glass could be seen, but blood smeared across half of the glass as the body slid off the side of the truck.

"Fucking Zeds." Jones used the remote turret to look behind them. "Zeds as far as the eye can see, dude. Shit. They're all coming to follow us."

The neighborhood street they were flying down stopped at a chain-link fence and a locked gate, both indicated by reflective triangles.

"What do you think, Jones, do we have time to stop and cut the chain?"

Jones swung the remote turret left and right, the viewfinder displaying in the cabin. "Uh ... no."

"Fine, fuck it!" Simmons pushed the gas pedal to the floor, the diesel motor pushing all four wheels as hard as it could. The depth perception was a little off with the NVGs, but Simmons lined up the center of the truck with the center of the gates as best he could, and was still accelerating when the front of the truck exploded through the chain-link gates.

Sparks showered around them, the ruined gate tumbling away from the truck into the desert. As fast as the big armored truck was moving, it bounced across the sandy ground, across the tarmac of disused taxiway, and onto the main pavement of the primary runway. Aymond had told them that the middle of the runway was where they should set up to do the most damage. On their left were rows and rows of containers, equipment, and parts; they didn't know what all was stored here.

"Look at all of that up there," Jones said, pointing through the windshield. More fencing held more vehicles, trucks, and military hardware. "I know where we'll go if we need parts, dude."

The truck flew down the runway, turning to head towards the flightline and a lone tanker truck sitting on the tarmac. Jones swept the turret from left to right, watching the display. "Looks like we have a little bit of time; the first wave is just making the gate now."

Simmons stopped the M-ATV next to the fuel truck. "Think it'll run?"

"No, but I'm going to try. All of this shit is supposed to survive a nuclear war so it should also survive an EMP."

"Fine, but can it survive shitty Navy maintenance and sitting around for a few months?"

Jones shrugged before he climbed out of the armored truck and into the green-painted fuel truck, not before slapping the side of the tank a couple of times with the butt of his rifle to see if there was jet fuel still in it. Scanning the dash, he made sure the truck was in a condition to start, flipped the switch to run and waited to see if anything lit up on the dash. Nothing illuminated. Shaking his head, Jones turned the switch over to "start," hoping to hear the truck turn over, but was rewarded with nothing but silence. Jones climbed out and waved his hand over his head in a circle to Simmons, who responded by turning the M-ATV around and backing up to the nose of the fuel truck. Simmons left his truck running and climbed out to help as Jones was dragging two large chains out of the back of the M-ATV. A few moments later the pintle hitch was chained to the recovery hooks on the tanker, the tanker was in neutral and, with a hard lurch, the convoy rolled slowly forward towards the center of middle of the runway and towards the approaching army of death left in the wake of their flight moments earlier. Simmons left off the accelerator and left the free-rolling tanker slam into the rear of the M-ATV before he pulled on the parking brakes to hold tension, the whole contraption bouncing along against the heavy tanker.

The dead were closing faster than they would have liked.

"What do you think?"

"Jones, you handle the turret, I'll pull the chains and take care of the demo."

"You sure you don't want me to?"

"No, this'll work and I'll be fast; just keep those fucking Zeds off of me, buddy."

Simmons climbed out of the driver's seat and ran around to the rear of the truck. The chains were easy; flipping the pintle hitch open, he pulled the chains out of the ring and left them on the tarmac.

Flame erupted out of the end of the M2's long barrel, the night air ripping open. In short controlled bursts, the heavy machine gun mowed through the nearest Zeds before Jones walked the line of fire up towards the gate they had come through. He estimated that the gate was nearly two thousand feet away, but that sort of distance didn't matter for the big deuce. Tracers arced through the night sky like a sci-fi laser blast until Jones had the gate entrance zeroed, small movements left and right obliterating any Zed that tried to shamble onto the airfield.

Behind the truck, under the tank of jet fuel, Simmons duct-taped six blocks of the putty-like explosives. Aymond told him to use one, Happy said to use two, and Gonzo said be safe and use three. Being the good Marine he was, he knew that if some was good a lot more was way better. Blasting caps, det cord, everything went together the way that he was shown; the timer set and armed, Simmons started the countdown timer on his watch as he ran back to the M-ATV.

"Out the way we came or what, Jones?"

"No way, man, the way we came is fucked. Head north."

Simmons turned the wheel and accelerated hard; they only had a few minutes to get the shit out of Dodge before the fireworks started. He drove fast around the buildings on the flightline and towards the walled edge of the main entrance to the facility. Jones controlled the turret and unleashed the M2 on the brick pillar to which the wrought-iron gate was attached.

"What the hell, that shit always works in the movies!?"

"Save the ammo, Jones, we'll try a gentle nudge first."

Simmons slowed as he approached the gate, pushing the front of the truck against the gate before slowly adding power. The gate bent and flexed before breaking free of its mount in the concrete and brick wall, falling to the side as they drove through.

Zodiac, Coronado, CA

The negligible sound of their Zodiac came faintly across the waves towards them, the dark form appearing suddenly. The boat passed them and looped back, the engine off, coasting to a spot a few dozen feet away from the rest of the team. Happy and Ski sat in the boat, helping to pull the rest of their team on board one at a time. Once everyone was aboard, the engine ripped to life and the Zodiac's nose stood out of the water. Save for Happy and Ski still warm in their wet suits, the team shivered in the night air as their boat roared along the coastline towards their beach, their compound, their home. Thirty minutes later, Aymond lay on the roof of the building, in dry clothes, the Zodiac sitting on the trailer and the UTV tracks in the sand on the beach covered by his team. He didn't hear the sound of his ship crashing through the shoreline and through all the boats tied to their docks, but he imagined it was spectacular. If he was lucky, in a day or two he would be able to admire their handiwork. Right now he watched the helicopters with search lights crisscrossing the area where the ship should have crashed. There were a lot of helicopters in the air and luckily none of them were near his compound or his team.

The muffle thump of the explosive charges could barely be heard; Aymond slowly moved the spotting scope left to look towards the other PANAMAX ships in anchorage. One of the ships began to list to the stern, slowly leaning steeper and steeper; the containers fell from their perch and onto the other ship. Both of the ships were still there and mostly floating, but even if they tried to salvage them the screws should be on the ocean floor. The PANAMAX ships were now oversized sea-going barges.

Behind him a fireball erupted into the night sky, the roof glowing orange and red in the sudden light. The pressure wave rippled through him before Aymond heard the explosion. He resisted the strong temptation to spin on the rooftop and look at where Simmons and Jones should be, but he remained perfectly still, watching the searching helicopters as one by one they turned and roared past him across Coronado towards the new explosion.

This is not a good evening for our Chinese and Korean friends ... it's a good one for us though.

Once the last helicopter roared past, Aymond slid backwards across the roof to the hatch, lifted it and crawled inside the building, closing the hatch behind him. So far tonight had been a complete success and none of his men were killed while executing the operations.

M-ATV One, Imperial Beach, Coronado, CA

The sky broke orange and red behind them before the pressure wave washed over the truck and the sound reached them. Seen over the homes, trees, and businesses was a fireball rolling and churning into the night sky.

"Holy shit, that's fucking awesome!" Jones gave Simmons a high five.

Slowing down so they could dodge the massive amount of Zeds heading towards the big fiery beacon, the pair of motor pool Marines were giddy from their first real Special-Forces-type mission and demolition job. Reaching the highway, Simmons turned to travel back towards Coronado and their home base.

"What's that?" Jones pointed through the windshield into the sky.

A search light screamed across the night sky along the same path as the highway from the north.

"That's the fucking PLA, man."

"Shit."

Simmons turned off the road and parked under the awning for a gas station.

"We can't stay here all night; if they have a helicopter up now, then they'll probably send patrols soon after."

Simmons nodded. "Yeah, I don't know, if we're seen we can't lead them back to where the team is."

"Do you think they have infrared?"

"Seems like they would be using it instead of a big spotlight if they did."

"We could take the bird out with the deuce."

"That would give us away too."

"Then why don't we haul ass after it goes past? Surely they're going to be more concerned with the huge fucking explosion than anything else, right?"

Simmons looked at his watch; only about two hours until sunrise. "You've got me, Jones, but you're right, we can't stay here, it's going to be daylight soon. Let's roll and we'll play it by ear."

Simmons drove out from under the awning and turned right towards I-5 and away from the highway leading back into Coronado.

Dodging the abandoned vehicles on Palm Avenue, Simmons rocketed west, bouncing over the raised median at full speed, the suspension soaking up the curbs with ease, following the exit ramp the wrong way. Suddenly his night vision goggles glowed bright, lights ahead of them blooming out the display before the high-tech devices could react and turn down. The truck shuddered hard to a stop, tires locked up against the asphalt, and they slid into the side of an abandoned car.

"Fuck, Jones, scan fast, we need to hide, fucking convoy headed towards us!"

Jones spun the remote turret, the display a green blur of shadows.

"Chopper behind us and closing fast!"

"Shit, OK ... hang on!"

Simmons selected reverse and stomped on the gas, front tires spinning against the car caught under the front bumper, the rear tires pulling the heavy truck backwards and into another vehicle. He turned the wheel hard left, put it in drive and stomped on the gas again. This time the truck bounced across the landscaping, crashed through a small tree and into the parking lot of a shopping complex.

"Talk to me, Jones!"

"Home improvement store. Head left about ten o'clock and fucking book it!"

The parking lot was surprisingly full, and the big M-ATV flew through the open areas, knocking carts and flatbed dollies out of their way in a shower of sparks. Turning hard right and stomping on the brakes, Simmons held on as the truck shuddered and slid towards the covered loading area for the store's customers.

Jones spun the turret to the rear, watching the green glow of the night vision sky glow violently with the spotlights on helicopters and the rushing convoy, all racing to the explosion, all racing to catch them. All racing to kill them even though the Marines were sure that the invaders didn't know exactly who or what they were.

"Do it Simmons, fucking go!"

Simmons yelled as he drove through the glass exit doors at forty mph, crashing through the cash registers and checkout lines before hitting the end of an aisle, the rack stacked high with rough lumber. The rack tilted away from the truck, slowly as if played back in slow motion, before crashing into the next tall rack of lumber, collapsing in a heap of metal and broken two by fours.

"Holy shit Jones, holy fucking shit."

"I know man, the shit they don't teach you at fucking Perris Island."

"Oh God, you know we'd get brought before the man if we did this back then."

"Before the man? Shit, we'd be in Kansas before the day was out, breaking big rocks into little rocks!"

Simmons used more finesse than before and backed the M-ATV out of the piled mess of lumber and shelving, running over a Christmas decoration display in the middle of the main aisle before turning to point the nose of the truck towards the gaping hole in the wall where the big glass doors once stood. Their NVGs turned off, the interior of the truck and the store were dark; they saw the sky beginning to lighten with the coming sunrise.

"And now we wait."

Jones nodded in agreement, turning the turret towards the opening as well. Their only chance at this point was to wait the daylight out and use the night to get back home. Movement in the shadows out of the side windows caught their attention. They flipped the night vision goggles down and turned them back on, only to be greeted with the face of death wearing an orange apron. Another appeared and another. In moments, surrounding the idling truck were dozens of dead, all pawing at the armored exterior.

"What are we going to do about that?"

"Nothing Jones, there's nothing we can do."

"You can turn the engine off, maybe they'll get bored and move on?"

"Maybe, but shit, man, what if the truck doesn't start again?"

"Simmons, you know this thing as well as I do; it's a roll but the secret squirrel commandos can come get us tonight if need be."

Simmons frowned and turned the truck off, the rattling hum of the diesel motor ceasing. They could now hear the muffled moans of the dead, fingernails clawing at the truck.

"Well if that isn't the suck, I don't know what is. I'm going to call it in," Jones keyed the mic for the radio mounted in the truck. "Dagger-Actual, Switchblade-One, copy SITREP, over."

MSOT Compound, Coronado, CA

"Switchblade, you let them name their call sign Switchblade? That's racist."

"Shut up Kirk, I'll fucking cut you, mang."

"Gonzo, eat shit and bark at the moon."

"Gentlemen, enough."

Kirk and Gonzo grinned but stopped talking at Aymond's order.

"Switchblade-One, Dagger-Actual, go 'head, over."

Aymond sat at the table taking notes, the room lightening with the coming day beginning to stream through the windows. Five minutes of back and forth later, Aymond had his questions answered, his notes scrawled across two pages of paper. "Switchblade-One, good copy, Dagger-Actual out."

"Chief, want me to go kick the team loose?"

"Not yet Gonzo, we're not going to roll until sunset, but I do have a project for you two ... remember the Shkin Firebase?"

"Shit, fucking Fort Apache, how could we forget, Chief?"

"Well Gonzo, it's time for you and Kirk to use what you all learned there for the forces of something other than screwing off."

"Fucking 'rah, Chief!"

Groom Lake, NV

"I don't know Jake, two women, one of them pregnant, and a teen?"

"You should have seen her, Bill, holy cow. I mean she nearly lit Brit on fire with nothing more than a look and some stern words."

"Still, what will they know?"

"Talk to them, Bill. Well I wouldn't talk to Erin, that's the teenager, unless she speaks first, but her mother Sarah, and Jessie, they've been out fighting and surviving since day one."

"So have we, Jake."

"Not like they did. We had the Chosen Tribe crazies, our losses were great, but still Cliff plucked us out of there. Sarah and Erin have fought their way across the country since the beginning, and after piecing together the details with that Special Forces group that went to Cortez ... Jessie was left for dead by a biker gang in Texas."

"And she's pregnant!"

"Yes Bill, I know that, and in a few weeks or another month or two I'm not going to want to let her topside at all, but for now I think this is the right thing to do. Besides, we need to get the rest of our fellow survivors ready."

Bill nodded.

"How has the exploration gone?"

"Interesting, no, interesting isn't the right word, it's borderline creepy and amazing all at the same time."

Jake poured more coffee from the carafe into their cups, anxiously waiting to hear what Bill had found.

"The facilities are basically separated into two separate areas. There isn't one but two closed-loop reactors. At least that's what Hal explained it as."

Jake furrowed his brow. "Who is Hal again?"

"Older guy from Kansas, ex-Navy. He was on subs, a senior enlisted guy. It was around the time The Hunt For Red October hit the theaters before he got out."

"Why Kansas?"

"Said he had enough ocean water for two lifetimes."

"Heh, OK, if he says so. So what did Hal tell you?"

"His explanation is that there are two power plants; one is running, the other is in standby, except that it's not really standby, there is no such thing as standby with a nuke."

Jake shook his head slightly. "Then what is it doing?"

"It's in standby. I mean to say that it's throttled all the way down."

"Is that why we keep having outages? Are we pulling too much power from the single nuke?"

"No, not from what Hal says at least. According to him, the two nukes together should be able to power Las Vegas and keep the neon signs glowing." Bill shrugged.

"How do we control it?"

"*We* don't. There is a complete computer system sectioned off, the whole thing is sectioned off like a giant lead bank vault. It's possible to shut the door and save everyone from the radiation if something goes wrong."

"That's good, I think, but the computer?"

"Yeah Jake, you should see it. The computer system down there is like something out of a dammed sci-fi movie. Impressive, absolutely impressive."

"And that controls the nukes?"

"No, I think it controls everything."

"What do you mean everything?"

"Jake, I mean *everything*, from the water, to the power, to the HVAC, to the lights, to which side the toilet paper goes on the roll, I mean it controls *everything*."

"Wow. So what happens if that computer system fails?"

"I don't know, there's not exactly a manual on this sitting around collecting dust ... at least none that we've found."

"Then we worry about that later. What about the other section, you said there were two sections?"

"Yeah, sorry, the other section is everything else, water, waste and air."

"Air? What waste and how much water, I mean, well ... Bill explain it to me, use small words; the coffee hadn't really kicked in yet."

"OK, Hal helped me with this too; it's like the cross between a big damn RV, a sub and the space shuttle. The cistern is massive, like epic, Great-Lakes-sized. If the readout on the terminal down there is right, we're sitting on roughly four billion gallons of water."

"Billion, with a b?"

"Yeah, billion, four billion gallons of water."

"How did they get that much water down there, in ten years or twenty years or whatever, and how will we refill it?"

"We don't."

"We can't?"

"No Jake, not we can't, just we don't refill it, the systems take care of that for us."

"Some sort of spring or something?"

"Yeah, something is right. The water is piped in."

"Piped in from where? We're in a dry lake bed, that's why this place exists is because it's dry and sucks so bad that it's in the middle of nowhere."

"I don't know where from yet, but I think it might be Lake Mead."

"Seriously? No ... Lake Mead as in the Hoover Dam and the Colorado River?"

"One and the same."

Jake shook his head in disbelief. "I don't know, Bill, I mean I might have an easier time believing you found alien bodies or something."

"Well we found those too."

Jake choked on his mouthful of coffee, turning red and coughing, trying to keep from spitting it out on the table.

"Seriously? I was joking."

"I am too, Jake," Bill said, his rotund stomach jiggling as he laughed. "Besides the water, the waste treatment is incredible, like the largest septic tank you've ever seen. I mean someone ran machines to dig all of this out, they built supports, it's like you're in a giant warehouse lit by glowing overhead gym lights. I don't know how they kept all of this a secret."

"Did they?"

"Yeah they did, Jake, people thought they really did have aliens or it was all just black aircraft and such. If for nothing else the facility itself is absolutely amazing."

"What about the air?"

"Scrubbers and generators. Like I said, it's like the Space Shuttle. Right now our air is exchanged and filtered with the air topside, but if we put the facility into lockdown, all the vents seal, all the doors seal, everything seals up tighter than a nun's habit and we breathe our own air."

"For how long?"

"That I haven't figured out yet. I say I haven't, *Hal* hasn't. He knows more about these systems than I do, so I passed the job along to him. He rounded up a couple of helpers of his own and they're systematically going through each area. He suspects there is much more that we don't know of yet. He thinks there might be tunnels."

"Tunnels where?"

"I have no idea, but if you believe the tinfoil crowd on the interwebs the country is crisscrossed with huge underground highways in giant tunnels bored by nuclear-powered TBMs."

"TBMs?"

"Tunnel Boring Machines, the big round rotating cutting snakes that make a tunnel as they creep along through the dirt; these were supposedly larger than what we know of and nuclear-powered, but I don't know if I believe that."

"Sure, and the SSC was dug by four guys and a shovel, while another couple of guys with a pickaxe took care of our home underground here. There has to be some technology at work that we're not aware of."

"Touché friend, but Jake, do we want to know?"

"I do."

The lights flickered and shut off for a few moments before blinking back on.

"All of this is neat, Bill, but why is that happening?"

"That we don't know, but I really do suspect it has to do with the computer system controlling the facility."

CHAPTER 13

MSOT Compound, Coronado, CA
March 16, Year 1

Night was quickly approaching with the falling sun. Thus far, Simmons and Jones had yet to miss any of the two-hour-interval quiet check-ins with two clicks of the transmitter, which was returned with a single click. The seven Marines and Aymond had their personal gear packed, checked and ready, and their M4s clean and oiled—not that their gear and weapons ever were in any condition but dialed in, but as part of the pre-operation ritual every piece of gear is checked, every weapon cleaned, oiled and checked, every place on their gear had a critical component and everything they carried had a purpose.

The gear was piled neatly in eight orderly stacks; the men knelt on the floor around a clutter of trash. At least that was what the clutter looked like. Trash from the dumpster at the back of the courtyard contained the biggest treasure trove of needed material, but some other gear scavenged out of the mission lockers and offices in the building rounded out their needs.

They sorted out aluminum foil, packing materials, soda cans, fuel cans, nails, bolts, nuts, screws, and they had a series of car batteries charging, linked with jumper cables from the M-ATVs. The time had come to bring the ways of the jihadist to the invading communists.

Each man worked quickly but carefully, shaping the hard clay-like explosives into the device that they were building. Each was as individually crafted and different as each of the men, but singular in focus and plan. The eight of them had three vehicles left: two M-ATVs and the one soft-sided Humvee that Simmons and

Jones had driven in from The Palms. Except that one of the M-ATVs was currently sitting in a store miles away. For the plan to work they would need all of the vehicles, and they had to be prepared to improvise a new FOB if they couldn't break contact and escape back to the SEALs' building undetected.

Returning from the vantage point on the roof, Happy walked into the room. "Chief, looks like the PANAMAX had the desired effect, and it's planted in the harbor by the airport. Looks like it plowed through a bunch of yachts and royally fucked everything. Even seeing it from all the way on this side of the harbor I'm impressed. Looks like fuel oil is spread across the water pretty thick, it was shimmering against the sunset."

"Roger, good idea on that one, guys. How about the other ships?"

"Looks like they toppled like dominos; some containers are floating in the water, others I assume sank, but all of them are listing really hard to port. They're going to need some serious gear for recovery operations. Even if they had the ships and they sent them to sea today it will still be a couple of weeks for them just to get here, much less open the harbor for business again."

"Outstanding!"

"Oh, the Coronado bridge is still fucked, Chief."

"Thanks Happy, we'll just have to ignore it. If it's impassable for us it is for our new neighbors as well."

"We could blow it, Chief." Gonzo smiled, holding up a small block of explosives he had shaped into a badly formed rabbit. "Just your friendly neighborhood rabbit coming by to visit."

Chief shook his head. "No, save your explosives for the golfers."

"You mean gophers."

"Whatever, the bridge doesn't matter right now. Not for this run and gun op." Aymond peeked through the blinds and then looked at his watch.

"Looks like we're good to roll in ninety mikes; get it right, wrap it up, and meet back here in sixty. Remember gentlemen, be prepared to not come back."

M-ATV One, Coronado, CA

Jones snored loudly in deference to the constant thumping on all sides of the armored truck from all the Zeds. Over the last few hours, Simmons had become accustomed to the gruesome faces peering in the armored windows and eventually came to terms with his safety in the big truck, although he still felt anxious and was ready to clear away from the undead.

The short radio transmission two hours ago only said to hang tight and the QRF would be en route. Simmons shook his head. *They sure put the quick in Quick Reaction Force. Jesus, it's been hours of this shit.*

As per the radio message, he responded with a single click of the transmitter to acknowledge the reception of the message. He had no idea what the plan was. *Come nightfall we could just drive over all of these dammed Zeds and out of here, if the fucking helicopters would leave.*

The muffled sound of a helicopter roared overhead. So far, hiding in the home improvement store had worked to their advantage, but Simmons was worried that the Chinese would eventually put trucks out and find them.

Really though, a home improvement store is a good place to be if it can be secured. Plenty of materials to make sure nothing can get in, other stuff to make improvised weapons, a garden center with potting soil and seeds to grow. There's even shit to keep the bugs out of the garden and help the tomatoes grow large. Shit, after this all settles down I'm going to talk to Chief about raiding some of these places and starting a garden. That would beat the hell out of these fucking MREs.

Simmons held the tackboard-like cracker in his hand, breaking off little pieces to chew on for a snack. The cracker was one of the more worthless items in an MRE and Simmons hated them, but he was hungry.

MSOT Compound, Coronado, CA

Aymond stood by the dry erase board, the assignments listed out by name. "Alright guys, each of you know your job, each of you know the rally point. If you get fucked, call it out. If you get stranded, hunker down and get safe, we'll come to you. This op has a lot of moving pieces; fucking Murphy will get you if you let him. Be smart, be fast, be accurate ... swift, silent, deadly."

The team gave a oorah in unison.

"Saddle up!"

The trucks were prepped with supplies: MREs, water, as much ammo and as many fuel cans as they could hold, the improvised explosives and some of the other combat gear scavenged from the SEAL Team's mission lockers.

Aymond climbed into the first M-ATV, Snow with him, and started the truck. Chuck and Happy sat in the soft-bodied Humvee, the trailer holding the Zodiac hooked to the rear of the truck, Hammer and Gonzo ready for the water.

"Dagger-Actual, commo check."

"Dagger-One."

"Dagger-Two."

"Dagger-Three."

Aymond smiled slightly. Snow rotated the remote turret, using the IR to scan the horizon for any blacked-out helicopters.

"Looks clear for now, Chief."

Aymond nodded and keyed the radio. "OK guys, go time."

Chuck climbed out of the truck and ran ahead of the short convoy to the gate securing the installation from the highway, pushing the gate open just as Aymond nosed his truck in position. Once back inside, Aymond took a right and drove hard, the Humvee with the Zodiac heading straight across the intersection and through Glorietta Bay Park, past the playset, to the beach and into the water. Hammer and Gonzo bailed out of the truck, unhooked the trailer from the Humvee, and released the Zodiac, the trailer sinking to the sandy bottom. Happy gave his buddies the bird before driving through the park and back onto the highway, driving fast to catch back up to the convoy ahead.

Glorietta Bay, Coronado, CA

The Zodiac came to life, Hammer and Gonzo piloting the craft carefully to the docks where the Chinese patrol boat had been left. Alongside the tied-up boat, the two of them carefully transferred the gas cans from the bottom of the Zodiac to the patrol boat. Gonzo stayed on the patrol boat and Hammer stayed with the Zodiac. The patrol boat coughed to life, Gonzo released the lines and backed the boat slowly out of the slip.

Motoring up, the patrol boat left a larger wake than the Zodiac, which Hammer used to mask his presence as he followed behind. They crossed under the Coronado Bridge, turning west and towards the cargo ship they'd run aground the night before.

Powerful spotlights illuminated the shipwreck; containers that had fallen to shore lay twisted, bent, and open. As they came closer to the wrecked ship it was obvious that what the Chinese and Koreans lacked in machinery they more than made up for in manpower.

Gonzo smiled. *God, I hope they haven't dumped the fuel tanks yet.*

The pair passed the USS Midway; Gonzo slowed the patrol boat and scanned the shore with binoculars.

There appears to be about a half-dozen of those radar trucks spaced on either side of the recovery, maybe another three dozen trucks that they're using to haul away the material from inside the containers.

Zeroing in on the containers that lay broken open on the shore, which coincidentally was near the original recon spot, Gonzo tried to figure out what the cargo was. It didn't appear to be military in nature; most of it appeared to be repair pieces, and some looked like electrical transformers one would see on power poles in neighborhoods.

Sure, fuck you guys, kill us off, fix the infrastructure and take the whole damned thing? Gonzo snorted in anger. He hadn't felt this angry since his first tour in Afghanistan. He pointed the nose of the ship towards the front of the wreck, where he saw the most people, tied the wheel to the seat, keeping the rudder straight, and looked at Hammer, who had pulled alongside the port side, away from the view of anyone on most of the shoreline. Gonzo took out a Zippo, flicked it twice, smiled at the dancing flame, pushed the red button taped to the can on the left and lit the rags hanging out of the four other fuel cans on the boat.

The lid of the Zippo lighter slapped closed before Gonzo put it in his pocket, pushed the twin throttles all the way forward, and jumped over the gunwale into the Zodiac. Hammer steered sharply away from the patrol boat and pushed the throttle as far open as it would go. The nose of the rubber boat stood sharply out of the water as it sped past the USS Midway. Rounding the corner of the north shore, a fireball erupted behind them, the dark sky glowing red. A hard pressure wave ripped over them, nearly knocking them out of the boat before the deep hard thump of the explosion could be heard. Hammer slowed the Zodiac while Gonzo held the binoculars to his face.

"Holy shit, buddy, there's a huge hole in the hull. It's ripped open like the fucking Titanic ... sinking like it too."

Gonzo scanned as much of the shoreline near the explosion as he could see; most of it looked absolutely destroyed, and the rest of it was on fire. Even some of the airport terminals looked damaged.

"Good kill. Another point for the good guys."

Hammer smiled at the comment, the two of them giving a quick fist bump before turning into the marina near the convention center. The motor off, they tied the Zodiac to a chain-link fence sticking into the water from shore and climbed out of the boat. Once on shore, they crouched back to back, scanning each direction for any threats, while gathering their bearings and preparing for what should be a short wait.

MSOT Convoy, Coronado, CA

The short convoy of two raced south on Silver Strand Boulevard before reaching the end of the bay and following the curve in the road into Imperial Beach. Approaching I-5, Happy and Chuck peeled off from the convoy and turned north on Saturn Boulevard before driving over the landscaping and into the parking lot of the home improvement store. Happy keyed the radio.

"Switchblade, time to roll."

The M-ATV started and drove out of the broken storefront, Zeds falling off of the hood and away from the doors as it rolled, more bodies falling and being pulled under the front bumper. There were dozens and dozens of Zeds. Once clear of the largest group, the armored truck sped up before stopping by the Humvee. Happy and Chuck stood on the hood of their truck, picking off the undead closest to them and no more, conserving their ammo. Once Simmons brought the truck to a stop, Happy jumped off the hood and climbed into the back seat of the M-ATV, tossing a large rucksack on the seat next to him before being pushed out of the way by Chuck and his large rucksack.

"Well hello, guys, finish all your shopping? Ready to go?"

"Dude." Simmons frowned at Happy, who was smiling like someone who couldn't wait to tell a secret.

"OK, in all seriousness, how much fuel do you have?"

"Three-quarters."

"Perfect. Fucking get going, we're racing west. This is going to be fun."

"What exploded?"

"It was the fun balloon."

"What about our Humvee?"

"If everything works out right we can pick it up after the party."

Simmons shook his head. Regular grunt Marines were weird sometimes in combat zones, but these secret squirrel commando types were a breed all their own.

Full MSOT Convoy, Coronado, CA

The truck rocketed down the flyover and onto I-5, which was surprisingly clear of Zeds. Snow scanned the route ahead with the remote turret, switching between night vision and IR; the Zeds didn't show up on Infrared due to their bodies being the same temperature as the air around them, but they would show up on NV.

Living people, trucks, aircraft, all of them glowed in IR, if there were any to be found. So far the few helicopters that Snow had seen were hovering around the site of the explosion, the powerful spotlights blooming out the night vision screen.

Zeds fell from the overpasses onto the Interstate as the truck rolled past. Simmons and Jones, their truck quickly catching up to Aymond and the lead truck, were listening to the details of the operation as Chuck explained them.

Jones shook his head. "That's the plan? We called those goat fuckers suicide jockeys on Route Irish for doing the same shit in Baghdad."

"How well did it work?" Chuck smiled.

"Great until air cover blew them to hell."

Chuck shrugged. He wasn't worried, he had no doubt they would win; if everything went to hell they would wing it and win no matter what.

The pair of armored trucks raced across the bridge down the ramp to Harbor Drive. As they bounced across the median, dodging the few abandoned vehicles and Zeds in their path, power poles and fences around huge naval support facilities flew past them. The army of the dead marched west with them, following the sight of the fireball, the sound of the massive explosion. A seemingly endless row of railcars appeared on their right, all full of new vehicles that had arrived by boat to be dispersed and sold all over the U.S. Every new car had been ruined by the EMP and was now worthless, left to rust and rot back into the earth.

Low-slung pedestrian walkways crossed over the roadway. Aymond in the lead M-ATV kept rolling at fifty mph, a blindingly fast speed as the trucks bounced through the median and around all the obstacles.

"Stop, stop here!"

Simmons slammed on the brakes, Happy yelling at him.

"Chuck and I are getting out for a second. Stay put."

Simmons gave a thumbs up Jones spun the remote turret, scanning for anything approaching that was a threat, but away from the direction of the other Marines.

Chuck and Happy climbed out of the truck, each holding a paint can and a garden hose. One hand holding the random supplies, they drew their pistols and ran quickly to either side of the heavy concrete pedestrian bridge. A paint can was placed against the concrete walls, the garden hoses unrolled across the roadway, wires and det cord sticking out of the end of the hoses by the paint cans; each man worked quickly, setting and arming their IEDs. The paint cans were each full of bolts and nails and a motorcycle battery to power the system, an improvised circuit that would squeeze together when a vehicle ran over the hose—hopefully not if a lone Zed stepped on it—and all of it set off with a pound of C4.

With a few more quick shots from their pistols to put down the closest Zeds, Happy and Chuck ran back to the running M-ATV and climbed in, Happy taking a glance over his shoulder at the blue sign welcoming everyone to the Naval Base San Diego. *More like fuck you for coming.*

Lead M-ATV, Coronado, CA

Aymond drove the truck hard, harder than they had driven the trucks from the MWTC to come here. In his mind that was a caravan, a simple convoy; this was a combat operation and they didn't have time to waste. Besides, two of his men were out in the open and a world of shit was about to go down. The truck practically flew under the overpass leading up the Coronado Bridge. The other ruined Chinese cargo ship lay across the spur lines and against the concrete pier.

Against the red sky in the distance the silhouette of the Hilton loomed towards his left. He couldn't remember the street names but he knew that was where he needed to turn, under another pedestrian bridge. He stood on the brakes hard before turning hard left, all four tires clawing at the pavement, trying to gain traction. The truck shuddered as it shot through the intersection and bounced over the concrete median. The massive convention center lay to his right, and the Zeds' activity was getting heavier, all headed towards the siren call of the glowing red sky and the remains of the Chinese ship.

A semi-truck stood across all the lanes of the road, jack-knifed, the cab lodged against the wall of the convention center. Aymond stood on the brakes, Snow yelling, "LEFT LEFT LEFT!"

Aymond jerked the wheel left, bouncing over the curb, the wheels churning through the dead grass before he jerked the wheel right and onto the wide concrete boardwalk. Snow spun the remote turret towards the marina park. "Got'em, Chief, they're running towards us from the left."

The M-ATV slid to a stop, tires leaving dark marks on the pristine concrete. Hammer and Gonzo piled into the truck, Aymond gassing it before they could even get their doors closed.

Trail M-ATV, Coronado, CA

Simmons slammed on the brakes again, the Coronado Bridge towering over the roadway. Happy and Chuck piled out of the back of the M-ATV with a handful of soda cans tied together with something that looked like a rope to Jones. This time Jones jumped out with an M4, taking shots to protect the other Marines while they rolled the rope across the roadway, the soda cans draped across the middle of the road on either side of the dirt median. Changing magazines, Jones kept firing, the Zeds coming in greater and greater numbers with each passing moment.

"Chuck, Happy, get your white asses back in the fucking truck!" Jones flipped to three-round bursts, burning through another magazine while holding protection. Simmons fired his pistol from inside the truck, shooting through the open passenger door, picking off Zeds that shambled up behind Jones, his attention directed to the rear, where Chuck and Happy worked fast.

An eternity later, mere seconds really, all three of them were in the M-ATV and Simmons had the pedal pressed all the way to the floor.

Lead M-ATV, Coronado, CA

"Gonzo, how many birds do you see up?"

"Only two, Chief; they're pretty much just circling the explosion, the spotlights are pointed down. They must have a hell of a mess."

"Well fuck'em."

Gonzo nodded. "How close do you want to get?

"Just past Hawthorn Street should do it, ya think, Gonzo?"

"Damnit Hammer, I don't know the streets over here like you and your little frat buddies do."

Hammer smirked. "Just past the courthouse-looking building, Chief, like a block and some change past it."

"See, those are directions I can work with."

At the next park entrance, Aymond steered right and back onto a real road, before turning left and back onto Harbor, where he needed to be. Moments later they passed the USS Midway on their left and then the San Diego County Building on their right.

"Tell me when, guys."

"Just a little further, Chief ... and stop."

Aymond followed Hammer's instructions and slowed to a stop. They were very close to the edge of destruction from the ship's fuel tanks exploding. Snow spun the remote turret again. "Still only see two; the IR on the ground is white-out due to the flames, so no idea on that one, guys."

Hammer and Gonzo climbed out and into the cargo box in the back of the truck, each unpacking their long 50-caliber rifles from the cases. Nearly in unison, they flipped the bipods down and braced the rifles on the roof of the truck. They were almost in reach of the Zeds; cold dead fingers clawed at their boots, trying to pull their prey to the ground for a feast. Behind them a legion of death approached, all the Zeds that Aymond had sped around and past now converging en masse.

"I've got left."

"I've got right," Gonzo responded.

Each of them concentrated on their breathing, letting the circling helicopters fly into the view of their optic instead of trying to chase the aircraft through the sky. The helicopters flying opposite each other, slowly circling, made the shot easier for the pair.

One then the other! Flames followed the heavy round out of the barrel, both Marines working the bolt to place another round into battery. For a moment it seemed as if neither Marine had made the shot, the helicopters continuing on their path, but then one began to spin, rotating faster and faster before rolling and falling into the debris of the ship and the fire. The other fell straight out of the sky and crashed into the runway opposite the ship. Both of the Marines quickly put their rifles back in the cases and raised their M4s, Gonzo pushing the transmit button on his radio.

"Chief, we're crawling with Zeds back here; splashed two, but we can't climb out yet."

"Roger, stay put. We continue as planned."

The turret and heavy machine gun faced forward, so both of them turned and faced the rear, flipping their NODs down from the front of their bump helmets. Each of their worlds became awash in a green and black glow from the night vision. The truck lurched forward, driving slower than it had been before, the mass of Zeds making it nearly impossible to drive any faster. They pushed on each side of the truck, far too many for Gonzo and Hammer to put down, their fingers still grasping at their boots. Both of them backed up against the cab of the truck, getting as far away from the openings of the cargo area as they could.

Trail M-ATV, Coronado, CA

Simmons drove quickly, but much slower than before, the concentration of the dead becoming thicker and thicker as they approached the fire.

"We're supposed to put another set of IEDs out with this walking bridge for the Hilton."

"Chuck, are you really going to climb out there and do that?"

"Fuck no, what about you?"

Happy shook his head. "No way."

Jones spun the turret, scanning. "I lost the helicopters, that's the good news; bad news is it is wall to fucking wall of Zeds as far as the eye can see."

Simmons tightened his grip on the wheel. "Any ideas or just keep driving?"

Chuck and Happy shouted at the same time, "Just keep driving!"

Lead M-ATV, Coronado, CA

Gonzo looked forward as the M-ATV pushed through the crowd of dead, reaching the edge of the blast radius. He held down his transmitter: "Radar truck, about hundred yards up and right twenty."

Snow replied, "See'em."

The heavy M2 machine gun ripped open the air around the truck, the tracer rounds following their path like lasers, a stream of heavy 50-caliber rounds in between the spaced tracer rounds. Five seconds later and the burst was finished, the stream of rounds walking up the front of the radar truck and through the radar face, the truck catching on fire and two men running away from behind it.

"I've got'em." Hammer braced his M4 on the truck and fired a burst, the green figures in his night vision crumpling to the ground. In front of the radar truck was a wall of death, stacked twenty yards deep; the Zeds fell to the ground along the arcing path of the truck's invisible destruction.

"Chief, think we can get one of those trucks?"

"Where, Gonzo?"

"Figure this one is one of a number holding a perimeter, right? Roll through here, race to the north, and find the next in line. If we reach the far edge of the airport we turn and burn. Their birds are down, by now they know someone is out there ... fuck it, do it live!"

Aymond looked at Snow, who shrugged before giving a thumbs up. Aymond keyed the radio. "Alright Gonzo, you two assholes are driving the damn thing since you're riding in the back anyways. Dagger-One, you copy?"

Chuck grabbed the mic, "Good copy Dagger-Actual, inbound from the northwest, five mikes."

Trail M-ATV, Coronado, CA

"Simmons, we're going to have to speed it up; use the fucking sidewalks if you have to, but when you get to the Embassy Suites go right instead of straight. That'll point us towards the end of the runway and where Chief is headed."

Simmons focused hard forward, Chuck and Happy pulling the remaining IEDs out of their bags in the backseat and working fast to modify their already modified explosives.

Lead M-ATV, Coronado, CA

The rings of fencing between the road and the airport were destroyed, making the drive onto the airfield much easier than it would have been before. Aymond turned right, looked at the compass and drove due north, straight across the runways, the pedal pinned to the floor. The open expanse of the airfield gave the illusion that they were crawling at a snail's pace towards the other side.

"Chief, go right ... RIGHT RIGHT RIGHT!" Snow yelled, pivoting the turret with the turning truck towards the northwest corner of the airfield. Just past the edge of the runway sat a radar truck. It was facing away from the fire; the IR on the turret worked and Snow could see two men standing beside the back of the truck, facing towards the front of the truck, rifles in their hands.

"They must be watching for anything that gets past the truck."

"Yeah, probably, Chief."

Aymond keyed the radio. "Two tangos, one each side."

"Copy, tangos in sight, straight approach, about a hundred meters and we've got them."

Hammer looked at Gonzo; they gave each other a quick fist bump and braced their M4s on the roof of the cab, waiting for Aymond to stop so they could fire with accuracy. Their bodies pushed against the back of the cab as Aymond stomped on the brakes, the heavy truck shuddering to a stop. Gonzo and Hammer both fired quickly, both men by the truck falling dead.

Gonzo and Hammer leapt out of the back of the M-ATV and ran forward in a combat crouch, their M4s pointed towards the truck. The back of the truck was a box, and on the box a door, much like the radar trucks that both of the Marines were used to seeing used by Coalition forces.

The door opened and a man got out, lighting a cigarette as he stepped off the bumper. The bright light from the interior of the box spilled out into the darkness. Hammer and Gonzo kept approaching, trusting the man's night blindness from the transition from light to dark to give them an edge; they needed him to step forward a little further so they could get the angle and not have a round bounce through the interior of the control box.

The soldier looked down and saw his fallen comrade. He spit out what sounded like an expletive and crouched to check on him. Hammer shot twice, the man's head rupturing across the tarmac from the bullet's impact. They continued towards the truck, Gonzo heading straight for the bright interior of the box, Hammer angling towards the truck's cab.

"Clear."

"Clear."

Aymond smiled. "Copy all clear."

The sharp staccato strikes of metal against the armored cab of the M-ATV caught Snow by surprise, as he'd been watching his buddies take down the truck through the remote turret's viewer; he spun the turret towards the rear, finding muzzle flashes from a truck barreling towards them on the runway.

"Technical approaching fast from the west, Chief."

Aymond keyed his mic. "Move it double time Dagger-One. ETA?"

"On the north, stand by, clearing fence."

Jones fired the M2 in a long burst, slowly rotating the turret, ripping through the mass of Zeds around the truck. "NOW!"

Happy and Chuck opened the rear doors and each threw a soda can at the fence, slamming the doors shut quickly. Simmons, the truck already in reverse, stomped on the gas, the tires chirping against the pavement as the truck launched backwards and across Pacific Highway. The IEDs in the soda cans exploded, blowing the fence backwards, opening a wide gap.

Simmons stomped on the gas again, this time in drive, and drove through the open fence, around the radar truck and towards the other M-ATV, the M2 firing short bursts at the pursuing PLA vehicle. Snow in the other M-ATV was doing the same, more rounds slapping the armor against the outside of both trucks. Snow and Jones turned their turrets outwards and each saw a half-dozen vehicles racing towards them, small arms fire flashing from each of them.

Simmons cranked the wheel. "Turning around, Jones."

Jones spun the turret to match the turning truck, both M-ATVs racing after the radar truck.

Radar Truck, Coronado, CA

Hammer keyed his radio, "Hey Gonzo, how far do you think the beam or whatever will reach?"

Gonzo, still in the truck box and separated from the cab, said, "I have no idea, guy."

"Is it turned on?"

"She just ordered the lobster so she better be."

"No, seriously asshole, what's your status."

"I can't read a fucking thing in here and it looks like the inside of the space shuttle, but I think it's on."

"Dagger ... uh, fuck, Gonzo, Chief."

Aymond drove behind the radar truck, Simmons' M-ATV behind him. "Go Gonzo."

"Chief, how slow can we go?"

Jones keyed the radio. "Not very unless you like eating Chinese food."

Gonzo keyed his radio. "Tell us when we can't keep the lead and we'll take the second position, but if you can keep them off our ass I want to start at a slow-ish speed and see how well this thing works on the roll; we can keep speeding up until we find the limit. Good to go, Chief?"

Aymond looked at Snow, who shrugged and fired off another burst from the M2.

"Sure Gonzo, but make the test snappy."

Hammer turned and followed the planned route back, even though he had a new ride.

Chuck keyed the radio. "When you get to the Coronado Bridge take the middle; at the Welcome Navy Base walkway go right lane, left lane, and watch for the goddamned garden hose."

Both of the trailing M-ATVs gave room to the radar truck, running interference from the chasing force, long bursts of the M2 ripping into the leading elements.

Spent casings from the heavy machine guns rattled off the roof of the truck, ammo links falling to the road.

The radar truck gradually sped up, an invisible hand in front of them slapping the dead to the ground, the truck having to swerve wildly to keep from running over the bodies as they fell.

Hammer keyed the radio. "This isn't working, the Zeds are falling right in our path! We need to form it up and haul ass ... Gonzo, can you get the transmitter down?"

"Working on it!"

Simmons sped up and took the lead position, Aymond falling in line and tight behind the radar truck. They all sped up, Jones sweeping left and right with the M2 as they drove along Harbor Drive.

Hammer: "Chief, are they taking the bait?"

"Snow?"

"Yeah Chief, they're trailing behind us, but we're gaining some distance, about three hundred yards now."

"Hammer, they're following, keep this speed if you can."

"Roger, Chief."

The further they drove from the airport and the destroyed ship, the fewer Zeds they had to drive around. Passing the Hilton, the road was practically clear. Moments later the convoy took the dirt median as they passed under the Coronado Bridge, the convoy taking the right lanes in preparation for the next IED line. Snow watched as the pursuing vehicles raced up both sides of the street. The first vehicles sped past the bridge, as did the second group of vehicles, but the third row of vehicles nearly disappeared in a cloud of dust, the vehicles behind them crashing into the rear of the destroyed vehicles ahead of them. Either unaware or indifferent to their comrades, the remaining four vehicles sped up, trying to gain ground against the convoy. Snow fired controlled bursts, trying to conserve ammo now that the worst of the fight was over, the following vehicles ignoring the machine gun fire.

Simmons approached the pedestrian bridge with the last IEDs, slowing and turning hard left to zig-zag around the barely visible garden hoses across the roadway. The radar truck and the last M-ATV did the same. When they slowed the chasing vehicles grew closer, small arms fire slapping against the armor. They were still spread across both sides of the street, and the IEDs detonated when the first vehicles reached the garden hoses, the concrete pedestrian bridge falling on the other two. Snow watched the dust settle and scanned ahead for more threats, and in the sky for any more helicopters.

"We're all clear, Chief."

Aymond smiled and keyed the radio. "Slow it down, Simmons, we're all clear. Good job Raiders." He thought about the radar truck, concerned that it could have a tracking device, as they'd thought the Jeep might have, *but no one came looking for the patrol boat ... no, not worth the chance.*

"Simmons, tell me about that home improvement store."

CHAPTER 14

SSC, Ennis, TX
March 17, Year 1

Amanda stood on the roof of the armored loader, facing the south, steam rising from her body in the cold air. Hands clutching her M4 rifle, she scanned her surroundings; the original gate for the park was behind her, and her shadow stretched long across the abandoned farmer's fields on the other side of the HESCO barriers. She was done with the first round of barricades and fence repairs. Waxahachie Creek Park, modified to conceal the facility's presence, was never meant to be a part of the facility's use. The designers had seen a different future in the facility's role and the survival of the country. The ability to step out of the underground bunker six months from the start of war to reclaim the abandoned land had changed, since the land had been claimed by the armies of marching dead.

The problem now is we need to begin sectioning off parcels of land, between pasture and plowed. The first few growing seasons will be rough and we'll have to start small; most of the work will have to be completed by hand. My hands alone can't do it. I need people, tens ... no hundreds of people willing to work hard to claim the land for the living once again.

Viewing the expanse of farmland stretching acres and acres from the left to right and nearly as far out as one could see, Amanda thought of the ancients, the first cities. *Walled to protect the people from invaders, surrounded by farmland, near a good water source and home to all who swore allegiance ... we've been thrust backwards in history thousands of years. The failed modern world surrounded by basic humanity attempting to survive ... God help us.*

People were one problem, the other was gear. Amanda knew about agriculture, but she wasn't a farmer, she was the SecAg—the *former* Secretary of Agriculture. As a manager, an executive, she *set* policy. She needed to be more hands on now. First she needed information, she needed equipment that survived the EMP, she needed people, and she needed supplies, seeds, knowledge, and labor.

Seeds. She wasn't sure where she could find seeds; they weren't a part of the stored goods in the facility, but looking at all the farmland she had to assume there was a co-op or a feed store nearby; surely there was. As for knowledge, wisdom of the land, that was most likely gone unless farmers had survived. She needed books, references. Her mind spun with a list of what she would have to learn: weather, planting rotations, planting seasons, planting techniques, harvesting techniques, preservation of crops, long-term storage of crops, repair manuals for old tractors and machinery ... she had to go into town and raid the library and maybe the next town over, and maybe a book store.

For all the technology she had underground, for all the supplies she had, for all the weapons of war at her disposal, Amanda needed the one thing that a prepper couldn't put in their long-term storage and let rest: skills.

Groom Lake, NV

"Bexar is better at this than I am."

"He should be here soon; when he arrives, then he can join you."

"Jake, how are we supposed to set up a range and training facilities when we don't even have the surface buildings cleared yet?"

"That's the problem we have, Jessie. We need people who are trained and able to take care of these sorts of problems on the surface, but in order to have room to train we need to be on the surface. I was hoping you and Sarah could come up with a solution."

"Who do you have that I could trust; someone who already has a clue?"

"On average we have twenty new people arriving every single day. That's nearly a hundred and fifty people a week. Some of those people should be able to help, I'm sure they have the skill."

"No Jake, who do *you* trust?"

Jake looked at Jessie for a moment before responding, the faces in his head flipping past like an old Rolodex, all of them with a dark red line across the photograph because they were dead, before stopping on one.

"Jason. Jason is someone I trust; he fought alongside of me in Cortez. He's someone who can help you."

"Jason, the teenager?"

"Yes him, he's our greeter right now, but we can rotate someone else into that job."

"He was like a leaf, shaking in the wind, and unstable when we arrived."

"Jessie, I promise you he's rock solid. His wife died as we fled Cortez, she 'came back' while on the plane and he watched as one of the PJ's, the Air Force guys, put her down for good. He's just been through a lot, but he did some incredible things under fire while fighting the cult in Cortez."

"He doesn't even look old enough to have been married; besides. we've all been through a lot, guy."

Jake's mind flashed with the image of his wife's face, the glow in his eyes dimming for a moment. "Yes Jessie, yes we have."

Coronado, CA

The PLA radar truck, now stashed in the home improvement store, was a safe enough distance away from the Marines even if it was being tracked. After retrieving the Humvee and getting back to their compound, they quickly hid the trucks and any evidence of where they were located. Just as Aymond suspected, the remaining helicopters, men, and trucks moved rapidly across the area.

Like an angry colony of fire ants after their mound was cut down by a lawn mower, the PLA swarmed, looking for the culprits from the attack and raid during the night. Aymond stood in the dark shadows away from the second-story window, the blinds cracked slightly, binoculars to his face. His gaze was towards the north, where the current operating base of the PLA was.

Fires still burned, but it looked like much of the damage they had caused the previous night was being repaired. He smiled at the thought. *No amount of repairs can reclaim all the damaged material the enemy needs; the ships, access to the harbor, and all the containers of equipment, food and who knows what else. This was a major setback to our enemy.*

The first enemy, the dead, had for a while become their ally. The Zeds overran the PLA's position and, as evident by the bodies being burned, had apparently killed quite the number of men.

All of this was great news, but Aymond knew for all of their success they would have to hunker down and stay invisible for a few days. Any activity might tip their hand, and even though they were ready to evac immediately, the resources left by the SEAL Teams were just too good; he didn't want to give them up. As far as he knew the PLA didn't even know what this building was.

Before rotating into a combat sleep schedule, all the men cleaned their gear and weapons, refilling magazines with fresh ammo and making notes for their known inventory. Although the supply cache was good, it was far from unlimited. *We could do a run to Pendleton for more ... but we would need to pass the PLA position. No, we need to simply eliminate the threat with what we have on hand; we need to be creative. We were creative and it was awesome.*

Exiting the office, Aymond walked along the hall to a window that faced away from the rising sun and out across the ocean, the sky falling into the water's edge far out into the horizon. *I still don't understand why the PLA's naval assets aren't here; it seems ludicrous that they would have a supply convoy with no escort ... unless they are fighting their own war further up the coast or somewhere else. I can't operate in the blind like this; I need information, I—WE need to make contact with other elements. This needs to be a coordinated fight.*

CHAPTER 15

Groom Lake, NV
March 18, Year 1

Jake offered a conference room for the training, but it seemed too enclosed, too much like something a corporation would set up, like someone was going to show a PowerPoint presentation. Instead, they chose the cavernous supply warehouse, which appeared to continue nearly to infinity, a black dot at the end of the rows of supplies and equipment. Shane, one of the earliest arrivals to Groom Lake, worked on the quartermasters' team, trying to not only inventory what was held in storage, but keep track of what each member of their underground community was issued and making sure it was signed for. The computer appeared new, but the all-steel desk he sat at appeared to be from the Eisenhower administration.

Jake made the introductions of the group before continuing. "So these guys are going to need whatever it is we have. Weapons, ammo, military gear ... frankly, I don't even know what all we have here." Turning to Jessie, he said, "For all I know we could have a colony of aliens living out of a flying RV in the back of the warehouse and we wouldn't know it."

No one laughed at the joke; Jake played it off and looked at Shane. "Once they have their own needs met, we'll slowly be adding more people to the project, although I'm not sure how many yet. Do we have everything they'll need, or do we even know yet?"

Shane ignored the computer and flipped through a smudged spiral notebook full of scratched-out writing. "Ammo we have—we have enough to fight off a goddamned invasion—same with M-16s ... whatever else they need, well, when they figure out what it is we'll have to figure out if we have it. We probably do, it seems like we have everything but vehicles."

Jason rocked back and forth on his feet nervously, not sure what to think of his new task or the women he had only recently met.

Sarah spoke up. "We're not soldiers; are there any manuals or books or anything on how to use any of this stuff?"

"Sweetie, we have a whole library on one of the servers, don't you worry your little head about it," Shane said casually.

"Talk like that to my mother again and I will cut off your tiny dick and shove it so far up your ass you'll chew on the tip."

Everyone gaped at Erin, who stood to the side of the desk, casually picking her fingernails with her knife. She stopped and looked at Shane. "And that will only be the beginning ... *sweetie.*"

Jake laughed nervously. "Right, well, I'm sure Shane here will be more than helpful, if not then Jason knows the systems, he'll take care of it."

Jason looked up from his shoes at Jake before taking a nervous glance at Erin. His voice cracking, he said, "You ... you bet, Jake."

Jake looked at the clock on the wall. "Well, I'm needed elsewhere about five minutes ago, so good luck and if any of you need anything, please ask."

The sound of his footsteps on the polished concrete floor seemed to be sucked into silence from the heavy tension in the room. After the door shut behind him, Shane glanced at Erin and turned to Jessie. "What exactly do you need?"

"We're not sure yet, but for now I know we need magazines for our ARs, some better cold-weather gear, lots of ammo, and in a perfect world we would have some plywood, a circular saw, some two foot by two foot wooden posts and some paper targets for when we are able to start up the training."

"The building materials I don't think we have, but I think we might actually have rifle targets ... the clothing is no problem. How many magazines and how much ammo do you want?"

SSC, Ennis, TX

Amanda tried to pull up the overhead imagery of the area, but the computer systems weren't responding and were giving strange errors. Frustrated, she was about to go find Clint when he walked into the command center.

"Hey, what's the deal with the computers? I can't get any of the satellite overhead imagery to pull up."

"That's because those servers aren't stored here."

"So?"

"We can only access systems that are physically located in this facility."

"Since when, and why? What about our chat link with Groom Lake?"

"Hackers. Chinese hackers might be targeting Groom Lake; Cliff is en route to find out. Depending on what he comes up with then we might be able to slowly start putting our systems back on-line."

Amanda sat at the terminal for a moment, anger flashing through her mind before she took a breath and a moment to carefully form her thoughts. "You've known about this and didn't tell me? That's not how this is all supposed to work ... so there might be Chinese hackers still alive, and rather than focusing on surviving their own societal destruction they're trying to penetrate our secure systems? That doesn't make any sense; besides, what about the Koreans?"

"Oh, the Koreans are involved, they're involved fully, but the Chinese have Unit 61398, among others. They're good, they're very good, and they're as good if not better than we are."

"I still don't understand why, though."

Clint sat down, nodding. "Madam President, there are some things that are classified so highly that even the sitting POTUS is kept in the dark. This was one of those things ... but times are changing rapidly, so please keep with me; this is going to cover a lot of ground."

Struggling to keep a neutral expression, anger flooded through Amanda. Clint was her confidant and friend, her lover and helpful guide through these drastic times, and yet he still kept secrets.

"First we have to start with the mindsets and population issues. The North Koreans, they're the labor after arriving. China is orchestrating the invasion ..."

"Wait, invasion?"

Clint held up a hand. "We'll get there, just keep with me for a couple of minutes. Yes, the invasion. Our own imagery showed China completely overrun; North Korea was the anomaly; most everyone vanished. China appeared practically destroyed, and North Korea, well, it appeared practically destroyed to begin with. The intelligence estimates indicated that China was willing to euthanize two-thirds of their population to make the plan work. They needed the reduction in people and they needed the false flag operation. The EMP, the Yama strain and what came next in the collapse of everything and extreme casualty rate, that is what they wanted. Think about what's left in the U.S.: most of the infrastructure remains intact but in need of repair. The electrical grid alone will take teams of people a few years to bring back on-line, but the lines are still run along poles to practically every building and home in the country. Same with phone service, sewer, water ... what wasn't destroyed during the collapse is all sitting here ready to be rebooted all over our country. And China wants to step in and take it all."

"But the dead, the reanimates, how are they going to overcome them?"

"We believed that's what they were still working on when we were attacked, the cure, a kill switch, whatever you want to call it; we thought we had more time, but obviously we didn't. Either they figured it out or are waiting trying to figure it out now."

"Then how did the Chinese and North Koreans survive?"

"Tunnels, facilities like this one, and careful government planning. Think of it as an ark to weather the storm."

"But I still don't get ... why the hackers?"

"They know that facilities like Groom Lake exist. Hell, just about anyone in the Western world knows about Area 51, although they don't really know what is out there. The Denver facility under the airport, well, quite a few knew about that. This facility is one of the newest and most secret. That's one reason why we came here, that's why we haven't broadcast for survivors. I'm trying to keep us hidden. We lost communications due to the Chinese; they either blocked our communications electronically or have physically destroyed those satellites with their own intercepting assets in space. Regardless, once that happened I knew we were in trouble; that's why I sent word to Cliff to check on the unit in Granite Mountain."

"The numbers broadcast, that was how you knew? That was Cliff?"

"Yes. I'm sorry I lied to you about that, but I had to."

Amanda frowned, staring at Clint. "What is Granite Mountain?"

"That's where the Mormons keep all of their genealogy records."

"So what?"

"So we helped them build that facility, along with a small addition in the back that only a few dozen people know exist. That's where our version of the hacker unit is set up; they live and work there. We keep them supplied with pizza, energy drinks, and whatever their vices may be, and together they are the man behind the curtain. Remember Stuxnet?"

"What?"

"Stuxnet, the computer virus?"

"I don't know, maybe, vaguely."

"That was these guys; it got out in the wild, which caused minor problems for people, but the virus destroyed centrifuges at the Natanz plant in Iran, setting their nuclear program back years. Those computer wonks are amazing, really."

"They're still alive?"

"We don't know, that's why I sent Cliff to investigate. They went dark recently and it was either due to their choice, the Chinese, or an accident. Hopefully it was something they did on purpose and they're working behind the scenes."

Amanda shook her head. "You said invasion?"

"Yes, the last intelligence estimate was that the Chinese would wait twelve to twenty-four months before attempting the invasion via the West Coast. That would give the Yama Strain enough time to kill off all but a few of the population, making their invasion basically as easy as walking into a vacant house. Nothing to do but clean the dust off the mantel."

Sitting back into her chair, Amanda quietly thought over what he'd told her.

"The survival of the country isn't enough; the survival of those people who aren't walking corpses isn't enough, but we have to be ready to fend off an invasion too."

"We have time."

"Maybe, maybe not. You all thought you had more time before and now look where we are! Can we get a message to Groom Lake?"

"Not without going back online, and I want to wait to hear from Cliff to do that."

"Then all we can do is keep on doing what we've been doing?"

"For now, the plan is that Groom Lake amasses the civilians while we gather up remaining military personnel from wherever they may be, and get them in position on the Wes Coast by next year."

"How—"

Clint interrupted her. "Amanda, Cliff and I are working on it; this is going to take some time, we'll get it, but first we have to wait."

"Wait? Wait for what?"

"Cliff will check in when he gets to Granite Mountain, depending on what the computer wonks tell him. If by some miracle some remnants of our military fighting force hasn't survived, he ... he may be heading to Wyoming."

"What's in Wyoming, more secret facilities you haven't told me about?"

"No. Minute Men III silos, ICBMs. You might be making a very important Presidential order soon."

Amanda stared at Clint, wondering if anything he told her could be trusted and what he believed her actual role was, regardless of her title.

"What about the farming and other preparations?"

"Complete waste of time. We have a war to fight first, but I figured it wouldn't hurt anything to let you play in the dirt and do your thing for a while."

Amanda paused; she wanted to tell Clint to go fuck himself, but now that she knew he wasn't going to be completely truthful with her, she felt like she needed to treat him with kid gloves, a soft, gentle grip on her situation.

"No, it isn't a complete waste of time and now we have something else I need to accomplish while we wait for your plan to come to fruition. I was trying to find imagery and information about the towns near here. I'm looking for a farmer's co-op, a feed store, anything along those lines. There are many supplies we need. I also need to find a library."

"A library?"

"Yes, I'm the SecAg turned President, but I was never a hands-on farmer. Besides the equipment, seeds, and fertilizer I'll need from the stores, I need information, books, planting schedules, reference materials. For all the technology this damned place has, it doesn't have any good reference material to help someone actually rebuild the country ... and this country was built through the labor of farmers and others like them."

"Fine. Go into the tunnel and get a truck ... get an MRAP, turn it over to make sure it cranks up, make sure the tires aren't flat and such. I'll put together what I can find for maps in the meantime. This evening we'll go over it all and work up a plan for tomorrow.

"That's a start, but what's an 'M-wrap'?"

"I'm sure you really care what the acronym stands for; it's a big armored truck we used in the last Iraq war. You can't miss it. There should be a few of them."

Amanda slung her rifle and walked out of the room, door slamming behind her. Clint watched her leave and checked the clock. He wasn't happy; if the Lazarus project had gone as planned he wouldn't be babysitting someone who didn't understand what she had to, no, *needed* to accomplish. He could have just delivered her to safety and let the interior teams take over. *I don't have time for these stupid games, I shouldn't have been weak and I should have kept my damn dick in my pants; I have a mission to accomplish.*

CHAPTER 16

Groom Lake, NV
March 19, Year 1

From the cold yellow glow of the morning light, new arrivals trickled into the hangar that housed the main entrance to the underground facility. Jason's typical duties of greeter had been handed off to a substitute, another seasoned survivor and resident of Groom Lake. The battered, tired and starved survivors stumbling past looked more like the dead than the living.

The team was gathered in their training area within the hangar. Jason was at the front of the line, and Jessie and Sarah were behind him with about three yards spacing between each of them. They weren't going to be kicking in doors like some SWAT team; they would open a door, bang on it, make some noise and wait for any undead to come to them. It was safer, even if it took slightly more time with each building. But they were only training at the moment. The three of them stood by an imaginary doorframe.

"Great, just like that one more time and I think we'll be ready to go."

Jessie and Sarah decided to start with the easy buildings first, or at least what they guessed to be the easy buildings. The dormitories to the south would be one of the last of the buildings they cleared. The FJ still sat in the hangar where they'd left it. The group drove out the front of the hangar, turning left towards the north and following the wide tarmac the short distance to the first cluster of buildings on the edge of the dry lake bed. They had no idea what was actually in the buildings; neither did Jake or Major Wright.

Keys were a problem, or key cards actually; they brought one that Major Wright's guys had programmed which should work on every door they found, but Jessie had Jason bring a short-barreled shotgun just in case. If the keycard didn't work, the twelve-gauge universal key would.

They left the FJ idling on the road by the first building. Erin opted to stay with the vehicle, and she sat on the roof rack with her M4 and her big rifle, just in case someone came shambling along looking for breakfast. No one knew whether there were any survivors in the buildings, but the general consensus was that there weren't any. With all of the commotion aboveground since the beginning of their stay—the comings and goings of the C-130, the daily arrivals—any survivors would have ventured out at some point. No, if there was anyone left in any of the buildings aboveground they would be dead and reanimated.

Jessie pressed the key card against the black square on the door frame; the small red light turned green and the door clicked. The card went back into her shirt pocket as she backed away from the door. Jason pulled the door open, held it open with his foot and slapped the metal door a few times, calling out to anyone inside the building.

They waited and made more noise, but nothing appeared in the dark hallway. Each of them switched on their headlamps and the powerful lights on their rifles and shotgun before stepping inside.

The night before, while they were kitting up in the warehouse-sized supply room, they'd found night vision gear. As excited as Jason was to play with the top-of-the-line items, the group decided to stick to regular lights. None of them had used or trained with night vision before and it could cause them more problems than they were worth. Jason was disappointed, but he kept a set to play with in his free time.

The trio stepped into the dark hallway, their lights cutting through the darkness, sweeping back and forth as they turned their heads, the metal door shutting behind them. Slowly they walked down the hallway to a row of closed office doors, but as they walked the lights clicked on, activated by motion sensors.

"Well that's helpful," Jessie said to no one in particular.

Jason stopped in the hallway, an office door on his left and his right. "What now?"

Sarah motioned down the hall with her head. "Jessie can watch the hallway, I'll keep an eye on this door, and you knock on your door. Wait for a response then open it. Depending on how big the room is we can either stay out in the hallway or we all can go in together. "

Jason nodded and rapped on the door with his knuckles, his other hand still clutching the pump action of his shotgun. They waited. Jason knocked again and they waited some more. No response came from the room or anywhere else.

"If there was any undead in here do you think they would have set off the motion lights?"

Sarah shrugged. "Probably, Jason, but I wouldn't count on it."

Jason pushed the door open slowly; the small office looked perfectly normal, with a cheap desk in the middle, a computer on the desk, a few photos on the shelves and desk, and a dead plant on top of the filing cabinet.

"It's small; I'll check it quickly and be back out."

Jason stepped into the office, checking behind the door and under the desk, the only places something could be hiding, and found nothing.

"Coming back out," Jason called out before stepping back into the hallway. He thought it was silly, but Jessie was very specific about how she wanted everyone to act and move. Jessie had said that she and Bexar had gone through some training, which was more than Jason had done. His training had been quick, fast, and dirty after the Cult declared war against them in Cortez.

Sarah started the same process Jason had done with the door on her side of the hallway.

Twenty minutes later, the first building was clear. All they found were a couple of empty offices and a workshop that had a fairly good complement of hand tools. None of them were sure what the building was for, but a little workshop might come in handy. Sitting back in the cab of the FJ, the heater on, Jessie labeled the building on the overhead image as "Building 1" and made some notes on a notepad about what they'd found.

Erin drove a few dozen yards forward and parked in an open area between three buildings and a huge satellite dish pointed towards the sky. They climbed out of the FJ and started the process all over again, one building at a time, leaving one person on guard outside.

Two hours later, the group was back in the FJ, snacking on some crackers and drinking the hot chocolate they'd brought with them. Jessie thought about Bexar and how he would probably want to clear the buildings at a faster pace, but she felt comfortable moving slowly and deliberately, trying to minimize their risks the best they could. She absentmindedly rubbed her small baby bump. *Get this crap cleared and set up a range, then I can relax and train others, let them do the hard work, the dangerous work. What a crazy world we live in.*

SSC, Ennis, TX

"These are the best we have on paper, top notch."

Clint set a series of large binders on the table and unfolded a large map of Texas that looked a lot like a regular road atlas. The large map was sectioned into numbered squares. Amanda scanned the map, working to find where they were located in the state, which Clint pointed to without being asked.

"Ennis, Waxahachie, Italy, and Corsicana are the four biggest towns near us, although none of them are all that large. There are more small towns though."

"That's fine, I don't need large towns for a farmer's co-op, I actually need small ones and there's a good chance the co-op wouldn't be in the town but just outside, nearer to the farmland. The towns I need for libraries, hell, maybe even some home improvement or hardware stores so besides just crops I can start a garden. Hands in the dirt farming I don't know very well, but gardening I know. We could have fresh tomatoes."

"Amanda you're going about this all wrong. If you're going to do this then we do it right. You don't have the first clue as to what you need to start up a farm. Books first, gear second, the last step before planting is gathering the actual seeds, fertilizer, etcetera. I'd look at libraries first. We don't even have the right kind of trucks to bring back any sort of large agricultural product. We don't have the tractors or equipment to work a large field; all we have is gear to survive, gear to fight, and gear to start towns back up. Farming was a whole separate group of people, a different compartment to the Lazarus project in a completely different facility."

Amanda glowered at him, but she knew he was right. Agricultural administration, large scale commercial farming management, the business side of things she knew; how to get out there like some homesteader in the 1840s and make a small scale farm happen was something she did not.

Clint smiled. "OK, libraries first. We can mark locations of any of the other things we might need while we're out. Happy?"

"No, but it's a start."

Groom Lake, NV

After clearing each of the buildings, they secured the doors and an orange circle was marked on the door with spray paint. Erin began driving west, where they found buildings scattered to the north, more large satellite dishes, and an endless dry lakebed. The majority of the buildings were to their left, the south, and they were going to save those for later. As slowly as they had been progressing, Jessie knew there was no way that they would finish in a single day. It might take them a week.

Erin turned right and drove past one large metal building before parking in between a group of buildings next to the dry lake bed where the group climbed out. Erin took her chosen perch on the roof of the truck, giving the team a security overwatch, although so far she had only stood on the roof rack, bored, scanning the area with a pair of binoculars.

The same process as with the first buildings was used, and an hour later the cluster of buildings around the FJ's parking spot were cleared, orange circles on each of the doors. Jessie marked the buildings on her map, making notes in her notebook for a report she planned to write later. Perhaps one of the more computer savvy of the survivors could make an interactive map. This time last year she would have used Google and placed markers with descriptions, but even the juggernaut of technology that seemed to have run her world before the attack hadn't survived.

Erin sat behind the steering wheel. "This sucks. I want to just drive around for a bit to get an idea of what that overhead photo really means; I can't tell what half of that shit is except for the buildings." She pointed at a brown smudge of dirt on the map. "What is that, is it dirt, is it something top secret, we have no fucking idea."

Sarah looked at Jessie, who shrugged. Jason sat quietly, looking at Erin, surprisingly happy to have a change of pace from the typical life he led in the facility. Also happy to see another girl about his age, even if she was a few years younger than he.

Jessie rested the map and notebook on the dash. "Let's go exploring; you've got the wheel, you drive us to where you want to go. We have a full tank of gas and another half-tank's worth of fuel in cans on the rack. I would suggest we don't drive further than we're willing to walk home, though. We never know what we'll find or what might happen."

Erin nodded, a faint hint of a smile on her face, the first Sarah had seen from her little girl in a long time. She turned the truck left and traveled south along one of the paved roads, slowly driving while each of them looked out the windows at the aboveground base so secret that everyone knew about it.

"Think we'll find any aliens?"

Everyone glanced at Jason, who hadn't spoken in a long time.

"No really, do you guys think that there might actually be aliens here?"

Sarah and Jessie both shook their heads no.

"Maybe. Who would have thought we would have fucking zombies or there would be this big underground base. At this point I think some aliens would simply fit in to our new reality." Erin glanced over her shoulder at Jason, who smiled bashfully.

SSC, Ennis, TX

The big brown MRAP, or Mine-Resistant Ambush Protected military vehicle, rattled up the ramp and onto the surface. Exiting the park, Clint drove the heavy truck south before turning left to head into Ennis. The map sections had been copied and taped to the dash of the truck for reference. Farming supplies weren't marked on the maps, but libraries were. Most civic buildings were marked, as were military installations; bridges were marked with their load capacity and clearance. The maps were high-detailed and very similar to the invasion maps of the U.S. that the Soviets had created, which Clint doubted Amanda had ever seen. They had all the information a military commander would need to fight his way into or through the country and occupy it.

Highway 34 was basically clear. Clint keeping the heavy truck to forty mph as he drove towards Highway 287. Not that they needed to take that highway, but the last imagery they had showed 287 and the surrounding major highways being completely overrun with a large herd of the undead.

Cars were pushed over the edges of the overpass from 287 to Highway 34 below. Clint turned the wheel a bit to the right and drove up the steep embankment to the highway above them. Scanning the scene outside the vehicle, Amanda and Clint couldn't see any of the undead, just a clear path of destruction where they had come through.

Clint merely grunted and continued driving, crossing the highway, the median, and then driving down the other side's embankment before turning back onto the roadway and towards town. Ignoring the map, where no route was marked, his route having been memorized as he'd been trained to do many years before, Clint took a left turn and rumbled past businesses and homes on either side of the highway. Some cars were still abandoned in the roadway, a sign that the herd of undead hadn't come through this way, but Clint drove on, sweeping the truck left and right, dodging the abandoned cars and trucks. Amanda looked at the side-view mirror on her side and saw a small gaggle of dead turning out from around the homes, trying to follow the truck as it passed.

"Looks like we have some stragglers following us."

"Yeah, they shouldn't be an issue for us right now. We'll have to see how the rest of the town goes."

Competing chain drug stores, a gas station and a grocery store marked each corner of the intersection they needed. Turning right on Ennis Avenue, Clint drove towards the library the next block up. The parking lot in front of the bright red brick building was empty, which Amanda took as a good sign that they might have the interior all to themselves.

Clint drove into the parking lot and came to a stop beside the large glass front arched entryway. Dozens of undead drew near to the truck, all of them shambling slowly towards the sound and movement of the truck; more seemed to stream out from the surrounding streets like water, starting with a trickle growing and into a flood.

Shaking his head, Clint put the truck in reverse and slowly reversed in the tight parking lot.

"You're not going to leave now, after we drove over here?"

Clint grunted, put the truck in drive and turned the wheels to the left. The front of the truck bounced over the curb at the end of the parking spots, putting the front wheels on the sidewalk. He turned the wheel again and put the truck in reverse before backing towards the glass entryway. The rear of the armored truck pushed through the thin metal framing of the doors and windows, glass fragments showering down around the truck as it stopped. At over eight feet wide, the truck took nearly the full width of the entryway, blocking anything from coming through unless it crawled over or under the truck. So far they hadn't seen any of the reanimates crawl or climb, so Clint felt reasonably safe with this solution.

"We have arrived, Madam President, although I think the local marching band may not have arrived in time to play Hail to the Chief."

Clint left the truck running, the parking brake set, and opened the troop hatch at the rear of the truck. He climbed down first, M4 in his hands, and quickly scanned the area. Amanda followed, her rifle sweeping the aisles as they passed, quickly clearing the interior of the library. Satisfied that they were most likely alone inside the building, Clint turned towards the idling rig and looked under the truck at all the legs of the dead; they were bouncing off each other and the front of the truck. He looked back at the heavy tables in the middle of the room before dragging one and then another to the back of the MRAP. Each of the tables was pushed onto their sides against the back bumper, blocking the gap between the bottom of the armored truck and the ground. He knew it wouldn't hold if really tested, but it still made him feel slightly better about their situation.

"Amanda, ten minutes tops. Get what you need and we need to pop smoke. The longer we sit, the more dead will arrive. I don't want to lose a tire or have the truck go down and be trapped with all of those damn things in town coming to visit!"

"OK!" Amanda shook her head. Obviously the computers were dead and the library had transitioned away from a card catalogue years ago. *Maybe decades ago?* Amanda wasn't sure; she couldn't remember when everything went digital, but it seemed like it had snuck up on her. Without a reference, she took a librarian's cart and walked the non-fiction aisles, back and forth, one by one, scanning for books that they needed or that might be useful. Books she hadn't thought to look for caught her eye and made it onto the cart, books about medical care, first aid, weather forecasting. She quickly realized that she would eventually need reference material on many subjects if the people who were experts in those fields didn't survive. Even if they did survive they still would use reference materials. A small town library wasn't really suited for what she wanted; it was great if you wanted to borrow novels or movies, or even audio books, but not so great for hard-core research. She needed a university's library. Regardless, this was where she was now and she had to get all she could; they could worry about the rest later.

Quickly Amanda transferred the cart of books into the back of the truck, just tossing them inside, moving quickly to fill the cart again. She couldn't see the dead, but the truck rocked from being pushed by the bodies.

Clint stood on the rear steps and looked through the truck and out the windshield. "Amanda, that's it, no more time, no more books, we have to roll. Things are getting ugly!"

Amanda didn't argue; even though she now mistrusted Clint, they had been through a lot together since that day in December, and she did still trust him when it came to tactics and security. She left the cart, grabbed the small handful of books off the top, and ran to the truck, tossing the books onto the pile in the interior as she shut and latched the door behind her. Climbing into the passenger seat, she was shocked to see the number of dead.

"Do you see the hatch in the roof behind you? Push the big button, then open the hatch."

"You want me to go outside?"

"Yes, well, sort of. The turret has an M2; it's a big 50-caliber machine gun. Open the hatch, stand on the platform, pull the charging handle on the right side of the weapon, grab the handles and push the trigger in the back. Only fire four- or five-second-long bursts, sweeping side to side. Best way to do it is grab the two handles, push the trigger button and say 'kill a family of eight' while sweeping left, let off when you finish saying it, take a deep breath and repeat the process to the right. You're not going to get all of them, but you'll help knock down the mob some so we can get rolling."

Amanda opened the hatch and found the charging handle; pulling hard she moved it to the rear and released it, putting the 50-caliber machine gun into service. The phrase was horrible, but it gave her something to focus on as she worked the heavy weapon, her ears ringing from the bursts.

Sweep to the right, *kill a family of eight*, sweep to the left, *kill a family of eight*. Repeating the processes and phrase again and again, the dead tore apart ahead of her, the large rounds ripping limbs from flesh, bodies seemingly disintegrating before her eyes. Like a giant saw blade had swung through and chopped down the masses. Slowly Clint drove forward, straight across the bodies, across the small parking lot, the sidewalk and grass and onto the street, turning left to head back towards the facility. Amanda rotated the turret, laying waste to the reanimates behind them as they drove off, and sweeping back and forth—*kill a family of eight*—with each pass. Eventually the heavy machine gun fell silent; the barrel glowed red and smoke rose in the cold air, the belt-fed ammo empty, brass casings falling off the roof as they drove.

Amanda's ears rang and she could barely hear from all the machine gun fire, but she felt a strange satisfaction in ripping apart the undead with such a powerful weapon. Standing high in an armored vehicle, with an armored turret enclosing her helped her confidence in being outside the truck, but she stood in defiance above the dead, cold air whistling past her as Clint drove back towards the facility. She had a front row seat to see what was left of little Ennis, Texas, feeling almost disconnected, like she was floating above it all as the truck rumbled beneath her feet.

I'm going to make this work, Chinese be damned, North Koreans be damned, the invasion ... Clint ... damn it all, I will make this work.

Groom Lake, NV

The FJ rolled slowly past the rows of twin blocked dormitories; they knew the number of rooms by looking at the overhead, but looking at them from the ground, windows gave view into how many rooms they would have to clear. It would take the four of them weeks to clear all of them and make sure that the dorms were safe for people to move into. Jessie strained to see inside the dark windows, seeing hints of movement in the shadows, but she couldn't be certain that it wasn't just her eyes playing tricks. She looked out across the desert mountains, the sun already high overhead, reaching midday, and smiled. She was happier outside than trapped far below ground.

They passed more buildings, more hangars, and large aboveground tanks that were fenced off from the rest of the facility. That struck Erin as odd; already they were in a top secret fenced-off facility that had supposedly been heavily guarded before the attack, and yet they felt the need to fence off the giant fuel tanks? It all seemed silly to her.

The road ended at what appeared to be a quarry operation; mounds of sand, dirt, and rocks were piled high, ready for construction. Erin turned the FJ around and drove back north. She could have followed the roads east and out towards the runways, but she decided to go left and travel a dirt road to the west. More fenced-off sections ...

"Stop the truck!"

Erin stopped, surprised at Jessie's outburst. The last half-hour of driving had been dead silent as each of them watched the abandoned aboveground facility go past, each wondering how many dead were left that they had to kill.

Jessie climbed out of the truck and walked to the fenceline on the right, opened a gate and walked past the chain-link fence. Sarah joined her, Jason staying with Erin, who sat in the idling FJ. A few minutes later Sarah and Jessie came back out of the fenced area smiling before walking a few hundred feet further west to another odd-shaped low structure. After a few more minutes they walked back to the FJ, still smiling.

"We're done for the day. Head back to the hangar."

"Why, Mom?"

"You saw those dorms, right? All the buildings. Do you think the four of us can handle all of that?"

"Yeah, it would just suck and take forever."

"Well, we won't have to. Over there is a rifle range, and that is a pistol range. We have a place to train. Jessie and I think that we could hold training out here and just have a couple of spotters for any approaching undead. We've been out all morning and not a one has been seen, so maybe we won't even need that."

"So what now, get a bunch of people together and train them? What are you going to do?"

Jessie turned in her seat. "Jason, we start with pistol skills, basic safety handling, then we teach how to shoot from cover and concealment, then we teach movement and then we do the same again with rifles. You've seen what we have in storage; we have enough of everything to outfit everyone living underground. Once we get enough people trained, then clearing the top side and using it for housing will be a snap! First we need to get back and talk to Jake, then we have to get volunteers, figure out transportation to the ranges from the hangar ... we have a lot to do before we can even fire the first round."

Coronado, CA

On the mainland, the remaining helicopters continued to circle and move from spot to spot. From what the observation post had been able to track, it appeared that a systematic search was underway, most likely looking for them and the stolen Zed-killing radar truck. Since the raid, Aymond had kept his team on lockdown. As Recon Marines, they continued doing what they did best, staying completely hidden and taking detailed notes of enemy movement, strength, abilities, vehicles, and material. The previous raids had been risky, ballsy, and run really loose. Now that they'd kicked the hornet's nest, Aymond wasn't ready to run any more raids like that. He wanted detailed planning; the stakes had been risen and it would be days before they were ready to strike again. One for gathering as much intelligence on their enemy as they could, but two for the enemy forces to become lulled into routine and boredom. Once enough time passed without an attack, they would become lax, and Aymond was counting on it. In the meantime, Aymond tasked Jones and Simmons to go over the M-ATVs. They didn't have all the tools they needed, they didn't even have any parts, but he was confident in those two to improvise as needed to keep their only two remaining armored vehicles reliable.

Aymond stood in what had become his office, staring at the low detail map of the U.S. on the wall. *There has to be more of us out there, there must be more Marines, soldiers ... we just need to find them, make contact with them. SATCOMs are down, we can't reach anything on any of the other freqs ... we need to disable the PLA's ability to use this area, destroy as much as we can, and evade and fade into the middle of CONUS. We can move from base to base, facility to facility if we have to.* Aymond looked at the calendar, counting off weeks and thinking about the last count of MREs they'd conducted. Already on reduced rations, they weren't going to make Coronado their home for much longer.

What good is all of the intelligence gathering without anyone to give it to? Roger's Rangers, bump and run; follow Major Robert Rogers to fight our way back into Indian Territory.

Aymond circled a date on the calendar that would be Move-Out Day. His mind was made and the plan would have to be set. Two plans. First, to leave the PLA devastated in their wake, and second, to have a concise plan to move on to bases in the interior, with a secondary plan and tertiary plan of movement. A discussion would have to be had with the men to choose a direction; north, up the coast, due east, or somewhere in between.

CHAPER 17

Bexar's first thought was that he could hear water running, water from a sink. It seemed strange but he couldn't think why; his head swam with confusion. Blinking his eyes open, he noticed they felt crusty, like he had a bad cold or an eye infection. Bringing his left hand to his face to wipe his eyes, Bexar hit himself in the face with something hard. Slowly his eyes came into focus, and instead of the back of his hand he was looking at a bright blue cast. Turning his head slowly, he looked at the room he was in. The curtains were open and sunlight streamed in, but the rest of the room was dark. A ceiling fan turned slowly on the ceiling above him, but the air felt dry and warm.

Still unsure of where he was and why, Bexar looked out the window. The room he was in appeared to be perched on a high hillside; on the edge of the drop-off were three gallows, two with empty nooses that swung lazily in the wind, the other with a man swinging by his neck, black bag over his head, hands and feet bound. A buzzard sat on the body's shoulder, picking meat from its neck as it swayed gently.

Panic flooded his body, his mind racing to the church in Cortez full of bodies hung from the ceiling, a human sacrifice on the alter. Bexar's right hand reached for his pistol; he didn't have it, and he was wearing a hospital gown. On a dresser at the foot of the bed were his clothes, neatly folded, his rifle propped against the edge and his pistol lying next to his clothes, magazines for each stacked neatly on the dresser. Bexar ripped the blanket back from his body, sat up and felt light-headed. He ignored it and stood for a moment before falling with a crash against the nightstand.

He looked at his legs; his right foot and ankle were also in a blue cast. Then he heard voices in the hallway.

A man's voice, no, two men ... one is approaching the room!

Bexar pulled himself across the tile floor, pushing with his good leg and pulling with his right arm, clawing his way to the dresser. Reaching up, he felt about with his right hand until he found his pistol.

The door opened and a man he had never seen before walked through, dressed in hiking pants and shirt, a pistol on his hip. Bexar pointed the pistol at his captor. "Stop and show me your hands!"

"That won't work, you'll have to also reach the dresser for a magazine for your pistol. I'll be happy to give it to you, but I do ask that you wait for me to introduce myself before you try shooting me."

His calm voice caught Bexar by surprise; the man smiled gently. Bexar relied on his instincts, his gut feeling, and set his pistol on the floor.

"No, I'm sorry, but who are you and where the fuck am I?"

"My name is Guillermo and you're in my home. Can I help you up? Maybe you would like to sit in the reading chair, or you can sit on the floor, it's your choice," Guillermo said, pointing to a comfortable-looking chair by the window.

Bexar looked at the chair. "The chair would be great, thank you."

Guillermo helped Bexar off the floor, squatting down and helping lift him from under his arms before shouldering his right arm to give support to the casted foot and leg. Although he was only about five foot five, he lifted Bexar easily.

"You've done that before."

"I'm a registered nurse ... *was* a registered nurse."

Guillermo picked up Bexar's pistol and set it on the dresser with his clothes. "Would you like this back or are you OK now?"

Bexar didn't answer, just looked at the man in puzzlement. As a beat cop working patrol, Bexar had stared down armed men before, men who he'd stopped in the act of a stabbing. Everyone teaches rookie cops to watch the hands—the hands are what will kill you—but Bexar would look at their eyes. The eyes tell you the person's intent. Guillermo's eyes looked kind, caring, and without malice.

"I'm OK now."

"Great. I'm sure you have a lot of questions. Let me start with what I know and we can take it from there. Both of the trucks were destroyed; your truck, well, that was a very bad wreck. I'm surprised you lived through that."

Bexar couldn't remember anything about a wreck and didn't know what Guillermo meant by both trucks.

"We saw the black smoke and saw the herd shift towards it and figured the worst. The gunfire afterwards was what surprised us; then we saw the second truck racing towards it. That was one hell of a gun fight, but there was no way out of it. We think that herd is in the thousands. If Angel hadn't got there when he did you would have been eaten. It migrated here last month and we've been trying to help it move on since then."

Guillermo walked to the window and looked out, pointing. "Your truck is that way, but you won't really be able to see it from here without binoculars. If you can see the overpass then the truck is just under it; you drove off the edge of the bridge. The other truck you can't see from this room, but it is equally destroyed, both of them burned completely to the ground. I'm sorry about your friend."

Chivo. Bexar's heart sank to think that his friend was dead. Putting his head in his hand, the one without a cast, Bexar took a deep breath. *I don't know if I can do this anymore; there's just too much ... too damn much for one man's burden.*

"Let me help you get dressed; I have some crutches for you and then you can check in on your other friend."

"My ... other friend?"

"Yeah, the guy that was dragging you, the one from the first truck ... you probably don't remember any of it, you didn't look like you were conscious."

"Short Mexican guy, really fit?"

"Yeah, well, a little taller than me, but that's him."

Bexar breathed a sigh of relief. "Yes, I would like some help, and I want to see my friend."

Guillermo helped Bexar out of the hospital gown, working to carefully thread the large cast on his right leg through his underwear, which had been washed. It had been some time since Bexar had put on a clean pair of underwear, and he smiled to himself as he reflected that sometimes the little things in life are the best. The right pants leg on the ACUs that Bexar had been wearing were cut, but with snaps added to fit and close around the cast. Obviously the right boot wouldn't fit, but the left sock and boot went on his left foot, and then he pulled on his ACU shirt. Guillermo loaded Bexar's pistol and handed it to him to holster; the heavy CM Forge knife he slid into the Kydex sheath on his belt. Guillermo left and reappeared with a pair of crutches, helping to adjust them before asking Bexar to follow him.

The home was nice, something that obviously cost a lot of money and was appointed well. It took a moment for Bexar to realize that the lights were on in the hallway.

"The lights ... how do you have electricity, how do your lights still work?"

"It's something we were prepared for. Your friend is in here."

Guillermo opened another bedroom door and in the room was Chivo, who still had an IV in his arm and was sound asleep. He too had a cast on his hand; his ribs were wrapped and it looked like he had a hard plastic brace on his back which wrapped around his chest. There were scars and old, stitched-up cuts on his face and arms. Bexar looked at the mirror on the wall and saw himself for the first time, realizing that his head was shaved and he had a number of stitches on his head and face as well.

"Frankly, it is amazing that he was still conscious and functioning, much less fighting and dragging you behind him after that wreck. I didn't see it all; you'll have to ask my husband to tell the story. It's intense."

"He's former Special Forces, everything he does is intense. His name is Chivo."

"Chivo, as in goat? Well that makes sense. I've treated those guys before; they're a different breed. Anyway, he's sedated for now. He regained consciousness a few days ago and simply could not function at all, wasn't coherent at all. The pain must be excruciating. Doc and I decided it best to help him sleep it off, if you will."

"Doc is your husband?"

Guillermo laughed. "Lord no, she is not. My husband is Angel, he was an architect," he said while waving his hand across the room, indicating that Angel had designed this house. "He is one of the ones who saved you. And your goat friend."

"Your group, how many of you are there?"

"There are just over a dozen of us in the compound."

"What is the compound?"

"That's just what we call it. It's a fenced-off and prepared site on our property. We have the high ground, we are protected, and we were prepared for this to happen."

"You were prepared for zombies?"

Laughing, Guillermo shook his head. "No, not zombies per se, but societal collapse. Angel always thought it would be an attack, an EMP, but I always thought it would be financial collapse, rapid inflation, etcetera."

"So you and Angel formed a prepper group?"

"You could say that. More accurately I would say that we had a group of friends with likeminded interests and the group chose our house and property because it was the best suited to fight off marauders, rioters, or other attacks. We never really thought it would be to fight off the living dead. Come with me; let us leave Chivo to sleep in peace."

Guillermo led Bexar down the hallway and into the spacious living room. The furniture was nice, all of it; the house, the furniture, it was worth more than Bexar and Jessie could ever afford. Guillermo gestured to an overstuffed chair and Bexar sat down, his new friend helping to raise his casted leg onto an ottoman.

Another Hispanic man walked into the room also wearing a pistol; he gave Guillermo a kiss before they sat down on the couch together.

"I'm guessing you're Angel."

"That would be correct, but we still don't know your name."

"Bexar, Bexar Reed."

"His friend's name is Chivo."

"As in goat? Huh. We have a bear and a goat, what else will the world bring us?"

"No, Bexar, with an X. B-E-X-A-R. It has to do with Texas history. As for Chivo, I have no idea what his real name is, I've only known him as Chivo since we met."

Guillermo stood. "I'm going to get us something to drink; what beer do you prefer, Bexar?"

"I'm partial to cold but will also take free."

With a chuckle, Guillermo walked out of the room.

"So Bexar, you've met us, you have an idea of who and what we are. What about you?"

"I am, was, a cop in Texas ..." Bexar didn't know why, but he felt relaxed and comfortable talking to Angel and proceeded to tell his story, beginning with his own prepper group with Malachi and Jack, to Cliff, Groom Lake, and now trying to get to his pregnant wife. A couple of minutes into the story Guillermo returned with cold beer in pint glasses; an insulated growler was placed on the coffee table and the story continued.

"So you have no idea who the man in the second truck was?"

"No idea."

A woman, in her thirties and fit, walked into the room. Both Guillermo and Angel greeted her as "Doc." She smiled and headed to Bexar.

"So you're awake? How do you feel?"

"I don't know yet."

"Well don't drink too much of John's homebrew, that will knock you on your ass."

"You treated my injuries?"

"Yeah, and your friend's."

"You're a doctor?"

"A veterinarian."

Bexar shrugged; he really didn't care. "What's my list, what's broken?"

"We're not really sure, we don't exactly have the ability to take x-rays anymore, but we're pretty confident that you fractured your radius in the wreck, as well as maybe a tib/fib. The cast is precautionary. As for your friend, the ulna, some fractured ribs, and I'm really concerned about possible fractures to two of his vertebra from the bruising he has. Both of you had serious concussions, abrasions ... thank God nothing became infected; the antibiotics probably helped."

"If you're not sure we fractured these bones, why the casts?"

"The bruising for one, but we gave you both detailed evaluations. Did you try to stand on your leg when you got up?"

"Yes."

"Did it work?"

"No, I fell over."

"That's what we call a clue, Dr. Watson. I'd leave the cast on your foot for at least four more weeks, and then we can cut it off."

"I can't wait four weeks; I'm trying to get to my wife, my pregnant wife."

Angel stood and walked to the window. "Have you looked outside yet? With this many zombies in the area there's no way you're going to be able to hobble your way out of here yet. We've found that these migrating herds of dead eventually move on after a while. This is the third herd we've seen come through in the last six weeks, each one larger than the first."

Doc nodded. "Besides, I'm not sure when your friend will be ready to be moved, much less walk out of here."

Cutting to the chase, Bexar asked what had been troubling him since he first woke. "What about the gallows, the man that's hung?"

After sharing a glance with Doc and Guillermo, Angel answered. "Our group is very simple; we welcome any who need help and are bringing a skill to the group. Leeches, people who want to use us as their own prepper supply house, are not welcome." Angel raised his hand, noticing the expression on Bexar's face. "No, that man was part of another group in the area, raiders really. They have tried twice, unsuccessfully, obviously, to take our compound by force. After your experience with the motorcycle gang, I assume you can understand."

Bexar nodded slowly. "Yes, yes I can."

"We know you don't intend to stay, but like my husband said, we welcome those who need help, so you and Chivo are welcome as long as you need. As you heal we will start assigning some of the daily tasks to both of you to earn your keep."

"That's fair, thank you. Thank you for everything."

Groom Lake, NV

"THREAT!"

Jessie watched as seven people standing on the firing line drew their pistols and fired twice into the paper target in response to her command. The pistol fire echoed softly off the mountains. She had trained with Bexar, been to the same classes, except for the police-specific training days, but Jessie still felt a bit like a fraud teaching a firearms class. She didn't feel all that qualified, but Sarah, who was walking down the line of students, watching to make sure that they all scanned a full three-sixty for any more threats before holstering, had encouraged her. She didn't have to be the best, she didn't have to be some sort of tactical ninja, she just had to help others who hadn't been exposed to good training. That boosted her confidence. It was one thing to feel confident in her own skill and use it well, but it was another thing entirely to try to teach it. Like Sarah told her, she was a teacher before the attack, so she could be a teacher now, although tactical firearms weren't typically taught in the public school curriculum.

While the class selection was underway, Jessie had spent many late nights with Sarah and Erin designing the class structure and lesson plans, and determining how much ammo and how many targets they would need. They also discussed basic logistical issues they might encounter for the pistol course and then the rifle course. The dorms still weren't cleared yet; after speaking with Jake, they'd decided to hold off until the pistol course was completed. They could use one of the already cleared buildings on the north end to practice room clearing and then set the newly trained teams out to clear the rest while the next class started.

Binoculars in her hand, Erin stood on the roof of the rifle range, her big rifle lying at the ready, bipod extended, and her short M4 at her feet. Turning slowly, she watched for any reanimates approaching. So far, since the class had started, the noise had brought two towards the range. She'd put them down before they became a threat. One of the survivors had arrived in a large fifteen-passenger van, which now sat pointed back down the mountain towards the hangar and facility. A handful of dead showing up was nothing to get excited about, but if a large number crested the mountain, they were ready to flee back to the safety of the underground facility.

Sarah was still trying to convince Erin to help teach the rifle class; she was just too good with one not to help, but Erin really didn't like the idea. She didn't like people anymore and would rather stand alone and be ready to fight. Jason had been talking to her more, and she didn't mind him so much, but everyone else really annoyed her.

The low pops of pistol fire sounded in a random cadence, all at similar times, but at different rates. Erin set her binoculars down and sprawled out on the cold metal roof, lying prone next to her big rifle. Another volley of pistol fire echoed in muffled pops just as the air was ripped apart with a hard boom. Erin fired her rifle, the sharp crack of the big 50-caliber round passing over the pistol shooters' heads, causing some of them to duck. Almost six hundred yards down the dirt road, a reanimate's skull vaporized into a red and black mist, the body collapsing to the ground.

Some of the members of the class clapped, some of them looked shocked, and two of them looked annoyed and were already facing the targets again, ready to train. Jessie watched the class reactions carefully.

Those two, those two want to be here, they want to bring the fight to the dead. These other five, they're here because it's something different, but they'll be content to live out their days cowering underground. There will have to be a test to be accepted into the rifle class for now, there are just too many people to train to be bothered with window shoppers. Jessie took a few notes down in a small Field Notes notebook and put it back in her pants pocket. She would have to organize a social for the class; that's how she'd get her read of them, that's what Bexar would do. *No, Bexar would pass out beer, pour drinks, and light a campfire. He believes you learn more about a person after a few drinks around a fire than any other way.* Jessie looked around and saw nothing in the way of trees, firewood, or liquor stores. She would have to make do her own way.

Coronado, CA

Hammer and Snow were yelling at each other; it wasn't really yelling but what the gunny in Aymond's first Force Recon platoon would call "recon yelling," which was more like an angry whisper. They deeply believed each of them was right, but they weren't willing to compromise OPSEC and give away their position by being loud. Although it was sort of humorous to watch, Aymond finally had had enough.

"Gentlemen, really it doesn't fucking matter because we don't actually have that boat anymore. The Zodiac is tied up across the bay. If, and that's a big if, the PLA haven't found it. I've written it off as a combat loss, so move on."

Both of the men immediately stopped their argument, each involving a better use for the Zodiac than the other. The Chinese patrols had slowed down the day before yesterday; now the Marines had observed the PLA settling into what appeared to be a routine. They were ready for another operation. The question was this: Would it be the last operation or could they come back to their makeshift FOB and do another. Aymond thought this to be the last and they would have to relocate; Kirk and Davis thought they could roll the dice again, and the rest really didn't care as long as they got to "blow some more shit up."

"We've crippled their ability to offload containers, we've disabled the runways at Halsey, and we've blocked major access to the harbor. That leaves one airfield available that we know they're using. We've seen that they have heavy lift operations. Do we try to disable the runway or just create havoc and strife before moving on?"

The team sat silent after Aymond's question.

"Wow, great help, guys. OK, first, what would it take to assault the air field and destroy the runway?"

"A battalion and an airstrike."

Aymond looked at Gonzo and was about to respond to his smart-ass remark, but Gonzo cut him off.

"Seriously Chief, think about it. We got lucky and pulled off one crazy operation, but we had a huge distraction to help. We don't have that anymore. We do this the old-fashioned way. First let's agree that our time at our brother SEALs' facility is over. We gather what we can for gear and we load to move out when we're done. Second, we cache our rides and set up for some old school psychological operations. Start snatching people out of their Jeeps while on patrol. Take their uniforms, and then do it again. Kill them, let them turn, and send them back as a Zed surprise. Maybe put down some leadership in the spirit of Carlos Hathcock: sneak in, get close, kill the general, and turn into a ghost."

"Anyone else?"

Simmons spoke up. "I like it, but do we even know where the leadership is? Where is their command post?"

Aymond agreed. "The corporal has a point."

"We scout it out, Chief, send out two scout/sniper pairs. The rest work the PSYOPS, body snatching and the like. Have a rendezvous time and date; if you're still alive you show up, if not you don't."

"That's great, Hammer, but I'm not really keen on losing any more of you."

"Well, I'm not really keen on becoming a fucking Zed either, Chief."

Aymond looked at his watch. The sun was setting; it was already too late in the day to launch any real night operations. "How far of a swim would it be from the closest end of Halsey to Shelter Island?"

"Couldn't be more than about a half-mile, Chief."

Aymond nodded, trusting Chuck to know; he was their best diver.

"How long to move in concealment from Shelter Island to the Recruit Depot, Chuck?"

"Moving only at night, including the swim, probably two days to get all the way around undetected."

"OK, this is our last operation. We pack to leave and we're heading east when we go. We saw San Diego. The PLA ended up here. I think they've screwed up, if not and they've established a strong beachhead at one of the other big ports, it's going to take more than just us to assault those positions. If the big ports are already claimed by the PLA, destroying one lone airfield where we've already shut down the bay won't matter. The operation launches in twenty-four hours. Take note, gentlemen, these are the assignments ..."

St. George, Utah

Bexar wasn't feeling much pain; perhaps Doc was right about the homebrew. They sat outside in the cold, crisp air, high on the hilltop; the beer tasted good and the fire felt great. If not for the moans of the dead in the distance and the cast on his arm and leg, this could have been a typical camping night before the fall of man.

Most of the rest of the prepper group was around, except for the two that were holding listening posts to sound the alarm if any of the dead or the other unfriendly locals came up to the compound. This group of preppers was all over the map. Guillermo and Angel made sense in that they were a family and this was their home, but how they'd all met and banded together was quite unlikely. From the stories it sounded like it had been a combination of groups overlapping between people, and more than a few nights around this fire pit with beers in hand. The original plan had been implemented after the group sent out the bugout signal to get to the compound.

The setup impressed the hell out of Bexar. Angel, concerned about an EMP much as Malachi had been, had designed his home with that in mind. Bexar couldn't imagine how much it cost to do all of that prep work during construction, but really, compared to the rest of the compound, it was probably the lowest cost item of the bunch. They had massive underground tanks of water and treated fuel for the backup generators; the water was fed by a well, which was an illegal well when it was dug, like that mattered now. The eight-foot-tall wrought-iron fence running the property line wasn't cheap fencing to look good, it was solid and ringed by steel pillions concreted into the ground, each camouflaged as large planters, with native plants growing in them. The wrought-iron fence was ringed with razor wire. The pillion planters would stop a vehicle, and the fence would stop the dead, even though they hadn't planned on the dead. The whole thing looked like a hardened Columbian drug lord's compound straight out of a movie.

Solar power panels and wind power kept the battery banks charged, and backup systems were in place for repair and eventual failures. The food, supply, ammo, and gear storage was staggering, and they also had large lockers stocked with personal gear and food. John told Bexar that the most perishable goods were going first—hence the homebrewed beer—but they were set for being there nearly indefinitely. Stocked with medical supplies and extremely stable food stores like wheat berries, these guys made Bexar feel like a complete amateur when it came to his group's prepping.

To be fair, the combined income of my group doesn't even come close to touching the single household income of Guillermo and Angel. We did the best we could ... which wasn't fucking enough.

Bexar let out a heavy sigh as he listened to the wood crackle and watched the fire dance. John took the opportunity to refill the nice stainless insulated pint glass in Bexar's hand.

"Bexar, I can't imagine being out on the road like that. How did you drive all the way across Texas, all the way to Colorado and now to here? We've been here since Day one. We have everything we need and have no intention of leaving."

Bexar looked at his pint of dark beer. *I'm not drunk enough for this bullshit; if he wants to know what it's like then he should take a trip, see the country, and fight some goddamned bikers or a cult ...*

"John, thank you for the beer, it's excellent, but I'm already bushed and should probably lie down ... with the crutches and all, I can't really carry the cup with me."

"Don't worry about it, we're just happy you're on the mend; do you want any help getting back in the house?"

"No, thank you, I think I'll manage."

John poured Bexar's beer into his empty cup and sat down to watch the fire, wondering how their two guests could have lived through so much. He didn't understand that by living, they'd died a little every day.

Groom Lake, NV

"Major, I'm trying, but a lot of the bands that would be the easiest for people to make contact with, things like CB and FRS, those little walkie talkies you buy at sporting goods stores to take hunting, they just don't fall into the right frequency to work over the horizon. Hell, they're not even good for more than a couple of miles."

"Bill, that's if you follow the rules. The rules are over, they may not be able to talk back, but could you broadcast on the CB frequencies at a high enough power to reach fifty miles? How about a hundred, or across the state?"

"Power, yes, but that's not how it all works; those frequency ranges physically don't work well over long distances. Blame God, blame Marconi, hell, blame Al Gore, but it doesn't work."

"What does work that we're not doing? What could be possible that we're missing? Have you talked with the survivors trickling in every day? Each of them says that every extra day spent out there with the dead is another day they would probably die. Hell, instead of cases of MREs they should have stored cases of Xanax; all of them are strung out from the intensity of this new life. So if there's some other way to reach survivors, some way we can help them get here, we need to do it."

"I don't know, Major, maybe a comprehensive advertising campaign, billboards, magazine ads and such?"

Wright glared at Bill.

"You're right, I'm sorry, Major, it's just that I'm running out of ideas too. If telegraph still existed then it would be simple to just tap out messages, dots and dashes ... CW across the airwaves ... that could work."

"See-W telegraph?"

"No, C-W, continuous wave. If we have any survivors with any sort of skill or knowledge they might make a spark gap radio!"

Wright still glared at Bill; he knew satellites, high-end technological communications methods, but radio history and design was one subject he'd slept through happily.

"Spark gap, it's old school, like original old school radio communications from the nineteenth century, but depending on how someone built their rig it could be transmitting in the medium frequency range, Top Band ... even as low as AM broadcast radio. It's hard to propagate over long distances, especially in the summer, but if I had nothing this might be something I would do. You could build it with goddamned car parts!"

Bill turned away from Wright and called over two of the airmen to help as Bill began to draw what he needed to build it. Just as well, the more they fought to get survivors safely inside their doors, the more problems they were having keeping the doors open and working. Jake told him he was working on a topside solution, Wright made a mental note to check in with *The Mayor* and see what that solution was and how it was going. He walked over to a small group of airmen he had working on their own communications problem.

"Well gentlemen, any luck tracking our birds?"

"Major, the ephemerides from the calculated projections we've been able to work out seem to be correct. We have tracking, the satellites seem to exist, but take the GPS constellation for example: they all exist, they all appear to be there, but the signal isn't reaching the ground, at least it isn't reaching us. Something is broadcasting on the L1 and L2 frequencies. We don't have the equipment here to work this out correctly, but we think the signal is being jammed."

"The Chinese?"

"I guess, but Major, we have no way to tell. If we were back at The Springs and all our gear was operational, we could, but we're really limited with what we've got here."

"What about SATCOM?"

"They seem to exist as well, so does MILSTAR and AEHF, but we're just not getting anything on those frequencies. We're not sure if the downlinks are being blocked, the uplinks are being jammed or what; none of the diagnostics we can do here are working. We can't even get a radio unit to lock onto signal, which makes me think that the downlink is being jammed."

"Then what about everything else? The Keyholes? What about the stealth satellites the National Reconnaissance Office swear don't exist?"

"For the stealth birds at this point, Major, it would do you well to go stand in the middle of the lake bed with a telescope. Our imaging satellites are gone, probably disabled or destroyed by China's hunter/killer satellites, but once again we don't have the gear here to track that fully. We have some radar tracking that would imply it, but we're still not one hundred percent."

Wright frowned. They were under attack, that much was certain; their ability to control and use their assets in space were systematically being shut down or blocked by someone. This wasn't some kid with a laptop at a coffee shop in Kiev, this was bigger. The lights and the computers in the room went dark again. Goddamnit, they couldn't even keep the lights on and Wright was getting mad.

First the satellites, then the systems here ... the connected systems here ...

The emergency lights shone in the darkness from above the door, but the facility lights still hadn't come back on. "Have we found all the computer systems for the facility?"

"We think so, Major, but we don't know, I'm not sure we could ever know for sure."

"If someone is fucking with our ability to use our assets in space, it would stand to reason that they have also gained access to our secure network and could be causing the system failures by way of the computers controlling them."

"Yes sir, it would, but I'm not sure how connected this facility is with the others."

"Whenever we're back up, try sending a message to Texas again and ask. Get me the answer."

"Will do, Major."

CHAPTER 18

Coronado, CA
March 22, Year 1

"Chief, we'll put in here." Chuck pointed to the undated aerial photograph of Halsey Field someone had found on the wall in one of the offices. "That's also right by the fuel farm, four large aboveground tanks. Hammer and I want to rig them to blow about a half hour after swim."

"Why?"

"Give the Chinese something to focus on, give us a diversion."

"That'll bring patrols this way from the mainland."

"I hope it does, Chief. You have Snow and Gonzo rig the Coronado Bridge and use the handful of remote detonators we found."

Aymond thought about the proposal for a moment. "Snow, how much would you need to drop the bridge?"

"You want the whole bridge gone or just a section?"

"Just a section, call it two of the concrete supports, maybe they'll think the bridge just failed by accident."

"Not as much as you would think, Chief, but it's going to take us some time to rig it. We have to do it from the water, so we'll have to swim out to it or find a canoe or something if you want to destroy the highest sections."

"What if you just rigged the first support on land this side of the bridge?"

"Less than five minutes to set it, plus insertion and extract time."

Aymond nodded. The plan was coming together; these were "extracurricular" activities that would help confuse the enemy and he liked them. The hills and parks near the California Tower were nearly in a perfect spot, a little close to the operational edge of the enemy, but they were the most heavily wooded and hilly section of the area near the airport that also had a quick exit to the east. The final preparations were being made; Simmons and Jones had the trucks ready and all the team could do was check their gear and take a nap until sunset, for once night was upon them the show would start.

St. George, Utah

The sun glared through the window, the defiant glow of mid-morning chastising Bexar for sleeping so late. Rolling to his side, Bexar was happy to be in a comfortable bed, in a warm home, even if he had two casts. He stared through the window at the gallows, a body swinging in the breeze. Bexar wasn't sure why the body hadn't turned, why it wasn't a reanimated corpse writhing against the sharp rope. The dark hood and the man's shirt were stained with blood. It took Bexar a few moments, but memories of crime scenes and past training came back, like a forgotten dream from a past life.

Blood stops when the heart stops, blood pools at the lowest point. If there is an escape from the body, then blood will flow out of the body, but gravity always wins. If there's blood on his shirt then it happened before or as he died. So they either shot him and hung him or hung him without a drop to break his neck, let him strangle on the rope before shooting him in the head. That would mean they put the dark hood on after they shot him. For a group that seems so happy and timid they sure took care of business with that guy. That's hardcore.

As nice as they were, as kind as they had been, the gallows gave Bexar the creeps and his gut instinct had saved his life more than once as a rookie working nights on patrol. He sat up, careful to pull his cast out from under the sheet and heavy wool blankets. Slowly Bexar dressed, pulling his pants on over his cast. His leg hurt, his foot hurt, his head hurt and his body ached, but his arm didn't hurt ... or didn't hurt as bad as the rest.

Bexar held up his arm and looked at the cast. *I need to get Doc to cut the cast off; I can wrap it if I need to or use a splint, but this damn thing means I can't run my rifle, I'm handicapped with my pistol, and I won't be much good in a fight.*

The realization that he might be wearing a cast as a form of control, a restraint, caused anger to flush across his face, but he thought of Chivo and how he'd acted in Albuquerque. *Smile, be kind, but have a plan to kill everyone.* That wasn't what Chivo said, what he'd actually said Bexar couldn't remember, but that was the lesson and that was the example Bexar would follow. The arm cast would be a test. If that wasn't an issue then perhaps Guillermo and his prepper commune were legitimately just trying to help. If what they said was true then he owed them his life, and Chivo's, if ... when he woke up.

Bexar hopped to the dresser, keeping the weight off the cast and his broken leg. He put his pistol in the holster then drew it, depressing the magazine release, which dropped the loaded magazine to the dresser with a clatter. His left hand useless for the task, Bexar hooked the rear sight on the back edge of his holster and pushed down hard, his thumb holding the slide lock up to catch the slide. A round ejected onto the floor. Bexar held up the empty pistol and gave it a visual inspection. It looked clean, like someone had cleaned it for him. He thumbed the slide lock, letting the recoil spring launch the slide into place. Bexar pressed the trigger and heard the click of the internal hammer falling on an empty chamber. He put the pistol under his left arm pit, picked up the magazine off the dresser, and pushed it into place in the pistol. Bexar heard it click into place, but took the pistol and hit the bottom of the seated mag against his thigh to make sure it was seated before repeating the motions with his holster to rack the slide, chambering a round. Bexar holstered a loaded pistol and pressed the magazine release button, pulling the magazine out of the holstered pistol and setting it on the dresser. After retrieving the ejected round off the floor, Bexar held the magazine under his arm and used his one good hand to press the round back into the magazine before replacing the now fully loaded magazine back into the pistol, slapping the base plate a couple of times to make sure it was seated. Satisfied he would be basically fully functional for one magazine's worth of a firefight; Bexar took his crutches and made his way to the living room.

Chivo sat on one of the overstuffed chairs, half-dressed, wearing only his pants and a pistol on his belt. With the torso brace covering his midsection, the bruising and cuts on his face, he looked like hell. Chivo smiled and held up a steaming cup of coffee to greet his friend.

"Buenos días, cabrón!"

Bexar smiled. "Good morning to you too, asshole. Apparently you wrecked that awesome truck."

"Hey mano, you know how it goes, can't have nothing nice."

"And we just got evened up after I pulled your brown ass out of the bus in Cortez."

"Never keep score. With you as my good luck charm I'm sure we'll keep going back and forth until we finally get welcomed home to the gates of Valhalla. Besides, I think Cliff was the one that came to our rescue first."

"Seriously?"

"Yeah mano, I really don't remember it, but from what Angel tells me happened and from his description it sure sounds a lot like our favorite asshole super-spook."

"But?"

"No idea ..."

Bexar wished he and Chivo could have just a few moments to talk this situation out, come up with a plan; he looked at his buddy, who sat in the chair with his legs propped up, arm and cast resting in his lap, coffee in his other hand and a smile on his face. Chivo looked at Bexar, and he knew. Bexar nodded slightly. *Smile and be kind but have a plan to kill everyone.*

SSC, Ennis, TX

Amanda organized the books she'd brought back from their raid. There were some real winners in the group; those went into their own special stack, but there were some serious hardbound trash too.

"Get any zombie books?"

"What?"

Clint smirked, peering over the edge of the desk at the President, who sat on the floor digging through the pile of books.

"Zombie books. Did you get any of those? They might actually be useful nowadays."

"Funny, you're really funny, you know that?"

"For all that work, did you find what you need to restart America's farming and save the world?"

She frowned at him. He was being a dick, but he was also right. She was more angry that he was right.

"What I need are people, lots of people. Without serious mechanizations this is a job that either consumes your entire day or takes a lot of people and still consumes your entire day. I did find some good references for a garden, so I could at least have fresh tomatoes soon. "

Clint just stood there looking at her; she couldn't read what he was thinking or what his plan was. *This man would kill in high stakes poker.*

"How many MRAPs do we have in inventory?"

Before responding, Clint cocked his head slightly. "Thirty-six, why?"

"With those we have the ability to practically drive wherever we choose, the reanimates be damned, right?"

"Well, sort of. They're not tanks, they break down. Worse, they get stuck because of how heavy they are. There's a reason why they were phased out at the end of the Iraq war, replaced with the M-ATV and other variations. What are you wanting to do with them?"

"We need people. You don't want to broadcast our position like Groom Lake is doing, but we could go there and bring people back. Take two and ferry as many people back as we can, then they all take one and go back for more. At last count there were over a thousand survivors at Groom Lake; with a couple hundred people we could really make use of the plowed fields just on the other side of the HESCO barrier."

"No."

Amanda leaped to her feet, furious. The anger had been building for some time, and she'd finally reached her limit, "WHAT THE FUCK do you mean no? You treat me like some goddamned child; I am the President of the United fucking States! No more secrets, no more lies, that world is gone! It died when we were attacked, and it reanimated to chase the living and it has been killed again."

"It isn't dead, not yet, it's only just beginning."

"What?"

"We're safe right now for a few reasons. First, the last intelligence reports don't believe that the Chinese have the imaging technology to really track or find this facility, even with the improvements you made on the topside, but in reality I should not have let you do that. It makes us a target if anyone notes the addition. Groom Lake isn't safe because they have made their presence known. That was a risk detailed in the Lazarus Project, it was understood and dealt with, except that the project, the entire operation was founded on the core belief that the U.S. military would survive. The low estimates had the survival rate at roughly fifteen percent of our fighting force. We practically have zero. The system problems Groom Lake are having, the loss of satellite imagery, the loss of communications, all of those things were expected, that is why I sent Cliff to Granite Mountain. The problem is they went dark shortly after we arrived here. We don't know if they died or if their systems were compromised, but regardless they're gone. Cliff should have returned or checked in from Granite Mountain by now, so I'm not even sure if he made it there."

Clint interrupted Amanda as she was about to speak. "Now the question is, 'what are the Chinese *doing?*' What they did was start this war, an attack as a prelude to invasion, and now it appears I'm shouldering the entire fucking operation by myself. As limited as I am, with only radio communication, I have no idea if any of our Navy survived; if they did then we have a chance. They can destroy Beijing, they can destroy Pyongyang and then clean up the afterbirth of this failed war. But the President, your predecessor, whose body is rotting inside his crashed fucking blue plane, ordered the Navy to man rescue operations for Americans abroad."

"It makes no sense, none of it does. Why would they start a war by destroying all the life on Earth? What's the end game?"

"The end game is that in a hundred years the Chinese and Koreans will own the whole Earth to be remade in their own image, their own beliefs, and all the natural resources they could ever need for the next thousand years as the population rebounds. The grasslands of the prairie, the thick timber of the northeast ... in a few generations the United States will nearly be what it was when the Pilgrims stepped off the boat."

"But the cities, the technology, the infrastructure ..."

"Some has been destroyed through the process, but think about it. The dams are still in place, the power plants, the sewer lines, much of the electrical service ... all the big pieces still exist and can easily be repaired with a little bit of time."

"But ..."

"But the dead? We didn't know, don't know, but the prevalent theory is that the bodies will rot, and in six months the last of the dead will be gone. As summer approaches, the thaw and natural processes will start up. Their sealed-in freshness from the freezer of the north will be expired. Another theory is that the Chinese had some sort of technology to kill off mass quantities at once or that there was another biological weapon they could use to exterminate the threat. It all just happened sooner than we thought it would."

"If we knew it would happen, why didn't we attack first?"

"Think about what you just said, think about it in the context in which you would have framed that statement on December 25th instead of after the 26th and the attack."

Nothing was said by either of them for a long moment.

Barely a whisper stirred the air as Amanda said, "You're right."

"I'm sorry, Amanda, I'm sorry this is how it is unfolding. Everything has unraveled at the seams. All we need is that one lucky break, that one surviving aircraft carrier, that one Ohio Class sub, something. Without a break we will either be overcome by the dead or die in the coming invasion."

"How long ... what ... when do you think the invasion will come?"

"I don't know, I was a part of the group that believed the Chinese would somehow corral the dead then kill them with conventional weapons, bomb runs and similar. So far as we can tell, no attempts to corral the dead have happened, but we just don't know. All we can do now is sit quietly and listen, hoping to hear it coming with enough time to act, if we can find the fucking means to act with!"

"What about Groom Lake? The survivors, we need to tell them."

"We can't even do that now. I've tried putting the systems back on line, but the terminal link is down, and all lines of communications have been cut. They're alone, we're alone, goddamned everyone is alone."

CHAPTER 19

The Humvee raced north along Strand Way. The Zeds were restless, they moved in packs, aimlessly, seemingly on the hunt for a fight. Simmons knew that was a ridiculous thought, not once had the dead shown any sort of thought or planning, just impulsive reactions, but the air was electric. Chuck and Hammer wore wetsuits under their utilities, the MK 25 rebreathers already donned; they were in full combat load and all of their battle rattle ready for a fight, but ready for stealth to get to the fight. The Humvee lurched left and right as Simmons dodged the groups of Zeds attracted to the truck roaring by. Eventually they were on Ocean Boulevard and still racing towards Halsey Field.

The gate for the Naval Air Station at the end of the road wasn't a problem; expecting to have to demo the gates to drive through, Hammer had a group of small, rigged explosives really to slap onto the hinges and lock, but one of the gates stood open. Simmons barely slowed as he wedged the wide combat truck through the narrow gate, the passenger side mirror slapping the concrete gate post, snapping inward and shattering the glass.

Simmons looked over his shoulder. Neither Chuck nor Hammer noticed or cared, they were in full operations mode. The jokes were over, the horseplay was over, and this was serious business for serious operators. Pipe hitters about to go do work. He checked his watch. Simmons had a tight schedule to keep. Playing taxi driver for the dive team was neat, but it was a hurdle to cross, something that had to be checked off his list before getting back to the rest of the team for the push.

The Humvee took a right at the end of the golf course, then a left and made it to a gate, the easiest crossing for the fence onto the flight line and runways. The unused small explosives were applied to the gate and moments later the gate fell backwards to the ground.

"That's impressive. I was expecting something like a movie, but that was smooth." Simmons only had silence as a response. Onto the taxiway and then to the runway, Simmons pushed the pedal to the floor, the big diesel motor roaring, geared for combat. The Humvee wasn't exactly a sports car, and in the wide expanse of the airfield it seemed even slower.

"Watch out for the bomb crater in the middle," Hammer said without looking up. Now done with his personal gear check, he was checking Chuck's gear, the rebreather, everything, and Chuck would reciprocate immediately after. Simmons swung wide around the dark spot quickly approaching. Without lights and with only the green glow of his NVDs it was hard to see the bomb crater for what it was at a distance, but as they came closer the damage was impressive, as it should have been for what they had exploded. These runways would be out of commission until some serious work could be accomplished.

Swinging to the right, he saw the fuel tanks were also surrounded by a fence, which was against another fence that separated the runways from the road on the perimeter. It may have been easier to drive the long way, but this was the fastest. Simmons drove around the small office building to the north side of the fuel tanks and where the gate for the fuel trucks was located. This time luck shined on the trio of merry men and the gate stood partially open, enough for Chuck and Hammer to squeeze through, but not large enough for Simmons and his Humvee. Both of them climbed out and dashed into the fuel farm. Simmons looked at his watch again and drove off. He had five minutes to get to the Coronado Bridge, his first waypoint.

Coronado Bridge, Coronado, CA

Kirk brought the M-ATV to a stop under the bridge. He hadn't even noticed the signs on the small sidewalk-sized path prohibiting their access to the bridge. On the remote turret, Davis was watching the Zeds they'd passed. He felt uneasy; during the planning of the operation the decision was made to refrain from firing a shot, if at all possible, before the explosives fired, just in case a patrol was near or a helicopter was close. Not that either would have missed the three vehicles scurrying across Coronado at high speeds, but they only wanted to press Mr.

Murphy's grace so many times, for they knew eventually that a roll of the dice would play out poorly.

Disembarking from the truck, Kirk watched the timer counting down on his watch. He stood overwatch while Snow and Gonzo rigged the massive concrete structure of the bridge. They'd spent time that afternoon shaping charges just right to get the maximum effectiveness, both of them also making the calculations for how much C4 it would take to accomplish the job and then doubling the amount. "If anything is worth doing, it is worth doing to excess" was the unofficial life motto for men like these. The fourth minute flashed by on Kirk's dim-faced watch. The Zeds shambling out of the nearby park and softball fields continued to close. Seeing that the gate stood open for the bike lane, which opened up to the park, Kirk ran to the gate, closing and latching it. *They might get close, but the Zeds are too stupid to open the gate. We have some time now.*

Sweat dripping from their faces, steam rising from their exertion in the cool air, Snow and Gonzo finally finished. They traded a quick fist bump and climbed back into the M-ATV. Kirk followed and drove quickly forward and away from the approaching softball Zeds; skipping the maintenance road he took the wide bike lane and drove hard.

"Dagger-Two, set, moving."

"Dagger-Actual, good copy Dagger-Two."

Halsey Field, Coronado, CA

Chuck and Hammer placed a ruck sack against each of the big white fuel tanks, det cord running out of each to a central ruck sack, which held the timer. Hammer worked quickly, arming the system, setting the triggers, and starting the timer. He winced slightly every time he used one of the timing systems; deep down he didn't trust it, but if it failed he wouldn't know anyway. The explosion would kill him instantly.

Chuck set a five-gallon jerry can of diesel about twenty yards behind the tanks, away from the shoreline. He pushed a shemagh into the fuel, soaking it before pulling the long scarf out of the can, draping it across the can and lighting it with his Zippo. A small flame glowed against the darkness, the orange and red colors dancing off the white painted tanks.

The fuel can was their piss poor attempt at a backup. If the tanks didn't blow, if they only ruptured one, then hopefully the burning can of diesel would ignite what fuel had escaped. A little something was better than nothing.

Chuck jogged to Hammer, who was finishing up. They ran out of the gate, climbed over the fence, and ran towards the long walkway out onto the small pier, towards the safety of the water and towards their destination.

"Dagger-One, set and moving!"

"Dagger-Actual, copy Dagger-One."

While they ran, the mouthpiece of the Mk-25 went into their mouths, swim masks were pulled down, and fins were on an arm and ready. Reaching the edge of the pier they never broke stride, both running off the edge and into the ink black water, sinking immediately to disappear. The rebreathers left no telltale bubble trail like a traditional SCUBA system, but they didn't want to linger in one spot too long, worried that they may have been seen dashing away from the impending explosion.

M-ATV 1, Coronado, CA

In the lead M-ATV across Coronado, Aymond drove the big armored truck, racing past the narrow shoreline and towards Imperial Beach. Jones felt a little like an imposter; wearing full combat rattle wasn't new to him, but being raced to his role in a Special Forces operation by a senior NCO like Chief, that was different.

Aymond steered the heavy truck around small pockets of Zeds on the highway as he rounded the curve in the road, heading towards the home improvement store where they had left the radar truck. The working theory was if the truck was still there and they didn't drive into an ambush, then it wasn't being tracked. If the truck was gone it was gone; if they drove into an ambush they would deal with it then. The simplest plans seemed to work the best, especially after first contact with the enemy. If this was a normal operation then a full MSOT would have been tasked with recovering the radar truck, other SOCOM elements handling the demo, the diving, the sniper work, and another MSOT probably handling the recon duties, but this wasn't a normal operation and these weren't normal times. Aymond wasn't worried about succeeding, he was sure they would succeed. They couldn't fail, wouldn't fail, but he was worried about losing another team mate, another brother.

Happy swung the remote turret, the infrared viewer searching for any signs of an ambush, any signs of bodies with temperatures higher than ambient. "Looking good so far, Chief."

Aymond only nodded, focusing on the driving, his task. The groups of Zeds were getting larger, gathering in numbers. It reminded Aymond of his old neighborhood. The neighborhood kids always knew when a fight was going to happen. No one seemed to say anything, everyone just appeared in their yards, then headed to the sidewalks and then to the streets, stirring, anxious, excited, and moving towards where the fight would be. Seeing the Zeds gathering like that made him a little uneasy, but he didn't have time for emotions or unfocused thoughts as the wheels of the M-ATV bumped across the curbs and sidewalk, into the parking lot of the home improvement store.

"Still nothing on the IR, Chief!"

Jones had the NVDs on his helmet flipped down, viewing the green and black world in front of him, the gaping hole in the front of the store, the swarming dead. Aymond was using his night optics as well. "Tell you what, Corporal, how about curbside service?"

Before Jones could respond, Aymond hit the gas, heading into the store through the open hole. Zeds bounced off the front of the truck, falling beneath it as he drove it like a snow plow towards the radar truck, which still sat in the middle of the lumber section.

"Happy, climb up top and help a man out."

Happy flipped open the roof hatch and climbed to the roof, taking a second to gather his bearings before raising his M4 and slowly taking head shot after head shot, working his way through the crowd of Zeds blocking Jones' route from the back side of the M-ATV to the door of the radar truck. The muzzle flashes would be hidden to anyone outside the store, which worked in their favor; the mounted M2 would have laid waste to the Zeds much quicker, but probably would have destroyed the radar truck in the process. This was precision work to be done by a professional.

"OK, on my count and go ... ready?"

"Oorah!"

Jones held the latch for the side hatch in his hand, cracking the door slightly, ready to bolt on command, trusting that Happy would take care of any Zed threats; his single focus was to reach the truck door and climb in.

In between rifle shots Jones heard Happy call out, "FIVE! *crack* FOUR! *crack* THREE! *crack* TWO! *crack* ONE! *crack* GO, GO, GO!" Jones bolted out of the M-ATV and towards the radar truck just ten feet away. The supersonic snap of rifle rounds passed near his head, Zeds dropping with each shot, fast shots coming more rapidly than before. Hand on the door, he opened it and climbed into the Chinese truck. The rifle fire stopped and Jones let out a breath, realizing he had been holding it. He scanned the dash, which was marked in Mandarin. It took a moment for him to figure out how to start the truck, but eventually it started and he was ready to drive. The M-ATV backed out, the remote turret swinging to cover its exit into an open area. Now the M-ATV was the armed escort for their special cargo, the radar truck. Since they had it and it wasn't being tracked, they were going to make sure it survived.

Aymond was confident that they would find more military elements as they made their way back into the interior of the country, and the radar truck, the Zed killer, could be reverse-engineered and implemented on a large scale to take his land back from the Zeds. The radar truck followed the M-ATV out.

"Dagger-Actual, package secure, moving."

Humvee, Coronado, CA

Simmons glanced at his watch; he was behind, not much behind but enough to make him worry. He drove his truck hard, giving it a good thumping, bouncing across the curbed median and across into the bike lane, using the entire road. He swerved to miss the Zeds coming into the roadway. The green black glow of the world in front of him was surreal, like a video game. Nearing the turnoff for the Coronado Bridge, and passing the beach resorts on his right, he felt a shockwave roll through the truck from behind him, and then the sound came, the deep thump and rumble of a large explosion. He glanced in the one good side mirror to see a bright red fireball boiling into the night sky and smiled. Looking up, he jerked the wheel to the left, a Zed slapping against his windshield head first and cracking the windshield. The Humvee plowed through a half-dozen abandoned cars in the parking lot and lodged against the wall outside of the swimming pool.

M-ATV 2, Coronado, CA

Kirk drove hard; if Chief checked on the radio that he was rolling then he knew roughly where he should be. If the systems had been up then the blue force tracker would have given him a precise location to the computer systems on board, as an overlay on their grid square, but the systems weren't up. At this point Kirk was just happy that the team radios still worked. The sound of the distant explosion was more felt than heard as he drove as fast as he could around the Zeds at Imperial Beach. In the green world ahead he could see the faint movement of vehicles just before the edge of darkness.

"Davis, hit the IR and tell me if those are our trucks up there about two thousand meters."

"Yup, looks like them alright."

"Dagger-One, Dagger-Actual, approaching from the rear, two-clicks and gaining."

"Dagger-Actual, clear."

M-ATV 1, Coronado, CA

The I-5 was mostly clear except for a number of abandoned vehicles. This made easy going for Aymond as he threaded his truck through the vehicles, from shoulder to shoulder, using the entire roadway and focusing forward. They would pass the area where they'd used their IEDs, during the chase after the last raid; he wasn't sure how well their IEDs had worked, and he was looking forward to seeing the damage as they passed, if he could see it at all.

Shelter Island, Coronado, CA

The lack of a good beach meant deeper water closer to the edge of land, which worked in Chuck and Hammer's favor. Passing under the keels of the sail boats all anchored in a group, the dark water gave them near zero visibility. Counting kicks as he swam and watching his navigation board glowing faintly, Hammer led the pair towards their spot. Although the swim was short, the underwater visibility was so bad that without the compass on the navigation board it would have been easy for a swimmer to become disorientated and swim in a circle.

On his hand signal, they stopped and pulled their swim fins off, securing them on their gear. They were near the edge of the island where rocks had been placed to prevent erosion. Making their way underwater up the rocks, they reached a point where they both had to crouch to stay below the surface. Slowly, leading with the muzzles of their M4s, they broke the surface of the water without as much as a ripple to give away their presence. Scanning back and forth, they saw no visible threats. They continued sweeping their fields of fire, scanning as they moved, and quickly the pair was out of the water and onto land. The squat brick buildings housing the public restrooms were the perfect place to stash their dive gear; the usefulness of the gear to their mission was over, but they couldn't leave it out to be found.

Through the dark of the night, using every bit of concealment they could, slowly Hammer and Chuck moved through the parking lot and towards the mainland. They had to get north; they had about two miles to cover and they needed to move as quickly as they could with as much stealth as possible. If they were found, they were dead.

MSOT Convoy, I-5, Coronado, CA

The second M-ATV took a position in the convoy at the rear, remote turret facing behind them for any following threat. Kirk worked hard to stay close to the radar truck and follow the turns and maneuvers it made to clear the vehicles and the growing number of Zeds in its path. Aymond drove hard and they were getting close to the destination, but he wasn't exactly sure how to get there from the Interstate. When he saw the tower over the hillside, he took the next exit, which the sign said was for downtown. He took the first right, saw the road open ahead of him and what was probably a gorgeous park on his right. Their destination. He mounted the curb and kept driving onto the grass, up the hillside, moving between the trees. The further he drove up the hillside, the fewer Zeds he saw.

Maybe the high ground will help ... but we had Zeds in the mountains, so that doesn't make any sense.

Taking the sidewalk, the convoy traveled north, to the high ground, to the less manicured part of the area and a wooded hilltop that was supposed to exist.

"This is it, Chief."

Aymond parked the lead M-ATV in a defensive position, turret pointed outward, obscured from above by the tree cover; the second M-ATV took a similar position on the other side of the hilltop, and the radar truck took a spot under the trees on the eastern side of the hill. This was to be their Forward Operating Base, their FOB, and their home for the next twenty-four to seventy-two hours. Just enough time to cause some havoc and strife, and from the response that the explosion had garnered from the airport less than two miles away, it was working.

Snow and Gonzo set off towards the Pan American Plaza to the south, a better vantage point from which to watch the Coronado Bridge. In the distance they could see the headlights of the Chinese trucks already heading towards Coronado. If they could get into position in time and luck was in their favor, they might be able to blow the bridge at just the right moment to cause some of the patrols to join that section of bridge on the way to gravity's harsh lesson.

St. George, Utah

Bexar flexed his hand and wrist.

"Now squeeze, release ... good." Guillermo poked at his arm gently but firmly. Bexar's left arm was a kaleidoscope of yellows and purple bruises but everyone agreed his arm wasn't broken. Doc had no issue with cutting the cast off; she seemed genuinely worried about his wellbeing, and her eyes were sincere. Bexar thought she might have been flirting with him, which she probably wasn't, but it didn't matter. Only one woman mattered to Bexar and he was fighting his way back to her.

Chivo's body and back brace were off as well. Doc explained for what seemed like the twentieth time that they were just trying to be careful, since they didn't have any ability to take x-rays. She said the group had discussed buying certain medical equipment, but even a low-end, older-generation x-ray device was expensive and those weren't even digital. They would have to store film and process film, so the group voted on it, as they did with all major group decisions, and had decided to make do without x-rays. To Bexar that appeared to be the only luxury item they didn't have. That and vehicles. Angel explained that they'd had two trucks in the garage, which were old enough to have survived an EMP on their own, but they were both destroyed during fighting the other group.

Bexar just nodded; he knew all too well. Being a well-stocked, fat and happy prepper was great, until TEOTWAWKI actually happened and someone not in your group found out. Immediately they felt entitled to your supplies, the very things you needed to survive. When you denied them they wanted it by force, or in Bexar's case with the bikers, they just wanted it because that was who they were, the wolves of society. Preying on others, even after The End of the World as We Know It, killing Keeley, splitting up his family, killing his friends and their young son. Bexar still seethed with rage, glad that the bikers were dead.

Bexar felt badly for Guillermo and Angel's group; the more he spoke with them the more it appeared they were all genuinely nice people, but if there was anything that Bexar had learned from being a cop, it was that nice people are often the sheep to the wolves. That's why sheepdogs like him had to exist. He looked at Chivo. *Now he's a fucking sheepdog; hell, he's the dog at the edge of the herd taking down wolves by himself before the other sheepdogs even knew the wolf was there. He and men like him are why the sheep believe their world is safe ... was safe. This fucked-up new life is anything but safe anywhere or anyhow.*

Later that night, as the fire crackled, Bexar's stainless steel insulated pint glass was full of John's homebrew once again, and this time Chivo was with him, their chairs pulled close to each other to chat. But these moments were fleeting. Each person in the prepper group wanted to talk, ask questions about the rest of the country, learn about Chivo's past and experience. They were genuinely curious, but there was tension in their voices. The questions about shooting ability, tactical skills, weapon usage were all too directed to be anything but a full-on group effort to interview them both. It felt like they were getting closer to asking for help with their assailants, since their efforts had worked inasmuch as they were still protected. Bexar got the impression they wanted to go on the offensive or were worried about worse attacks.

"Mano, we need to get back to the truck to see if my other rifle survived."

"The truck burned, dude."

"Yeah, but it was in the bed of the truck. If we're lucky it was thrown free as we went off the bridge."

"That's a huge amount of luck, guy. Besides, what about the swarm? It appears like the herd of undead is growing larger, pushing towards the compound ..."

"They are, they're being driven. What did you say about the bikers doing that before?"

"They would lead the dead like a pied piper of gore to the survivors they were going to raid, let the dead kill them off and then take what was left ... you don't think ...?"

"I do. That is exactly what I think and I think I'm really going need my other rifle."

"How do we do it?"

"We ask for help. These guys want our help, they can earn it."

"Chivo, they did save our lives."

"No, Cliff saved our lives, they just came to the rescue after that. Besides, in their minds that was just the right thing to do. We talk to them about their problem, see if they think the push of the dead is for the reasons we think it is, then tell them about our gear. See if they have any ideas. I mean, they did get through the herd to pull our ass to safety, they have a few horses."

"I'm sorry to interrupt." Guillermo approached where they sat. "Can I join you?"

"Come and join us, Willy, please. We're your guests, enjoying your fire, drinking your beer and staying at your house." Chivo smiled.

"Guys, you've been told about the other group, the raiders, bandits or whatever you want to call them, right?" Guillermo looked at them each gravely.

"Something might have been said, but we don't really know the full scoop. Did you know them before the end?"

"Yes, no, well, sort of. A number of years ago there was a large group, sort of a club or lunch group, nothing very formal, of likeminded people in the area. The leader was in that group. We met a few times and there were some serious disagreements so Angel and I never went back."

"Because you're gay?"

"Mostly, but that guy was unstable. An absolute extremist, even for a group of preppers."

"Well fuck'em, their loss. So after you split from that group what happened?"

"This group formed up. It was really loose at first, a couple of dinner parties, but everyone really hit it off and we realized that we could be really helpful for each other."

Bexar sat silently and watched the discussion, impressed. Chivo was a master interviewer; put him in a trench coat and have him say "oh one more thing" and he could have been a character in a detective show on TV.

"How did you end up picking your house for the group compound?"

"We have the high ground; we also had some of the necessities already in place. The water and fuel tanks were put in when we built the house, the water reclamation system to the secondary cistern as well. The fence and the planters, which you may have noticed are really heavy barricades, went in last, after we had formed. The basement was turned from a movie room with high-end entertainment equipment to storage with lockers for individuals in the group, as we quickly outgrew what Angel had designed for our own pantry and long-term storage in the house."

"Have the dead ever been this concentrated at your gate and fence?"

"No, never. Before, the herds would pass on the Interstate below; we would see them go by, the massive clouds of flies, the smell, but no more than a few came up the hillside. They usually just marched one way or the other following the road."

"I don't think that the uptick in the number of dead bodies walking up to your fence is just a random coincidence, Willy."

"What do you ... no, you don't think ... that's just evil."

"Well, you have what they want and they don't approve of who you are. Six months ago it would have made national news; now, since the fall of mankind, it's just something we have to deal with."

"How do we deal with it?"

"Did anyone go check out our wrecked truck?"

"No, why?"

"Is there a way that you guys can get out and down the mountain to the truck? We had some gear in the bed that might be useful for your needs."

"Angel uses fireworks, like black cats, to distract the dead to gain a way through by using the horses, but I don't know if it would be enough to get through our gate."

"What if we don't go through the gate, what if we went out the back?"

"Over the edge of the hillside? The horses couldn't go that way."

"Are there any dead at the fence there?"

"No."

"Then that is the path we take. A trick I was taught as a young soldier is that in a combat zone be like water, take the path of least resistance, flow past your obstacles and, if something stops you, well, you overcome that with brute force."

"Chivo, you're a piece of work. Let me get Angel, we'll have to have a group meeting."

Guillermo walked away from the fire, calling for his husband.

"That was impressive."

"What's that?"

"The way you directed the conversation, the questions. He had no idea he was being interrogated. Did you go to a class for that?"

"Actually yeah, but the class sucked, that's more from years outside the wire working with the locals. You learn how to get a feel for people really quickly and approach the situation as needed. No need to go all good cop bad cop, Bexar."

"I always preferred doing it bad cop, bad cop, more fun that way."

Chivo laughed. "You're not right, you know that?"

Bexar shrugged and drank his beer.

SSC, Ennis, TX

Amanda checked on Clint; he was asleep, or appeared to be at least. She had to start, she needed to take action, but she would have to do it in secret until the right time came. Dressed in her normal jogging and physical training gear, Amanda headed towards the tunnel.

The MRAPs were located near the entrance to the tunnel, which was handy as there was nearly twenty miles of tunnel going all the way back to where the original Superconducting Super Collider's offices were located. Many of the other things she wanted were stored in tunnel sections as well, but those were further away than the big armored trucks.

She climbed into one of the electric carts, like a beefed-up industrial golf cart with a flatbed, and drove as quickly as the electric motor would allow through the echoing chamber.

Food, ammo, clothing ... fuel, this time the trip is done right; it is completed without having to scavenge for fuel, for clothes, for ammo, for food while en route. No, this time I'm taking everything I'll need.

The running clothes would be her cover; if Clint found her she could claim she couldn't sleep, went for a run and decided to explore the tunnel. Her M4 rested on the seat next to her, but the chances of a reanimate getting into the tunnel was as remote as waking up and this entire world only being a bad dream.

Radio Hut, Groom Lake, NV

Bill wrote the directions clearly on a yellow lined pad of paper, step by step on how to build a spark gap radio out of car parts and other items that survivors would have or could scavenge wherever they were. The antenna was the hardest part because of the mast. The good HAM radio guys would use a telescoping fiberglass mast, but the survivors would have to make do with what they had. At least the co-ax could be scavenged from any home that was wired for cable TV, which was practically every home built in the last fifty years. At the end of the instructions for constructing the radio was an explanation on how to use it, how to tune it, and how to communicate via Morse Code, including the breakdown of what the alphabet was. If any survivor knew CW communications, then that survivor would have probably built a rig already.

"Do I just say dot and dash?"

Bill nodded. "Yeah, keep it simple. Make a recording and loop it on the shortwave every hour in-between the normal broadcast, but don't start playing the message until I tell you. Jake is going to get those new commando women to take me topside to put together the antenna."

"Got it."

Bill walked out of the radio hut, shaking his head at the technical explanation. It was the most MacGyvered piece of work he had seen in a while.

Jake's Office, Groom Lake, NV

"No Brit, I don't."

"Jake, those women are playing you for a fool; they haven't paid their dues and you've put them at the top. You've let them start training their own little army, all the while they're waiting to take you down and take over our nice underground city."

"Brit, they did pay their dues, they paid their dues like every other citizen that has reached us for safety, they paid their dues out there fighting and surviving every single day they weren't safe with us."

"You're wrong and you know you're wrong!"

"Brit, I'm not going to argue with you. These women don't belong in the kitchen doing dishes, I've put them in a position to do what they're meant to do. If you're so damn sure I'm wrong, go with Bill and keep an eye on them while he erects his new antenna."

"I'm not saying I should ..."

"You should. Go. Get outside and get some fresh air for a change, you need to remember what sunlight feels like. Besides, you need to spend time with them. If you would give them a chance you might find that Jessie and Sarah aren't bad people, they've just been through a lot ... we've all been through a lot."

MSOT, Coronado, CA

Snow and Gonzo were more bushes than men in their ghillie suits on the hillside. The heavy sniper rifle wasn't with either of them this time; they took turns with a spotting scope watching the Coronado Bridge while the other maintained security. A helicopter was already circling Halsey Field; it wasn't spending much time over the fire, though.

Gonzo whispered from behind the spotting scope, "There's a convoy of those Chinese Jeeps racing that way. What do you think that the helicopter is hoping to find?"

The helicopter stopped and hovered near the building and compound they had been using, the spotlight trained on the ground in a single spot. The helicopter began circling, the spotlight staying on the same spot.

"Whatever they were looking for, he found it."

"Gonzo, has the Humvee joined the FOB?"

"No ...shit."

"Dagger-One, Dagger-Actual."

Their ear pieces crackled with the radio traffic. "Dagger-Actual, go with traffic."

"Chief, has Simmons arrived?"

"No ... Simmons, check in."

The radio was silent, the call repeated.

"There's a problem. Roll the QRF."

Snow's radio traffic would spur a lot of activity on the other side of the park; they were only about a half-mile away from what a few of them had begun calling Fort Apache, the joke more real than they would have liked.

"They're taking the bridge; get ready with the clacker."

It really wasn't a clacker, it was a sophisticated digital long-range wireless detonating device, but ever since Vietnam, when the Force Recon Marines would put out Claymores for their night camp, the triggering device had been referred to as a clacker.

Snow couldn't see what Gonzo was watching; the Chinese Jeeps had lights on, or he assumed they did, but they were too far for him to see without the scope.

"On my mark ... three ...two ...one ... mark!"

Snow pushed both buttons, one being a part of the safety mechanism.

"Good kill ... oh shit, man, I wish you could have seen that ... like six of those Jeep things and a radar truck drove off the missing section of bridge."

The sound of the explosion finally rumbled past them.

"Wow, those guys are flipping shit! There are still another dozen Jeeps on the bridge with a radar truck behind them, but it doesn't look like they know what to do ... looks like they're waiting for a commander or some sort of direction."

"Gonzo, now I wish we would have rigged the second support so we could blow that and send all of those fuckers to their virgins or whatever it is they believe in."

The helicopter left station to where the bridge collapsed, shining the spotlight on where the vehicles drove off of the missing bridge

Gonzo keyed his radio. "Chief, the bridge bought you some time, but probably not much."

Watching through the scope, he could see the Chinese and Korean soldiers standing at the edge of the bridge, firing their rifles at the ground.

"I think the Zeds from the softball fields are causing them some problems; there's a lot of small arms fire."

Snow smiled. "They don't know what to do without their radar trucks ... I bet if we killed the trucks they would get overrun after the fence failed."

"How do we do that?"

"We don't, but fucking Chuck and Hammer do. Put a BMG round through the center of each of those radars, and we can figure out how to blow some more shit up on this side."

Snow keyed his radio. "Chief, the PLA really doesn't know what to do with the Zeds without the radar trucks. If we hard kill their trucks the Zeds might take care of them for us."

"Dagger-Actual, Dagger-Two, status."

"Dagger-Two is nearing position one, approximately sixty mikes."

"Dagger-Actual, clear, do not proceed to position two, destroy any radar trucks you can locate."

"Dagger-Two is clear, out."

Snow watched one of the M-ATVs roar past on 6th Avenue, towards I-5 and the long way around to find Simmons. Aymond attempted again to raise him on the radio, but there was no response.

SSC, Ennis, TX

Amanda picked an MRAP at random; the one they took to the library hadn't been refueled or rearmed, so she passed on that one. Into the back of the big truck she loaded a dozen cases of MREs. Two hundred and forty-four meals in all; that was her conservative guess for what she would need and others might need, even though Groom Lake had their own supplies. Five thousand rounds of XM-193 for her M4 took less room than she would have expected. The machine gun on the turret was something she really wasn't familiar with, except that Clint had called it a "fifty" and also an "M2"; the ammo was also linked together. It took her a few tries of opening green metal ammo cans, but she finally found one that was stenciled as being 50-caliber. When she opened the can she found the surprisingly large rounds linked together like a metal belt. Although she wasn't sure the ammo cans went with the big machine gun, she loaded them onto the flatbed golf cart and drove it to the MRAP.

She looked at her watch and saw that three hours had elapsed in her supply excursion to the tunnel; the water, clothing, and fuel would have to be taken care of a different night. Amanda wasn't sure when she would leave, but she knew it would be at night, which was really subjective as there was no night or day underground. At the very least it would be when Clint was sleeping.

I better set a date in my mind or I'll keep dawdling around with supplies and get caught before I go. Should I leave a note?

Amanda plugged the cart into the charging station, did some burpees to get a little sweaty to fit her cover story, and opened the hatch back into the climate-controlled facility.

Coronado, CA

Aymond drove the M-ATV, the laughably undermanned QRF comprised of only three Marines. In the last wars the Quick Response Forces would consist of more men, with air support, significant firepower, and more vehicles. In the land of the Zed it was one truck and three Marines, although they were motivated and angry.

The drive seemed to take forever, which was understandable due to the distance they had to cover, but it seemed even more so in that they were racing the PLA to save one of their own.

"Chief, the Chinese pulled their head out of their ass and are heading back down the bridge."

"Copy."

"Shit. Well how do we look, Kirk?"

"Nothing following, Chief."

The armored truck roared past the home improvement store, through Imperial Beach and towards Coronado. Zeds were a problem; Aymond spent most of his time driving across curbs and medians to dodge them, driving as fast as he dared.

"Gonzo, where was the chopper spotlighting?"

"About where the SEAL compound is, maybe a bit further north; couldn't really see much more than that."

The narrow stretch of land separating the ocean and the bay was mostly clear of the dead, but as they closed in on the more populated part of Coronado the Zeds grew in numbers rapidly.

"Chief, the Chinese are entering Imperial Beach; more coming out of the airport."

Busy driving, Aymond yelled at Davis over all the noise, "Tell Hammer to start engaging as soon as they can, anything to keep more of those fuckers busy and off our ass."

Davis keyed the radio, "Hammer, Chuck, Chief says start blowing shit apart as soon as you can, sooner the better."

The radio clicked once in response, which Aymond took as a good sign, since his scout sniper pair was too close to the enemy to talk on the radio. The Zeds were a mob, like rioters looting a store; they all gathered around the outside of the community center and the pool. In the green black world of the night vision goggles he wore, Aymond saw the tall whip antenna of the Humvee sticking out of the crowd like a narrow flag.

"Humvee is in the crowd. Kirk, check the IR and give me some good news."

"One warm body and one warm engine."

"Is the body moving?"

"No."

"OK ... light 'em up, make us a path."

Kirk walked the fire from the M2 back and forth, moving slowly forward in quick bursts with the remote turret, Aymond driving slowly into the path he made, the rest of the Zeds swarming around the back of the truck as it passed. Too close to use the M2 anymore, Kirk opened the top hatch and climbed through the turret, using his M4 to put down the Zeds standing in their way.

"Davis, what do you think?"

"I think we're going out through the roof hatch and making a jump from the hood of the M-ATV; put our bumper against the fucking Humvee."

Aymond drove forward until the Humvee rocked from the M-ATV bumper pushing it.

"Kirk, coming up, climb out!"

Kirk climbed out, Davis climbing out behind him, and they went over the front of the M-ATV, dead hands reaching and clawing at the side of the truck, trying to reach them. They jumped the small gap onto the roof of the Humvee, getting to the middle of the wide truck while attempting to stay out of reach of the cold fingers grabbing at their boots. Davis gave cover, putting down the Zeds closest to Kirk and the Humvee as Kirk knelt on the roof and peered into the windshield at Simmons.

Simmons lay slumped over the steering wheel, head pushed back at a sharp angle and his eyes unblinkingly open.

Kirk stood, tapped Davis on the shoulder and jumped back onto the hood of the M-ATV; Davis followed and they climbed their way back into the safety of the armored truck.

"Simmons is dead, Chief; broken neck, eyes wide open."

Aymond nodded somberly. Their band of ten was down to nine. Although Simmons hadn't been a Recon Marine or a part of the MARSOC community, he'd still been a Marine and someone he had grown to like since finding him and Jones at The Palms.

"Kirk, make it so Simmons doesn't come back as a Zed."

"Aye, Chief," and Kirk centered a burst from the 50-cal at the passenger window, destroying Simmons' body.

Aymond keyed the radio. "Simmons is KIA. Dagger-Actual returning to FOB. Gonzo, update."

"You've got about two dozen trucks headed your way just making the turn from Imperial Beach onto Coronado; the helicopter is starting to move off station too."

Aymond held the radio handset, not transmitting. "Fuck."

"What do you want to do, Chief?"

"Kirk, I don't know, we blew the bridge ...ideas?"

"Fuck 'em."

Aymond looked at Davis. "I'm serious, Chief, fucking drive at them, do it fast and we light everything we come up on with the Deuce. We'll have to pop smoke on Fort Apache if we can't shake the air support, but we can deal with that after we clear the trucks."

Aymond shrugged. "Kirk, you got the Deuce?"

"Ready. Let's blow some shit up, Chief."

Aymond keyed the radio. "We're making a run for it through the advancing PLA. Set to exfil the FOB. Happy, Jones, extract Chuck and Hammer."

The Zeds thinned as they left the Humvee and Simmons behind; as much as Aymond wanted to retrieve his body, he couldn't, but at least he wouldn't be coming back as a Zed. Getting into more of a clearing on the road, Aymond pushed the accelerator pedal to the floor, scowling, intensity radiating from his body as he concentrated on the green world outside his NODs, sweeping the big truck around the Zeds as they came upon them.

Kirk slapped his hand against the door. "LEROOOOY JEEENNNNKINNNNS!"

St. George, Utah

"The fence is breached!" Doc yelled from the front of the standalone shop by the gate.

Chivo looked at Bexar. "To the roof, mano! You can't walk, you can't fight on your feet, come on!"

Chivo stood, Bexar wrapping his arm around his shoulder, and they hopped/ran together towards the expansive house. Chivo's M4 bounced on the sling, his armor carrier on, magazines full; he would have a hard time due to the cast, but Bexar had no doubt Chivo would still be deadly. Bexar's AR bounced between them from his sling, but he only had two spare PMAGS for his rifle in his cargo pocket, the chest carrier lying on the dresser in the house.

Reaching the house, Chivo stopped and helped Bexar onto the roof, the heavy cast hitting him in the head on the way by. Bexar leaned over and held a hand down for Chivo. Rifle fire could be heard.

"In a minute. You get to work, I'll be back." Chivo ran towards the shop, rifle up, braced on the back of the cast on his left arm.

"Dead in the compound!" Chivo yelled as he ran forward, firing his rifle. Bexar sat up on the roof, his left arm propped on his leg, his two spare magazines on the shingles between his legs. With only ninety rounds between three magazines, plus the one in the chamber, he had to make every shot count.

Chivo came around the corner of the detached garage, the fire in the fire pit lighting his face in reds and yellows, Doc over his shoulders. Bexar took a deep breath and let it out slowly, letting the red triangle of the Acog rifle sight come to rest on the face of the corpse closest to Chivo before pressing the trigger to the rear and moving to the next target. One by one Bexar, took down every walking corpse in the courtyard that was near Chivo as he ran into the house with Doc. The entire sequence felt like it took a half-hour, but in reality it was less than five seconds.

Angel came out of the house firing an AK-47 on full-auto, changing magazines quickly and firing another full magazine's worth. "Bexar, get down here; you've got to get inside."

"What?"

"Come here Bexar, trust me!"

Bexar slid to the edge of the roof, his magazines falling to the ground as he turned and lowered himself, Angel helping catch him as he fell. He threw his arm over Angel's shoulder, and they hopped towards the door. Moments later they were in the house. Guillermo pushed a red button in the vestibule for the front door and, with a hard thunk, heavy metal shutters fell into place at each of the windows and doors, turning the house into a bunker.

Bexar looked a little bewildered.

"The shutters were my idea. Angel designed them. The walls are CMU with reinforced concrete, too."

"Impressive." Bexar couldn't imagine what all of this cost to build, much less how they'd kept it a secret. If they'd kept it a secret during the construction process.

Angel did a head count and everyone was accounted for, but Doc was in trouble. She lay on the kitchen table, blood pooling across the table and on the floor.

"Was she bit?" Chivo asked anxiously.

"No, shot ... where is your trauma bag?"

John ran off to get it, returning quickly. With the EMS shears Chivo cut the clothes off of Doc, leaving her nude on the table, blood pooling.

"Blood check. Guillermo, help me out here, I'm a hand short."

"What's a blood check?"

"Run your hands on her body. There's too much blood to see injury; I need you to feel for injuries, bullet holes, bites, anything through the blood."

"Got it!"

Guillermo checked Doc front and back, finding an entry wound just above her right shoulder blade. The bullet had come out the top of her chest, ripping the top half of her right breast off.

Chivo was trying to work fast, but the cast was in the way "Angel, John, someone get me a fucking Dremel or saw or whatever the fuck you can cut and cut this fucking cast off!"

John ran out of the room.

Chivo ripped open a package of gauze with his teeth and handed it to Guillermo. Rolling Doc onto her side, Guillermo pushing the gauze hard against the entry wound. More packages of gauze were packed into the destroyed flesh of the exit wound.

"Bexar, come here and hold pressure."

Doing what he was told, Bexar hopped to the table and held pressure on the wound, the bandaging quickly becoming soaked with blood. A thin silver space blanket came out of the bag, which Chivo threw at Angel. "Open this and cover her before she goes into shock."

John returned.

"Cut this fucking cast off my hand!"

Chivo sat down and held his left hand on his leg, John steadying it and holding what looked to be a battery-operated angle grinder. Ignoring what was going on with his left hand, Chivo called more of the group over to help, giving curt instructions, while Guillermo started an IV.

Angel ran into the other room and returned with a case, opening it. The case contained small glass vials. "We have just about anything you could want, just tell me what you need."

Chivo rattled off some quick names of the medicines Doc needed, running the same process a highly trained combat rescue man does. More bandages, more blood, another IV; the tile floor became slippery from all the blood. The cast was off of Chivo and, although in pain, he moved quickly and precisely, his hands those of a man trained and practiced. Guillermo matched his fast but calculated movements with the well-practiced hands of a medical professional.

Doc coughed once, spraying blood on all who were near, before her body shuddered and stopped.

"Goddamn it!"

Chivo leapt onto the table, kneeling over Doc's body, giving hard chest compressions. Guillermo used a bag-valve mask to give breaths to the CPR process. The whole table shook with each chest compression, with every attempt to save her life.

Doc's head snapped forward, her arms grabbing Chivo by the shoulders and pulling him hard to an open mouth, startling Guillermo, who dropped the BVM. Bexar's hand went up and came down hard on Doc's forehead, burying the heavy CM Forge knife through her skull and into the wood of the table below.

"Fuck!" was all Chivo said as he climbed off the table, nearly slipping on the blood-slick floor.

The rest of the group stared in horror at Doc, then at Chivo and then at Bexar.

"I'm sorry," was all Bexar could say. He thought of retrieving his knife, but instead pulled the space blanket up over Doc's face and head.

No one spoke a word; the muffled sounds of the dead could be heard against the reinforced house.

Chivo broke the silence. "Do you have any body bags?"

Angle shook his head no. He appeared numb.

"How about a tarp?"

Guillermo stepped out of the room, returning a few minutes later with a plastic blue tarp. Together they moved Doc's body from the table onto the tarp, wrapping her and her ruined blood-soaked clothes in the tarp before moving her to the garage for the time being. John and the rest of the group took to cleaning the floor and table of all the blood and medical debris. Guillermo returned a few minutes later, holding Bexar's knife in his hands; he had retrieved it and cleaned it.

Tears on his cheeks, Guillermo whispered "Thank you," presenting the knife to Bexar with both hands, obviously grateful for all they did to try to save his friend and also thankful for Bexar's quick reaction to her reanimation, even though it had been devastating to witness.

Coronado, CA

Hammer lay on his rifle. The low, three-story building's roof wasn't where they had originally planned to set up. The original plan was for a rooftop at the Marine Corps Recruit Depot, but Aymond's radio traffic spurred them into action before they could make their way to their destination while staying concealed. Just a few hundred yards from the west end of the runway, they were in a good location, just not as good as the one they'd wanted.

The ship they'd run aground and subsequently demoed had left a heavy scar on the ground and had damaged the buildings, which was useful in that it pushed the enemy forces closer to where their sniper position. Rooftops were not their first choice; dark rooms, where they could set up away from the window, in the shadows, was preferred. Here they lay in the open, practically exposed; they would have to work fast and hope that Happy could get there before the Chinese or Koreans rallied to find and kill them.

From the roof they could see that a commercial aircraft had crashed off the end of the runway at some point; they assumed it had occurred on the day of the original attack, but they really had no idea. The other end of the runway was towards the bay; any aircraft that crashed in that direction had sunk to the bottom long before they came to Coronado.

The rifle barked sharply, even with the long suppressor on the end of the barrel. The big 50BMG-round center punched the large square surface of the transmitter on the first truck, and moments later men came out of the back of the truck to look at the transmitter. Neither Chuck nor Hammer saw the men; they were already adjusting for the next truck, Chuck calling out distances and elevation quietly to Hammer, working seamlessly as a team. The transmitter of that truck experienced a 50-caliber hole through the middle as well. In less than two minutes, six trucks were disabled. The only trucks they could see that they hadn't disabled were on the far east end of the runway.

"Range?"

"Thirty-four hundred yards."

"Damn."

Since they were unable to reach the far trucks, instead of wasting time trying for a shot which would more than double the last known world record kill shot, they turned their attention to any officers and other trucks they could find.

"Dagger-Two, we're en route, coordinates ... err, I guess describe where you are."

GPS was down, had been down for some time, and normally for the team precision was paramount to their safety, but these were odd times.

"Far west end of the airport, south of the runway, will rendezvous, give us a few mikes."

"Officer ..."

"I see him."

The Chinese Jeep stopped behind the line of radar trucks, a man from each running up to the Jeep as the driver opened the rear door to let his passenger out, the driver most probably the officer's aide. The man stepped out of the Jeep and took a half-dozen steps towards the front of the vehicle and stopped, waiting for the men from the radar trucks to give a report as to why their machinery had failed. Just before those men made it to the Jeep, the officer's head vaporized in a red mist, his body falling to the ground. Hammer's follow-up shot went through the aide's chest and into the engine block of the Jeep. The rest of the men dove to the ground, each taking to a different side of the Jeep for cover.

The helicopter hovered in the distance on Coronado, something that Chief would have to worry about since it was also out of range for Hammer. The sound of a turbine engine spooling up caught their attention, though. Close to a thousand yards away another helicopter was preparing to take off.

"I got'em."

Hammer watched through the big optic mounted on the rifle, waiting for the bird to spin up and start to leave the ground. Once the wheels were off the tarmac, Hammer led the movement and fired. A moment later the round impacted just below the helicopter's swash plate, and the bird shuddered before pitching wildly then rolling left, the rotor blades striking the tarmac, the helicopter rotating violently across the ground towards a fuel truck. Not one to waste an opportunity, Hammer fired a round into the large tank of the fuel truck, helping to start the large fire that followed.

Switching magazines, Hammer was sure he was overheating the barrel with this rate of fire, possibly ruining the rifle, but it didn't matter. All that mattered was the now and the now was to lay waste to as much of the enemy as he could.

"Center mass shots, Hammer; give them a chance to turn Zed."

"Good call."

Scores of men drove and ran to the fire decimating the truck and the helicopter; any time one of them looked mildly important Hammer made sure they were given a hardy 50-caliber welcome to America.

"Last mag."

Chuck keyed the radio. "ETA, Happy?"

"Five mikes, update position."

Chuck gave a better description of their location and a street intersection they would move to.

Hammer didn't need any more convincing; only five rounds in a magazine, five more opportunities to create havoc and strife. Ninety seconds later five more important-looking people arriving to take charge were laid to waste, center-punched in their torso. Soon they would be back to haunt their friends.

"Happy, exfil."

"Two mikes!"

Chuck and Hammer climbed down the maintenance ladder; hitting the ground, they began to run. They were supposed to be a fourth of a mile south for pickup in two minutes. Running south on McCain Road, they saw a vehicle turn northbound from Harbor Drive. They both dove for the shadows, the overgrown bushes near the buildings giving them cover.

"It's me, you assholes."

They climbed out of the bushes and ran to meet their coming ride.

Climbing in, Chuck and Hammer found Happy alone. "Where's Jones?"

"With the radar truck, picking up Snow and Gonzo."

"Get to the east end of the airport and we can destroy the last two radar trucks they have!"

Happy turned the wheel and pushed the M-ATV hard; the dead were already flocking towards the glowing sky of the fire at the airport, making it more difficult for Happy to drive as fast as the truck could go.

M-ATV 1 Coronado, CA

Aymond drove hard, Crown Cove passing to his left, the incoming convoy of vehicles visible to Kirk using the remote turret, their engines glowing on the IR view.

"Two miles, Chief."

Kirk swung the turret back and forth to check the view, watching the glowing engines grow in size as they neared. Switching to the night vision view, the scene turned green and black, the outline of the convoy growing distinct just as the night vision went to white out.

Above them the helicopter's spotlight lit them up from above, pinpointing their position to the coming enemy forces, but also rendering the night vision devices useless. Kirk switched to IR on the view; there was nothing any of them could do about the helicopter, but they could do something about the convoy ahead.

"Looks like they're stopping and setting a hasty ambush, Chief."

Davis shook his head. "It's like watching a police chase, except we're in it."

"No shit, dickhead."

"Fuck you, Kirk, at least you have something to do!"

"Guys!"

Muzzle flashes could already be seen in the distance, the small arms fire still too far away to be of any danger and the armor of the truck being heavy enough to stop it.

"Chief, bike lane!"

Aymond veered left, bouncing over the median, across the other lane of traffic and onto the large bike lane. The helicopter followed easily, Kirk watching the men ahead scramble to shift their positions, more small arms fire flashing before them, some of it now skipping off the armor plating.

"Weapons hot, Kirk."

Kirk didn't reply to Aymond, only opening up the big M2 mounted to the turret, strafing the vehicles and men, the unarmored vehicles laid waste by the heavy machine gun. As they passed the skirmish line, Kirk rotated the turret and continued to fire on the men and Jeeps until passing out of range. The helicopter continued to follow, spotlighting the M-ATV as they drove, Aymond bouncing back onto the roadway again.

"Chief, follow 75 to the I-5, I'll take care of the helicopter."

"Chief, we're en route, same location."

Aymond keyed the handset. "Clear."

Racing again through Imperial Beach, they neared I-5, Kirk calling from the rear seat, "IR showing vehicle and personnel on the bridge."

Nearing I-5, they saw a single large muzzle flash; the spotlight above them pitched, and the helicopter turned away before spinning and crashing into their favorite home improvement store. Aymond slowed and stopped his truck next to the Chinese radar truck, the transmitter erected and facing east. They were happy to see their teammates. All they lacked were Happy and his crew.

M-ATV 2 Coronado, CA

Happy slowed as he followed the road around the east end of the runway, turning left and away from their rendezvous point. Hammer rotated the turret, using the night vision display to aim the M2 at the first radar truck. Small arms fire flashed in the display; rounds thumped against the armor. A single burst from the 50-caliber machine gun ripped through the transmitter and some of the men near it.

Happy sped up before slamming on the brakes at the last radar truck, Hammer repeating the machine gun sweep and destroying the truck.

"Happy, drive over the fence, knock it over."

Happy smiled; even Chuck had a good idea on occasion. Careful not to harm his truck, Happy slowly drove across the parking lot and nosed up against the chain-link fence, driving forward. The fence bowed then buckled, folding inward with the weight of the truck. Careful not to drive over the barbed wire, he backed up, moved further down the fenceline and repeated the process, Hammer raking Chinese and Korean soldiers with heavy machine gun fire. Satisfied the fence wouldn't hold, Happy turned, bounced over the curb and sidewalk, across the road and median, before turning east and putting his foot to the floor on Pacific Coast Highway. A few blocks later he turned and drove up an on ramp for I-5. The number of dead on the Interstate was thicker than before, all moving north, towards the gunfire, explosions, and sound. Twenty minutes of careful driving later, he took the exit for 75, turned right and found his team.

MSOT Coronado, CA

"We have one radar truck, two M-ATVs, fuel, food, water, although we're shorter on ammo now than we were ... we're not that bad off."

Chuck, Hammer, and Happy each gave reports of the Chinese activity at the airport. Although they had created havoc and destroyed the radar trucks, there were still too many men, too much for nine men and limited resources to handle. After the night's raid it was doubtful any spot in the area would be safe to hide. With the sun rising and some discussion, they agreed on a plan to travel east to Marine Corps Air Station Yuma. What they would find they didn't know, but it was a start. With a silent prayer for their fallen comrade, Aymond gave the signal for them to move out.

CHAPTER 20

Groom Lake, NV
March 23, Year 1

Jessie, Sarah, and Erin rode in the FJ, Bill and Brit following in another survivor's vehicle, a worn old Suburban. Tied to the roof of the Suburban were two sections of heavy PVC pipe that Bill had made into a pole, a spool of wire, coaxial wire, rope, and stakes; a large amount of items for such a bizarre project.

"Baby, I have no idea why she's here, but at least she's riding in the other vehicle."

"She doesn't like us because we're not her little happy house elves doing her every bidding."

"I think Erin is right, Sarah; she had her perfect little underground fiefdom and we're the Vikings pillaging the supplies and taking control, her little village destroyed in our wake."

Erin wasn't happy; Brit had somehow made it along for this trip. As it was explained that morning by Jake, the three of them were going to escort Bill aboveground to install a new radio antenna that he'd built, and being mission critical it had to be installed immediately. Brit hadn't been mentioned; when they saw her Jessie argued with Bill about her coming along, that she hadn't been through any of the firearms training yet; Bill assured her that Brit had survived long enough to make it to Groom Lake and that she would be OK. Still, the mood in the FJ was dark and unhappy. Since starting the firearms classes they'd had fresh air and sunlight, and had enjoyed getting outside and away from the frequent power and system outages plaguing the facility underground.

"Look, we can't do anything about it now, and this isn't supposed to take too long. Let's just hope it doesn't so we can get rid of her and he can go play with his radio." Jessie frowned, gripping the steering wheel. It took her a second but she took a deep breath, trying to relax. The dirt road to the antenna site wasn't that bad, but it made for slow going. Eventually they arrived. Jessie, Sarah and Erin fanned out, scanning the area around them for threats. They didn't see any, but lately there seemed to be an uptick in the number of dead making its way into the middle of nowhere.

Brit wore a strange mix of layers, including a huge, ugly red scarf and matching red knit gloves; where she had found them none of the women knew, but even in the cold March air they didn't find the temperature all that uncomfortable outside. They all made fun of her for the impractical cold weather gear.

"How is she going to grip a pistol with knit gloves on?"

Jessie frowned. "I don't know, Sarah, I'm not even sure she brought one."

"But the rule?"

"I'm not sure she cares. Remember, she's better than the rules, she *is* the rules."

The wind and dust was another problem all together. The three of them wore goggles and each had shemaghs pulled up over their faces. The wind gusted with more intensity as time wore on, and none of them understood why Bill wanted to try to get an antenna up with the wind so strong; but he'd been very insistent that the antenna be put into service immediately. The antenna wasn't their problem. They were to stand around while Bill worked and take care of any *real* problems that shambled their way.

Bill took his PVC-pipe-antenna-mast off the Suburban and began working on attaching the long loop of wire. The small buildings by the other antennas hadn't been cleared yet, the group having stopped the process of building clearing until they trained more people to help. They appeared to be secure, and none of them really wanted to deal with clearing them today; the wind was just getting worse and blowing dust became more miserable.

After about an hour of trying to set up the mast, Bill came to the girls and asked for help. Ready to get things done and leave, they agreed. Brit just stood outside the Suburban with her scarf wrapped tightly around her mouth, her eyes squinted shut against the wind and dust. Two more attempts to push the mast up failed.

Jessie yelled over the wind, "Bill, it just isn't going to work today. You can tie off your gear here or you can put it back on the roof of your truck, but you're done, we're done, the conditions are only getting worse!"

Bill nodded, although he looked disappointed. He began uncoupling his home-built antenna, packing it away to carry back to the hangar. Erin went back to sit in the FJ, angry for having to be out in the miserable conditions and angrier about Brit coming along, even though there hadn't been a chance to say more than two words between them.

Jessie and Sarah helped Bill as best they could and tried to hurry along the process. A strong wind gust rocked the FJ. Erin looked up and saw Brit fall over and started to laugh, stopping abruptly when she realized that Brit hadn't fallen, she had been pulled down. She hit the FJ's horn frantically and Jessie and Sarah turned to look, seeing Brit on the ground with a reanimated corpse clawing at her. Her hands pushed against its face and neck, trying to keep the rotted gnashing teeth away from her. Jessie ran to Brit and kicked her boot hard against the corpse, knocking it to the ground while raising her rifle and firing a single shot into its skull.

She reached down and helped Brit up, yelling over the wind to be heard, "Are you OK, are you hurt, are you bit?"

Brit shook her head and angrily stomped off to the Suburban to sit in the back seat while the rest of the group finished packing up the antenna. Ten minutes later they were driving back towards the facility, the wind rocking the vehicles as they drove.

"Brit, that was close, are you sure you're OK?"

"Yeah Bill, I'm fine, I'm just shook up. It's been a while since I've had to deal with one of those ... those things."

For a man who loved HAM radio, Bill wasn't much for conversation unless via radio, so not prodding any further, he drove in silence, the wind whistling through the PVC sections on the roof. The FJ ahead of him led the way down the dirt road, which was hard to see for all the dust, back to the hangar and the comfort of the underground facility, Brit looked at Bill from her spot in the back seat, making sure he was watching the road before gingerly pulling the glove off her right hand. The side of her hand and her pinky finger was bleeding from deep teeth marks in her flesh. Her hand ached badly like a bone might be broken. Frowning, she carefully pulled her glove back over her hand and stuffed both hands into her coat pockets.

Safe from the wind in the hangar, the group climbed out of their vehicles, Jessie, Sarah, and Erin slapping the dust off each other's clothes. They watched Brit get out of the Suburban. "Brit, are you ..."

Brit ignored Jessie and walked past her towards the open blast door to the underground facility, Jason standing inside the entryway to the facility, the greeter once again.

"What a bitch."

Erin and Sarah looked at Jessie, surprised she'd said what they were all thinking. Bill shrugged and walked past, thanking them for trying. After they all were inside, Jason closed the door and locked it into place.

St. George, Utah

With daybreak they saw the damage wasn't as bad as it could have been. Angel used some fireworks as a distraction to get some of the dead away from the house. Guillermo opened one of the heavy steel shutters and the window it guarded. Chivo sat in a chair, his M4 propped on the window frame, and slowly picked off nearly forty undead as they shambled about inside the fence. The gate was damaged but the group was able to rig it into place temporarily. Miraculously the horses were unhurt in their pen behind the garage.

With the courtyard cleared and secure, the group took to the task of pulling the corpses into a pile next to the fence. They hadn't planned for such an occurrence, so there was some discussion as to what they should do with the bodies. For Doc's body there wasn't any discussion. The group took turns digging a grave near the house in the hard soil. Once dug, they had a small service and buried their friend. Hugs were exchanged, and one by one each of them thanked Chivo for doing his best and Bexar for his quick reaction, but they both felt like intruders in a private family moment. After the burial, Bexar followed Chivo across the courtyard on his crutches. Chivo flexed his hand; it obviously hurt him, but he didn't utter a single complaint.

They stopped at the gate, where Chivo surveyed the damage and the temporary repair. "This will probably hold against a few undead, but another swarm like last night and it's coming down again."

"Think that's how it failed last night?"

"No, see here and here? This was sabotaged. Someone set the gate to fail, then corralled the dead here, pushed them through like cattle and shot Doc. No, mano, we need to see if my other rifle survived, get some wheels and get the shit out of Dodge before this gets any worse."

"What about these guys?"

"Your call, mano. Remember, I ride with you."

"No brother, we ride together."

The End

ABOUT THE AUTHOR

Dave Lund is a former Texas motorcycle cop with nearly a decade in active law enforcement. Previously he was a full-time skydiving instructor and competitor (in Canopy Piloting, aka swooping) with over 3,000 skydives. He also has a love for air-cooled VWs, including the 1973 Superbeetle that he built and drives.

Website: **http://www.winchesterundead.com**
Facebook: **https://www.facebook.com/winchesterundead**
Twitter: **@WUzombies**
Instagram: **https://instagram.com/f8industries/**
Tumblr: **http://winchesterundead.tumblr.com/**
Pinterest: **https://www.pinterest.com/f8industries/**

The *Author Dave Lund Winchester Undead Newsletter*, the place for unique content, special contests and tales of adventure can be found here: http://winchesterundead.com/main/winchester-undead-newsletter/

ACKNOWLEDGMENTS

When I first began writing Winchester: Over it didn't even have a title; it had a plan, a story and a process, but it was rough. I dreamed of someday publishing it and maybe selling one hundred copies to friends and family who might be kind enough to buy a copy. The idea of actually writing the sequel, much less having the opportunity to see the whole story arc through each place I wanted it to go was only that, a dream. However, here we are and thank you for joining me on this journey. All of you who reach out to me on my website, via social media, e-mail, at events and leave reviews, I can't thank you enough for the encouragement and support. None of this would have happened without all of my friends, new friends and readers getting behind a story with excitement, telling their friends about the Winchester Undead series.

My wife Morgan. Without her love, support, and faith in me I could have never even started on this journey, much less made it to this point. Her willingness to not only say "go" but to be in the trenches as my front line first rough draft reader, biggest fan and cheerleader when I needed it most is a big reason you have the fourth book of the series in your hands. She is my rock and my best friend and without her help the first step of this journey would never have been taken, nor all the steps since then.

Numerous friends have reached out and helped me chase down details and given advice. Thank all of you, James, Mark, Jerry, Jason, the other Mark, Brains, Freeflier, my friend I gave a promotion to, DFA 1 and DFA 2 ... the list continues. Thank you, thank all of you.

So far the characters have been right as they have led me down this rabbit hole in directions I didn't realize it needed to go. I hope as the series continues that the characters become your friends as they have become friends to me. The foundation of the story began twenty years ago, blessed by campfire smoke and star-filled nights camping with my close friends who still remain my close friends, finding new tales of adventures with our families around a campfire to this day.

Keep your go-bags packed and be ready, I ride with Bexar!

-Dave

PERMUTED PRESS

needs **you** to help

SPREAD (THE) INFECTION

FOLLOW US!

f | Facebook.com/PermutedPress
🐦 | Twitter.com/PermutedPress

REVIEW US!

Wherever you buy our book, they can be reviewed! We want to know what you like!

GET INFECTED!

Sign up for our mailing list at
PermutedPress.com

PERMUTED
PRESS

KING ARTHUR AND THE KNIGHTS OF THE ROUND TABLE HAVE BEEN REBORN TO SAVE THE WORLD FROM THE CLUTCHES OF MORGANA WHILE SHE PROPELS OUR MODERN WORLD INTO THE MIDDLE AGES.

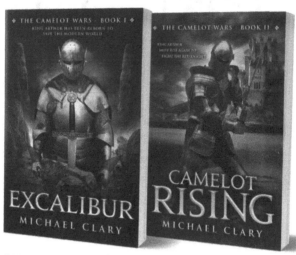

EAN 9781618685018 $15.99   EAN 9781682611562 $15.99

Morgana's first attack came in a red fog that wiped out all modern technology. The entire planet was pushed back into the middle ages. The world descended into chaos.

But hope is not yet lost— King Arthur, Merlin, and the Knights of the Round Table have been reborn.

THE ULTIMATE PREPPER'S ADVENTURE.
THE JOURNEY BEGINS HERE!

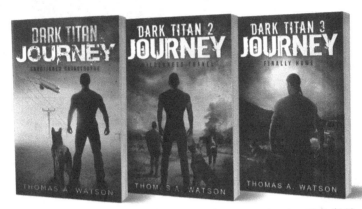

EAN 9781682611654 $9.99   **EAN 9781618687371** $9.99   **EAN 9781618687395** $9.99

The long-predicted Coronal Mass Ejection has finally hit the Earth, virtually destroying civilization. Nathan Owens has been prepping for a disaster like this for years, but now he's a thousand miles away from his family and his refuge. He'll have to employ all his hard-won survivalist skills to save his current community, before he begins his long journey through doomsday to get back home.

THE MORNINGSTAR STRAIN HAS BEEN LET LOOSE—IS THERE ANY WAY TO STOP IT?

An industrial accident unleashes some of the Morningstar Strain. The

EAN 9781618686497 $16.00

doctor who discovered the strain and her assistant will have to fight their way through Sprinters and Shamblers to save themselves, the vaccine, and the base. Then they discover that it wasn't an accident at all—somebody inside the facility did it on purpose. The war with the RSA and the infected is far from over.

This is the fourth book in Z.A. Recht's The Morningstar Strain series, written by Brad Munson.

PERMUTED
PRESS

GATHERED TOGETHER AT LAST, THREE TALES OF FANTASY CENTERING AROUND THE MYSTERIOUS CITY OF SHADOWS...ALSO KNOWN AS CHICAGO.

EAN 9781682612286 $9.99 **EAN** 9781618684639 $5.99 **EAN** 9781618684899 $5.99

From *The New York Times* and *USA Today* bestselling author Richard A. Knaak comes three tales from Chicago, the City of Shadows. Enter the world of the Grey–the creatures that live at the edge of our imagination and seek to be real. Follow the quest of a wizard seeking escape from the centuries-long haunting of a gargoyle. Behold the coming of the end of the world as the Dutchman arrives.

Enter the City of Shadows.

PERMUTED
PRESS

WE CAN'T GUARANTEE THIS GUIDE WILL SAVE YOUR LIFE. BUT WE CAN GUARANTEE IT WILL KEEP YOU SMILING WHILE THE LIVING DEAD ARE CHOWING DOWN ON YOU.

EAN 9781618686695 $9.99

This is the only tool you need to survive the zombie apocalypse.

OK, that's not really true. But when the SHTF, you're going to want a survival guide that's not just geared toward day-to-day survival. You'll need one that addresses the essential skills for true nourishment of the human spirit. Living through the end of the world isn't worth a damn unless you can enjoy yourself in any way you want. (Except, of course, for anything having to do with abuse. We could never condone such things. At least the publisher's lawyers say we can't.)

PERMUTED
PRESS